# A
# FAMILY
# AFFAIR

## Books by Caro Peacock

A FAMILY AFFAIR
A DANGEROUS AFFAIR
A FOREIGN AFFAIR

# A
# FAMILY
# AFFAIR

## Caro Peacock

**AVON**

*An Imprint of HarperCollinsPublishers*

First published in Great Britain in 2009 by HarperCollins Publishers under the title *A Corpse in Shining Armour*.

FIRST U.S. EDITION

Library of Congress Cataloging-in-Publication Data is available upon request.

ISBN 978-0-06-144749-5

10   11   12   13   14      OV/RRD      10   9   8   7   6   5   4   3   2   1

# A
# FAMILY
# AFFAIR

# PROLOGUE

*Dry lightning flickered over the black waters of the lake, throwing the pine trees on their rocky promontories into relief against a copper sky then back into darkness, like some gigantic experiment in stage lighting. No thunder could yet be heard, but to a sensitive ear the whole atmosphere seemed to hum with the electric charge, setting nerves on edge and making repose an impossibility. The dark tower at the very edge of the water might have been designed and built to suit the humour of the coming storm. It stood at the tip of a rock ridge that stretched out from the land like the arm and claw of some great lizard of prehistoric time. Silhouetted against the pulses of lightning, the blunt column of the tower seemed as old as the rock it stood on, though it had been built five hundred years before, in a time of feud and warfare that had raged round the lake shores.*

Nothing in the wildness and antiquity of the scene would have told the observer that time had moved on five centuries or, to place it with precision, to the night of 26 August, 1816.

Nothing, that is, unless the observer had been daring and impudent enough to scramble up the steep rocks from the lake and peer through the window that made one narrow rectangle of lamplight in the dark bulk of the tower, to the room inside. The young woman who sat on a chair by the window, staring out at the lightning, wore a loose dress in pale silk quite in the latest style. Her travelling trunk and hat boxes piled by the wall, the writing case open on her desk, her lamp on the table, were all of the best and most modern quality. The novel that lay face-down on the table beside her was the latest production of the Author of Waverley. Although not perhaps quite in the first rank of beauty, the young woman was pleasant to the eye. Her light brown hair, let down for the night, hung over her shoulders in a shining cloak. Her hands were white and well-shaped, her features refined and regular, although her somewhat square forehead and determined chin hinted at strong opinions and a certain stubbornness.

The hypothetical observer at the window might at first glance have taken it for a picture of domestic repose. Closer observation would have revealed quite the reverse. The young woman was anxious, even perturbed. Perhaps it was the effect of the storm on a highly strung nature that made her restless. She would get up, walk a few paces round the room, pick up a pen from her writing case and put it down unused. Then she would return to her seat by the window and take up her novel, but even The Antiquary seemed unable to hold her for more than half a page. She ran a hand idly through her hair then withdrew it as if stung by the tiny crackle of electricity that the contact generated. Several times she sighed. Once she said softly to the empty room: 'Is this what the rest of my life will be?' And sighed again, as if giving herself the answer.

When the storm broke at last and rain beat down on the waters of the lake, throwing up miniature stalagmites of water back to the dark sky, it seemed to bring some relief to her restlessness, though not her sadness. She blew out her lamp and, illuminated only by lightning flashes, moved over to a day bed set against the wall, heaped with quilts and cushions. She slid off her velvet slippers and covered herself over with a quilt, as if intending to sleep only a short time. Her eyes closed. For a while there was no sound but distant thunder and the hiss of rain into the lake. The lightning ceased. Tower, rocks and fir trees sank into darkness.

'Who's there?'

She was suddenly awake, not knowing how long she'd slept. The room was almost totally dark. She knew at once what had woken her. Heavy footsteps were coming towards her door, thudding on the stone flags of the ante-room that led from the outside of the tower. She jumped up, heart thumping, clutching the quilt to her chest with chilled hands.

'Is that you, Cornelius?'

The door opened. A shape came in, darker than the darkness of the room.

'Cornelius?'

No answer. The darkness came towards her.

# CHAPTER ONE

*London. June 1839*

At one end of the lists the Knight of the Green Tree was fighting to control his horse, a raw-boned chestnut hunter of sixteen hands or so, over-bitted and nervous of the flags fluttering in the breeze. The knight's helmet was too big for him, threatening to tip down over his eyes, but with the reins and shield in one gauntleted hand and a lance in the other, he couldn't do anything about it. At the other end of the lists his opponent waited patiently on a wall-eyed roan that looked as if it might have done a morning's hard work pulling a brewer's dray. The opponent wore no helmet, only his own thatch of hair the colour of good hay. He'd buckled a dented metal breastplate over his waistcoat, but unlike his opponent he had no arm or leg armour. His shield was plain wood. When his blue eyes caught mine he grinned like a schoolboy.

'Are you ready, gentlemen?'

The man in the top hat acting as marshal sounded impatient. It had taken ten minutes or so to get the chestnut facing approximately the right way, with the wooden barrier of the lists on the rider's left hand.

'Yes.'

The knight's voice echoed round his helmet. The man on the roan simply nodded, then they set off down their own sides of the barrier, lances pointing across their saddles towards each other's shields. The chestnut pranced and curvetted like something out of a circus. The roan came on at a heavy canter, slow but straight as a steam piston and was past the halfway point when they met. A crack of wood, a noise like a shelf-full of saucepans falling, shouts from the spectators and a scream from one of the ladies. The Knight of the Green Tree was on his back in the sawdust, the chestnut up on his hind legs and the bare-headed man cantering on as if nothing had happened, tossing away the butt of his shattered lance. Muted applause and laughter broke out from a group of grooms standing near me.

'Got 'im fair and square.'

One of their own had triumphed, although they couldn't make a song and dance out of it with all the gentry panicking about the unhorsed knight.

He lay there on his back, helpless in his armour as a foundered turtle. Men of his own class ran to him, shedding their hats and the air of polite amusement they'd shown so far. The bare-headed man threw the roan's reins to another groom, jumped off and ran to calm his opponent's horse. I arrived at the fringe of the group as somebody managed to take off the knight's helmet. It revealed a head of dark curly hair, matted with sweat, a face that would have been unusually hand-some if it hadn't been as red as a boiled lobster from being tin-canned, a pair of merry brown eyes.

'A shrewd blow. Well done, Legge. Where is the man? And where's Marmion?'

He was still pinned to the ground by the weight of his armour, his friends kneeling in the sawdust round him fumbling to unbuckle it piece by piece. In spite of that, he managed an amused drawl. The other man had managed to get the chestnut down on all four feet by now. He came up leading it, so that the horizontal man could see that it was unhurt.

'He's well enough, sir. How about you?'

Amos Legge's Herefordshire accent was as strong as when I'd first met him, in spite of two years as the most popular groom in Hyde Park.

'Well enough too, I believe,' said the knight. 'Thank you, all. I might just manage to stand up now.'

This to his friends, who had succeeded in unbuckling breastplate and greaves. They helped him cautiously to his feet. He took off his gauntlet and shook Amos Legge by the hand.

'I believe by the rules of tournament my horse and

armour would be forfeit to you, Legge, only I'd be devilish glad if you don't claim them.'

Amos laughed.

'We'll get him schooled to it all right. He's a bit green, that's all.'

'Green as my green tree. I suppose you'll tell me I am, too. What did I do wrong this time?'

Since as far as I could see the answer to that was 'everything' I was impressed by Amos Legge's moderation in replying.

'You need to sit deeper in the saddle, like I was telling you. Get your seat right and it doesn't matter how hard somebody clouts you, you'll stay put.'

'Give me ten minutes to get myself in order, then we'll take another run at it, if you're agreeable.'

Amos seemed willing, but the man in the top hat shook his head.

'Your time's up. The Knight of the Black Tower's booked in next.'

The face of the young man changed. He was still smiling, but the smile had become hard and mocking.

'So he is. I suppose I should leave the field to him then.'

The faces of his friends had changed too. Until that moment, they'd been laughing and relieved to find him unhurt. Now they seemed embarrassed. One of them actually took him by the arm and seemed to be urging him to come away. He shook the hand off.

'Don't worry, I'm not going to make a scene. Same

time tomorrow then, Legge. Brown will take Marmion back.'

Moving stiffly, still wearing his arm and shoulder armour, he strolled with his friends into the Eyre Arms Tavern by the jousting ground.

While Amos Legge was handing over the chestnut to the man's groom, I sat there on my own horse, Rancie, wondering why a crowd of rich young men, in this summer of 1839, should develop this craze for jousting – a sport that had died out around four hundred years ago. As far as they'd bothered to give a reason, it had to do with Queen Victoria's coronation the year before. Some of the upper classes and a few newspaper editors had whipped themselves up into a state of annoyance because the ceremony of the Queen's Champion had been neglected. From time immemorial, so they said, a knight in full armour had ridden into Westminster Hall at the coronation banquet and thrown down his gauntlet in challenge to anybody who denied the new sovereign's right to the throne. Little Vicky had contrived to get herself crowned without this. A good thing too, I thought. The coronation had cost enough as it was, and besides it's not fair to a horse to ride it into a building full of the over-excited upper classes. But some of the young bloods fancied themselves as Queen's Champions. With their heads full of Walter Scott and antique ballads they'd decided to hold a tournament in the old style.

The tournament was fixed for the end of August, two months away, at the Earl of Eglington's castle in Scotland.

9

But this was June, the height of the London season, and the would-be champions needed somewhere to practise without leaving the pleasures of the capital. The ideal place turned out to be the extensive gardens of the Eyre Arms Tavern, just north of Regent's Park and conveniently close to the leafy lanes of St John's Wood, where men of fashion kept their mistresses. There was even a terrace on the roof of the tavern where spectators could enjoy the fun. Fashionable London found it a great diversion from the usual round of afternoon calls or drives in the park. It was my first visit. I'd collected Rancie from the livery stables on the Bayswater Road, where Amos Legge worked, and ridden the short distance out there on my own.

Amos Legge strolled across to me, now freed from his breastplate.

'I'd no idea you were such a knight at arms,' I said.

He grinned and patted Rancie's shoulder.

'Back home, we'd go at each other on cart horses with kitchen mops, riding bareback too. Wasn't a lad between Ledbury and Leominster could have me off.'

I guessed that his barnyard experience was earning him a lot of extra guineas. The young bloods might have been born in the saddle, but they couldn't compete with Amos in terms of horsemanship.

'Your Knight of the Green Tree seems a good-humoured fellow,' I said. 'Who is he?'

He glanced up at me.

'Miles Brinkburn.'

Amos Legge missed nothing and must have seen the change in my face.

'You've heard of him?'

In fact, Miles Brinkburn – whom I'd never met – was one of the two reasons for riding out there that afternoon. I wasn't quite ready yet to admit that, even to Amos.

'He has an elder brother,' I said.

'That's right. Stephen Brinkburn.'

'Is he here?'

'Should be. He's the one who's supposed to be going next, only he's late.'

'Stephen Brinkburn is the Knight of the Black Tower?'

'That's right.'

Which explained the change in Miles Brinkburn's expression.

'Is the brother a pupil of yours too?' I said.

'Not a pupil, no. He rides better than his brother. But he wants me to look out for some new horses for him. He's just going to take a run or two against the Railway Knight.'

'Railway Knight?'

It was true that people who cared about money were talking up railways as the next thing to make everyone's fortune, but as a title it was hardly medieval.

Amos laughed and pointed towards the back of the tavern. Two servants were trundling out something that looked like an enormous version of a child's toy. It was a life-size wooden horse with a wooden knight

11

in the saddle, the whole thing mounted on a wheeled platform.

'They give it a push and it runs on rails down the list,' Amos explained. 'Comes in useful if a gentleman wants a bit of extra practice.'

The Knight of the Black Tower still hadn't arrived, so most of the spectators were watching three riders in normal costume but carrying lances, taking it in turns to charge at a figure like a scarecrow with a shield on its chest, set up at some distance from the lists.

'What's that?'

'They call it a quintain,' Amos said. 'You have to hit it square in the middle of the shield. If you hit left or right it swings round and clouts you with its arm, like that.'

One of the riders galloped at the scarecrow figure and just caught it with his lance on the outside of the shield. It swung out a jointed arm with a flail on the end, hit him in the chest and almost had him out of the saddle. The spectators on the roof laughed and jeered. It sounded as if some of the men had been drinking already. The second rider tried and missed the target entirely. The third dropped his lance.

'Want a try?'

At first, I didn't realise that Amos was talking to me. He must have seen something in my face that I hadn't intended to show.

'Well, why not? I don't suppose we could do any worse.'

I was half-appalled to hear myself saying it, but it had been in my mind that Rancie and I could do better, even though I did have the disadvantage of riding side-saddle. He gave me one of his mischief-making grins, walked over to a pile of lances stacked against a tree and came back holding one.

'Like this, see. Point it across her withers and ride straight at it.'

If it were to be done, it must be done without thinking about it. I tightened my right knee round the pommel of the saddle, pressed my left heel lightly against Rancie's side. It only needed a touch. As usual, she read my thoughts and cantered straight as a swallow towards the quintain. I kept my eyes on the centre of the shield and concentrated on keeping the lance steady. It was lighter than I expected and when the point of it hit the shield square in the centre, the top of the lance broke like a barley straw. Amos's whoop of delight told me that we'd got it right first time.

I don't think the spectators on the roof had realised I was going for the quintain until I struck it, but now laughter and cheering broke out. I knew my face was going red. I hadn't intended to make a spectacle of myself. I'd felt as if Amos and I were two children in a barn-yard together, daring each other, and for a moment had forgotten everything else. I glanced up at the terrace and blushed even more hotly when I saw that the loudest cheers were coming from the young man who'd ridden as the Knight of the Green Tree. Miles Brinkburn was actually on his feet, applauding. Since the thing had to be carried off somehow, I bowed from the saddle to acknowledge the applause and, carrying my splintered lance, walked Rancie back to where Amos was standing.

Luckily, a new arrival distracted attention from me. Another knight had appeared at the far end of the lists on a useful-looking dark bay, a group of friends with him on foot. He was in armour and carried a shield with the device of a black tower. Stephen Brinkburn. He had not yet put on his helmet, so I had the chance for a long look at his face. He was less striking than his younger brother, though by no means bad looking. His hair was light brown and worn quite long, his nose an aristocratic beak. Above all, he looked serious, as if this craze for jousting were no game. More than that, he looked like the kind of man for whom nothing was a game. I thought that when they'd played cricket at their public school, the younger brother would have sent balls flying in all the wrong directions while the elder one frowned over the rule book. One of the friends handed up his helmet. He settled it carefully on his head, not moving until he was satisfied that the eye slit was at exactly the right level, then took his lance from another friend.

Meanwhile, at the other end of the lists, the servants were manoeuvring the Railway Knight on to his set of rails. When they were ready the marshal looked inquiringly towards the Knight of the Black Tower. The silver helmet gave one heavy nod and he levelled his lance.

'The shield!' somebody yelled at the servants. 'Take it off.'

The shield of the Railway Knight had been loosely covered with a piece of sacking, presumably to protect it. It was dangerous because if it had flown off when the wooden knight gathered speed it might have caused his opponent's real horse to shy. The servants were just giving the Railway Knight a good shove to set him off on his career down the lists, but at the last moment one of them managed to twitch off the piece of sacking.

The metallic bellow that sounded when the shield was revealed was louder than the galloping hooves of the dark bay and the hiss of wheels on rails. It sounded like some furious and gigantic elephant in a cave. It took us all a moment to realise that the bellow was coming from inside the helmet of the Knight of the Black Tower. As he bellowed, he drove his horse towards the Railway Knight at a speed that looked suicidal. When his lance struck the Railway Knight's shield square on, the force splintered the lance like kindling and rocked the wooden rider. The artificial horse trundled on to the end of its track. The rider reined in the bay at the end of the list with a force that brought his forelegs off the ground, then spun him round like a circus trick-rider. He rode across the grass, over a flowerbed and straight at the back of the tavern as if he intended to propel himself and his horse inside. The spectators on the roof had been too stunned by his bellow to applaud what had, after all, been a very accurate hit. Now some started

15

shouting at the rider to stop and others screamed. Only one of them seemed unalarmed. Miles Brinkburn sat there with a smile on his face like a child at a pantomime.

Stephen Brinkburn drew his horse up by the steps that led to the spectators' platform, dropped the reins and began taking off his helmet. It revealed a face white with fury, jaw set. He dropped the helmet, flung himself out of the saddle and – still in armour – started clanking up the steps to the platform. By then, some of his friends had caught up with him.

'Leave it, Stephen, he's not worth it.'

'For God's sake, Stephen, you'll get into the newspapers.'

He took no notice of them. Miles Brinkburn had left his seat now and was standing at the top of the steps, the smile still on his face. From several steps down, Stephen launched himself at his brother. For a man encumbered with metal plates, it was an astounding feat of athleticism or fury. Miles hadn't expected it and was knocked off his feet. The two of them slithered all the way back down the steps, Stephen clanking and Miles yelling something about taking a joke. They hit the ground with Miles underneath. Stephen aimed a punch at him with a gauntleted hand that would have knocked him senseless if it had connected, but one of Stephen's friends managed to push it aside at the last moment so that it clanged against the bottom step, knocking splinters out of it. One of the splinters pierced Miles's face, just below the eye socket, drawing blood. He yelled, managed to pull himself out from under his brother's weight, struggled upright and delivered a kick to Stephen's jaw. Stephen saw it coming and rolled aside so that the kick struck the back of his neck and was partly deflected by armour plating. As Miles drew his foot back for another try, Stephen grabbed his ankle so Miles hit the ground again.

They lay there for a moment, panting and exhausted, their faces only inches apart. Blood was pouring down Miles's face and on to his teeth, his lips drawn back in a snarl. No pretence about jokes now. Stephen's expression was intent, almost blank. It seemed a battle out of space and time, like a tiger fighting some plated monster from a prehistoric era. The sheer oddity of it must have paralysed the friends surrounding them, because after that one attempt to intervene they'd stood gaping, mouths open. At first they might have regarded it as part of the afternoon's diversion, but now raw hatred was in the air, like the smell of blood. Miles rolled over, grabbed two handfuls of Stephen's hair and started thumping his head against the ground. Stephen's hands clawed for Miles's throat. One of the friends let out a shrill yell.

'Stop them, somebody. They'll kill each other.'

Up to that point, Amos Legge had been watching with the air of a man who'd seen worse. In his book, if the gentry wanted to fight among themselves, that was up to them. Now, moving in his usual unhurried way, he pushed through the crowd of friends and stood over the two writhing bodies.

17

'That's enough. Just calm yourselves down now.'

I'd heard him use exactly the same tone in parting a couple of fighting terriers in a stable yard. The sheer solidity and calmness of him froze the two men. He bent down, untwined Miles's fingers from his brother's hair, set him on his feet like a nursemaid dealing with a fractious child and delivered him into the hands of a group of friends.

'Take him inside and get that face sponged off.'

He watched as they walked him into the building, then hauled Stephen to his feet.

'You all right then, sir? Best get out of that armour so they can take the dints out of it.'

Like a man in a daze, Stephen clanked off with another group of friends. The rest of the crowd gradually melted away, though some of them still looked shaken. I rode over to Amos, who'd started collecting up lances as if nothing had happened.

'Has Stephen Brinkburn gone mad?' I said.

'Well, he's not very pleased at the moment, is he?'

'Really mad, I mean.'

'Not that I've heard. His dad is though, so they say.'

'He seemed calm enough before the Railway Knight started. Did something about that annoy him?'

The wooden horse and rider stood alone at the end of the list, abandoned by the servants who'd run to watch the fight like everybody else. I rode over to it, Amos walking beside me.

'Fair dinted the shield, he has,' Amos said.

I looked at it.

'Oh God, that's why.'

Amos looked puzzled.

'Just a copy of his own shield, isn't it?'

A black tower on a white ground. Stephen Brinkburn
would have seen his own device speeding towards him,
but something else as well. A black diagonal bar that
had not been on Stephen Brinkburn's shield cut across
the one carried by the Railway Knight from left to right.

'It's the baton sinister,' I said.

'What's that when it's at home?'

Amos's many abilities did not include heraldry. I was
not much better myself, but knew enough to recognise that
black bar. It was the heralds' sign for a man of illegitimate
birth. I explained to Amos and he gave a whistle.

'And he thinks his brother did that?'

'Yes, and he's probably right. Did you see the grin on
Miles Brinkburn's face? I suppose he'd bribed one of the
servants to substitute the shield.'

'So he's telling the world their mother was no better than
she should be,' Amos said. 'Not surprising he got upset.'

I didn't answer, thinking of that metal fist so nearly
smashing into Miles Brinkburn's unprotected face. It
looked as if what I'd been told was true, and I didn't
like it.

'I'll ride back with you, if you're going,' Amos said.

As usual, he'd picked up my mood and sensed that I
wanted to get away from there. I said I should like that,
please, and he went to fetch the roan.

It took him time because one of his other jousting pupils wanted to speak to him, so it was about twenty minutes later when we rode towards the gate on to the Wellington Road. Miles Brinkburn was waiting by the gate on his chestnut hunter, in normal dress of dark jacket and tall hat. The blood had been sponged from his face, but the left side of it was raw from his slide down the steps and his left arm hung awkwardly. He smiled when he saw us, but with the shame-faced air of somebody who knew he'd lost control of himself. He wasn't exactly blocking our exit, but had positioned himself so that we couldn't pass without noticing him. I thought he might want to apologise or justify himself for the fight, but he spoke to me with an attempt at a jaunty air, as if nothing had happened.

'I say, that was a most capital blow at the quintain. I only wish I could do half so well.' Then, to Amos: 'Would you be kind enough to introduce me, Legge?'

Amos did it correctly enough, though I sensed he wasn't pleased.

'Miss Lane, this is Mr Miles Brinkburn. Mr Brinkburn, Miss Liberty Lane.'

Miles Brinkburn's shapely eyebrows flicked up and down. He might have been surprised by my first name – a cradle gift from my two radically minded parents – or perhaps he was registering my unmarried state. Under my gloves, he couldn't have seen whether I was wearing a ring. Either way, there was a hint of speculation in

20

those eyebrows that made me annoyed enough to speak my mind.

'That was a downright unchivalrous trick you played.'

He bowed in the saddle.

'Then I am rebuked. Should I have challenged him to single combat?'

'If you do, you'd better stipulate that it's on foot,' I said.

He winced. It had been ungenerous to remind him that his brother was the better rider, but I wanted to see how he reacted.

'Beauty has a right to severity, Miss Lane. I hope I may be permitted to alter your poor opinion of me.'

I gave him a cold bow and moved my hand on the rein, indicating that we wanted to ride past him. He stood his ground.

'You obviously have an interest in knightly pursuits, Miss Lane.' (I hadn't particularly, but didn't interrupt.) 'I wonder whether you might be interested to see my ancestral armour.'

I'd heard some unlikely lines of invitation from gentlemen to ladies, but this was the most blatant yet. I decided he was mocking me and replied accordingly.

'I believe I've seen it already, Mr Brinkburn. Brought low in the sawdust.'

He kept his good temper.

'That was only hired stuff. I'm having my own ancestor's armour sent from home. It's arriving at Pratt's in Bond Street tomorrow. There's any amount of interesting armour

21

and things at Pratt's. Perhaps we'll even find another lance for you to break.'

From his smile, he seemed to think that he was irresistible. It suited me to let him think he was.

'What time at Pratt's?'

'Would twelve o'clock suit m'lady?'

'I'll think about it.'

He nodded as if the thing were settled and at last moved aside to let us through the gate.

'So is it in the line of business, then?' Amos said, as we rode along the west side of Regent's Park.

He knew me well enough to guess that I hadn't been bowled over by Miles Brinkburn's charm to the extent of losing all discretion. A lot of my friends were embarrassed by the singular way I made a living, but Amos was unsurprisable.

'Probably, yes,' I said. 'I've been asked to investigate something connected with his family. I can't decide whether to agree or not.'

'I don't think there's much harm in him,' Amos said. 'But he's a touch impudent, like. He wants watching.'

Was that meant as a warning to me to watch my reputation? Mr Brinkburn had indeed been impudent in trying to make an assignation with me when we'd only just been introduced. There were two possible reasons for that. The obvious one was that he'd taken me, from my unmarried state and apparent readiness to attract attention, as a woman whose business it was to make assignations with gentleman. The other was more worrying. Was it possible that he knew already, by some means, that I'd been approached to investigate his family's extraordinary problem? If so, Amos was right and the younger Mr Brinkburn certainly did want watching.

# CHAPTER TWO

The approach had come, as was often the case in my investigations, from that rising young Conservative MP, Mr Benjamin Disraeli. He'd told me about it two days before, at a private viewing at an art gallery in Pall Mall that I was attending with the family of one of my singing pupils. He'd come up to me in the refreshment room.

'What a pleasant surprise to find you here, Miss Lane.'

I was sure he would have had sight of the guest list in advance and knew very well that I'd be there. He was a man who preferred surprising other people to being surprised. But I played him at his own game, making social chat.

'I understand I am to congratulate you on your forth-coming marriage, Mr Disraeli.'

To a plump chatterbox of a widow, with a more than

comfortable income, a dozen or so years older than he was. At least that should take care of his debts.

'Yes indeed. Mary Anne has consented to make me a happy man very soon. I only wish all unions could be as well starred.'

While we were talking, he was deftly steering us towards two empty places on a sofa at the far end of the room, under a landscape in oils so gloomy that nobody was likely to come for a closer look. When we were settled he inquired politely how business was going.

'Reasonably well, thank you,' I said. 'I'm doing more private intelligencing than music teaching these days.'

'Yes. I understand the Staffords were more than grateful about that regrettable business with the statue.'

He was entitled to know something about my work. It had been Mr Disraeli who'd invented my metier for me, pointing out that I seemed to have a talent for investigation and might make a living by using it on behalf of people whose problems were too delicate to go to the police. His network of acquaintances was wide, growing all the time, and he cheerfully admitted that favours to friends were useful currency for a politician. We were useful to each other. Far more than that – and in spite of our political differences and my knowledge of his failings – I liked the man. He took his risks gallantly and was never dull. Even now, sipping lukewarm tea under one of the most dismal paintings in London, I felt my pulse quickening.

'So you want to talk to me about somebody's ill-starred

marriage,' I said. 'It's no good asking me to collect evidence for a divorce. I've tried that once and it was my only failure.'

'Yes, but that was because you decided to take the wife's part. If you'd stayed on the husband's side . . .'

'He was a liar, an adulterer and a bully. I'd rather teach music to tone-deaf five-year-olds all my life than work for people like that.'

'Then we must hope that my unfortunate friend's morals come up to your high standards. It really is a most unusual case – quite possibly a unique one.'

He had me there, of course. I could no more have refused to listen to him than a child could walk away from a sweet-shop window. The need to earn money was strong, but curiosity stronger. So that was how I first came to hear about the Brinkburn brothers, although Disraeli didn't mention their names until at last I'd agreed to consider taking on the case.

'It's an old family,' he said. 'They've been living on their estates in Northumberland since the Conqueror. Until quite recently they had no money to speak of; they've made good marriages in the last couple of generations so they own considerable property near Newcastle, including four or five coal mines. With the railways coming up so fast, that's almost as good as gold. Then there's a smaller estate on the Thames in Buckinghamshire. The heir will be more than comfortably placed.'

'But the family are unhappy?'

'By most accounts, the father, the old lord, is happy enough in his way. He's sixty or so, hale and hearty until recently, but the word is that he's been out of his mind for some months. He spent quite a lot of his life travelling and had a villa in Rome. Apparently he now believes he's the Emperor Hadrian. They've stored him in a private asylum near Kingston upon Thames and I'm told he's perfectly easy to manage, provided the attendants drape themselves in bed sheets and remember to say good morning in Latin.'

'Is he likely to recover?'

'No. I understand he's paying the penalty for being too ardent a worshipper of Venus in his youth and is not expected to live long.'

So the mind of the old lord had been eaten away by syphilis. Even though Disraeli and I talked pretty freely, he couldn't say that outright.

'And the wife?'

'She lives mostly on the Buckinghamshire estate. She's twenty years younger than he is. It was never a love match. The present lord's father had gambled away quite a lot of the money he'd married, so the son had to do his duty and marry some of it back again. I gather he was reasonably good looking in his day and there was the title, of course. He married a woman from his own part of the world. She was considered a beauty by local standards; amiable, although inclined to be bookish. She inherited fifty thousand a year and the four or five coal mines, so it seemed suitable enough.'

27

He pretended not to see the grimace I was making. When it came to old families and new money, the usually irreverent Disraeli came too close to being serious for my liking.

'So were there children of this perfectly suitable union?' I said.

'Two sons. One of the sons is twenty-two now and the other's twenty. That's where the problem lies.'

'Sowing wild oats?'

If so, I couldn't see how I was expected to trail a young man, or two of them, through the gambling clubs and brothels of London.

'Nothing like that, no. The elder one's sober as a judge. The other's probably had his moments, but nothing out of the way.'

A thin woman in ill-advised purple wandered our way, peering short-sightedly at the picture through a lorgnette. Disraeli greeted her politely and they held a meandering conversation about apparently mutual acquaintances before she drifted away.

'Who was that?' I said.

'I haven't an idea in the world. Nobody important, or I'd have known her. So, may I tell him you'll take it on?'

'Tell whom I'll take on what?'

He was deliberately teasing me, trying to provoke my curiosity.

'Oh, haven't I explained?'

'A twenty-two-year-old man who's as sober as a judge

is about to inherit a title and a fortune. I can't see how that poses a unique problem,' I said.

'It might be if his claim to the title were in question.'

'How is it in question?'

'The usual way – that he might not be his father's son.'

'This sounds even worse than the divorce case. Am I meant to be going through rumpled sheets from twenty-three years ago?'

'If only it were that easy. It's a matter of hints, gossip – nothing tangible.'

'So people have been hinting and gossiping for twenty-three years?'

'No, that's the strange part. The hints and gossip have only begun quite recently.'

'Since people knew the old lord was going to die soon?'

'Yes.'

'Do we know who started the gossip?'

'We have a very good idea.'

'Who?'

'The young men's mother.'

I nearly dropped my teacup.

'The elder boy's own mother is saying he's not her husband's son?'

Disraeli nodded.

'But why should she admit it after all these years? And what about the younger one?'

'She's quite adamant that the younger son's legitimate.'

'But that doesn't make sense. If a woman's going to be unfaithful, it's usually the later children who . . .'

I didn't finish the sentence because it was straying into things that should not be said.

'Indeed.'

'Does she say who the father was, if he's not her husband?'

'As far as I'm told, she takes a somewhat legendary line,' Disraeli said. 'There was a storm one night on their honeymoon tour. She was alone in her room in a tower by a lake in Italy, waiting for her husband to return from a visit. A man entered, at the height of the storm, without lighting a candle. She naturally assumed it was her lord and master come home and . . . well, you can guess the rest. In the morning, his place in the bed is empty and she thinks he's gone out early to admire the view. Imagine her horror when her husband arrives some hours later, mud-splattered on horseback, explaining that he decided to stay the night with friends because of the storm.'

'It's like something from a bad Gothick novel.'

'I gather the lady in question is fond of novels. She also paints and writes poetry.'

I stared at him, still disbelieving.

'Of course, there is precedent for it,' Disraeli said.

'Precedent?'

'You may remember that something very similar happened to the lady in the Greek myth of Amphitryon. And our own King Arthur was born of just such a visit by Uther Pendragon.'

30

'May we please keep to the nineteenth century. Are you suggesting that this woman's head has been so turned by novels and myths that she's denying the legitimacy of her own son? Is she insane too?'

'That's probably the question the case will turn on.'

'Case?'

'Miss Lane, you can surely see what will happen if the old lord dies before this question is resolved. It will end up in court, and not just any court, either. A question like this would have to be submitted to the House of Lords.'

He sounded serious again, so I had to put out of my mind the entertaining picture of their lordships in coronets and ermine debating the story I'd just been told.

'What about the younger son? He surely wouldn't want to see his mother and his brother put through this.'

'I understand that there's no great brotherly love between them. The younger boy has always been his mother's favourite. He takes after her, while the elder brother bears some resemblance to the father and took his father's side when husband and wife fell out.'

'But that would make no sense at all, if he's supposed not to be the father's son,' I said. 'And if he looks like his father, surely that settles the matter?'

'Not conclusively. There's a fairly general family resemblance within the English aristocracy, wouldn't you say?'

He smiled at me and flicked one of his very un-English

raven ringlets back from his face with a hand that glinted with gold rings.

'So it's quite possible that the mother is making all this up to try to ensure that the younger one inherits,' I said.

'Yes, that's the other possibility.' Disraeli sighed. 'It almost makes one wish that there were some way of testing the blood for paternity, the way that scientists test for acid or alkali.'

'If such a test existed, the whole of *Debrett's* would probably have to be re-written,' I said.

I was doing some hard thinking. There was no doubt that he'd succeeded in piquing my curiosity. At that point, I'd met none of the people involved and it presented itself as an interesting puzzle.

'If I were to investigate, who would be my client? The elder son?'

'Not directly. I've been approached by a lawyer of excellent reputation who was the elder son's trustee, up to his twenty-first birthday, and is still trustee for the younger son for another few months. He's a family friend as well as their legal adviser. He's very concerned that the thing should be halted in its tracks before it becomes public knowledge.'

'But if it's gossip already . . .'

'Gossip is one thing. Lawsuits are another.'

'So the lawyer would be paying my fee?'

'Yes, and I don't think there'd be argument about anything you considered reasonable.'

32

'What exactly would he expect me to do?'

'He hoped you might make the acquaintance of the lady in question and encourage her to talk to you.'

'To a complete stranger, about the most intimate things in her life?'

'People usually seem willing to talk to you. You have a gift.'

'And having gained her confidence – goodness knows how – I'm supposed to report to you and the lawyer on whether she's mad or scheming?'

'That's a reasonable summary. I'll admit, we haven't given much thought to the details. I simply promised my friend to see if I could persuade you to take an interest.'

I stood up.

'I'll think about it,' I said, not knowing that I'd be saying the same thing to another unorthodox invitation two days later.

That was when he told me, in confidence, the family name. I left him sitting under the picture, alone for once, looking like a man who thought he'd done a good evening's work.

I walked home that evening to Abel Yard, my dear but rackety home in Mayfair at the back of Park Lane. The front of Park Lane is one of the most desirable addresses in London, facing directly on to the eastern side of Hyde Park, with dukes by the dozen, peers ten-a-penny and the whole of society coming and going in carriages with liveried footmen on the back. But spin those mansions round, like a child with a doll's house, and the scene at the back is altogether more domestic, with narrow slices of workshops, sheds and dwellings crammed with carriage-makers, carpenters, glaziers, bonnet trimmers, pastry cooks, cows, chickens – all the things that the great houses need for their comfort but don't want to know about. A stone's throw from Park Lane, in between grand Grosvenor Square and the parish workhouse, is Adam's Mews. Carriage horses are stabled all along the cobbled street. Grooms and drivers live overhead, some in rooms so low-ceilinged that even jockey-sized people can't stand upright in them, with hay stores in between and pulleys for drawing up hay bales from the carts that are so often blocking the narrow mews. There was one standing there that afternoon. I managed to squeeze past it without snagging my dress and went through the gateway into Abel Yard.

The carriage-mender at the entrance to the yard had the forge roaring and was hammering at something on his anvil. Chickens scratched around the door at the bottom of our staircase. The door was locked, which meant Mrs Martley was out. Good. Mrs Martley might, I suppose, be described as my housekeeper, except I'm not grand enough to have a housekeeper and she's far too opinionated to be one. A more accurate description might be that she's my resident respectability. A woman can't live on her own and keep up any reputation, especially if, like me, she sometimes has gentleman callers.

Mrs Martley, a retired midwife in her forties, cooked and cleaned and nagged me about everything from forgetting to hang up my bonnet to still being single at twenty-three years old. As I was fumbling in my reticule for my key, something jogged my elbow.

'Enerunds?'

The girl Tabby had appeared from nowhere, standing there in her old stableman's cap, her assortment of shawls that never varied, winter or summer, her stockingless feet in shapeless boots too large for her. She was, I guessed, around fourteen or fifteen years old and slept in a shed next to the cows at the end of the yard on piles of sacks and old blankets. As far as she made a living, it was doing small jobs for dwellers in the yard. She'd just asked me if I had any errands for her. I thought quickly.

'Would you run along to the baker's and see if there are any loaves left. Here's sixpence. Keep the change for yourself.'

Her eyes glinted. She took the coin and ran off, boots flopping, before I could change my mind.

I found my key, unlocked the door and walked upstairs to our parlour. There was a note from Mrs Martley on the table: *Have gone round to Mr Suter's. Your supper is in the meat safe.* Better still. My best friend, Daniel Suter, had married a dancer named Jenny the year before. Mrs Martley had expected me to marry him and was furious. With me, not with him. Then Jenny had done the only thing that could redeem her in Mrs Martley's eyes and become pregnant. All Mrs Martley's professional instincts, as well as her kindness, had been aroused. She now spent as much time at their rooms in Bloomsbury as she did at Abel Yard. I hoped Daniel and Jenny were grateful. I knew I was.

I went on, up a narrower flight of stairs, into a room that was one of the delights of my life. The afternoon sun gleamed on the white walls, scattered here and there with rainbows, from the light filtering through a glass mermaid that I'd hung in the window. My second-hand couch, newly upholstered in blue to match the curtains, stood by the window. I knelt on it as I took off my bonnet, enjoying the view over waves of gleaming roof tiles with pigeons basking in the sun, to the tops of the trees in Hyde Park. Besides the couch, I had a trunk and a row of pegs for my clothes, a set of shelves over-flowing with my books, a cheval mirror, a table to write on. There were still a few strawberries left in the chip punnet on my table, an extravagance from yesterday. I took off my gloves and ate them, then rummaged under the bookcase for the box where I kept my accounts. It took only a few minutes to establish what I was nearly sure of in any case – that if I wanted to keep my precari-ous comforts, I couldn't afford to turn down a case as profitable as this one might be. That was true enough, but only an excuse. I'd known before I'd left Mr Disraeli that his appeal to my curiosity had been successful, and he knew it too.

*     *     *

36

The events at the jousting practice two days later only increased my curiosity. As it happened, I had another social engagement that evening after I came back from the Eyre Arms. Often weeks might pass when I didn't go to functions except on business, but this was June, with the season at its height. An embossed invitation card had come from a former pianoforte pupil of mine, an aristocratic young married woman whom I didn't care for greatly, who had decided that my efforts weren't on a par with her genius. I'd heard she'd found herself a professor instead. She now intended to delight the world with a soirée of Chopin and Miss Liberty Lane was cordially invited. I didn't much look forward to it, but my career as an investigator was not so secure that I could ignore an event which might provide rich pupils.

When I got home after returning Rancie to the stables I warmed a pan of water for a good all-over wash, then dressed in my new ribbed silk, the colour of bluebells. It had two rows of lace down the bodice and wonderful sleeves that puffed out from shoulder to elbow, then came tight to the wrist with a row of three silk-covered buttons. It was a struggle doing up the buttons on the right sleeve with my left hand, even with the help of a button-hook, but when I looked in the mirror I knew it had been worth it. The event was in Knightsbridge and I'd decided to walk there across the park to save a cab fare, so I tucked a cloth into my reticule to give my shoes a surreptitious wipe before I faced the front door and footman.

My former pupil hadn't improved greatly as a pianist, only added a layer of affectation to her modest competence. I sat there in her over-decorated drawing room on an uncomfortable gilt chair, wishing I hadn't come. Then, in a pause between nocturnes, a woman's voice hissed from the row behind.

'Elizabeth.'

It seemed to be directed at me, even though it wasn't my name. I ignored it. It came again, more urgently, actually in a note's rest in the music. I turned round and saw a face I'd never expected to see again. A lovely face, framed in red-gold hair dressed with a rope of creamy pearls, a little fuller than when I'd last seen it two years ago, cheeks soft as peaches. Celia. When she saw she had my attention, she beckoned and flicked her eyes towards the room next door. She thought we should get up there and then, in mid-nocturne, and go and talk. She always had been impatient. I put a finger to my lips, tried to sign wait and turned round, but I could feel her eyes on the back of my neck, hear the silk hiss of her dress as she fidgeted.

I sat oblivious of the music, hurled back suddenly to a time I revisited as seldom as possible. Celia and I belonged in different worlds. She had a rich husband who adored her, a London house and a country estate. She was as good natured as a child and just as self-centred, without a thought in her lovely head about society, art, politics or anything outside her own circle. In spite of that, and even after a gap of two years, there was something that bound us as closely as sisters. I'd met her at the lowest point in my life, a few hours after I learned my father had been murdered, and she'd been kind. The events of the weeks that followed had deprived her, too, of people she'd loved. I'd played a part in that. I knew I wasn't to blame. Or if there had been any blame at all, I'd cancelled the debt by helping her elope to a marriage that even London gossip admitted had become a by-word for happiness. I'd been pleased when I heard that. If I'd wanted to meet her again, it could have been arranged easily enough, but I was scared of the feelings that meeting her might bring back. There was no help for it now, though. When the music finished at last, she was waiting at the end of my row.

'Elizabeth! I don't believe it.'

She'd first known me under an assumed name, and although I'd told her my real one she'd never managed to remember it. The soft lisp was still there in her voice, the grace in the way she moved. She was wearing pale apricot silk with a wide sash in a darker tone. A triple necklace of pearls and diamonds gleamed against her skin. She put her hand on my arm, laughing at the wonder of it.

'Where have you been? What have you been doing? I've been thinking about you so much since . . . since that night.'

The night I'd helped her elope. The night I'd seen her brother die. Her brother had killed my father. Celia would never know that. If she'd tried, she could have found me over the last two years, but Celia lived by impulse and didn't look far under the surface of things. There was nothing but pleasure at seeing me again in her voice and face, no tension in the hand on my arm.

A slow tide of people was carrying us towards the next room where refreshments were laid out. She kept her hand where it was, talking all the way.

'It really is a miracle. We've been in town so little this season, just a couple of appearances at court and so forth. Have you been presented to Queen Victoria yet? Isn't she quite charming, and she talks so amusingly. But it's such a labour to get Philip to leave the estate for more than a week at a time. He's totally devoted to agricultural improvement, especially pigs. How many other women do you know whose chief rival for their husband's attention weighs thirty stone and grunts?'

People were beginning to turn towards us. She was laughing about her husband, but her voice was full of love for him and she was clearly happy. My dread began to melt away. Celia might claim to have been thinking of me, but she lived almost entirely in the present and after that first reference she didn't want to talk or think about the past. She brought her face close to mine.

'And I must tell you, I'm breeding.'

It took me a while to jump from pigs to people and offer her my sincere congratulations.

'Yes, it will soon be showing, so there won't be many more parties this season. It's due in November – isn't that convenient, such a dull time of year with no parties.'

We'd reached the doorway. Our hostess was standing at the other side of it so before we were allowed to reach the refreshments we had to pay tribute to her performance. Celia told her the mazurka thing was so cheerful you wanted to dance to it, meaning it as a compliment, and got a sour look. I said the performance was charming, meaning it as an insult, and received a thin smile. We progressed to the buffet and a gentleman who knew Celia fussed round us with plates and glasses. Skilfully, she managed to keep the food and wine but lose the gentleman, and found us two chairs on our own. She forked up poached salmon with eager appetite.

'And you, my dear, are you . . .?'

She glanced at my ring finger. I shook my head. She gave a disappointed pout.

'I was sure you would be by now. I hope you have friends looking out for you.'

I laughed.

'My friends know all too well what I'd say if they did any such thing.'

'Is there somebody?'

I shook my head and forked up salmon. She looked into my face.

'Was there nearly somebody?'

'Well, yes, perhaps nearly.'

'And did he marry somebody else?'

'Yes.'

'Oh, my dear, I'm sorry.'

'Not at all. I'm glad of it. She's a far better wife for him than I'd ever have been.'

She put down her fork and touched the inside of my wrist.

'My dear, I admire you for putting a brave face on things. So it's up and on with the hunt.'

'Celia, it isn't a hunt. You don't bring a husband home over your shoulder like a haunch of venison.'

Her laugh brought people looking towards us again.

'Oh, how convenient if one could.'

'Celia, you married for love. My mother and father married for love. If I can't do the same, then I shan't marry at all.'

'Nonsense. You're far too pretty and agreeable to be an old maid. But one really can't be too fussy.'

I finished my salmon, remembering that with Celia the impulses to hug her and hit her with a heavy object were never far apart. What I couldn't explain to her, because there was nothing in her life that would help her understand, was the delight that I was beginning to take in my independence. I'd fallen into it by accident, and the shock had been like a plunge into cold water, but now I'd learned to swim in it and the water didn't seem so cold after all. It would take a more remarkable man than any I was likely to meet on the social circuit to understand that.

Luckily, something had happened to change the subject. Two women had arrived late and, instead of being annoyed because they'd missed her performance, our hostess was fawning over them like royalty. The older one was tall and middle-aged, the younger one in her early twenties. Celia caught her breath.

'Look, it's Rosa Fitzwilliam.'

She was staring at the younger woman like an astronomer seeing a comet. Rosa Fitzwilliam was a little above average height, slimly built but with a good bust and beautiful sloping shoulders. Her face was a perfect oval, complexion like alabaster with moonlight on it. Her chestnut brown hair, swept up into elaborate spirals, was pinned with a diamond aigrette that caught the light from the chandeliers as she graciously nodded at her hostess's words. Celia wasn't the only one looking at her. A hush had fallen on the room. Some people were staring at her openly, others trying to carry on their conversations while looking at her sidelong.

'Who is she?' I said.

'Oh, my dear, where have you been? She's positively the Beauty of the season. Just come over from Dublin, or everyone would have known about her long before. Just look at those eyebrows. Do you suppose she plucks them?'

They were two flawless arches; her lips, equally flaw-less, could have come from a classical statue. I looked and puzzled about this question of beauty. In my opinion, Celia was at least equally beautiful, and there were several other women in the room of whom you could say the same. And yet they were staring at Rosa Fitzwilliam without envy, as if she came from another planet and they could not be expected to compete. For some reason, every now and then, society chooses to pick out a lovely woman and raise her to the status of the Beauty. There was no arguing with it.

Rosa Fitzwilliam graciously accepted a glass of champagne and moved across the room to talk to a group of people she obviously knew. Conversation swelled again, but there was an excitement in the room that hadn't been there before she arrived, the way the air quivers after lightning strikes.

'I suppose they'll have to put off the marriage if his father dies,' Celia said.

'Whose father?'

'The whole thing is terribly hard for her, although you'd never guess it to look at her. After all, she couldn't possibly have known when she accepted him at Christmas time. Nobody had the least idea then.'

'Least idea about what?'

'If it came to it, I suppose he'd have to release her from the engagement. It would be the only honourable thing to do, don't you think?'

'Celia, I haven't the slightest notion what you're talking about.'

She stared at me.

'Surely you've heard about the Brinkburns? Everybody's known for weeks.'

I bit my tongue. Even if everybody had known for weeks, my promise to Disraeli of secrecy still held.

'Known what?'

She handed her empty plate to a passing servant and brought her head closer to mine.

'Rosa's engaged to Stephen Brinkburn. His father's madder than poor old King George was, and he's going to die any day now. Only there's some doubt about Stephen's right to inherit . . . apparently his father wasn't . . . well, you know.'

If I hadn't heard the story already from a more coherent source, no, I shouldn't have known. But one thing was clear. However hard Disraeli and his friends were trying to keep the scandal within a small circle, it was already the talk of the London drawing rooms.

'But she's still engaged to him whatever happens, isn't she?' I said. 'She can't just send him back like a pair of gloves that aren't the right colour.'

'My dear, what pictures you're painting. It seems quite clear to me. If it turns out that he isn't and the younger brother is, then strictly speaking it's the younger brother she should be engaged to, and since he's supposed to be in love with her too, like all the other young men, it wouldn't make a lot of difference. Except to poor Stephen, of course, but then . . .'

She stopped talking because another of those sudden silences had just fallen on the assembly. Celia turned towards the door.

'Oh look, it's him.'

A young man was standing just inside the doorway, his posture stiff and his face serious. He was in correct gentleman's evening wear of black and white. The last time I'd seen him he'd just rolled down a flight of steps in full armour and was trying to do serious harm to his brother. From the silence, and the set expression on his face, many of the people in the room had heard about it already and he was all too aware of that.

Everybody seemed to have noticed his entrance except Rosa Fitzwilliam. She had her back to the door and was talking to one of her group. Stephen started walking towards her, like a man who expected to come under fire. One of her companions must have said something, because she turned and smiled at him. To me, there seemed a hint of strain in her smile, but it must have been good enough for him because he smiled back and relaxed a little, as if the other people didn't matter so much after all. He walked up to her, took her hand and raised it to his lips. Celia caught my eye and gave an upward jerk of her chin.

'Still on, then,' she murmured to me.

It was safe to say it now, because people were talking again and pretending to disregard the couple. From Rosa's gestures, it looked as if she was rebuking Stephen playfully for being late, tapping his coat sleeve with her fan. The gesture was charming, vivacious, just a little too stagey, as if she knew very well that everybody's attention was on them. A footman had appeared at our side and was waiting for Celia to notice him.

'Your carriage is outside, ma'am.'

Celia stood up.

'Darling Philip is so concerned I shouldn't stay out late. Do let me drop you off.'

We said our goodbyes. Her own footman helped us into their comfortable carriage, upholstered in pink. When Celia asked where I lived I suggested that she should put me down at the corner of Mount Street. I had no shame about living among the artisans and animals, but I knew it would puzzle her terribly. On the short journey she chattered on about the endless good qualities of her Philip, so there was no opportunity to get back to the problems of the Brinkburn family. As I was getting down, she kissed me.

'Oh, it's been so pleasant. Let's meet again soon. You must come and see me. Do say yes.'

'Yes, but I don't even know where you live,' I said.

She produced a tiny pink notebook from the pocket of her evening cloak and a silver pencil as thin as a flower stem.

'You'll come tomorrow, or the day after, promise? The doctor says I must rest in the afternoons and you've no idea how achingly dull it is, Elizabeth.'

Clearly my name was a lost cause with her. She tore the page with her address out of the book and pressed it into my hand. I watched as her coach pulled away, pleased things had turned out well for her. Also, I was glad to have set eyes on the possibly transferable fiancée. Altogether, it had turned out to be a more instructive evening than I'd expected.

# CHAPTER THREE

You can buy anything in Bond Street. Anything, that is, except what a person might need in everyday life. Ironmongers, cobblers or grocers have no place on these elegant pavements. But if you want, say, a painting reliably attributed to Fra Lippo Lippi, a marble Aphrodite from Delos, a sacred scarab once owned by an Egyptian pharaoh, you may stroll up and down Bond Street and take your choice from several of each. You could also equip yourself with a full suit of armour, a crested helmet, sword, battle-axe and caparisons for your war horse.

I'd walked past Samuel Pratt's shop at number 47, on the corner of Maddox Street, almost every day, stopping now and then for a glance when he had some particularly elaborate suit of armour or flamboyant banner in his window.

His customers, I'd assumed, were people who wanted

these things to add historical tone to the halls of their newly built gothic castles. The knowledge that he was now supplying them to men who intended to wear and use them gave the place a new interest for everybody. When I walked down Bond Street on a sunny morning to keep my appointment with the younger Mr Brinkburn, there were so many people looking in Pratt's window that they blocked the pavement, and two carriages were waiting outside. I pushed my way through and went into the shop. The high walls of its salesroom were hung with banners, shields, battle-axes and dozens of swords and daggers arranged in symmetrical patterns. Suits of armour on dummies flanked a door to an inner room. Two gentlemen and a black-coated salesman wearing white gloves were standing at a table gravely examining gauntlets. There was no sign of Miles Brinkburn.

'Fifteenth-century German,' the salesman was saying, 'hardest steel that was ever made, but they're supple as silk.'

A younger salesman came towards me and asked if he could help. I told him that I had an appointment with Mr Brinkburn.

'He's through there in our workshop, ma'am, seeing his armour unpacked. He said you were to be shown through.'

He opened the door between the two guardian suits of armour and stood back to let me pass.

Miles Brinkburn was down on his haunches beside a crate surrounded with wood-shavings, studying what

49

looked like a piece of leg armour. He stood up when he saw me.

'I'm so glad you could be here, Miss Lane. It arrived just before they closed last night and they haven't had time to unpack it all yet.'

A well-dressed man in his mid thirties whom I took to be Mr Pratt himself was standing beside the crate, supervising an apprentice who was removing more wood-shavings. It struck me that Pratt looked worried. Miles, on the other hand, was glowing with enthusiasm. He showed me the piece of armour.

'Just look at the great dent in this greave. Pratt thinks it's old damage. It might have happened when my ancestor Sir Gilbert was wearing it in a tournament four hundred years ago.'

It struck me that it could have just as well resulted from some domestic accident twenty years ago, but I didn't say so.

'The armour's been standing in our gallery all my life,' Miles said. 'I used to dream about it as a boy. I never imagined I'd be wearing it in action one day.'

Pratt looked even more worried. Miles pushed the apprentice aside and delved in the case like a child in a bran tub, bringing out another greave and two or three more pieces I couldn't identify. Pratt took them and inspected them gravely, nodding his head.

'Yes, they have every appearance of being authentic fifteenth century.'

'Of course they're authentic. They've never been out

of the family. Now, where's the main part of it, the what d'you call it?'

'The cuirass,' Pratt said. 'It's over there by the wall.'

He nodded towards the back and breastplate that would cover the upper part of the body.

'It will have to be altered to fit me,' Miles said. 'Our noble ancestor must have been on the small side. I'll need it done well before the tournament so that I can practise in it.'

Mr Pratt coughed.

'When it comes to alterations, I think I should say that your brother may have . . .'

It sounded like the start of a speech he'd been preparing. Miles broke into it impatiently.

'It's nothing to do with my brother. I was the one who had the idea of sending for Sir Gilbert's armour. He'll just have to make other arrangements. Where are the spurs? They'll need new straps.'

Mr Pratt looked anything but reassured, but must have realised he could take the subject no further at present, so signed to one of the apprentices to drag out another crate from where it was standing next to the cuirass. The lid was still nailed down and they had to use a crowbar to lever it off.

While the work was going on, I had a chance to look round. A craftsman was hammering delicately on something at a bench by the window. Wooden dummies stood along the walls, wearing various bits of armour. A full-size wax model of a leg dangled from a peg.

Other pegs held leather tunics that were presumably for wearing under the armour. It might have been ancient sweat and blood from those that, in the heat, gave the workshop a pronounced animal smell. I noticed Mr Pratt looking round and wrinkling his nose. Wood splintered. The apprentice wrenched off the lid of the case, disclosing a layer of wood-shavings. Miles Brinkburn stepped forward eagerly, then fell back. The smell was suddenly much worse.

'What the . . .? Have they gone and put a dead rat in with it?'

Mr Pratt took his place and scooped out double hand-fuls of wood-shavings, dumping them on the floor. Something rat-coloured, but not as solid as a rat, appeared among the shavings in the crate. Wispy, like human hair.

I was only a few steps away at the time and my heart gave a thump. I don't know why, but I think I guessed before anybody else in the room what was happening, even before Pratt turned pale and drew his cupped hands back as if he'd been bitten.

'No,' he said, as if the thing could be made to go away.

As the shavings in the crate settled, a yellowish dome appeared as if it were rising by its own will. Pratt staggered back. The apprentice screamed.

'What is it?' said Miles. 'What's happening?'

His view of the crate was screened by Pratt. He sounded impatient. When nobody answered he pushed past Pratt then came to a sudden halt.

'Oh God.'

In spite of the heat of the day, I was shivering. I told myself: *You've seen worse than this*. It was true, but that didn't make it any better. I wanted to look away, but there was a terrible fascination about that head. The shavings had settled now, just at the arch of the eyebrows. The skin of the forehead was shiny and tight-stretched, with a small liver-coloured birthmark shaped like a map of Ireland on what would have been the hairline when the person was younger. A man, certainly. A man going bald but not grey yet. A middle-aged man who did not go to expensive barbers. I wished my mind would stop working like that, coolly forming conclusions while the rest of me shivered. It registered too that there had been a peculiar tone about Miles's 'Oh God'. It sounded like recognition as well as shock.

To his credit, Pratt must have been cool enough to notice that too.

'Do you know him, sir?'

Miles retched out a 'yes'. Then added, 'I think so.'

'We'd better get him out.'

When it was clear that he'd get no practical help from Miles, Pratt reached into the packing case. The head flopped forward. The hair at the back of it was black and clotted.

I thought: *Head wounds bleed a lot. There's no blood on the shavings, so he was dead before they nailed him up in the crate*. It seemed a relief to know he hadn't been shut up in there alive and suffocated. I don't think

53

I said anything out loud, but I must have made some movement that reminded Pratt I was there.

'Get the lady out of here,' he said to the apprentice.

In fact, the apprentice needed help far more than I did. He looked near to fainting and I had to guide him towards the door to the shop. Just before we got there, he leaned over and vomited. I jumped aside in time or it would have been all over my shoes. When I glanced back, the body was out of the case and Pratt had laid it on the floor, surrounded by pieces of Sir Gilbert's armour. It was a man in black trousers and jacket and what looked like a coarse, yellowish shirt. He seemed rather shorter than average and younger than I'd guessed, perhaps in his mid thirties. Above the retchings and gaspings of the lad, I heard Pratt repeat his question:

'Do you know him, sir?'

And Miles Brinkburn's answer, as if he couldn't believe what he was saying:

'It's Handy. My father's servant, Handy.'

I'd have liked to hear more, but had the apprentice to look after. Several well-dressed gentlemen took backward steps as I propelled him through the door into the shop. I sat him down in a chair meant for customers and told the gauntlet salesman to bring him a glass of water. The man looked so horrified at this breach of protocol that I thought it was just as well he didn't know what was happening in the workshop. He was still dithering when the door from the workshop opened and Pratt told him to go and find a policeman.

'A policeman, sir? Has something been stolen?'

'Just go and do it,' Pratt said.

The man gulped and left the shop at a run. Pratt went back into the workshop. Before he closed the door after him, I heard a snatch of Miles's voice, saying shouldn't they wait before calling the police? Wait for what? I wondered. The customers were asking each other and me what was happening. I had no idea, I said. One of the gentlemen said his armour was out in the workshop and he hoped to goodness it wasn't one of the things stolen. He showed signs of wanting to go through for a look, but luckily the shop assistant was back within minutes with a police constable in tow. There are always plenty of police in Bond Street. The assistant opened the door and let him through to the workroom. The customer worrying about his armour tried to follow, but Pratt barred the way.

'I'm sorry, gentlemen. A situation has arisen and we are having to close for the afternoon. Our apologies. We shall be open tomorrow morning as usual. No, sir, I assure you that there's been no robbery. Nothing is missing, nothing at all. An accident, that's all.'

They filed out, slowly and reluctantly. I was lingering with the last of them when the door to the workroom opened again and Pratt came out.

'Miss . . . Miss Lane, is it? I do apologise most sincerely, but for some reason the constable wishes to speak to you. If I may send him out to you . . .'

'I'll come in,' I said and walked past him, through

the door and into the workroom. Partly it was an act of bravado to prove to myself that my nerves were under control, partly that I was curious about the reaction of Miles Brinkburn. He was sitting on a chair at one of the work benches by the wall, head bent, arms hanging between his legs. He stood up and looked at me with the expression of a dog in a rainstorm, hungry for pity, and started apologising for bringing me into this. The constable cut across him, polite but authoritative. If he was surprised that I'd come into the room instead of waiting outside, he didn't show it.

'I am sorry to cause you any further distress, Miss Lane, but the coroner will need to know who was present when the body was discovered.'

He seemed well spoken and intelligent for a mere constable. His grey eyes looked me in the face and I was sure he'd recognise me if we met again. The body was on the floor behind him, covered with a caparison ornamented in black and silver chevrons that must have been meant for the back of a warhorse.

I gave him my name and address and he wrote them down in his notebook.

'I understand you were here at the invitation of Mr Brinkburn, Miss Lane?'

'Yes.'

'May I ask if you are a friend of the Brinkburn family?'

'I met Mr Brinkburn for the first time yesterday.'

A flicker of surprise in the grey eyes.

'And other members of the family?'

'I have met no other members of the family.'

He was trying to place me, I could tell that. I was unmarried, with an address in Mayfair (he might not know that it was on the unfashionable side) and I accepted invitations from gentlemen I'd only just met. The conclusion might seem obvious.

'Had you met Mr Handy?'

'The man in the crate? No, to the best of my knowledge, I've never seen him before.'

That seemed to be all. He thanked me.

'I'll see Miss Lane to a cab,' Miles said.

The constable shook his head.

'I'd be grateful if you'd wait, sir. There are formalities. I'm sure Mr Pratt will take care of Miss Lane.'

Miles seemed about to protest. Pratt took my arm and I let him guide me towards the door. Miles called after him.

'Pratt, will you get somebody to send for Lomax. Oliver Lomax of Lincoln's Inn. He'll know what to do.'

Pratt nodded and we went through to the shop. I told him I didn't need a cab and walked into the sunlight of Bond Street, wondering why Miles Brinkburn's first coherent thought had been to summon a lawyer.

# CHAPTER FOUR

Back home in my room at Abel Yard, I opened the window to let in what passes for fresh air in London. It came in with the familiar smells of sun-warmed grass from the park, of the cow byre where the yard's resident herd of four Guernseys was kept, of hot iron from the carriage mender's workshop, with the usual faint whiff of cesspit underlying them. Still, it was sweeter than the memory of that smell from the crate. I mixed some fresh ink and wrote a note to Jimmy Cuffs at the Cheshire Cheese, Fleet Street, asking him to find out when and where the inquest into a servant named Handy would take place and let me know by return. When I went back down to the yard, the boy who blew the bellows for the carriage mender's forge was willing to carry out the errand for sixpence.

Jimmy Cuffs was a man I'd met in one of my investigations. I suppose he might be described as a journalist of a kind, though that was rather a grand title for his trade of picking up snippets from the coroners' courts that might make a paragraph or two in the newspapers. He was no taller than a twelve-year-old child and lurched along at a fast limp because of a club foot. He must have had a lodging somewhere, but his seat in the corner of the Cheshire Cheese was his true residence and he was always to be found there in the evenings. It was hard to tell his age and nobody knew his surname. Jimmy Cuffs was the name given to him by the other scribblers who were his drinking companions, because once, when the coroners' courts had been unusually dull, he couldn't afford to have his shirts washed, so took to wearing his rusty black jacket buttoned right to the neck, with a pair of respectable white cuffs sticking out from the sleeves. Only the cuffs, with no shirt attached to them.

Jimmy Cuffs was a cultivated man. I'd seen him in St Martin's Lane with his nose pressed to a bookshop window like a starving boy at a pie shop. He claimed to know all the Odes of Horace by heart. Late one night, when business had taken me to Fleet Street, I'd heard him trying to prove it by reciting one of them to a crowd of drunken friends. He was just as drunk himself and had to cling to a lamp post to stay upright, but his Latin sounded as clear as Cicero's. He and I were occasionally able to do each other professional favours. Although

I'd never betray a client's confidence, I could sometimes put a story Jimmy's way that did him good and nobody else any harm.

In not much more than an hour, the bellows boy returned with his reply, written on the back of a few inches of newspaper proof in his fine Italic hand: *Day after tomorrow, Thursday, 10 a.m. at Marylebone. Would have been tomorrow, but they have to wait for a witness to come up from the country.*

While I was reading this, Mrs Martley returned from her daily visit to Jenny and Daniel, with two warm pies for our supper in her basket because she hadn't had time to cook. I'd opened a bottle from our small store of claret in celebration of having a case that might pay well and poured two glasses to go with the pie. As we ate and drank I asked her how Jenny was.

'I've never known a woman so happy. Mr Suter fusses over her that much, he'll hardly let her lift a finger. I told him not to worry. She may be only a little scrap of a thing, but she's strong as oak.'

'The baby's due soon, isn't it?'

She gave me a reproachful look for not knowing.

'Four weeks this Sunday. It's often late with the first, especially if it's going to be a boy. She's carrying it high, so . . .'

Tides of midwife's technicalities drifted over my head. Mrs Martley had got over her reluctance to talk about such matters, with me in my unmarried state. There were

60

times when I wished she hadn't. I thought about the Brinkburn family, and how the death of Handy might affect my investigations.

'. . . so I told her if she did it again I'd pitch her down the stairs and watch while she bounced.'

'What?'

It took me a while to realise that she'd changed the subject. While I was away, she'd caught the waif Tabby inside our part of the house.

'Right up here in the parlour, looking round like somebody at the zoo. The girl's so alive with lice and fleas it makes my flesh creep to look at her.'

It made my flesh creep too. Still, I felt an interest in the girl.

'Did she say what she was doing here?'

'She said she wanted to know how people lived. Can you imagine the insolence of it? I told her I had a good mind to call the beadle and have her put in the poorhouse.'

'Oh, don't do that.'

I didn't want Tabby in the house uninvited either, but it sounded as if the girl had been guilty of nothing but curiosity. Since that's a sin of mine as well, it gave me something of a fellow feeling for her. I decided not to tell Mrs Martley about the day's events. She thoroughly disapproved of my way of earning a living, even though it did pay our rent and put food on the table. A few months before, I'd lost patience and told her roundly that she must either accept it or go. To my surprise, she

61

stayed. To my even greater surprise, I was glad that she'd stayed. So we'd come to a truce on the subject. I tried not to intrude my professional concerns on her, while she tried hard not to nag about my irregular comings and goings. When, after the meal, I fetched my old black bonnet down from my room and asked her help in steaming it back into shape, she didn't even ask why I needed it at the height of summer.

Anybody may attend an inquest. It's a public event like any other court case. Still, a woman among the spectators tends to be conspicuous and I didn't want to attract attention. I wore the re-shaped bonnet tilted well down to shade my face and a black cloak, hoping to pass for some obscure mourning relative. The usher didn't give me a second glance as I took my place at the end of the back row in the stuffy courtroom. The windows were set so high that the dusty sunlight coming through them made little difference to the dimness of the place. When Jimmy Cuffs limped in, I kept my head down. He walked past to a seat at the front without noticing me. From the sideways glance I had of him, he looked to be the only cheerful person present. The oddity of the body's discovery combined with the current jousting mania should pay his wine and laundry bills for another week. The coroner arrived and we all stood up. The jurors were sworn in and immediately sent out again for the formality of viewing the body in a room next door. After a two-day delay in this heat, I didn't envy them. Several were holding handkerchiefs to their noses as they came back.

While most of the attention was on them, two men walked in and sat down on the end of my row, with eight chairs between us. The elder one looked to be in his early fifties and had an air of distinction that set him apart from anybody else in the room. He was slim and upright, with a firm profile, iron-grey hair and clean-shaven face. His black jacket and trousers were finely tailored, his shoes crafted by a master boot-maker to flatter long and narrow feet. The younger man was Miles Brinkburn. He too was carefully dressed in black, but in contrast to his companion he looked uncertain and ill at ease, all his vitality and confidence gone. The coroner told the jury that the first business of the court was to establish the identity of the deceased.

'Mr Brinkburn, please,' the coroner said.

Miles glanced at the grey-haired man and got a nod from him, as if his orders mattered more than the coroner's. He got to his feet steadily enough and walked to the front of the court.

'Mr Brinkburn, have you viewed the body of the deceased?' the coroner said.

Miles nodded.

'Answer yes or no, please.'

'Yes.'

'Are you able to identify him?'

'Handy. Simon Handy.'

'In what capacity was Mr Handy known to you?'

Miles swallowed, glanced towards the grey-haired man and away again.

'He was a family servant.'

'At what address?'

'Brinkburn Hall, in Buckinghamshire.'

'How long had he been employed there?'

'Only for a few months, but before that he'd been my father's servant for twenty years or more. Then my father didn't need him any more, so . . .'

His voice trailed away. The coroner may have been aware why Lord Brinkburn was no longer in a position to employ servants, because he didn't press the point.

'How recently before his decease had you seen him?'

'Back . . . back sometime in the spring, I think. The last time I was home anyway.'

'Were you present when his body was discovered?'

Another nod. Another reminder that the question must be answered in words.

'Yes. Yes, I was.'

It took the coroner some time to get an account of what had happened in Pratt's workroom out of Miles Brinkburn. It added nothing to what I knew from being there.

'Do you know of any reason why Mr Handy should have been inside the crate?' the coroner said.

'No, of course not. I'd told Whiteley to have the armour packed up and sent to Pratt's. Handy shouldn't have had anything to do with it.'

'Whiteley being?'

'Our steward.'

After a few more questions the coroner thanked him and asked the jurors if they had any questions. They hadn't, so Miles was allowed to stand down. He walked back to his seat, blowing out his cheeks with relief, said something to the grey-haired man as he sat down and got a brief nod in reply.

The next witness was the intelligent policeman. He described how he'd been called to Pratt's premises and what he'd found there, without adding anything to what I knew already. Then it was the turn of a doctor employed by the police to give evidence on the cause of death. Translated into layman's terms for the benefit of the jury, Handy had died from being struck several times on the back of the head by a heavy object. The injuries to the skull had been such that death must have been almost instantaneous. The doctor's opinion was that he'd almost certainly been dead before he was put into the crate. There was a perceptible feeling of relief in the court. The coroner asked the doctor if he'd been able to establish when Handy had died.

'Not with any degree of certainty. I examined the corpse the day before yesterday, soon after it was brought to the mortuary. By that point, rigor mortis had entirely passed off. From the state of the internal organs, it's likely that the deceased had been dead for something between twenty-four and forty-eight hours.'

The coroner made a note, writing slowly.

'You said that death would have been almost instant-aneous?'

'Yes, sir.'

'In your opinion, is there any possibility that the deceased might have climbed inside the crate after receiving the blows to the head?'

The doctor hesitated.

'In my opinion, it is extremely unlikely. The brain is a peculiar organ. There are cases on record of people performing actions which seem to imply some form of consciousness after receiving what subsequently prove to have been fatal blows.'

'So it can't be ruled out entirely?'

'Not entirely, although I repeat it would be very unlikely. For one thing, head injuries of that nature bleed profusely. The crate and its contents would have become so suffused with blood that anybody attempting to move it would have noticed.'

The coroner sat forward.

'So you are saying that the bleeding must have taken place elsewhere, before the deceased was put into the crate?'

'In my opinion, yes.'

The doctor was followed by the steward from Brinkburn Hall, Wilberforce Whiteley. He was a middle-aged man who seemed to be made up of circles, like a child's drawing; a rounded figure, neat little paunch bulging out of his waistcoat, round head with sleek brown hair combed carefully over the bald patch, slightly protuberant brown eyes that reminded me of a guinea-pig's. He held himself stiffly upright, showing his nervousness by blinking often and quickly. The coroner asked him how long he'd been employed as a steward by the family.

'Twenty-six years, sir.'

He spoke with a country accent.

'Were you well acquainted with the deceased?'

'He joined us quite recently, sir. Before that, I only saw him when his lordship came to visit us.'

'And how often was that?'

'Once a year, sir.'

The coroner raised his eyebrows. I noticed that Mr Whiteley glanced towards the grey-haired man after answering.

'Are you able to tell the court anything of the way in which he met his death?'

'No, sir. I didn't even know he was dead until we got word from London.'

'Had he not been missed from his employment?'

'The housekeeper told me he hadn't been seen all day Monday and Tuesday morning, but that wasn't entirely out of the way with Handy.'

His tone of voice made it clear that he hadn't thought highly of the man.

'He was accustomed to absent himself from his employment?'

'From time to time, yes, sir.'

The coroner made another note.

'Is it a fact that you were instructed to pack up a suit of armour and send it to Pratt's in Bond Street?'

'Yes, sir. Sir Gilbert Brinkburn's armour. I received a note from Mr Miles saying I was to have it crated up and sent off as soon as possible. I asked her ladyship and she was entirely agreeable, so I started seeing to it that same day.'

'How long ago was this?'

'I received the note last Saturday morning. As soon as her ladyship gave permission, I had the armour dusted and moved from the gallery to the old dairy for packing. We had to wait for crates to be got down from the attic and wood-shavings brought from the carpenter's shop, so by the time we finished packing and nailing them down it was too late to send that day. There was no point in sending the armour up on Sunday, with the shop not open, so I gave instructions that our carter was to come first thing on Monday morning and collect the crates.

'And did that happen?'

'Yes, sir.'

'Did you check the crates when they were loaded on to the vehicle on Monday morning?'

'No, sir.'

The coroner looked surprised.

'Wasn't that part of your duties?'

'The carter came early, sir, and I was engaged else-where on the estate. My instructions to him were quite clear, so there was no great need to be there.'

'So nobody counted the crates when they were loaded and realised there was one extra?'

'It seems not, sir.'

'You said the armour was packed in the old dairy. Where is that in relation to the house?'

'A hundred yards or so away, on the far side of the back courtyard.'

'Why choose to pack the armour there?'

'We don't use it as a dairy any more, now we get our milk and butter from the farm, so it was just convenient, sir.'

'Was it locked overnight while the armour was in it?'

'No, sir.'

'Wasn't that somewhat lax? I assume ancient armour has some considerable value?'

Whiteley glanced across at the grey-haired man again and hesitated.

'I suppose we didn't see the need for it, sir.'

'So anybody could have gained access to the crates during Saturday night and all through Sunday?'

'I suppose so, sir.'

'When did you last see those crates?'

'Just after eight o'clock on the Sunday evening.'

Whiteley seemed sure of his ground again. The coroner looked at him over his glasses.

'Had you gone to check that they were safe?'

'Not exactly, sir.'

'What do you mean? Either you did or you didn't.'

'The fact is, sir, I looked out of my window and saw Handy leaning against the outside wall of the old dairy. Knowing him, I thought he might be thinking of getting up to some mischief with the armour, so I went out and asked him what he was doing. He said he'd only come out to smoke his pipe and wasn't doing anybody any harm. In my opinion, he'd been drinking. I said he could go and smoke his pipe elsewhere, so he took himself off.'

'Did you see where he went?'

'Towards the vegetable garden. To be honest, I didn't take a lot of interest. I looked through the window at the crates. Everything seemed to be in order, so I didn't think much more about it.'

'You said you feared he might be thinking of getting up to some mischief with the armour. Why was that?'

'He was a bit of a one for practical jokes, sir. I wouldn't have put it past him to get it out and dress up in it.'

'But as far as you could tell, he didn't?'

'No, sir. It was still in there, all nailed up.'

'Did you see him again?'

'No, sir.'

'As far as you know, did anybody else in the household see him again?'

'No, sir.'

'So to the best of your knowledge, Sunday evening just after eight o'clock was the last time anybody in the household saw Handy alive?'

'Yes, sir.'

'And you're sure of the time?'

'To within five or ten minutes, sir. It was just before

the servants sit down to their supper. We have it at quarter past eight, on account of her ladyship dining early.'

The coroner seemed to go on writing for a long time, occasionally glancing across at Whiteley, who stood staring ahead, face flushed. When the coroner had finished writing, he asked Whiteley a few more questions. Had he been aware of any disturbance on Sunday night or early Monday morning? Had anybody in the household reported anything out of the way to him? The answer was no to both questions. The coroner wanted to know if the deceased had any enemies.

'Not enemies as such, sir. But the other servants were none too friendly.'

'Why was that?'

'They thought he gave himself airs on account of working for his lordship so long.'

'Did anybody ever make threats against him?'

'Oh no, sir.'

Finally Whiteley was allowed to stand down and he took a seat in the front row. There was a long silence. The coroner nodded to his clerk to come forward and the two of them conferred for some time. The clerk sat down and the coroner addressed the jurors.

'As you may have gathered, it is an unsatisfactory situation with regard to the evidence. There would seem to be several possible verdicts open to you: death as a result of accident or misadventure, or by manslaughter, unlawful killing or murder by person or persons unknown. As things stand, there is not enough information available to you to reach a conclusion. The chief officer of the Metropolitan Police, in whose area the body was discovered, may well wish to order further investigations. These may take some time, so I am adjourning this inquest *sine die*. In the meantime, I direct that the body of the deceased should be released to his next of kin for burial. Thank you for your patience, gentlemen.'

The coroner and his clerk walked out. The jurors, taken aback by the sudden ending of the case, started asking each other if that meant they were free to go. They decided they were and filed out with a disappointed air. Jimmy Cuffs had already gone. The adjournment was good news for him and the rest of the press, for it would mean two stories instead of one. After a word with the grey-haired man, Miles Brinkburn left the courtroom, still looking dazed. There were only three of us left now: Mr Whiteley, the grey-haired man and myself. I sat quietly unnoticed in my corner as Mr Whiteley walked over to the grey-haired man.

'Did it go as you expected, Mr Lomax?'

Whiteley's voice was low and respectful. So, as I'd guessed, the grey-haired man was the lawyer that Miles had summoned from his chambers in Lincoln's Inn: the man who would know what to do. I was certain, too, that I was looking at the man Disraeli had described as the Brinkburns' family friend as well as their legal adviser. Mr Whiteley wanted his good opinion. That was clear from the way he stood looking up with his round brown eyes, like a spaniel waiting for a biscuit. He was rewarded with a curt nod and a few words.

'Probably as well as could be expected.'

'Do you think my evidence was satisfactory, Mr Lomax?'

'You did the best you could, Mr Whiteley.'

When the steward saw that this morsel of biscuit was all he could expect, he wished the other man farewell and walked slowly to the door.

Before Mr Lomax could follow him, I stood up and called his name. He turned. I don't think he'd been aware of me. I pushed back my bonnet to give myself a less funereal look.

'Will you allow me to introduce myself, Mr Lomax. My name's Liberty Lane. I think Mr Disraeli may have mentioned me.'

There was a flicker of surprise in his eyes. He took his time in replying, weighing me up.

'I had expected you to be older,' he said.

'A fault which the years will correct. I believe we might have things to discuss.'

Another pause as his eyes locked on mine. The intentness of his look would have been offensive in a normal social situation, but this wasn't one, and neither of us was pretending otherwise.

'Can you come to my chambers at four o'clock this afternoon, Miss Lane?'

It stopped just short of being a command.

'Very well.'

I turned and walked out. Had Miles Brinkburn told him that I'd been present when Handy's body was discovered? From the way Mr Lomax looked at me, I suspected that he had. He'd been asking himself whether I was the solution to one of the Brinkburn family's problems or a part of another.

That put us on an equal footing, because I didn't know either.

# CHAPTER FIVE

I went home and changed into my blue cotton print dress and straw bonnet with ribbon trim, both more appropriate to the season. When I came downstairs, Tabby was loitering by the pump at the end of the yard where the cows were kept. She came running up to me, stumbling over the cobbles in her too-large boots.

'There's a hen got her foot caught up in some string. I can't get her out of it.'

I followed her reluctantly back down the yard. I didn't want cow-byre smells clinging to my clothes, and the hens were the property of Mr Colley who kept the cows and ran a milk-round. Naturally, there was no sign of him or his idle son-in-law.

'There.'

A big red hen had got her leg tangled in a loop of

old string attached to the wooden bars of the chicken coop and was flapping and clucking.

'How in the world did she manage to do that?' I said.

'Dunnow.'

There was nothing for it in all humanity but to crouch down in the dust and try to free her. I put my reticule down on top of the coop.

'Can you hold her?' I said to Tabby.

Her brown and grimy hands enfolded the hen. The string was frayed and terribly tangled round the scaly leg. I broke a fingernail and was set coughing by the warm dust from the hen's feathers, but at last she was untangled.

'It doesn't look as if the leg's hurt,' I said. 'Let her go and we'll see.'

The hen stood for a while, not realising she was free, then shot off to join three or four others that were pecking by the manure heap. I watched her go and laughed.

'Well, there's nothing much wrong with her. It's a good job you saw her before she died of thirst.'

'You got straw on your dress now,' Tabby said.

She kneeled down in the dust and started brushing at it with her hand.

'No, never mind. I'll do it.'

I picked up my reticule, adjusted my bonnet and hurried out of the yard, knowing that I'd have to walk fast now to get to Lincoln's Inn by four.

Mayfair was crowded and in sociable mood under

the blue skies. I had to weave a zig-zag course among the gentry strolling and looking into shop windows or standing in the middle of the pavement, talking in the loud voices of people who have nothing much to say but are determined the world should hear it. As I went, I tried to plan in my mind the interview with Mr Lomax. Through Disraeli, he'd offered me an intriguing and well-paid case, and I'd been minded to accept. But that had been before the discovery of Simon Handy's body. Did I still want to accept the case? Yes. Would Mr Lomax still want me to accept it? That was another question altogether. Simon Handy's death might have changed the situation for him too. There were things about it that the Brinkburns wanted hidden, or why had Lomax gone to so much trouble to coach the steward in his evidence? And he had coached him, I was as sure of that as if I'd heard him doing it.

I was still thinking about it when I got to High Holborn. The crowds were less fashionable there, but just as annoyingly inclined to drift along the pavements or make sudden changes of direction to watch two cab drivers arguing or avoid argumentative drunks.

'Hey, stop! Stop, miss.'

The voice came from behind me, a husky female voice. I thought it might be a beggar or an unusually importunate posy seller, so didn't turn round.

'Miss, you lost this –'

I turned round and there was Tabby, red faced and

77

panting. Her shawl had slipped, leaving her bare-headed. She was holding something in her hand.

'Your purse, miss. You must have dropped it when you was seeing to the chicken. I've run all the way after you with it.'

She held it out to me. Her eyes were as appealing as Whiteley's had been.

'You followed me all the way here?'

'Yes, miss. There's still all your money in it. I haven't opened it.'

All my money. Seven pence halfpenny, as far as I remembered. I took it from her.

'Thank you, Tabby. I'll see you when I get back this evening.'

Disappointment clouded her eyes. A plump woman who'd stopped to listen looked at me reproachfully. She thought I should at least give this honest girl a penny for her trouble.

'Is that all then?'

'All for now. I'll see you later.'

I turned and hurried on, aware of a pair of hurt eyes at my back.

Oliver Lomax had not given me his address at Lincoln's Inn. Was that arrogance, or did he assume I knew it from Disraeli? If arrogance, it might have been justified, because the first person I asked at Lincoln's Inn – a clerk weighed down with bundles of papers – pointed out his staircase at once. I climbed the stairs and knocked on his door just as a clock was striking four. He was waiting in his clerk's room to meet me and led me through to his office. It was simply furnished, but the furniture, carpet and curtains were of fine quality, with touches of comfort that suggested he might spend more time there than at home. Two leather armchairs with brocade cushions stood either side of an empty fireplace. Instead of a conventional desk he had a big mahogany table, with books and papers in tidy piles. A drawing in a simple gold frame of a Roman centurion's head in a crested helmet was the only picture in the room. It looked to be Renaissance and expensive. A smaller table held a tray with a silver teapot and two bone china cups. He invited me to sit down at one of the upright chairs by his table.

'Tea, Miss Lane?'

China tea, served without milk or sugar. That was the way he liked it, so that was the way his business associates would have to like it.

I sipped and put down the cup, deciding to unsettle him from the start.

'Did the adjournment this morning surprise you?'

For a moment he let his annoyance show, but his voice was level.

'In the circumstances, the coroner had little choice.'

'I was surprised he thought misadventure might be a possible verdict,' I said. 'It would have to be a strange kind of misadventure, wouldn't it?'

He turned the force of his slate-coloured eyes on me. The temperature seemed to drop by a few degrees.

'Miss Lane, you know very well that this is not the question on which I wish to consult you. I'm surprised you attended the inquest.'

'Why? I was there when they found the body. Did Mr Brinkburn tell you that?'

He gave the faintest of nods.

'He naturally regrets having caused you to be present at such a distressing occasion.'

I doubted that. Miles Brinkburn still seemed far too shaken to indulge in conventional politenesses. I didn't say that because I'd only intended to unsettle Mr Lomax, not antagonise him.

'The unfortunate death of Handy is not your concern,' he said. 'I want to make it clear from the start that, if we do come to an understanding on the other matter, you are not to ask questions about it or take advantage of your position in any way.'

I let my eyes drop and picked up the teacup. If he wanted to interpret that as agreement, it was up to him. From the way he settled back in his chair, he did. The atmosphere became less frosty.

'Mr Disraeli seems impressed by your talents and your discretion, Miss Lane. I've made inquiries in other directions that seem to confirm his good opinion . . .' He paused, then added: '. . . on the whole.'

So he'd heard that I'd once refused to complete an investigation when I took a dislike to the client. I said nothing.

'I take it that your presence here means you're prepared to accept the commission?'

I met his eyes again.

'To find out if Lady Brinkburn is mad or misguided?'

'In a nutshell, yes.' He sighed. 'Miss Lane, you should understand that it's almost impossibly painful for me to have to talk in this way. I've been a friend of Cornelius Brinkburn's since university days. I was present at his marriage. I've known both sons since they were born. Only the most pressing necessity could persuade me to engage a person to spy on a gracious lady who has been my hostess several times in the past.'

The distress in his voice sounded genuine. He'd picked up a penholder and his fingers were clenched round it as tightly as if he wanted to break it.

'But there are some situations, Miss Lane, in which we have to accept one evil to avoid a worse one. The consequences if Lady Brinkburn persists in her allegation would be unimaginable.'

I decided to swallow his implication that I was an evil, for the time being at least.

'If I've been informed correctly, these rumours that Stephen Brinkburn is not his father's son have begun quite recently,' I said.

He nodded.

'And their source is Lady Brinkburn?'

A pause.

'Apparently, yes.'

'How recently?'

'This spring, only a couple of months ago.'

81

'Before that, had she suggested the possibility to anybody?'

'As far as I'm aware, no.'

'You'd known her socially since they were married?'

'Even before that. To be honest, Lord Brinkburn asked my opinion before proposing to the lady.'

'And your opinion was . . .?'

'There was a difference of some twenty years in their ages, but when the gentleman is the elder party, that's no great objection. Apart from that, nothing could be more suitable. Her family owned estates adjoining his family's in the north-east. She brought a very considerable settlement with her and was an accomplished and good-natured young woman.'

'That's hardly the language of a passionate love match.'

'Why should it be? It was an arrangement beneficial to both parties. In many respects, it has been a good marriage.'

'Except that they've spent a lot of it living apart.'

'It suited them both. Lady Brinkburn preferred a more secluded life and Lord Brinkburn found the Italian climate beneficial to his health.'

'And in more than twenty years, she'd never mentioned the matter of the stranger on her honeymoon until a few months ago. Can you account for that?'

He'd abandoned his attempt to break the penholder. It was in front of him on his blotter, and he was sitting back in his chair. Now that the decision had been made – to employ me, though not to trust me completely – some of the tension seemed to have gone out of him.

'Yes, I think I can account for it. Lord Brinkburn returned from Naples last January. Before he left Italy he wrote me what I regard as a very courageous and honourable letter. He said he'd been conscious for some time of a decline in his physical and mental faculties. He had consulted several distinguished physicians who had told him that his malady could only become worse. What had up to then been occasional alarming episodes were becoming more frequent. He was facing the prospect of a permanent derangement of the mind, probably in the quite near future, and increasing physical incapacity. While he still had his reason left, he was determined on making his own arrangements. He selected an establishment in Surrey where he knew he would be permitted to live out his days with all possible comfort and dignity, returned to England accompanied only by his valet, and took up residence there much as a gentleman might settle into a hotel.'

'The valet being Simon Handy?'

'Yes.'

'Did Lady Brinkburn know about this?'

'It was my sad duty to tell her. I visited Lord Brinkburn at the establishment. It was all too clear that the doctors' prognostications had been borne out by events and his mind was irretrievably affected.'

I decided not to mention what Disraeli had told me

about the Emperor Hadrian. In spite of the lawyer's dry manner, he was clearly distressed.

'I went down to Buckinghamshire to see Lady Brinkburn,' he went on. 'She was naturally affected by what I had to tell her, but seemed at first to take it quite calmly. I broached with her, as tactfully as possible, the question of who was to take on the considerable task of managing the estates now that Lord Brinkburn was incapable of doing so. I suggested that, since Stephen was of age and would inherit, probably within months rather than years, I should set about arrangements for giving him power of attorney. Lady Brinkburn made no objection to the proposal at the time, but in retrospect I believe it may have started her on this potentially disastrous course.'

'How did the story of the honeymoon get into circulation?' I said.

'I'm afraid there is no doubt at all that it came from Lady Brinkburn herself. Two weeks after I visited her at Brinkburn Hall, she came up to London unexpectedly and asked to see me.'

'Was this an unusual event?'

'Yes. I shouldn't want to give the impression that Lady Brinkburn is a recluse, but she prefers country life to the city. Although she lives a little over twenty miles from London, she usually comes to town no more than two or three times a year at most, to visit relatives or old friends. I assumed she wanted to discuss some business matters. It would have been quite reasonable, for instance, for her to want assurance that her tenancy of Brinkburn Hall would continue after her husband's death. I looked forward to being able to reassure her on that point.'

'But that wasn't what she wanted?'

'No. The moment she came in and sat down, she launched into the story that you have heard. Needless to say, I was horrified.'

'Did you believe it?'

'Not a word, neither then nor now.'

'Did you tell her you didn't believe it?'

'Not in so many words. One doesn't accuse a lady of lying. I assumed that she was distraught owing to the illness of her husband and needless uncertainty about her future. I hinted, as gently as I could, that this fancy was the result of being overwrought and she should return home and rest.'

'How did she react to that?'

'Calmly enough, but she didn't budge from her story. She asked me what I thought she should do about it. In the circumstances, I thought it would be best to pretend to take what she said seriously. I told her that, before any other steps could be considered, I should have to ask her to swear an affidavit that every detail of what she'd told me was true. I offered to prepare the affidavit for her then and there.'

'And did she swear it?'

'No. My offer had exactly the effect I'd intended. She refused to consider an affidavit and brought our interview pretty rapidly to an end. I was seriously concerned for her and decided that I must visit her at home as soon as I had the opportunity, to see if she needed any form of help.'

'Did you tell her sons what had happened?'

'At that point, no. I decided that it would distress them needlessly. I believed I'd dealt with the immediate crisis and we'd hear no more of the matter.'

'But you were wrong.'

'Yes, I was wrong. Within a few days, alarming rumours came to my ears. Lady Brinkburn must have used her circle of acquaintances in London to spread the story. As you can imagine, you could more easily stop a forest fire than a rumour of that kind, once it takes hold.'

'And of course Stephen and Miles must have heard the rumour.'

'Inevitably. Both came to consult me.'

'Separately?'

'Separately.'

'How did they react?'

'As I'm sure you know very well, Miss Lane, there is confidentiality between a lawyer and his client. I've come very near the line in describing my meeting with Lady Brinkburn. I've only done so because I choose to regard her visit to me as social rather than professional.'

'Have Stephen and Miles always hated each other?' I said.

He considered, and must have decided that this was a social matter too, though he remained wary.

'I wouldn't say *hated*. But it's fair to say that from boyhood there has been some friction between them.'

'Well, they hate each other now,' I said. 'Three days ago they were fighting each other in public.'

'I'm sure that incident has been much exaggerated.'

'I was there.'

He sighed and said nothing.

'I'm told Miles Brinkburn was always his mother's favourite,' I said.

'That's true. He was a charming, sunny-natured child, more inclined to show affection than his elder brother. Then, in his first term at public school, he caught diphtheria and nearly died. He had to spend the next year at home with his mother, convalescing. That naturally brought them closer.'

'And Stephen was not so charming and sunny-natured?'

He frowned.

'I'm implying no criticism of Stephen, none at all. He was a most satisfactory boy in every respect.'

That sounded like criticism to my ears. Any boy so described must be either very good at hiding things or insufferably boring. I said nothing, and Mr Lomax went on reciting his praises.

'He was a steady worker at school, never top of the form but always above the average. He captained his house's cricket team. By comparison, Miles was never good at applying himself to anything for long. Their schoolmasters used to hold Stephen up as a good example to him. I'm afraid that didn't make for friendship between them.'

'Did Lord Brinkburn have a preference?'

'He didn't spend much time with his sons, but on his visits to England he did encourage Stephen to take an interest in managing the family estates. He took him on tours of their property in the north-east on several occasions and Stephen visited him once in Italy.'

'Without Miles?'

'Yes. Lord Brinkburn told me that Stephen had a good head for business. He's very competent.'

'So Lord Brinkburn had no doubt that Stephen was his son?'

'None whatsoever, I'm certain of that.'

'And Lady Brinkburn didn't begin to cast doubts on it until her husband was in no state to contradict her?'

'That's true.'

Silence for a while, apart from the sound of feet walking heavily down the staircase outside.

'So what you want from me is evidence that can be produced in court showing Lady Brinkburn is mad?' I said.

'Let us say that her memory and judgement are less than reliable. It would be better than the alternative of suggesting that she's trying to advance one son's interests against those of his brother, and her own honour.'

'There is a third possibility,' I said. 'Suppose she's telling the truth?'

The slate eyes met mine and held them for what seemed like a long time.

'Miss Lane, we may suppose many things. We may suppose that this table will grow wings and fly away, or that the River Thames will run uphill. On the whole, I'd suggest it's a better policy to stick with what is likely.'

So my brief was narrower than Disraeli had suggested. It seemed that it wasn't a question of testing one version against another, only of providing support for the line already decided. Plus, I was not to concern myself with the strange death of a servant. I felt like a horse between shafts and in blinkers. Still, horses have to eat.

'How am I to set about introducing myself to Lady Brinkburn?' I said.

He actually smiled. This was where he wanted to be.

'I've been giving that some thought, Miss Lane. The Buckinghamshire estate is a small one, no more than two hundred acres or so, just across the Thames from Maidenhead. The views are less charming than they used to be, owing to the Great Western Railway's insistence on building a monstrously large bridge over the river, just next door to the Brinkburn property, but it's still a pleasant area. The estate includes a riverside cottage, about half a mile away from Brinkburn Hall. It was built as a residence for a water bailiff, but Lady Brinkburn doesn't care for fishing so it has been standing empty for some time. Rather than let it go to ruin, the estate lets it out occasionally to suitable people. Provided you look away from the railway bridge, it's a picturesque spot, and much favoured by artists. You paint or sketch, I suppose?'

'A little.'

'I've already written to Whiteley saying that an artistic acquaintance of mine is interested in taking it for some weeks. It's unfortunate that you attended the inquest this morning, but I don't suppose for a minute that Whiteley will recognise you. Lady Brinkburn is fond of painting and often walks in the woods or by the river. I'm sure you could arrange things so that the two of you meet.'

And go from there to proving her a weaver of fantasies? It was a tall order, but then tall orders were my business.

'Very well,' I said. 'When am I expected to move in?'

'Within the next few days, I told him. There really is no time to be lost. From the latest report I had, Lord Brinkburn is sinking fast.'

He picked up some papers from the desk.

'There are instructions here on how to get to the cottage. You may find it best to take the stagecoach to Maidenhead and hire a chaise. There's also a banker's draft for forty pounds towards your expenses. I'd be grateful if you'd sign a receipt.'

I signed. He was almost cheerful by now.

'It really is a very pleasant place,' he said. 'I'm sure Whiteley will find a woman from the village who will clean and cook for you, and of course there's a bedroom for your maid.'

'Of course.'

I folded the papers into my reticule, stood up and shook hands with him, which he didn't seem to expect, and walked in the early evening sunshine back to Abel Yard.

Tabby was sitting on the mounting block by the carriage mender's store-shed. As I approached, she looked up, half hopeful, half apprehensive.

'If you'd hurt that hen, I'd have had nothing more to do with you,' I said.

I could see a succession of possibilities passing over her face like cloud shadows: run away, brazen it out, pretend she didn't know what I was talking about.

'I didn't do it no harm, I took care of that.'

'It must have been awkward, tying all those knots.'

I must have let some softness into my expression, because her face lit up.

'It was, too. I didn't want you undoing them before . . .'

Then she realised what she was admitting and looked scared again.

'Before you could take my purse out of my reticule. Then you kept me in sight all the way to Holborn and ran the last part. That wasn't so clever, you know. You couldn't have known where I was going, so you must have had to follow me quite closely. In that case, why would you have to come running up, hot and breathless?'

She worked out what I meant immediately and nodded

at the justice of it, biting her lip. Her teeth were whiter and more regular than you'd have expected from her way of life.

'Why did you do it?' I said. 'Did you expect a reward?'

She shook her head, her knotted locks whipping round her face like Medusa's snakes.

'I just wanted to do you a good turn, that's all.'

I looked at the eagerness in her expression and thought that beneath her cunning there was truthfulness of a kind. Amazing though it seemed, the charade had been because she wanted me to like her, or notice her at least. Was that so wrong? Quite recently, in my own life, I'd been without family, money or a roof over my head. Admittedly, my circumstances had never been as poor as hers. The fates had been kind to me, so who was I to turn away from her?

'Mrs Martley said you came into our rooms the other day,' I said.

'She thought I'd come to take something. I hadn't. I only wanted to see where you lived, that's all.'

'Still, you shouldn't . . .'

But she was launched on a sense of grievance and wouldn't be interrupted.

'She called me names and threatened to throw me downstairs. She said I was lousy and flea-ridden. That's not my fault. The queen and all her ladies in waiting would be lousy if they had to sleep where I sleep.'

I burst out laughing. The picture of Little Vicky and her retinue of ladies in their satin and diamonds, couching in a shining heap in the shed next to Mr Colley's midden, was too vivid to contemplate straight-faced. Tabby was startled at first, then she started laughing too, so that we were more like two schoolgirls than wronged householder and vagrant.

When we stopped laughing we looked at each other, caught off-balance.

'Tabby, would you like to work for me?' I said.

It was a ludicrous idea. Anything less like a lady's maid than the ragged girl standing in front of me would be hard to find in the whole expanse of London. Still, I had a problem and needed a quick solution to it. Mr Lomax's casual assumption that I'd be bringing a servant with me reminded me that any kind of gentle-woman – and a person seeking acquaintance with Lady Brinkburn would have to be some kind of gentlewoman – would not stay in a country cottage unattended. There was no question of removing Mrs Martley from Jenny at this interesting stage, even if I had wanted her company, and I couldn't afford or endure a conventional lady's maid. Tabby grinned as if I'd given her a present, nodded her head and kept nodding it. I wished she wouldn't. It reminded me about the state of her hair.

'It will only be for a week or two,' I said. 'It means living outside London for a while.'

'Further away than Hackney?'

'Yes. More than twenty miles away. A day's journey.'

She knelt down and started tightening one of the laces on her wrecked boots.

'We're not walking,' I said. 'And not at once. It will be the day after tomorrow, probably. And there's something you must do first.'

I opened my purse and gave her the seven and a half pence.

'You know the bath house, round the corner from the workhouse?' She nodded. 'I want you to go in there tomorrow morning and have a first-class bath. That will cost you threepence. The rest you can keep for yourself. Wait there.'

I ran upstairs and rummaged at the bottom of my clothes chest, turning up a grey cotton dress, much creased but quite respectable, cotton stockings and garters, a plain chemise and petticoat, corsets that were too fancy and frivolous for the purpose but the only ones I had to spare, and a woollen shawl. Down in the parlour, I stuffed them in a clean potato sack, took a bar of carbolic soap from the cupboard and raided Mrs Martley's box of herbs for the mixture of dried rosemary and fleabane that she said was good against lice. Another raid on the food cupboard produced half a loaf of yesterday's bread and a lump of cheese. When I got back downstairs with my armful, Tabby was standing just where I'd left her.

'You can put the clothes on tomorrow after you've had your bath,' I said. 'You'd better keep them in the sack till then. Rub this into your hair in the bath and make sure you wash it really thoroughly.'

She accepted the sack and the instructions with the same calm she'd shown when she thought we were

going to walk twenty miles. I said I'd meet her in the
yard after she'd had her bath and wished her good
evening. When I looked back from the doorway she
was still standing there with the sack in her hand,
looking after me. I thought I'd probably live to regret it.
And the same applied to the other commitment I'd made
that day as well.

# CHAPTER SIX

The next thirty-six hours were too busy to worry about whether I'd done the wrong thing: to a bank in the Strand to cash the lawyer's draft, to a little shop in Soho for sketchpads, charcoal, a set of watercolours and brushes, to Bloomsbury for a quick visit to Daniel and Jenny to let them know I'd be away for a while, to a stage-coach office to take two inside seats on the *Emerald*, from the Spread Eagle in Gracechurch Street to the Bear at Maidenhead on Saturday morning. Of course, it should have been one seat inside the coach for me and one on the top outside for my maid. But I guessed that it would be the first time in Tabby's life that she'd been outside London and I could hardly condemn her to a lurching and uncomfortable journey among total strangers. Besides, there was no telling what she might say to those strangers.

When I got back to Abel Yard, arms loaded with packages, she was waiting for me, face shining with cleanliness, hair damp and – from a not too close look – free of animal life. My grey dress was too long for her so she'd gathered it up at the waist with a piece of string. At least it was clean string. A strong smell of carbolic hung round her. She tried to give me back the diminished bar of soap.

'I'm sorry, I used a lot of it.'

'Don't worry. Keep it.'

I checked that Mrs Martley was not at home and then took her upstairs to help pack. Naturally, Mr Lomax hadn't given me any helpful details like whether the water bailiff's cottage had its own linen, so I took some of our second-best sheets, pillowslips and towels and folded them into a trunk. By the time I'd added a tin of biscuits and a slab of portable soup, the spirit stove and kettle, my clothes, a few books and the painting materials, it was some weight. With difficulty, we manoeuvred it down the stairs together and put it near the gate to the yard, to be collected by a carter's service as I'd arranged, and deposited to await our arrival at the Bear. There'd be no room for such bulky luggage on the stage. Then I took Tabby to my favourite second-hand clothes shop, where we fitted her out with another grey cotton dress nearer her own size, two white aprons, two white caps, a nightdress, and a carpet bag to carry them all. None of the second-hand shoes would do, so some of Mr Lomax's money had to go on a pair of new black shoes from the cobbler's shop. (I comforted myself that it all came from the Brinkburn family's coal mines in the end, so I should feel no guilt.) The shoes looked lumpish and clumsy to me, but after the boots they seemed to her ridiculously light. She capered a few steps on the pavement.

'I feel like my feet's flying away from me.'

'People are looking at us,' I said.

I didn't like to curb her exuberance, but in my business I often needed to blend into the background. A dancing lady's maid wouldn't help.

By the time I'd got her back to Abel Yard it was late afternoon. I remembered that Celia was expecting me to call, so dashed off a note to her saying that I'd be out of town for a few days. In case she wanted to write to me, letters could be addressed care of the mail office in Maidenhead. I gave the note to Tabby to deliver. That left just enough time for the most important part of my preparations. I went alone, crossing Park Lane, walking northwards through the park in golden sunlight, towards Bayswater Road. There weren't many people in the park because the fashionable had finished their afternoon promenades on horseback or in carriages and gone home to change for dinner. That meant the end of the day's work for their horses. By the time I reached the livery stables where Amos Legge worked and Rancie lodged, the grooms and boys were in the middle of the evening's routine, cleaning tack, filling hay nets and water buckets.

I asked for Mr Legge and was directed to the fodder room. He was measuring out buckets of oats, barley, bran and split peas to each horse's individual needs, giving them to the boys to distribute as instructed. It was responsible work. Amos was one of the mainstays of the stable now, paid accordingly, as you could guess from the fine quality of his boots and breeches. I stood outside the fodder room until the last of the boys had gone. Amos put the lid down on the oat bin, secured it with a lead weight to keep out the rats, and turned to me, beaming.

'Haven't seen you for a few days, Miss Lane. You all right, then?'

He dusted down an old wooden chair and invited me to sit down.

'Yes, thank you. I've been pretty busy.'

'That business of the man in the crate? I heard you were there.'

Nothing escaped Amos. As long as society depended on horses, grooms would be at the hub of everything. They might be silent in front of their customers, but they listened and gossiped over their pints in the evening. Thanks to Amos, I had access to that network and often found out more there than in offices or drawing rooms.

'What else did you hear?' I said.

'Not a lot. He was a bit of a bad 'un by most accounts – drink and so forth.'

'Did you hear that from Miles Brinkburn?'

'No. He didn't talk about it and neither did I. Just what people are saying.'

'You've met Miles Brinkburn since it happened, then?'

'I was out at the Eyre Arms with him this morning, having another practice.'

'How did he do?'

'No better than middling. I had to hold back, otherwise I'd have had him out of the saddle again.'

'Did he seem downcast or worried?'

'I wouldn't say so, no. His normal self, quite cheerful like.'

So Miles Brinkburn had good powers of recovery.

'What kind of armour was he wearing?'

'The same you saw him in, the suit he'd hired from Pratt's. I took particular note of that.'

Because he knew I'd ask. It would have been callous of Miles Brinkburn to wear the ancestral armour after what had happened.

'What about Stephen Brinkburn – was he there?'

'No. I heard their friends have been trying to keep them apart, after what happened. I'll be seeing Mr Stephen tomorrow. He wants me to look out for a couple of new horses for him.'

By common consent, we got up and strolled across the yard to Rancie's box. She was eating her feed, but looked up and blew hrrrr through her nostrils when she saw me. Her black cat watched her, golden-eyed, from the hay manger.

'I'm going out of town for a few days,' I said to Amos.

'So I hear. The *Emerald* to Bristol, seven o'clock tomorrow morning, getting down at Maidenhead. They're trying out a new lead horse as far as Hounslow, so I hope you have a smooth journey.'

'Now how did you know all that?'

'I've got a friend helps out here sometimes, sold a horse to the man who works at the Spread Eagle. He knows the lad who's a clerk in the office where they keep the passenger lists.'

No point in asking why the lad noticed my name. Amos's network could probably tag each individual sparrow.

'I don't know how long I'll be away,' I said. 'Do you think you could keep an eye on the Brinkburn brothers for me, and let me know if anything else happens?'

'Surely. I can send word down by my friends as far as Maidenhead. Can you pick messages up from the Bear? If not, there's probably a carter goes out to Brinkburn Hall.'

'But I haven't told you where . . .'

I stopped. He was laughing at me. It wasn't often, these days, that he could surprise me by what he knew or guessed.

'Well, that's where the man in the crate came from, isn't it?' he said, pretending innocence.

'I'm not supposed to be thinking about him. It's the other matter.'

'Well, I hope you get it fettled, then. It's a bad business.'

Rancie had finished her feed now and come up to the half-door to join us. I stroked her head, tracing the comma-shaped blaze with my fingers.

'I wish I could take you with me,' I said to her.

'Don't you worry, I'll look after her,' Amos said. 'And I'll make sure nobody rides her unless she's got hands lighter than the feathers in a lady's hat.'

I gave her a last stroke, said goodbye to Amos and walked back home across the park. The carriage mender was just shutting up his shop. He kindly agreed that Tabby could spend the night in an old landau awaiting repair in his store shed. I didn't want to spoil the good work by having her curl up in the shed by the midden, but I knew Mrs Martley wouldn't tolerate her in the house. I fetched an old blanket, introduced Tabby to her temporary lodgings and reminded her that we'd have to start out at five o'clock in the morning to get to Gracechurch Street in the City in time to catch the stage. Upstairs, Mrs Martley had prepared Irish stew for our supper.

'You're gallivanting off again, then?'

'Yes, I'm gallivanting. Not very far and not for long, I hope. I'll call at the mail office when I can, in case there's any news of Jenny.'

'I hope you'll bring our sheets back.' Then, as an afterthought, 'And you look after yourself.'

Tabby and I walked to Piccadilly in the morning and took the local stage to the City. At this hour there were few people on the streets apart from crossing sweepers, patrolling policemen and costermongers trundling their barrows out early to secure the best pitches. Tabby clutched my arm when the horses broke into a fast trot along the Strand.

'Are they running away with us?'

'Of course not. Haven't you ever ridden in a coach before?'

She bit her lip and shook her head. We got down at Gracechurch Street and walked to the Spread Eagle, with Tabby carrying my carpet bag as well as her own. The huge coaching yard there was in its usual state of bustle, full of passengers anxious in case they were put on the wrong coach, harassed clerks with boarding lists and ostlers yelling to people to get out of the way as they backed horses into shafts. As well as our *Emerald*, bound for Bristol and points between, there were half a dozen coaches due out at about the same time: the *Courier*, heading for Birmingham, the *Sovereign* for Brighton, the *Magnet* for Cheltenham, the *Retaliator* for Gloucester, the *Star of Brunswick* for Portsmouth, the *Express* for Gosport. The air was full of horse smells and all the excitement of the start of journeys. I left Tabby on a bench by the wall with our bags and strolled from coach to coach, admiring their bright paintwork and the glossy coats of the horses, matching the shine of the coachmen's boots. After a while the cry of 'Passengers for the *Emerald*' went up, and we took our places on board.

The Spread Eagle coachyard was one of several in the

same area, all contributing their coaches to the morning rush, so the congestion, whinnying and shouting when they all ground on to the narrow streets, manoeuvring for precedence, was beyond belief. It was one of the reasons why coaches very seldom achieved the journey times advertised by their proprietors. But the new lead mare must have been good at her business because, once clear of the confusion, we covered the twelve miles to the first stage at Hounslow in an hour and a half. After Hounslow, the only other inside passengers were a middle-aged couple and a man in black who looked like a lawyer or a doctor. Throughout the journey, Tabby sat by the window, eyes wide, carpet bag clutched on her lap. She was so quiet that I thought she might be terrified by the experience. We arrived at Maidenhead Bridge only ten minutes behind time, three hours and twenty minutes after leaving London. Our coach had to halt in the middle of the bridge because of some obstruction at the other end. I looked down at the river bank, wondering if a roof visible among the trees to our left might be Brinkburn Hall. Then Tabby let out a cry, the first sound she'd made since leaving London.

'Look. What is it?'

We all looked where she was pointing. The thing we saw was as strange to me as it must have been to Tabby. On a level with us, perhaps half a mile away, a great horizontal column of whiteness was heading across the river, like a cloud that had somehow developed a sense of purpose and the speed of a bolting horse. A black line moved under the cloud, keeping pace with it. Below the black line, a more solid line of red remained motionless, the whole thing standing out against the blue sky. In that first surprised moment, I couldn't have answered Tabby's question. It was the middle-aged man who said: 'It's the *North Star*.'

I remembered then. The *North Star* was the Great Western's locomotive. I'd even seen it close to, standing at the end of its track in Paddington, but I'd never witnessed it in motion and certainly not in this phenomenon of flying, apparently in mid air. Once the first visual shock had worn off, I thought of what Mr Lomax had said about the Great Western's monstrously large bridge over the Thames. Only from here it looked more wonderful than monstrous, a breathtaking leap of red brickwork over the wide river from bank to bank.

'That must be one of their trial runs,' the middle-aged man said. 'They're not opening the Maidenhead to Twyford section to passengers until next month.'

So far, passengers could be drawn behind the *North Star* only from Paddington to the riverside opposite Maidenhead. I supposed Tabby and I could have travelled that way, but it simply hadn't occurred to me. The cloud of steam hung over the bridge for some time after the locomotive had gone, then gradually melted away. The obstruction cleared itself and the *Emerald* trotted on over the old stone bridge that seemed so undramatic in comparison, up the main street to the yard of the Bear Hotel. It was well accustomed to the needs of coach travellers and when I asked about transport to the cottage on the Brinkburn estate, a curricle and driver were promised within an hour. I checked that my trunk had arrived and ordered lamb chops to be served to us in a side room. After such an early start, we ate with a good appetite.

By noon, we were driving back across the bridge in the curricle, to the Buckinghamshire side, with Tabby perched on the groom's seat at the back. There was no locomotive to see this time, only young men on the river, racing each other in rowing boats. For a few hundred yards we ran back along the main road to London, then turned right on a road between fields and neat hedges. We must have been going more or less parallel to the river, though it was out of sight. We passed a fine wrought-iron gateway on our right, and a drive curving to an imposing red-brick house.

'Is that Brinkburn Hall?' I said.

'That's right, ma'am.'

'Do you often have to drive people there?'

'Not very often, ma'am. They keep their own coachman.'

Just past the entrance to the drive, we came to a village with a church, a duck pond and a public house called the Farrier's Arms. The houses were mostly brick-built and thatched.

'They had a funeral there this morning,' the driver said cheerfully, pointing with his whip at the church and its surrounding graveyard.

'Oh yes?'

A funeral was hardly a rare event, after all.

'The coffin came all the way down from London overnight,' the driver went on. 'They buried him straight away, six o'clock in the morning.'

'Who was he?'

'Servant from the hall, from what I heard.'

We turned on to a rutted track through woodland, and came to a halt in a clearing just wide enough for the curricle to turn round, with a view of sunlight glinting on water.

'Here we are, ma'am.'

The cottage was like a child's playhouse only slightly enlarged, built in the picturesque style with a steep tiled roof and gables too large for it, like eyebrows raised in surprise. The garden was a mass of hollyhocks, penstemons, roses, all growing higgledy-piggledy together, with a row of red and white flowered runner beans on poles. Beyond the garden, a patch of rough grass sloped down to the river. In winter the cottage must be damp and probably quite often flooded, but in June it was so beautiful I wished I really were there on a holiday. I found a key left ready in the front door, opened it and let the driver and Tabby carry the trunk inside. A note was lying on the stone flagged floor inside the door from the steward, Mr Whiteley, addressed to me by name, trusting I would find everything satisfactory and recommending a woman from the village who would clean and cook. The curricle rumbled away and I set Tabby to unpacking.

There were just four rooms, none of them large. The main one downstairs looked out on the garden and the river, with a cubbyhole of a kitchen at the back. Upstairs was a bedroom and a box room, both with beds and wash stands. I set up my spirit stove, found my tea caddy and sent Tabby to dip a kettleful of water from the river. We drank our tea without milk, sitting on a bench by the porch. Tabby started talking again and it was a relief to find she hadn't been terrified by the journey as I feared, simply noticing everything. She could describe almost every building of any size we'd passed on the way, and imitated the nervous cough of the lawyer-like man so perfectly that he might have been sitting beside us. I was almost envious. I've had to cultivate my powers of observation as a professional necessity. Tabby seemed to have them as naturally as a bird sings.

'So what do we do now we're here?' she said.

I'd been wondering that myself.

'I think we'll walk to the village to see if there's anywhere we can buy bread and milk,' I said.

It was about four in the afternoon by then, the air warm and languorous. I could happily have sat there for hours, with the bees buzzing in the hollyhocks and the murmur of the river in the background, but there was work to be done. The first thing was to find a way into village gossip and ascertain, as delicately as possible, the local opinion of the lady of the manor's sanity.

We walked together up the path through the woods, Tabby carrying my empty travelling bag for our shopping.

The village seemed almost deserted, with most of the men likely to be out working in the fields because it was hay harvest time. There was a village shop of a kind, consisting of the front room of one of the cottages, with a drowsy-looking young woman behind the counter. When Tabby and I went inside, the three of us filled up the small room almost completely. Of the small stock available, I managed to buy a pint of milk, with the loan of a lidded can to carry it, some cheese, a none-too fresh loaf of coarse bread and about half a pound of strawberries, over-ripe and weeping their pink juice. I reminded myself not to be critical. It was a Saturday afternoon in a village probably not much used to visitors. I paid for the groceries and told Tabby to carry them home.

'Can you find your way back all right?'

'Yes, I think so.'

She sounded doubtful. I saw her to the start of the path through the woods then turned back to the village, looking for the cottage of the woman who would clean and cook. According to Mr Whiteley's note, she was called Mrs Todd and lived next to the church.

Mrs Todd came to the door with a scarf round her hair, a child clinging to her skirt and another one yelling in the background. She looked so tired that I felt guilty about asking her, but she was eager to work every day from ten till one, Sundays excepted. Goodness knows what I'd find for her to do in our tiny residence. A side gate into the churchyard stood open opposite her cottage.

109

There was only one fresh grave there, a hump of brown soil in the closely mown turf, in the far corner of the churchyard by the wall, in a space on its own. I was almost certain I knew who was lying under that hump of soil. Naturally there was no cross or headstone on it, as the burial had taken place just that morning, but what was odd was the complete lack of any floral tributes, not a flower or a laurel leaf. I stood for a while, then strolled away from it, past gravestones recording many generations of the same family names, and out of the main gate back to the village street, just in time to see something happening.

It would have been no event at all in London, simply a builder's wagon, loaded with pieces of squared stone, drawn by a cobby grey. The horse was standing quietly with nobody holding it, while two men unloaded a few pieces of stone and some tools from the wagon into a handcart. When the handcart was half full, they dragged it across the road and through the churchyard gate, straining to pull it up the incline. Then they manoeuvred it past the gravestones towards the hump of fresh earth. At first I thought that people were concerned about the new grave after all, and these were memorial masons come to give it a stone surround. But they dragged their cart past the grave, right to the corner. They set it down, produced a hammer and chisel from the cart and set about demolishing the existing wall. It looked to me a perfectly good wall as it was. I went closer and watched, unnoticed, as they removed a course of stone blocks from the top of the wall and piled them up neatly. They'd started on the second course when an elderly man came running out from the church porch, shouting at them.

'What do you think you're doing? Leave that alone.'

The two men stopped work briefly.

'Ladyship's orders.'

'You can't go taking down the wall.'

'We're going to build it up again, just on the other side of this.'

The workman indicated the grave mound. The elderly man gave them another scandalised look and hurried back into the church. He came out again with a young and nervous man in clerical bands.

'Stop it at once. What do you think you're doing?'

The vicar's voice came out as a high bray, but respect for the cloth made the two men stop work again. The one who did the talking touched his cap.

'Excuse me, Reverend, but we had instructions from her ladyship it was to be done at once. She said she'd be sending to you to explain.'

'Explain what? Why in the world does she want the wall taken down?'

'Because she wants him outside of it,' the workman said, nodding towards the mound of earth.

Comprehension and embarrassment flared on the vicar's face.

'You can't, you know. You really can't . . .' he began.

'I'm sorry, Mr Headingley, but it's necessary.'

111

A new voice, a woman's voice from behind us. We all spun round. She was dressed in floating green silk, with the inside of her bonnet green-trimmed to match. She was probably in her late forties, with a square forehead, high cheekbones and a determined chin, her hair showing streaks of grey. Even in youth, she would have lacked the softness of conventional beauty but age had given her face authority and distinction. Her voice too. There was a tone of command in it that struck the men to silence. She took a few steps towards the clergyman, speaking more softly.

'But I do beg your pardon. I'd intended to come and speak to you before they started work, but something delayed me.'

'But why . . .?' he said.

'It's all been an awful mistake.' She gestured towards the burial mound, a full-armed gesture, theatrical. 'He should never have been buried in the churchyard. He should never have been brought back here at all. I'm afraid my son totally misunderstood my wishes. I sent word to you as soon as I knew what had happened, but evidently it came too late.'

Beads of sweat ran down the clergyman's forehead.

'I . . . I didn't receive your message until after the ceremony.'

'So early. Why did it have to be so early?'

He swallowed, trying to cling on to his courage. Almost certainly, the living of the church was in the gift of the estate. Lady Brinkburn's husband had appointed

112

him and, even if she couldn't dismiss him, her patronage was important.

'In any case, I had no reason to bury him outside the churchyard,' he said.

'No reason? Why should a man like him lie alongside these good people?' Another gesture took in the gravestones as witnesses. 'He has no business in sacred ground, and you know that as well as I do.'

'But since it's done now . . .'

'I don't suppose you'd let me have him dug up, so this is the next best thing.'

The workmen stood stolidly by the wall, hammers and chisels ready to start work again. The clergyman looked from her to them and back again.

'It *is* parish property,' he said apologetically.

'Of course it is, and I'm willing to make a more than fair exchange. I'll give the parish that acre next to the school. I know they've had their eye on it for years.'

Land-greed on behalf of his parishioners shone in the vicar's eyes.

'Where would you want the wall to go?' he said.

She looked at him, then slowly paced a line a few feet from the inside of the grave, running diagonally to connect with the existing wall in the corner. A perfectly reasonable line that would leave Handy's remains in the next-door pasture with the cows. The land lost to the parish had nothing else on it but a heap of broken flower-pots, and it was only a small fraction of the acre she'd offered in exchange. She turned at the corner and walked back to us, face calm. Under the floating hem of her silk dress she was wearing plain cotton stockings and sensible brown leather shoes for walking.

'I'll have to consult the parish council,' the clergyman said, admitting defeat.

She smiled for the first time.

'Of course you will. But when they see where the new wall runs, I'm sure they'll realise it's no loss. I'll have the deeds for the school acre drawn up at once.'

She nodded to the workmen. Two hammers clinked on to two chisels simultaneously, like figures on a German clock.

Satisfied that her orders were being carried out, she turned and noticed me for the first time. Her eyes looked a question. She knew everybody in the village. I introduced myself and explained that I was staying at her cottage. Her expression changed in an instant, the planes of her face softening from determination to polite sociability.

'Whiteley did mention it. You are comfortable there?'

'Very. It's a beautiful cottage.'

'I'm glad you think so.'

Her eyes were an unusual shade of pale blue that gave an other-worldly quality to her look. She began to walk towards the gate, disregarding the vicar who was still hovering, perhaps hoping to make a last appeal. I went with her.

'Whiteley tells me you paint,' she said.

'Sketch a little. I have no great talent.'

'Great talents are granted to few of us. Still, me must do the best we can, mustn't we?'

Her mind wasn't on what she was saying. I sensed in her some of the drained feeling that comes after an argument. She'd won, but wasn't enjoying her victory. We went through the lych gate on to the road. The builder's horse was dozing in his shafts. Two women in the porch of one of the cottages were pretending not to look at us. The story of her ladyship and the wall was probably running round the village already.

'You must come to tea,' she said. 'Monday at four o'clock. We shan't talk about this miserable business.'

It was more of a command than an invitation. I said I should be glad to. I thought there might be a carriage or at least a horse waiting for her, but she simply wished me good afternoon and turned along the road in the direction of the hall, walking purposefully in her sensible shoes, silk skirt fluttering.

# CHAPTER SEVEN

Next day was Sunday. I decided against going to church in the village, although the bells were ringing out their invitation over woods and fields. I left Tabby washing up after our breakfast and went for a solitary walk along the river bank with my sketching things. A narrow footpath ran upriver from the cottage. I followed it between swathes of meadowsweet and purple loosestrife, past clumps of yellow irises, thinking hard about what had happened in the churchyard. I'd got what I wanted, my invitation to Lady Brinkburn's home, but it was hardly necessary any more. If I reported what had happened to Mr Lomax, he'd probably say that my task was accomplished already. A woman of wealth and title has a churchyard wall knocked down and moved, which probably amounts to sacrilege, argues with her vicar in public and parts with an acre of land, all to make sure that an unsatisfactory servant rots under the hooves of her cows, rather than decorously among the gravestones. When that story was told, any court in the land would be likely to judge Lady Brinkburn as mad as a March hare. If I'd only heard the story without meeting her, I'd probably have agreed.

And yet, and yet, and yet. Looked at in another way, this was a woman of more than common strong-mindedness. Faced with something she believed to be wrong, she'd weighed her alternatives and come to a solution. If Handy once buried couldn't be taken from the churchyard, then the churchyard could be taken from Handy. Within hours, she'd organised her workmen and set about it. When faced with opposition from the vicar, she'd used both bullying and bribery effectively. The offer of the school acre had apparently been made on the spur of the moment and showed an impressive capacity to improvise. If this was madness, then it was of a disturbingly rational kind. What weighed with me as much was her air in those few minutes when we were walking across the churchyard together. There'd been a sadness about her that seemed at odds with the rest of her behaviour. I wasn't sure whether I'd like her or not on closer acquaintance, but I didn't have the impression of a hard-natured woman.

After half a mile or so the river bank became a more orderly affair, faced with stone, and the path wider. A wooden jetty with a rowing boat moored to it stuck out into the river. To my right, an expanse of smooth lawn sloped steeply upwards to a gem of a Queen Anne house: Brinkburn Hall. It wasn't large, by the standards of the aristocracy. An indoor staff of ten or so could probably maintain it quite easily. It stood among the lawns and shrubberies as if it had an age-old right to be there, overlooking the river from behind its balustraded terrace, its mellow red brick and white stone facings glowing in the sun. Nobody was visible except a single gardener, trimming the lawn edge. A path ran up to the house from the jetty. A smaller gravel path led across the lawn at a diagonal towards a copse. I followed it. I was tres-passing on the Brinkburn estate, but that might be permitted to a tenant of their cottage.

Every step confirmed the first impressions that this was a well-tended estate. The gravel was freshly raked, the bushes on either side cut back just enough to let one person in full skirts pass easily, while still giving the path a natural woodland look. Now and then the trees would part and at every one of these places a wooden bench was placed precisely to give the best view down to the river. Beyond a doubt, the lady of the house walked this way. At every turn, I thought I might see her sitting on a bench with her sketchpad, but apart from scurrying squirrels, I had the path to myself. After a while it curved towards the house. I turned and went back down through the trees to the river-bank path, sat on the trunk of a fallen willow tree and realised that I'd come to a deci-sion. Before rushing back to report to Mr Lomax, I'd keep my appointment with Lady Brinkburn. She'd been polite to me and was owed that at least. With that decided, I thought I might as well try out one of my new sticks of charcoal and began a sketch of an alder tree slanting down to the water. The angle wasn't quite satisfactory, and when I shifted along the willow trunk I saw the fisherman. He was on his own, standing so still that he might have been a tree branch himself. Since I like sketching people more than scenery, I included him in my composition.

By the time I'd finished my sketch – as far as it would ever be finished – he still hadn't moved. I'd have to walk past him to get to the cottage. If he turned out to be from the village, or one of the servants of the estate, it might be useful to talk to him. I packed away my sketching things and walked softly along the bank so as not to scare his fish. I was only yards away when he caught something, a large roach, the red of its fins flashing as it was hauled into the sunshine. Expertly, he disengaged the fish from the hook and slid it back into the water, where it stayed floating for a stunned second then whisked away. He turned, aware of somebody on the path. I stared, knowing I'd seen him somewhere before but not able to place him. Then the picture came to mind of a policeman's tall hat, set respectfully down on the coroner's table as its owner described being summoned to number 47 Bond Street. Just in time, I remembered his name.

'Well, good morning, Constable Bevan.'

'Good morning, Miss Lane,' he said, not missing a beat.

He showed no surprise that I remembered his name from the inquest and came out with mine as if we were old acquaintances. His smile was perfectly friendly, but I didn't quite like his air of being pleased with himself.

'You're obviously a skilful fisherman,' I said.

'I'm sure I could say the same about you as an artist, Miss Lane.'

Again, that slightly mocking use of my name, and he wanted me to know that he'd been aware of my watching him.

'So what brings you here, Constable Bevan?'

'I had some days' leave owing to me. As you see, it's a delightful spot for fishing.'

As at the inquest, his voice and manner struck me as more cultivated than you'd expect in a constable. I knew very well that the Metropolitan Police were not generous in giving leave from duty.

'Nothing to do, then, with the coroner asking for further inquiries into Mr Handy's death?'

'These things are decided above my level. Are you staying with Lady Brinkburn?'

'No. I've rented the cottage back there.'

He must have passed it on his way to his fishing place. I was under no obligation to answer his questions, except I needed answers to some of my own.

'At the suggestion of the younger Mr Brinkburn, I take it.'

The remark came very near to being offensive.

'Mr Brinkburn had nothing to do with it,' I said. 'I'm simply renting it from the estate.'

He didn't believe me, and let me see that from his face. Then he turned aside and baited his hook.

'At any event, you've missed the funeral,' he said.

'Handy's funeral? Were you there?'

'There were four of us: Mr Whiteley, a woman from the village, the sacristan and myself.'

'You representing the Metropolitan Police Force?'

He flicked the hook into the water.

'Representing myself. Did it surprise you, Miss Lane, that Mr Whiteley was so anxious to blacken Handy's reputation at the inquest? Drunk, disrespectful, likely to absent himself for days on end . . .'

'And I suppose you've found out that he was none of those things?'

'As far as I've been able to find out in the village, he was all of them and worse.'

He looked at his float on the water. The question 'Well then?' hovered in the air unasked.

'I gather that there have been some alterations to the churchyard wall since then,' he said.

He'd obviously heard the story. Did he know I'd been present at the time? He seemed to expect some comment from me, but I was determined to disappoint him.

'I mustn't interrupt your fishing,' I said, making a move to walk past him.

'I assure you, you're not interrupting it in the least, Miss Lane.'

I thought that was probably all too true. I kept walking, forcing him to step back. He wished me good morning and raised his hat to me, looking altogether too cheerful for my peace of mind.

Back at the cottage, I said nothing about Constable Bevan. The rest of our Sunday passed quietly enough. I helped Tabby wash her hair again in a solution of Mrs Martley's herbs and showed her how to spread it to dry on a towel across her back. It struck me that the roles of mistress and lady's maid were being reversed, but she knew no better so was entirely unselfconscious about it. Later, we ate our supper of soup, bread and cheese, then strolled to the bottom of the garden and sat on the river bank. I rolled my stockings off and dabbled my feet in the water, feeling minnows tickling between my toes, watching swallows darting low over the surface to catch midges. It helped to cool my annoyance about Constable Bevan. But even the thought of him brought back all too vividly that day in Bond Street and the smell of Handy in the crate, blotting out the freshness of the river. What had the man done to deserve so much dislike, first from Whiteley at the inquest, then from Lady Brinkburn? If he were that bad a servant, why not simply dismiss him? And which of Lady Brinkburn's sons had decided to bring him back to the village for burial, so much against her wishes?

After a while the biting of the midges drove us back inside the cottage. It was after ten by the chimes of the church clock, but only a few days away from midsummer so the last glow of the sun was still on the sky.

I told Tabby she should go up to bed, but she lingered.

'It's quiet here, isn't it?' she said.

'Yes, isn't it wonderful after the noise at home.'

'This quiet's noisy. It gets inside my head.'

I asked her if she meant the sound of the river, but she said no. I lit a candle in a holder for her, warning her to blow it out before she went to sleep, then watched as she made her way up the steep stairs, her shadow wavering against the wall. Leaving the door open to let in fresh air, I went and sat in the room's most comfortable chair. It was not very comfortable, but even so I must have dozed, because when I was next aware of anything it was dark.

There'd been no noise, I was sure of that, but I knew at once there was something outside. It was no more than an animal instinct, made sharper by the darkness. A faint light of a kind was coming from the direction of the river, starlight on water perhaps, just enough to make out shapes in the part of the garden I could see through the open door. Hollyhocks, nothing else, and no movement. A sheep or cow perhaps? No, the fields were well fenced, and why should a lone cow or sheep stray into woodland? A dog? It had sounded bigger than that. I was on my way out to look when a scream sounded from upstairs.

'Tabby, what is it?'

I rushed upstairs, thinking she was having a nightmare or perhaps had woken and seen whatever it was in the garden. The white shape of Tabby in her nightgown came flying downstairs and knocked me backwards.

'There's a ghost out there.'

I staggered down the stairs and caught her as she tripped over the nightgown. Her heart was thumping. The urchin who'd seemed scared of nothing in London was terrified now.

'Tabby, of course it's not a ghost. It's some animal come into the garden. I was just going out to look.'

She clung to me.

'It's not an animal. It spoke to me.'

'Spoke?'

'About somebody coming back to haunt somebody. I didn't understand it.'

I'd have taken it for part of a nightmare, were it not for the way she said it with such flat certainty.

'In that case, it will be some wretched boy from the village playing tricks,' I said. 'I'm going out there to give him a piece of my mind.'

Tabby wouldn't stay in the cottage alone, so I had to wait while she found her shoes. We went out together to the space where the curricle had turned round. She pressed close to me as we stared into the dark woodland.

'Who's there?' I shouted. 'Why are you playing stupid tricks?'

No answer but the rustling of leaves. Then faint sounds

came from the direction of the river, the creak of rowlocks and the dip of oars in water.

'The wretch must have come in a boat,' I said.

I turned and stumbled across the garden with Tabby close behind me, the sharp scent of trampled marigolds rising like a gas. By the time we reached the river bank, a rowing boat was in mid current some two hundred yards away, heading upriver towards the old Maidenhead bridge. The person rowing, sitting backwards to the direction of travel, must have been pulling hard against the current. I could make out nothing except a white oval of face in a dark hat or hood, rising and dipping. Soon even that was out of sight.

Tabby and I went back into the cottage and I lit the lamp. She kicked off her shoes and sat in the chair, curling her bare feet under her.

'Tell me exactly what happened,' I said. 'Were you asleep?'

She shook her head.

'I heard somebody downstairs, under the window. I thought it was you. Then something hit the window. I think it was a pebble. I thought it might be you letting me know I'd left the candle burning.'

'Why in the world would I do it that way? Go on.'

'So I got up and opened the window, and this ghost sort of hissed at me.'

'Did you see it?'

'No, there's this thing that sticks out under my window. He was on the other side of that.'

125

'The wood shed. Tabby, what did he say? As exactly as you can remember.'

She frowned, then spoke in a low rasping voice.

'He said "Are you a friend of hers?" I didn't answer. I didn't know if he meant you or what. Then he said, "Tell her he'll come back and haunt her. She won't get rid of him as easily as that. He'll come back and haunt her, tell her."'

'Then what?'

'Nothing. That's when I screamed and ran downstairs. What does it mean? Is it you that's going to get haunted?'

'Tabby, nobody's going to get haunted. It wasn't a ghost, just a silly trick.'

'Is it to do with the man they buried yesterday? Perhaps he was angry because he got put outside the churchyard, so his ghost has come back looking for vengeance.'

'That's nonsense. Besides, who ever heard of a ghost rowing a boat?'

She was quick-minded, for all her superstition. I'd already come to the conclusion that the warning had to do with Handy. Whoever had come to the cottage had seen one candle-lit window and assumed it was mine. I was intended to carry the message – but to whom? The obvious answer was Lady Brinkburn. Anybody could have seen her talking to me in the churchyard and not known we were only meeting for the first time. Some friend of Handy's resented the exiling of his body to the cow pasture and was trying to use me in a crude attempt to scare the person responsible. It was mean and ugly,

126

and I wished more than ever that I could have got my hands on him. Then something else about what Tabby had said occurred to me.

'How did you know about a man being put outside the churchyard?'

'The fisherman told me. He came past this morning while you were out. He comes from London.'

She made it sound like meeting a countryman after a long exile.

'Was he quite tall, with brown hair and a long nose?'

I hardly needed her nod to confirm that our visitor had been Constable Bevan.

'What else did you talk about?'

'He wanted to know all about you, where you lived and what you were doing here.'

Tabby hardly knew anything about me – or nothing that mattered, at any rate. Still, I was furious.

'If he comes again you're not to talk to him. Just tell him to go away.'

She didn't argue, but her face fell. Simply, she had no notion of privacy or discretion. I made some tea for us then told her to go back to bed and be sure to blow the candle out this time. It would soon be daylight in any case. Then I wrapped myself in my cloak and went out to sit on the bench by the porch. Was this a piece of village malice, or something worse? Tabby's impersonation sounded as if our visitor had been trying to disguise his voice. I wondered whether Constable Bevan might be responsible. If so, goodness knows what game

127

he was playing. Could it have been one of the staff from Brinkburn Hall? Quite possibly. In which case, should I warn Lady Brinkburn that she had an enemy in her household, or did she know that already?

I stayed on the bench, alternately thinking and dozing, until the sky turned pale. There were no further disturbances other than water voles plopping into the river and the white underside of a barn owl swooping soundlessly out of the woods. The rowing boat didn't come back.

# CHAPTER EIGHT

'I see some of your household enjoy rowing,' I said.

On my way up the lawn at the hall for tea with Lady Brinkburn, I'd noticed a boat moored to the landing stage. As a social occasion, our meeting could hardly have been more conventional. I'd been greeted at the door by a neatly dressed manservant and led through to a drawing room overlooking the lawn that sloped down to the river. Lady Brinkburn was standing just inside the doorway, smiling what looked like a perfectly genuine welcome. A King Charles spaniel slid down from a cushion and licked my hand.

'If you don't care for dogs, don't let him . . .' she'd said.

'I love dogs.'

'His name's Lovelace. Animals are such a comfort, aren't they? Indian or China tea?'

Everything about the house and grounds radiated order and neatness, even cheerfulness. The maid who brought in the tea things had given me a smile as if genuinely pleased to be taking trouble for a guest. There'd been nothing in her manner to suggest either fear or mockery of her employer. Scared servants move awkwardly and look sidelong. Servants who despise their masters have a satirical, slightly exaggerated way of moving and standing, like actors in a bad play. No sign of either at Brinkburn Hall. We'd sipped tea and talked conventionally: how delightful to be by the river in summer, especially for an artist. Wasn't it difficult to sketch or paint the flow of water convincingly? How did Turner manage those marvellous rough seas? I launched my seemingly innocent remark in the wake of these watery topics.

Lady Brinkburn smiled.

'Sometimes if one of the gardener's boys is not needed elsewhere I'll have him row me up to the old bridge and back. If there's not a boy to spare, I sometimes lie on cushions in my little boat moored to the landing stage, look up at the sky and imagine I'm floating along like the Lady of Shalott. Don't you adore Tennyson? Such a talented young man.'

'I prefer Shelley.'

'My dear, such old-fashioned tastes for a young woman. You make me feel quite modern.'

She smiled, offered more tea. We were getting on well. I was getting nowhere. I might have been talking to a different woman from the one in the churchyard. Even the oddness of her footwear was gone. Today her high-arched feet were sleek in white silk stockings, encased in blue velvet house-shoes embroidered with silver cockleshells. She was wearing white and blue silk, with three stems of white sweet peas pinned to the shoulder. If there was anything unconventional about her manner or surroundings, it was only that her dress and the furnishing of the room showed leanings towards the artistic. The room's colour scheme of soft green curtains, green and dusky pink upholstery and lighter pink cushions was unconventional but surprisingly restful. A revolving bookcase in light wood was full of poetry books and novels. Her piano had music sheets scattered untidily over the top of it, for use rather than effect. Not a detail came anywhere near eccentricity, let alone insanity.

She'd said we shouldn't talk about the business of the churchyard wall, so that approach was closed to me. I'd decided, for the present at any rate, not to refer to the matter of the ghostly warning. If somebody were trying to scare her, why should I do his work for him? Still, I needed to find a way to break through this crust of politeness into whatever was happening underneath. While thinking about it, I looked at a pottery trough on the windowsill, planted with things that looked something like primroses, but with shiny leaves and strange-coloured flowers. Her eyes followed mine.

'I see you're admiring my auriculas.'

'Auriculas, yes.'

I wasn't admiring them. Their stiffness and their purple-brown petals, bordered with yellow, made them look like plants in a waxworks. But a tenderness in her voice warned me to bite my tongue.

'Would you care to see my greenhouse? That's where I keep my collection.'

'I should love to.'

The spaniel and I followed her, through a small dining room with a table set for one, into a corridor leading to the back of the house. Clashing of crockery and a low murmur of voices came from the kitchen next door.

'I hope you don't mind coming out this way. It's much quicker.'

She tried to turn a door handle. It resisted and she clicked her tongue impatiently.

'Whiteley's always locking things. It's a positive mania with him.'

She felt in her pocket, produced a key and opened the door. We were in a cobbled courtyard at the back of the house. Various outhouses stood round it, one more substantial than the rest.

'Is that your dairy?' I said.

'Was. We don't use it any more – so wasteful.'

She answered absently, as if her thoughts were elsewhere. I edged sideways so that we passed close to it. The door was shut with an iron bar and a heavy padlock. The hasp and staple of the padlock gleamed with a film of new oil. We walked out of the courtyard, along a path and into a free-standing greenhouse. The air was heavy with the scent of jasmine. Raised benches down both sides held hundreds of pots of the strange flowered plants. She led the way between them with the confidence of somebody on her own territory, plunging a hand into the masses of pots to pick out those for my attention.

'This one's our own cross. You see, the border is much deeper than the others. And this one has the most extraordinary streaks in the petals. If it breeds true, it could lead to most exciting developments.'

*If it breeds true.* She'd said it without a trace of self-consciousness. At the end of the bench, somebody had set up a small painting area. Brushes and a well-used box of watercolours stood on a board alongside an open sketchpad. I looked at the pad and gasped.

'That's beautiful.'

'Do you really think so? I try to keep a record of all our new ones. It's very amateur stuff, alas.'

It looked anything but amateur, the kind of beautifully detailed painting you might find in a book of flora, every line of the petal clear and accurate. If she needed a certificate of sanity, she couldn't produce anything much more convincing. We walked back through the greenhouse. Next to the auriculas, I saw some old friends.

'Saxifrages.'

'Yes. I keep them to remember the Alps,' she said.

We started talking then, not the constrained conversation of the drawing room, but as two people with a

133

shared enthusiasm. Did I know the Alps? Those amazing silenes that cling to the rocks like moss and suddenly cover themselves in pink flowers.

'And those martagon lilies,' I said. 'The way they stand up on a ridge.'

'Yes, like candelabra. And those white St Bruno's lilies, whole slopes of them moving in the wind like waves.'

We stared at each other. I thought, 'I like this woman,' and wished I didn't. From her eyes, I saw that she had her doubts too. The enthusiasm was gradually fading away, and caution following, as if she thought: 'Can I trust this woman?' Without saying anything, she led the way back to the drawing room. Instead of inviting me to sit down again, or giving me a polite signal that it was time to go, she stood looking at me in a considering way. She seemed to come to a decision.

'If you're interested in Alpines, there's something in the library you might care to see.'

The spaniel and I followed her out to the hall and along a gallery that looked as if it ran the length of the house. The walls were hung with swords and battle-axes in patterns, paintings of stern men posing in court dress or riding wild-eyed horses. She passed without looking at them.

'My husband had these brought down from Northumberland. He said the boys should be reminded of their heritage.'

It was the first mention of husband and sons, thrown off casually in apology for the pictures.

At the far end of the gallery was a low rectangular plinth. The basket of flowers on it was too small for the plinth. I guessed that, until very recently, that had been where Sir Gilbert Brinkburn's armour had stood. She went past it without a second glance, turned a corner and opened a door.

The greenish light of the library gave walking in there the feel of being submerged in a soothing warm sea. Olive-coloured blinds, pulled half down over long windows, protected the books that covered most of the walls from floor to ceiling. In alcoves between the book-cases, white marble busts and pots of flowers stood alternately on white pillars. There was no mustiness about this library. The smell was wax polish, flowers, old leather. Lady Brinkburn led the way past busts of Shakespeare and Milton to the far corner of the room. A slope-topped desk stood there with a straight chair in front of it. She pulled out a red leather-covered volume from a shelf next to the desk, put it down on the sloping top and undid the faded tapes that held it shut.

'There are your martagons. The colours have faded, I'm afraid.'

The double-page spread was composed of handwritten paragraphs in small rounded script and pencil and water-colour sketches, mostly of flowers. A train of mules, some with riders, others loaded with painting equipment and picnic things, walked across the bottom of both pages, so beautifully observed that I couldn't help smiling.

When I looked up, she was smiling too but nervously, as if my opinion mattered.

'This is beautiful,' I said. 'Yours?'

She nodded.

'I did it a long time ago, more than twenty years. Some of the sketches are very amateurish, I'm afraid.'

In comparison with her auricula painting, that might be true, but the pages had the vigour and freshness of a young woman's work.

'Was it your first time in the Alps?'

'First and only. I was almost mad with the beauty of it. The men would bring the mules round as soon as it got light and up we'd go, through the pinewoods and on to the mountain pastures where they graze the cows. We'd be all day up there, no sound but the streams and the cowbells.'

'Were you travelling with your family?'

She gave me a sidelong look, not smiling now.

'It was my honeymoon journey.'

Knowing how things had turned out, I didn't know what to say to that. She touched one of the mules gently with her fingertip.

'We stayed in Chamonix for three weeks. I truly believe they were the happiest weeks of my life.'

So they'd been happy once, this couple who'd spent most of their married life apart. I didn't know whether to be glad or sorry about that. I imagined them sitting on the grass together by some mountain stream, she sketching, he watching her with the pride of a man newly wed.

'My husband had managed to pick up some infection of the stomach,' she said. 'He was bedridden for the entire three weeks, so I was able to do pretty much what I wanted.'

Another sidelong look, testing my reaction. She'd quite deliberately led me down a wrong path. She had something in mind, I was sure of that, and the ruthless woman of the graveyard didn't seem so far away any more.

'Did you go on across the Alps to Italy?' I said.

It was an innocent question on the face of it. Most people did. The encounter with the daemon lover had happened in Italy.

'Yes, we spent most of the summer by Lake Como.'

Her face and voice were bland again. I looked at the book. The Alpine pages were only about halfway through.

'And you kept up your journal for the whole journey?'

'Of course. What else was there to do, all those hours in hotels?'

She turned a page. I admired her gentians. We agreed that no paint on earth, not even lapis lazuli, could match that heart-stopping blue. She was playing for time, trying to come to a decision.

'If you're really interested, you'd be welcome to come back tomorrow and have a longer look at it,' she said.

A sound came from the other end of the room, a creaking of wood.

'Mr Carmichael, come down and be introduced,' she said.

She was looking up towards a corner by the door. I followed her look and saw a man crouched at the top of a library ladder, with his back braced against the corner, his head folded under the ceiling and a book on his bent knees. He managed to look perfectly comfortable, as if that were a normal position for reading. I'd no idea he was there, but she must have known. He looked down at us, unhurriedly replaced the book on the top shelf and climbed down the ladder, unfolding as he came. He was tall and very slim, in his late twenties or early thirties. His dark hair, worn quite long, was pleasantly untidy, face clean-shaven, eyes bright behind a pair of black-rimmed spectacles.

'Miss Lane, may I introduce Robert Carmichael. Mr Carmichael's our librarian.'

'A grander title than I deserve,' he said, touching my hand. 'I suppose I'm a kind of shepherd of books.'

His voice was low and pleasant.

'Some of the family's books have been shockingly neglected,' Lady Brinkburn explained. 'They've been buying them since Caxton and never looking at them, let alone reading them. Mr Carmichael and I brought two carriage-loads of them down from Northumberland and are doing what we can to repair the damage.' She turned to him. 'Miss Lane has been kind enough to take an interest in my poor travel journal. I've invited her to come back tomorrow for a longer look.'

I thought he'd probably heard that anyway, perched

up on his ladder. He nodded politely, but did not seem enthusiastic about the idea.

'I should love to read all of it,' I said. 'If you're sure it's not an intrusion.'

I put a little emphasis on the 'all' to let her know that I was aware of what was happening. I wasn't sure if she caught the implication, but he did. The look he gave me was both surprised and alarmed. She must have noticed it, because there was a touch of defiance in her voice when she spoke to me.

'Would ten o'clock suit you? Excellent. Did you walk here, Miss Lane? May we offer you a ride back in the pony gig? The driver is going to the village in any case.'

This was the polite dismissal I'd expected an hour ago. I gratefully accepted the offer of the gig and Robert Carmichael said he'd go and have it brought round to the front door. That was hardly a librarian's job. I sensed that he wanted to see me off the premises and have a serious word with his employer. Lady Brinkburn and I lingered for a while, looking at some of her books on botany, then followed him out of the library. She pointed out a flight of polished wooden steps next to the library door.

'That leads straight up to my own rooms. So convenient. When I have trouble sleeping I can come down to my books without disturbing anybody.'

Her tone was surprisingly intimate. It was as if she were playing some kind of game with me, inviting an advance in friendship, but ready to draw back.

139

She and the spaniel came with me to the front door. The pony gig and driver were waiting but there was no sign of her shepherd of books. She saw me into the gig beside the driver and waved me off, the perfect hostess.

All the way up the drive and on to the road, I wondered what she wanted from me. Was she grasping the opportunity of using anybody reasonably intelligent from London to add to the gossip about the family? The other possibility was that she knew exactly who I was and why I was there. If she knew I'd come to judge her sanity and the worth of her evidence, her move would have more point to it. Mr Lomax and I had assumed that Mr Whiteley hadn't noticed me at the inquest, but suppose he had and then had happened to see me when I arrived, or even have somebody from the village describe me? If so, Lady Brinkburn's invitation to tea had been anything but impulsive.

Before we came to the village, I realised I might be wasting an opportunity. A relatively modest establishment like Lady Brinkburn's would only run to one driver. This one was a plump and red-faced man, genial-looking. I made some comment on the state of the roads and we got into conversation. It wasn't easy, with the noise of the wheels, so I had to speak at the top of my voice.

'Do you drive to London much?'

'Not if I can help it. They all drive like madmen up there. Run straight into you as soon as look at you. I've had enough to last me a twelvemonth.'

'You've been up recently, then?'

'Just a week ago, in the old landau, with their armour.' He flicked the reins and added, 'And him. Not that I knew it at the time.'

'Simon Handy?'

'Yes. I said to the policeman, "Do you think I'd have driven a corpse up there if I'd have known? Do I look like a bleeding undertaker?"'

'Policeman? When?'

'Day before yesterday. Didn't look like a policeman, but reckoned he was. All those questions. Had I gone straight to London? Had I stopped anywhere and left the crates without anybody looking after them? I said, sarcastic like: "Oh no, I went by way of Wigan and Manchester." Of course I went straight there, or straight as I could in London. I was driving up and down Oxford Street three or four times, looking for the way into Bond Street.'

'And did you bring Simon Handy's body back again on Saturday?'

He looked as if he were going to spit then thought better of it.

'No, I did not. Somebody from London did that.'

Once we'd turned into the track to the cottage he had to concentrate on steering among the ruts and potholes, so there was no chance to ask anything else. When we reached the turning point he got out to help me down, then spun the gig in an expert circle and went back up the track, waving to me with his whip.

॥      ✢      ✢

There was no sign of Tabby at the cottage. Plenty of things showed that she'd been active in my absence, from breakfast plates roughly washed, a broken cup on the table, a pile of sticks for kindling by the door. I decided there was enough time for me to walk into town before supper. I needed to keep my communications with London open, and though I wasn't expecting any letters yet, I could at least find the mail office. It was a walk of two miles or so, but I discovered a footpath that cut through fields to the old bridge. The mail office was next to the Bear and still open. I made myself known and, to my surprise, was handed a letter that had arrived that morning. It was on scented pink paper with a silver wax seal, addressed in curly feminine handwriting. Evidently from neither Mrs Martley nor Amos Legge, the two people I thought might write to me. When I sat down on the edge of a horse trough and broke the seal, the first three words solved the mystery.

*My Dear Elizabeth . . .*

Celia. The date on the top was Saturday's so her letter must have followed me down.

*It really is too provoking of you to be called to the country, just when you and I had met again. Is it some sick old aunt? If so, I only hope she leaves you a fortune in her will to make up for being such an inconvenience. It could not have*

142

*come at a worse time. When I reached home after the party where we met on Monday night, Philip gave me such a lecture for being out late. Then, in the morning, he thought I looked pale so would insist on calling the doctor and the doctor said I must lie on my couch and not move a finger for days and days or the baby might suffer. So what can I do? I really had no idea that this whole process was so achingly tedious. Why is one not warned? So here I am, being waited on like a Sultana in a harem (is it really Sultana? It sounds more like something from a pudding, but Philip says that's right) positively forbidden to move. My only refuge is to write letters like this one and have my friends visit with the latest gossip, which I'm glad to say they do. A propos of which, I have a bone to pick with you, my dear. Why didn't you tell me when we met about what happened at the Eyre Arms? I assure you, the whole town is talking about it. The Brinkburns, of course, but you as well. Is it really true that you put on armour like the woman in that long and rather tedious poem, challenged Miles and knocked him out of the saddle?*

I groaned. I should have known that my moment of foolishness would be gossiped up into something quite ridiculous. After cursing myself, Amos and all the people in society who had nothing better to do, I read on. Wafts of perfume rose from the pages.

*In any case, you have made a conquest in every sense. They say that Miles has been asking every-body about you. You know, if things turn out one way, you could do worse. He's the younger son, of course, but more than comfortably provided for and certainly one of the twenty most handsome men in London. (Some people say one of the ten, but the list keeps changing.) A sudden thought – is he why you left town so suddenly? I wonder. It can sometimes be good tactics to absent oneself for a while after provoking a man's interest, but two or three days are enough unless he is staying somewhere remarkably quiet and without distractions, like a Scottish castle, in which case he may be safely left for a week or two.*

I felt like scrunching the letter up and throwing it in the drinking trough, but the smell of it might have frightened the horses, so I read on.

*But, of course, things are complicated by La Rosa. Stephen seems to be behaving very oddly in this respect. Nobody has seen him for three or four days. He has not been practising at the Eyre Arms and has missed two dinners, an opera and a ball – all of which he was expected to attend with Rosa. She went to the dinners with some old male cousin, but wasn't to be seen at the ball or the opera. It is practically unheard of for an engaged man to desert his fiancée like this at the height of the season, unless he's an officer called away to the army, and even then the best regiments can be quite accommodating. They say Rosa is absolutely furious with him, and so should I be in her shoes. Perhaps she's hoping that Miles will turn out after all to be The True Heir. (Isn't there a play called that?) Of course, that might be disappointing news for you, if I'm right in my guess. I often am proved right. Philip says I have an instinct. In any case, if it really is your aunt, I do hope the old lady gets better or dies very quickly, so that you can return to town and to your affectionate friend who misses you and wishes very much that you were here to entertain her in her captivity,*

    *Celia*

By the time I got back to the cottage I'd walked myself into a better temper and was even ready to laugh about Celia's fantasies. She was right about one thing. Stephen's absence from fashionable London was puzzling. If ever there was a time to brave it out, it surely was now.

There was still no sign of Tabby and I was beginning

to worry. The back streets and yards of London were her element, but the country was new to her. She might have got lost in the woods, fallen in the river. The sun was well down towards the treetops before the sound of a voice singing came along the path from the village. The voice was not beautiful and the song was a bawdy tavern ballad that a girl her age shouldn't have known. (I probably shouldn't have known it either.) Still, in my state of worry, it was sweeter than a nightingale.

'Tabby, where in the world have you been?'

She looked surprised at my annoyance.

'Up at the houses. Polly said I could go and look at her bees if I wanted.'

'Polly?'

'The woman who came and cleaned this morning. She keeps thousands of them in a sort of upside-down basket thing in her garden. She says they make honey. Was she pulling my leg, do you think?'

'No. Tabby, it was kind of Mrs Todd to invite you, but I was worried. If you'd left a note for me . . .'

She gave me an angry look. I deserved it. Where in the life she'd led could she have learned to write or read?

'You didn't tell me I was supposed to stay here,' she said sullenly.

Which was true, because I'd assumed she'd be too intimidated by her new surroundings to go far.

Our supper was ham and eggs fried in a pan over the fire, the slices of ham plumper and pinker than in London, egg yolks golden as the evening sunlight coming

146

through the window. Tabby ate with appetite, elbows on the table, egg on her chin. The fear that she was missing had started me worrying about what I was doing to her. It was all very well taking her with me on a whim. As far as I'd thought about her future, I'd supposed that working for me for a while might ease her path into proper domestic service, with her knees under somebody else's table and a roof over her head. In time, she might even rise to the heights of a real lady's maid. Now, obeying her casual request to pass the salt, watching her hack at the loaf of bread, I knew that was as unlikely as water running uphill. Tabby had never learned deference, a far graver defect in a servant than lack of reading and writing, and I was not the person to teach it to her. Instead, once her hunger was satisfied, I let her rattle on about her visit to the village. She seemed to have struck up an instant friendship with Mrs Todd.

'Five children, she's got. She said she wanted to stop at four, only her husband wouldn't. He works at the public house. It's his brother what's married to the woman whose sister was friendly with the one what got killed.'

'With Simon Handy?'

I was trying to keep up with this tangle of relationships. As far as I could make out, we were talking about Mrs Todd's husband's brother's sister-in-law.

'Yes. I told Polly about what happened here last night. She says it might have been his ghost walking, because of being shut out of the churchyard like that.'

147

She looked at me triumphantly.

'Did you mention that he was rowing a boat as well?'

She disregarded it.

'Polly says it gives her the shivers, with her living right next to the churchyard, in case he decides to walk in on her one night. She says she wouldn't have him in the house when he was alive, but she doesn't know what she could do about it now he's dead.'

'She didn't like him, then?'

'Nah, she said nobody liked him, except her husband's brother's wife's sister – Violet's her name – and even then they were always quarrelling because he wouldn't give her any money for herself or his kids.'

'What children?'

'Violet's.'

'By Handy?'

'Yes.'

'So was Handy married to Violet?'

'Not in the church, no. That's what Polly said to her: that she couldn't do nothing about it in any case because of them not being married in church.'

My head was spinning.

'Let's go outside,' I said. 'Put the plates in the sink and you can wash them in the morning.'

We sat on the bench by the porch. The flowers of the evening primroses were still glowing yellow in the dusk as if they had their own source of light, the warm-animal smell of them filling the air.

'So you were there when this woman Violet came to talk to Mrs Todd?' I said.

'Yes. She came when we were looking at the bees. Polly wasn't any too pleased to see her, you could tell that. She said they shouldn't be arguing in front of strangers.'

'They argued?'

'Yes.'

'Tell me about it.'

'Polly and me were out in her garden, then Polly looks over the wall and says, "Here comes trouble." This woman comes in, hair all over the place and petticoat trailing in the dust, goes straight up to Polly and says, "What are we going to do about it then?" So Polly says she doesn't know what she's talking about – only you can tell she does really – and Violet says, "You know very well. Getting that wall put back in its proper place."'

'Meaning the churchyard wall?'

'Yes. Violet says, "Lady or not, she can't do that," and Polly says, "She can, and she's done it." Violet says she had no right, and Polly says her husband owns all the houses in the village, so she can do what she likes.'

'What did Violet expect Mrs Todd to do about it?'

'Violet had this idea that all the men in the village should go out at night and put the wall back where it had been. She wanted Polly to tell her husband to help. Polly said it was a daft idea and she wouldn't. That's when she told Violet she had no rights anyway, because of not being married in church. Violet started shouting at her about having no respect for her own flesh and blood. Polly said, "You're not my flesh and blood, and Handy certainly wasn't. He didn't even come from round here. In any case, he was only ever in your bed when he couldn't find a warmer one."'

Tabby reported all this with complete tranquillity. I think it had even made her feel at home to find that people could quarrel every bit as fiercely in the country as in London.

'Do you know where Violet lives?'

'Two down from the public house. Keeps hens and sells eggs.'

'I'm going to the big house tomorrow morning,' I said. 'If there's time when we get back, you and I will go and buy some eggs.'

'But Polly brought a dozen . . .' Then she looked at me and grinned.

'I see. All right then.'

Reading and writing weren't everything. Nor was deference.

# CHAPTER NINE

Next morning Lady Brinkburn must have seen me walking down her drive, because she was already in the hall when a maid opened the front door to me. She seemed genuinely pleased to see me and led me straight to the library. The journal was ready on the sloping desk, with a chair drawn up to it.

'Betty will be in soon with coffee, Miss Lane. Is there enough light for you here? We can draw the blind up higher, if you like.'

The light was perfect, I assured her. She lingered. Now the moment had come, she seemed nervous about leaving me with the journal.

'Mr Carmichael has had to go on an errand into town,' she said. 'He won't be back for an hour or so.'

Was that intended as reassurance to herself or me? I

151

wondered if her librarian had taken himself off as a sign of his disapproval.

'So I'll leave you with it then,' she said, and went.

The first page of the journal carried simply its title, in capitals and under-ruled: *Journal of a Continental Tour, 1816.* The year after the battle of Waterloo, the first year that British travellers had been able to visit Europe for pleasure, after it had been closed to them for so many years by the Napoleonic wars. I decided to start at the beginning and read all the way through instead of skipping straight to the part that mattered. I wanted to know more about the young bride Lady Brinkburn had been twenty-three years ago. I turned the page.

*16 March 1816, Rotterdam*
*We embarked at Newcastle yesterday morning, arriving late and almost losing the tide. The sailors managed to have our travelling chariot taken on board quite easily, but there was a terrible pother with the fourgon that will carry all our luggage for more than six months, as well as Edward and Suzy. The gangway shifted and for a while it appeared that it and all our belongings were doomed to be an early tribute to Neptune. But the brave sailors pushed and pulled with a will and eventually we were all safely on board, just in time. I was sad to say goodbye to*

*the horses that had pulled our carriage, but God willing they will be waiting for us when we return in the autumn. It was a turbulent crossing, although the sailors said we were making faster than usual progress because of the strong wind from the west. Poor Suzy and C were overcome with mal de mer before we were out of sight of the coast of England, and spent the entire voyage down below. I was mercifully unaffected and stood at the rail with the spray from the waves bursting over my head, feeling a thundering in my ears and all through my body as huge waves battered the oaken sides of our good ship.*

The page was ornamented with a cloaked figure at the ship's rail – presumably a self-portrait – and a ship wallowing in a trough of sea with a wave rearing above the mainmast. Probably some artistic licence. On the next page they landed at Rotterdam, secured rooms in a hotel that was *so spotlessly clean and orderly that one might have eaten dinner off the flagstones in the hall* and were met by a Mr Schwarz who was to be their guide for the first few weeks of their journey. So they'd decided to hire guides as they went along, rather than take one with them. I knew a little about these Continental tours because one of the many ways in which my late father managed to make enough money to keep us was by occasionally escorting rich young men around the cultural sites of Europe, as a final gloss to their expensive educations. Mr Schwarz's task would have been to smooth the way for the young couple, advise them on the best hotels to stay, the art galleries, notable buildings and best views and quite probably tell them what to think of them as well.

They had rested at Rotterdam for three days while Mr Schwarz went ahead with the fourgon containing the luggage, along with Edward and Suzy (presumably valet and maid) to prepare things for them on the next stop of their journey towards Antwerp and Brussels. It seemed that they were avoiding Paris and most of France; hardly surprising at a time when the majority of English people still thought of it as a country of bloody revolution. The journey to Brussels, in easy stages, seemed to go smoothly, apart from occasional worries like a hotel where the beds had fleas – *I told Mr Schwarz that it simply would not do and unless they replaced the mattress and bolsters as well as all the linen we should move to another place* – and a lame horse – *I insisted on getting out of the carriage and walking the two miles to the staging post, rather than burden the poor creature with my weight.*

As I turned the pages, I started to like the young Lady Brinkburn very much. Every night without fail, after what must have been exhausting days of travel, she wrote a few lines at least in her journal and usually added a sketch. She had a good eye for the unremarkable things

154

as well as the approved sights – two women in shawls walking to market with baskets of root vegetables, an old man leaning on a stick and drinking beer, even a line of washing blowing in the wind. The excitement of an intelligent young woman, abroad for the first time, shone on every page of her journal. She was kind to people as well as animals. The last stage into Antwerp had been a pouring wet one. *Our poor boy riding on the back of the coach was wet as a herring when we arrived, teeth chattering. I told Suzy to dry him and wrap him in a blanket and I made him some tea with my little spirit lamp.* So their entourage had included a boy to ride on the back of their travelling carriage and help with the luggage, which would have been below the dignity of Edward the valet. There was even a drawing of the boy on the Antwerp page, blanket wrapped, with his steaming teacup. Every detail of the journey was there. Or almost every detail. Only one thing was missing: any sign of affection for, or even interest in, her new husband.

Lord Brinkburn always appeared simply as 'C' for Cornelius, his first name. Usually, as in that first entry on the crossing, when there was something wrong with him. At Antwerp, where they stayed for a week, *C brought low with a cold, so Mr Schwarz showed Suzy and me around the city on our own. I purchased a set of painted plates and Suzy begged a small advance of her wages from me to buy a new lace cap with ribbons.* At Brussels, making the obligatory visit to the battlefield

155

of Waterloo, C *angry because the man who was to have been our guide did not meet us, but fortunately an officer who had taken part in the battle was also visiting and gave us a most vivid account of how our hero the Duke of Wellington defeated the French tyrant, so C mollified.* A conscientious plan of the battlefield accompanied the entry. Although the new bride might be bashful about going into raptures over her husband in a journal that friends and family might read, all this seemed unusually cool. Shouldn't they, for instance, have watched the occasional sunset together, walked together, shopped for luxuries for their home together? Come to think of it, should a young woman on her honeymoon tour have been quite so assiduous about keeping up her journal every evening?

'Lady Brinkburn says would you like some more coffee, Miss Lane?'

The maid had come into the library so softly that I didn't notice until she was standing beside me. I'd let my coffee go cold in its cup, hardly tasted. I said no thank you, waited while she took the tray away, then turned back to the journal, following the Brinkburns' leisurely progress across Europe.

From Brussels they went eastwards to Cologne, then up the Rhine Valley, sometimes making diversions and often stopping in one place for days at a time. I was looking for something else in the journal now, and not finding it. Lady Brinkburn had no great fondness for her husband, but had she met another man she liked better on their travels? That might explain, if anything did, the preposterous story of the stranger in the night. If so, there was not the faintest trace of it in the journal. Mr Schwarz, from her sketch of him, was fifty, had ears that stuck out and wore a *pince nez* on the sharp ridge of his nose. As arranged, he left them at the Swiss border where plump and cheerful Mr Lebrun took over the management of the Alpine stage of their journey. Occasionally the Brinkburns would meet other travelling British parties and go on excursions or picnics with them, but these associations lasted a week at most before they went their separate ways.

One thing that was clear, as they travelled over mountain passes and had to survive simpler accommodation than they'd experienced so far, was how much Lady Brinkburn was growing up on the journey. The young bride, still in her early twenties, was learning to manage people and events. One evening when they arrived tired at a mountain inn to find the cook incapably drunk and the prospect of a bread-and-cheese supper looming: *I told Edward and the boy to carry the wretched cook into the yard and hold his head under the pump, then Suzy and I took charge of his kitchen and succeeded in constructing some quite satisfactory omelettes, which Mr Lebrun pronounced as good as any he'd ever eaten in France. Since the cook had managed to lose the keys to the wine cellar, we broached some bottles from the store we keep for emergencies under the floor of our chariot and did well enough. In the morning, when the proprietor presented his bill, I told him roundly that we'd no intention of paying anything for our dinner beyond the value of the eggs and butter.* And where was Lord Brinkburn in all this? I imagined him lounging with his legs under the table, complaining of having to wait for his dinner. Perhaps unfairly, I was beginning to dislike the man.

They spent some days at Geneva and made a daring foray into France, to see the glaciers at Chamonix. Then came the pages I'd seen already, when Lord Brinkburn was taken ill and his wife had the happiest three weeks of her life, painting and botanising in the Alpine meadows. Various new names occurred over the next few pages, but most of the men mentioned were travelling Britons or guides, with no indication that her heart had been stirred by anything apart from lilies and gentians.

Once recovered, the party seemed intent on making up for lost time and hurried over the St Bernard Pass into Italy. Because of the pace of travel, the journal entries were shorter, mostly just a few lines recording the more spectacular sights and the miles travelled, with the occasional sketch. But once in Italy, they expanded again into whole pages. The Brinkburns had rented a villa on the shores of Lake Como for most of July and the whole of August and Lady Brinkburn was enchanted with the place.

*It really is the most romantic of all possible dwellings, like something from a fairytale. Although it is a villa, most comfortably and properly appointed, it is also a true castle. A small peninsula juts into the lake, crowned with the ruins of what must have been a formidable small fortress three or four hundred years ago. Its walls are mostly crumbled into falls of stone down the hillside, but the original round tower remains. The architect has most cleverly worked it into the design of the villa, so that the room downstairs is a round sitting room looking out over the lake, so close to the water that one might almost feel oneself afloat. Above it, a smaller room is fitted out as a bedchamber. It is not large and may have been intended for a servant, but the minute I saw it I appropriated it as mine. (Suzy may sleep more spaciously in the main body of the villa.) I have my drawing and writing things set out on a table by the window and a view of the lake that a soaring eagle might envy.*

For the next few weeks, she didn't tire of drawing and painting that castle from all angles: from the shore, from a rowing boat on the lake, against the sunset, by moonlight. She wrote poems in her journal too, about the castle and the lake, much influenced by Wordsworth and not as good as her drawings. Although the poems were full of fashionable melancholy, every page of the journal suggested that Lady Brinkburn was enjoying those summer weeks by Lake Como. Small sketches of their household practically danced from the margins: the maid Suzy with a basket of peaches, the boy from home grinning at the back of the travelling coach, along with a smaller lad who might have been the child of one of their Italian servants, the Italian cook waving a ladle – everything and everybody, in fact, but her new-wedded lord. That might have been because her lord was not often there to be sketched. Soon after their arrival, he took off on his own for Milan, where he stayed for a week. When he got back, some of his old university friends had arrived in a villa a few miles away, part of what seemed to be a British migration to the shores of the lake. Reading between the lines, Lady Brinkburn didn't much care for these old friends and dryly recorded when C was off boating or driving with them. She made her own friends and established a new round of picnics, lunch parties and sketching expeditions. Altogether, it seemed an enviably sunny interlude.

The breaking up of it was gradual at first. Some of her picnic friends began to turn their travelling chariots towards home. It was mid August by now and the grouse moors were calling. The long summer days began to fray into rain and thunderstorms. She loved the storms at first.

*Here, the lightning often begins long before the rain. Last night after dinner I sat at the window of my little round drawing room and watched pulse after pulse of white light flickering over the lake. The effect is quite beyond my powers of drawing. No thunder was audible, but the air seemed so charged with electricity that I could feel the small hairs at the back of my neck rising. A silk handkerchief became magnetised and clung to the sleeve of my dress. When I touched my paper-knife, a perceptible shock ran up my fingers and along my arm. The phenomenon has a remarkable affect on one's nervous organisation, as if waiting anxiously for something but not knowing what. Later, when it was quite dark, the storm broke in earnest, with downpours of rain so heavy that it looked like a second glass pane on the far side of my window, copper-coloured lightning forking down to the water and tumultuous thunder. It is the most sublime of Nature's effects, and I privileged to see it here from my window suspended between land and water as the elements raged all round.*

More of their holiday friends packed up and headed home. Lady Brinkburn began to acquire packing cases for some of the china and pictures she'd picked up on their travels. There were fewer sketching expeditions.

Her journal entries began to take on a regretful tone about the people and places she would miss and the darkness and cold of an English winter in prospect, but there was still nothing to give any hint of what was to come. August 26 started as a normal day in the journal.

*Sky overcast, the heat heavy and oppressive. The Italian seamstress called this morning, about the alterations in my blue travelling costume. C has taken the carriage and gone to the Desmonds, where they are getting up a party to play bridge.*

A few more domestic details followed, then a later entry:

*Evening. C not back, so I had a light supper of poached chicken and fruit brought to me here in my drawing room. I have little appetite and my head is aching from the heat. I tried to sketch boats on the lake this afternoon, but could not get them to come right. Even now that the sun is going down, there is no sense of relief from the oppressive atmosphere. A storm is brewing, preceded by thunder echoing from the hills like a big bass drum. Now and then, distant lightning illuminates the undersides of the clouds on the far side of the lake with a sullen kind of glow, nothing like the bright pulses of previous storms*

*I have witnessed from this window. I suppose it
is Nature signalling the end of the summer.*

Unusually, there were no sketches on the page. I hesitated before turning it, knowing we must be very close now to the entry that mattered. Outside, two gardener's boys were kneeling on the gravel drive, rooting out weeds invisible from where I was sitting. Further away in the fields, men and women were turning over lines of mown hay to dry in the sun. When I turned the thick paper it made a creaking noise that sounded loud in the library. There was just one line of writing on the double page. The hand was the familiar one that had led me all the way from Newcastle to Lake Como, but it slanted across the paper as if the writer lacked the strength or energy to hold the journal straight while she wrote.

*August 27*
*This morning, Lord Brinkburn has told me
something terrible, terrible.*

Nothing more. I turned the page. The next two pages were blank. The journal resumed, after a fashion, two weeks later when they were on the far side of the Alps and on the way home. But it was a different journal altogether, a mere record of miles travelled and hotels where the party stayed. No descriptions, no poetry, no sketches. The last entry recorded *Arrived*

*Brussels 5.30 p.m.* After that, only more blank pages. Not a word about the return to England or whether the same horses were waiting. I felt as if the talented, resourceful young woman I'd been travelling with had suddenly died.

A door opened. A man's footsteps came across the floor. When I turned there was Robert Carmichael. My face must have shown my distress. He came and stood beside me. On an impulse, I moved to shut the journal, with some obscure idea of protecting her secret, even though I still didn't know it.

'It's all right,' he said. 'I read it some time ago, at Lady Brinkburn's invitation.'

His voice was quiet, with the same sense of loss that I was feeling. I turned back to the page with one line of writing, then forward again to Brussels, not knowing what to say.

'You're wondering if that page could have been inserted afterwards?' he said.

I hadn't been, but the suggestion brought me back to my investigative senses. I thought about it.

'I don't think so, no. It would have been hard to tamper with the stitching of these pages, and you'd need silk yellowed with ageing, as this is. The binding is scuffed just as it would be from travelling.'

'Books may be restitched and bindings changed,' he suggested.

He didn't add, '... *as I know very well*', but the suggestion was in the air. His work among the family's

164

books would have brought him into contact with the trade.

'In that case, somebody did an expert job. Then there's the question of the ink.'

'Yes?'

He was listening politely, head on one side. He'd thought of all this in advance.

'If you look at that one sentence on the twenty-seventh and then the passage about the storm the day before, the ink is exactly the same colour and the same degree of fading,' I said. 'Those short entries at the end of the journal are in a variety of different inks, as they would be in different hotels.'

'So you conclude . . .?'

'I don't conclude anything yet.'

I closed the book and tied the tapes. He picked up the journal and slotted it into place on a shelf near the desk, among bound volumes of maps. I stood up, feeling wearier than was reasonable from a morning in a library.

'I'm sorry to say Lady Brinkburn is indisposed,' he said. 'She has one of her headaches. She sends her apologies and hopes to meet you again soon. I hope you've been offered coffee.'

'Yes, thank you.'

'May I call the pony chaise for you?'

'I'll walk, thank you. I need the fresh air.'

'In that case, perhaps you'd permit me to walk with you, as far as the top of the drive at least.'

It would have been rude to refuse. Had it been her

decision or his that I shouldn't talk to her after reading the journal? He escorted me to the hall and asked me to excuse him while he went to fetch his hat. It took him several minutes, long enough to talk to Lady Brinkburn, or perhaps I was being unfairly suspicious.

At first Robert Carmichael didn't attempt to talk as we walked up the drive together, leaving me to my thoughts. The amazing thing about the journal was how close it came to bearing out Lady Brinkburn's story. All the elements were there: the storm, the tower, the husband's absence, the shock in the morning so appalling that it had crushed the life out of her. Hearing the story for the first time, in Mr Disraeli's voice with its hint of mockery, it had been so clearly a romantic woman's fantasy that I hadn't believed it for a moment. Now, that disbelief was wavering. I was sure that the journal was genuine and that the entries had been made at the time events were happening. Either Lady Brinkburn had gone mad quite suddenly, with nothing in the journal to give the slightest warning of it, or something terrible had happened in the course of that night and day beside Lake Como.

'So what did you think of the journal?' he said.

'Fascinating. Observant and beautifully illustrated.'

We were fencing with each other, and these were no more than opening moves. He made no attempt to follow up his question, so I tried one of my own.

'Have you worked for Lady Brinkburn long?'

'Longer than I care to admit. I was engaged as tutor to Miles when he was ill and away from school. When he went back, Lady Brinkburn asked me to stay and help with the library and tutor both boys in their holidays.'

Tutors were often engaged straight out of university, so that would make him perhaps ten years older than Miles, therefore in his early thirties. In spite of his occupation, he had the look of an active and athletic man.

'Are you happy with a life among books?' I said.

His eyes widened in surprise, as if at an unexpected move, then he smiled.

'You think I should be out in the great world? "'I am half sick of shadows,' said the Lady of Shalott.'"

'She died, out in the great world,' I said.

'And Sir Lancelot lived and had no notion what he'd done. It hardly seems fair, does it?'

'He didn't mean her any harm,' I said.

'I suppose no man ever does – no normal man, anyway. In answer to your question, yes, I am content with my life here. There's the river to row on and swim in, a horse to ride, paths to walk and a perfectly adequate library. What more could I ask?'

Somehow, we'd already passed the boundaries of normal conversation. The gateposts of the hall were behind us and we were out on the public road, alongside a field were women were still turning hay with long wooden rakes. He showed no sign of turning back.

'Lady Brinkburn's not mad, you know,' he said.

I stopped and stared, wondering if he'd really said the words, or if I'd imagined them. He stopped too and stared back at me. He'd taken off his glasses before leaving the house. His brown eyes were sad.

'But I think you've come to that conclusion anyway,' he said. 'I think you like her.'

I hesitated, so as to be clear on what I did think. We started walking again.

'Yes, I do like her. And from what I've seen and read so far, I don't think she's mad either,' I said.

'Will you be reporting that?'

He knew or had guessed so much that there was no point in pretending.

'In all conscience, I can hardly do otherwise.'

I was sure that was not what the family's lawyer, Mr Lomax, wanted from me. He might refuse to pay my fee, which would be a hard blow, but I could do nothing about that.

'On the other hand, she may be misguided,' he said. 'As you'll have seen, she's a strong-willed lady.'

'Misguided and mad are two different things. If they weren't, most government ministers would be in asylums.'

He laughed. We'd passed the hayfield now and were alongside a copse.

'And there's a legal difference,' I said. 'A court won't listen to a person who's known to be mad, but it has to decide for itself who's misguided.'

I was sounding him out, trying to see what side he

was taking in the family quarrel. He must have guessed that, because it was some time before he spoke.

'I like both the young men – though they both have their faults – and I hold no brief for one against the other. If I have any interest in this, it's to see that the family doesn't inflict more damage on itself than it has done already.'

'And to protect Lady Brinkburn?'

'Yes, that especially.'

A jay flew out of the woods on one side of the road, into them on the other. His eyes followed the blue flash of its wings into the leaves.

'Miss Lane, you implied that I'd chosen to live a retired life . . .

'I didn't mean any criticism of –'

He pressed on, as if he'd nerved himself to say something and wouldn't be distracted.

'As it happens, that's largely true. But I've some experience of the world and I pride myself on being a good judge of character. That's why I'm about to take a step which may be a mistake. Whether it is or not, depends very largely on you.'

I said nothing. We walked on a few paces.

'I don't think you should ask Lady Brinkburn any questions about the journal or anything else.'

I didn't reply. That was a decision for me to take.

'And I think you should report back to Mr Lomax that Lady Brinkburn is, unfortunately, not in her right mind,' he said.

'What!'

For the second time, I came to a halt. The minor surprise – that he knew that Lomax had sent me – was outweighed by the greater one.

'But we've just agreed that she isn't mad.'

'Not mad, exactly. Certainly not mad in the sense that she'd need to be restrained or confined in any way. Simply subject to delusions, fixed ideas, eccentricities. I'm sure you could gather evidence quite easily. You'll find plenty of people in the village with stories about her – wandering in the woods reciting poetry to herself and so forth.'

He was speaking fast now, like an inexperienced barrister who senses he's lost the sympathy of the court but is determined to get through his piece. I started walking, so that he had to fall into step beside me.

'Mr Carmichael, you know as well as I do that walking in the woods reciting poetry is not evidence of insanity. Eccentricity and insanity are not the same thing. Are you asking me to perjure myself?'

'No, of course not. In any case, we hope it won't come to anything as serious as perjury.'

'So I'm to lie, and hope it won't have to be in court?'

He blushed from hat brim to collar stud, but kept doggedly to his brief.

'Miss Lane, this whole affair has been fed by gossip, most of it in London. At least, let's try and use gossip against gossip. If enough people in society become convinced of Lady Brinkburn's mental instability, perhaps

170

it will die as quickly as it arose, before any more harm is done.'

He was talking as if I were already part of this conspiracy.

'But why?' I said.

'Surely you see? You tell me that you like Lady Brinkburn. Can anybody who has any consideration for her at all bear the thought of her standing up before the House of Lords, telling the story we both know about?'

'Even if the cost of preventing it is having her thought mad?'

'Yes. Even at that cost.'

We came to the track through the woods that led to the cottage and turned on to it.

'There's something you should know,' I said. 'There's a policeman down here from London who's trying to find out what happened to Handy. He was there just after they found the body. He's not the usual sort of policeman.'

He went tense.

'How do you know that?'

'He spoke to me. Not that there was anything I could tell him.'

I didn't add that he'd spoken to the family coachman as well. Let him find out some things for himself. He didn't speak again until the chimney pots of the cottage were in sight.

'Well, are you going to do as I suggest about Lady Brinkburn?'

'I can't do it,' I said. 'I want to help her, I think, only I can't do it this way.'

He said nothing, just raised his hat to me and turned back along the track.

# CHAPTER TEN

When I reached the cottage, Mrs Todd was just preparing to leave. Goodness knows what she and Tabby had found to do all morning in so small a place, but it looked tolerably tidy.

'Polly says that fisherman you didn't want me to talk to has gone back to London,' Tabby told me as soon as I came through the door.

She sounded regretful. Mrs Todd nodded.

'Went first thing yesterday. He told the landlord he'd be coming back as soon as he got another day off. He likes it here.'

'Oh, he does, does he?'

I wondered what news Constable Bevan was carrying back to the coroner.

'Ever such a nice man,' Mrs Todd went on, unwinding the scarf that she'd worn like a turban over her hair.

'He wanted to know all about the village and the hall and Lady Brinkburn and so on.'

'Polly says he spent a lot of time talking to Violet,' Tabby put in, with a sideways glance at me.

Mrs Todd's expression changed. She crammed the scarf violently into the pocket of her apron.

'Goodness knows why he bothered talking to her. I suppose she was leading him on as usual.'

'Leading him on?' I said.

Mrs Todd looked at Tabby, as if questioning whether she could speak freely in front of me, and got a nod.

'Anything in trousers. Now she's lost one man – not that she had much of him in the first place – she's looking round for the next.'

Eventually she went away up the path, promising to be back in the morning.

'Well, are we going to get the eggs?' Tabby said.

'Not before you've made a pot of tea. My throat's parched.'

'Polly says she saw you walking up to the hall. Have you been calling on the lady again?'

'Yes. Go and fill the kettle.'

She fidgeted all through our lunch of bread and cheese and wasn't happy until we were walking up the path to the village together. She walked well, at a good swinging pace that matched my own, our skirts tucked up out of the dust. I had to remind her to pull hers down again at the edge of the wood, or she'd have shown her lower legs to the world like the girls in the hayfield.

Violet was out in her front garden, a space of scuffed earth and vigorous weeds, mostly thistles and Good King Henry. Hens scratched in the bare patches. She looked at me suspiciously, narrowing her eyes against the sun.

She was no more than five foot tall and thin as a stick of kindling, sharp cheekbones pushing at the skin of her pale face. Hair that might have been an attractive chestnut brown when clean was scraped into an untidy knot at the nape of a neck that hadn't seen soap for a while. She wore a grey cotton dress, stained at bodice and shoulder, and the milky whiff of infant clung round her. At the open door of the cottage a child of three years old or so crouched in the dirt, playing a game with pebbles.

'We want some eggs,' Tabby told her.

Violet stayed where she was, still staring at me. I introduced myself, explaining that we were staying in the cottage by the river. It seemed to take a while for the information to reach her brain.

'There's not many. They haven't been laying on account of the heat,' she said.

'That doesn't matter, just what you can let us have.'

She led the way along the side of the cottage, passing the child without looking at it, to a shed leaning unsteadily against the back wall. Her bare feet were narrow and high arched, seeming more elegant than the rest of her. Inside the shed, five eggs nestled on soiled straw in a cracked bowl.

'They'll do very well,' I said. 'But that won't leave any for you.'

'Don't matter.'

I took a shilling from my pocket and laid it on the shelf beside the eggs. It was at least twice as much as they were worth. I signed to Tabby to pick up the eggs. She looked at me.

'We haven't got nothing to put them in.'

I sighed, and produced another shilling.

'Then we'll have to buy the bowl as well.'

It wasn't worth a halfpenny and yet, surprisingly, Violet hesitated.

'It was a good bowl until it got cracked. It's one he gave me.'

I moved it into the light from the cobwebbed window space. Under the grime it was fine porcelain, delicately patterned.

'Mr Handy gave it to you?'

She nodded.

'Could we talk about him, do you think?' I said.

'What's he to you?'

'I was there when they found his body.'

She said nothing, but flinched and drew in her breath as if I'd punched her in the stomach. I hadn't intended brutality, but her question was a fair one and didn't deserve a lie.

'I never knew him alive,' I said. 'I'm sorry for what happened.'

'He wasn't a bad man,' she said, as if begging a reprieve for his reputation, if not for him.

'I'm sure he wasn't.'

'Is it true they stuffed him in a packing case and had him sent to London?'

'I'm afraid it was. Who told you about it?'

I decided not to ask who 'they' were at this point.

'Janet, she works up at the hall, in the kitchens. She came running down here, full of it, how Mr Whiteley had had to go up to London in a hurry because of him being dead. She made sure I knew about it, little cow. "Well, thank you very much for telling me," I said. I wasn't going to let her see me crying.'

But she was near to tears now.

'Do you think we might sit down?' I said.

She led the way through the back door, into a kitchen-cum living room that took up the whole ground floor of the cottage. A baby slept in a wooden cradle by the window, wrapped in a reasonably clean blanket. A heavy oak table took up most of the floorspace, with three roughly made chairs drawn up to it. Apart from that, the only items of furniture were a dresser with a few cheap plates and oddments, and a rocking chair with one broken rocker. Flies circled in the shaft of sunlight coming through the front window. Violet sat at the table and signed to me to take the chair opposite. Tabby perched carefully on the broken rocking chair.

'Had you known Mr Handy long?' I said.

'On and off, four or five years.'

After that first question of hers, she seemed to take it for granted that I had a right to ask anything I wanted.

'On and off?'

'He came when he could, only he wasn't here very often. That's what none of them here allow for, you see.'

'Away with Lord Brinkburn?'

'Yes. Italy, mostly, and France. Up in Newcastle sometimes. All over.' She stood up, went to the dresser and came back with two things clutched in her hands. 'He always brought me back something, like these.'

She put them carefully on the table: a carved wooden bear of the sort they make in Switzerland, and a bracelet of red glass Venetian beads. When I picked up the bracelet the beads caught the sunlight and threw scatterings of light like blood drops round the walls.

'It's pretty,' I said.

'Yes, he was always thinking of me, see, whatever they said.'

'How long had he been working for Lord Brinkburn?'

'All his life, since he was a boy of ten. His family were coal miners, up north where Lord Brinkburn's family comes from. His lordship picked him out for a bright lad and took him into service, then later he made him his vally. Handy by name and Handy by nature, his lordship said.'

'And Handy travelled abroad with him?'

'All the time.'

'But . . .'

I looked at the baby in the cradle, the bear and bracelet on the table.

'But when did you . . . did he . . . ?'

Tabby rescued me.

'Are they his children?'

'Yes.'

'From when he came back here?'

'Yes. Every year, Lord Brinkburn would come here for a week or ten days to go over the estate accounts with Mr Whiteley. Sometimes it was nearly two weeks at a time.'

She was smiling at the thought of it. I felt like crying at the desperate patience of some women.

'So Handy never worked at the hall until now?' I said.

'Only for his lordship when he was there, and for these last few weeks, after they put him in the madhouse. Handy was the man who had to take him there – not his wife or his sons. Handy was the only one he'd have near him.'

'So once Handy had left him in the asylum, he came here?'

'That's what Lord Brinkburn told him he should do. When they were still in Italy, he could feel his mind going. So he gave Handy a letter to give to Whiteley if anything happened to him. Handy read it out to me three or four times, so I know by heart what it said. *Handy has been my most faithful servant. He is to be given suitable employment at Brinkburn Hall as long as it suits him.* He signed it and sealed it with his ring, all legal.'

I hazarded a guess.

'I suppose Mr Whiteley wasn't too pleased about that.'

She laughed.

'Handy said he looked like he'd been butted by a bull in the backside. But he couldn't do nothing about it.'

'So after all the travelling, Handy settled at Brinkburn Hall. How long ago was that?'

'Nearly two months. Only I wouldn't say *settled*. The last time I saw him, he told me he was so fed up with them all that he was thinking of moving on. He'd have done it already, he said, only he was waiting for some money.'

'Weren't his wages paid, then?'

'It wasn't wages he was talking about. A tidy sum of money, he said.'

'Do you think he expected to be left something when Lord Brinkburn died?'

She shrugged. I asked where Handy had been thinking of moving.

'Back up north, where he came from. He'd have sent for us when he got himself settled, I know that.'

But she sounded far from sure of it.

'Why was he fed up at the hall?'

'The other servants didn't like him. Jealousy, it was, because of him having travelled and knowing more about everything than they did. They'd do little things to spite him, like the cook giving him the piece of meat with all the gristle. And they were making him work too hard. "I'm being asked to do too much," he kept saying to me. "It's not fair on a man."'

'And he didn't get on well with Lady Brinkburn?'

'She couldn't abide him. She gave orders that he wasn't even to come within sight of her, only he took to popping out of hedges and round corners now and then, just to show her. It was his lordship he'd worked for, not her.'

I was forming a poor opinion of Handy, but tried not to let her see it.

'Have you any idea why she disliked him so much?'

She shrugged.

'The way she felt about her husband, anybody he liked, she didn't.'

'Surely there must have been more to it than that. She wouldn't have the churchyard wall moved just because she didn't like him.'

'Sheer spite, that's all,' Violet said.

Clearly there was no progress to be made in that direction. I tried another tack.

'When was the last time you saw him?'

She looked down at the table.

'On the Sunday.'

By Monday morning, Handy had been dead and in a crate on his way to London. Hardly the moving on he'd have expected.

'What time on Sunday?'

'He came and had his tea with us. Eggs mostly, it was, and a bit of mutton I'd managed to scrounge for him, but he said it was still better than what they gave him up at the hall. He sent me across to the Farriers with the jug for some beer, gave me the money for it, too. We had a good time.'

181

She smiled at the memory of it, but her eyes were glazed with tears.

'Then I suppose he had to go back to the hall?' I said.

I remembered that Mr Whiteley had seen him by the old dairy just after eight o'clock, around the servants' supper time. I supposed that having filled his stomach with eggs and mutton, he wouldn't have needed to eat with the rest of them.

Violet's smile faded. She looked down at the table.

'I thought he didn't have to. I thought we were tucked in for the night, all cosy. I said, "What do you want to be going back there for at this time of night?"'

'Night?'

'When he got out of bed and started putting his trousers on, I thought it must be morning already, then I heard the church clock striking eleven.'

'Did he say why he was going?'

'He said there was something he had to do and he'd see me in the morning. Then he put on his trousers and his shoes and went. That was the last I ever saw of him.'

She was crying in earnest now, tears dripping on to the table. I spoke as gently as I could.

'And that was eleven o'clock on Sunday night?'

She nodded.

'He'd had his tea with you. Did he go away after that and come back later?'

'No, he was with me all evening. It was the longest time we'd had together since . . .'

She glanced across at the baby.

'Did he talk much about things at the hall?'

'Not much, no. But you could tell he wasn't happy there.'

'You said the other servants didn't like him. Was there one in particular he thought of as an enemy?'

She thought about it.

'Not in particular, no.'

'And he didn't give you the idea that he was in danger in any way?'

'Of course not. Why should he?'

'Did he say anything about the suit of armour?'

'He mentioned they were having to pack up an old suit of armour and send it to London for Master Miles, that's all.'

'And he didn't say any more about whatever it was he had to do when he left you?'

'No.'

'Did you ask him?'

'He never liked a lot of questions.'

The baby started whimpering. Violet went over to the cradle and scooped it up, rocking it in her arms and murmuring to it. There was a new moist patch broadening on the bodice of her dress. I caught Tabby's eye. Time to go. We stood up and I said we'd see ourselves out.

'But he was up to some sort of mischief.'

She said it as much to the bundled baby as to us.

'Mischief?'

'He liked a joke – they both did, him and his lordship, that's why Handy suited him so well. Why he didn't stay with me that night, he was up to something.'

'Did he say so?'

'He didn't have to say so. I knew him.'

'And he didn't say what it was?'

'No. I thought it might be some way of paying out them at the hall for not being friendly to him. I thought tomorrow he'd come and tell me whatever it was and we'd have a laugh about it. Only he didn't.'

Her eyes were on the baby. We went out the back door, paused to prevent the toddler putting a worm in its mouth, closed the gate behind us. An old man was watching from the street, leaning on a stick, and I guessed the whole village would soon know about Violet's visitors. We were halfway back to the cottage before Tabby said, 'We forgot the eggs.'

'So we did.'

'And you left all that money.'

'Never mind.'

We walked in silence for a while, Tabby deep in thought.

'Are you trying to find out who killed him then?'

'Yes.'

No point in denying it, to her or to myself.

'Did her ladyship do it?'

'Don't be silly.'

'Well, she didn't like him, did she?'

'Not liking somebody doesn't mean you want to kill him. I don't suppose I'd have liked him myself.'

'Why not?'

'Look at the way he treated that poor woman. A few days a year with her, two children and a couple of cheap souvenirs. Why in the world did she stand for it?'

'Well, he must have suited her, and they had a laugh together,' Tabby said. 'And he did give her the money for the beer.'

Simply, she didn't expect men to behave any better. But she'd taken us to the nub of the matter: why Lady Brinkburn literally couldn't stand the sight of Handy. Dislike of anyone connected with her husband surely wasn't enough to account for such a strong reaction.

'Do you want me to try and find out?' Tabby said, as if offering to run an errand.

'Who killed Handy? No, most certainly not.'

Goodness knows what she'd do if let loose. At least I could divert her energies on to one of the things that had come into my mind since reading the journal.

'More than twenty years ago, Lady Brinkburn had a lady's maid called Suzy. She'd probably be in her forties or even fifties by now. Most people in the village will know somebody who works at the hall. You might try to find out if Suzy's still working there, or what became of her.'

It was clear from the journal that Lady Brinkburn and her maid had been on good terms. With nobody

185

else to confide in, she might have talked to Suzy on the journey home about whatever calamity had happened by Lake Como.

'Nothing else?'

Tabby sounded disappointed.

'Definitely nothing else.'

I left Tabby at the top of the track to the cottage, with instructions to start preparing our supper, and walked into town to check at the mail office. There was nothing for me, but Matcham's coach from London to Reading had just pulled in to the yard of the Bear to change horses. A servant from the inn came out with a tankard of beer for the driver. He downed it in two gulps and handed back the tankard for a refill.

'And you might give this to the landlord while you're in there,' he said, producing a note from his pocket. 'To be sent on next time anything's going out to Brinkburn Hall.'

'Excuse me, but is it addressed to a Miss Lane?' I said.

The two men spun round and noticed me.

'Well, so it is,' the coachman said. 'Was you waiting for it?'

Trust Amos. If it had come by the mail coach, I'd have had to pay for it. He preferred his own network. I thanked the coachman and unfolded the paper. Amos's communications never took much reading.

*Has anything been seen down there of*
*Mr Stephen? Neether hide nor hair of him up*
*here since what happened.*
  *Yrs ruspectfully*
  *A. Legge*


His writing style might be more terse than Celia's but the message was much the same: Stephen Brinkburn's absence from his normal haunts had been noted. What was more, if I understood *what happened* aright, he hadn't been seen since Handy's body was discovered.

I walked back to the cottage and found Tabby on the river bank, throwing bread-crusts to ducks.

'Tabby, I have to go up to London in the morning. I shan't be away long, I hope.'

I'd been coming to that decision even before I read the note from Amos. I needed another talk with Mr Lomax, whether he liked it or not.

'I'll come with you then.'

'No, I'd like you to stay down here.'

Her face fell, but I didn't need a companion.

'I suppose you won't want to stay in the cottage on your own,' I said.

'Nah.'

'When Mrs Todd comes tomorrow, ask if you can stay with her until I come back. I'll leave some money on the table.'

'Give me more chance to ask her things, won't it?'

'Yes, I suppose it will.'

There was no point trying to stop her. I sent her up to bed with a stub of candle, then packed a few necessities into my bag. I'd planned to walk back to the Bear in the morning and take the first stagecoach for London, but it struck me that there was another way now, and I should try it. By six o'clock next morning, with some apprehension, I was following the railway line back from the new bridge in the direction, I hoped, of the *North Star*.

# CHAPTER ELEVEN

The service for London started on the Buckinghamshire side of the river from an inn called the Dumb Bell. To that extent, at least, it was not so different from the stagecoaches, except instead of dozens of horses there was only the one great beast standing on the iron tracks, fuming gently through its funnel and smelling of coal, with a hint of sulphur. At least six men were ministering to it with oil cans and polishing rags so that the shine on it was like the hindquarters of a thorough-bred. Through the noise of the steam hissing and coal being shovelled, they told me the service for Paddington would be leaving in half an hour and directed me to the inn to buy my ticket. There was a choice of first, second or third class. Since it was Mr Lomax's money and I was in a bad humour with him, I chose first and was glad of my decision when I saw that the third-class

189

accommodation was no more than open trucks. The first-class carriages were much like any horse-drawn vehicle, only mounted on iron wheels. By the time a man walked along the tracks clanging a bell and shouting to everybody to get on board, there were about a dozen other passengers waiting, all of them men. I shared a carriage with a middle-aged gentleman who seemed already so well accustomed to railway travel that, after a civil good morning to me, he opened a newspaper and stayed immersed in it for most of the journey.

When we started, with a clang and a jerk, I managed not to cry out. Clouds of steam billowed past the window, so that at first the sensation was of clanking through a thick fog. Then, as we gathered speed, the steam cleared and we were rushing between green fields under a blue sky so fast that it felt as if our great puffing and clanking beast had unfurled dragon's wings. Once I'd recovered from the surprise of it, I tried to take cooler note of how the trees and gates were flashing past, and decided that we were going about as fast as a good horse could gallop. A very good horse, like my Rancie. If I'd been alongside the *North Star* on Rancie, jumping hedges and ditches, we might just have kept pace with her, for a mile or so. There was the difference. Even the best of horses couldn't have kept up that pace for long, but the tireless locomotive did it for mile after mile. The sensation was so thrilling that I resented it when we had to slow down and stop at stations, but the other passengers seemed to regard it as an opportunity for socialising, putting their heads out of windows to shout to passengers in other carriages, or even getting down and walking along the tracks for a chat.

In spite of the stops, we reached Paddington in just over an hour, about a third of the time even a fast mail coach would have taken. By then, a thought had struck me: with this dragon to carry him, a man could almost be in two places at once.

I walked from Paddington to Lancaster Gate and across Hyde Park in the sunshine, stopping at a water fountain to dip my handkerchief and wipe smuts from my face. I was aware that my clothes smelled of smoke and I'd need to go home to change before visiting a lawyer's chambers.

'Are you back for good or just visiting?' Mrs Martley said.

'Just visiting.'

I changed into my rose print with the tucked bodice and took a cab to Lincoln's Inn. The clerk looked up, startled, when I knocked at the door of Mr Lomax's outer office and walked straight in.

'Mr Lomax is in court.'

'When will he be back?'

The clerk ran his tongue over his lips.

'I'm not sure. Probably not for some hours.'

'I'll come back this afternoon, then.'

'Mr Lomax has an engagement out of town this afternoon.'

I didn't believe him. Mr Lomax was probably sitting in the inner office, only yards distant. He probably had few female callers, and it would be easy enough to describe me and instruct the clerk to turn me away. But if that was the case, who had warned him that I might come asking awkward questions?

'When Mr Lomax does return, will you please let him know that Miss Lane needs to speak to him urgently,' I said, speaking loudly enough to be heard on the other side of the door. 'A message will find me at this address.'

I took a pen from the clerk's inkstand and scrawled my address on a spare scrap of paper. The clerk picked it up gingerly as if he expected it to burn his fingers. I stamped down the stairs and took a cab to the Bayswater Road.

At the livery stables, I drew the second blank of the morning. The owner informed me cheerfully that Amos Legge was out at the Eyre Arms with the jousting gentlemen. He had good reason to be cheerful because the tournament craze, and Amos's expertise, were bringing plenty of custom to the stables. I asked him to have Rancie tacked up for me and took to the saddle as I was, in my rose print and town shoes, rather than face another trudge home to change. As I rode out of the yard, the owner told me I should get to the Eyre Arms in nice time to see the fun.

'They're calling it the Day of the Fair Ladies,' he said. 'All the ladies were annoyed because of the gentlemen spending so much time jousting, so the gentlemen have had to set up something to pacify them.'

This didn't improve my mood. I needed to talk to Amos and it sounded as if he'd have his hands full. Sure enough, the congestion of carriages as we came near the Eyre Arms showed that this was a full-blown fashionable occasion. At least Rancie's suppleness and obedience meant we were able to weave in between them, past landaus and barouches so full of ladies in bright silks and muslins that they looked like huge flower baskets on wheels. Occasionally somebody I knew by sight would call out to me from a carriage, but I simply acknowledged them with a wave and rode on. At the top of the line, carriages were queuing to turn in to the inn yard. The spectators' stand on the roof was crowded with people and a dozen knights on horseback were waiting by the pavilion at the end of the lists. An extra platform under a white-and-gold canopy had been added at ground level, exclusively populated by ladies. I recognised several society beauties, among them Stephen's fiancée, Rosa Fitzwilliam, in white silk with gold embroidery that just happened to match the canopy.

The ladies were chatting to each other in that studiedly casual way of people who know they're being watched, leaning their sleek heads on slender white necks towards each other and back again. They reminded me of swans on the Thames. As I watched, the heads turned to one of the knights, riding helmetless towards their platform. He stopped in front of it, dismounted, went down awkwardly on one armoured knee and said something to one of the ladies. She pretended surprise and reluctance, then untied a pink ribbon from the bodice of her dress and handed it to him. (It struck me that it came undone so easily that the request couldn't have been much of a surprise.) Amid 'aaahs' and a pattering of applause the knight pressed the ribbon to his lips, remounted his horse and cantered back to his friends. I noticed that many of them had similar ribbons of various colours hitched to parts of their armour. Rosa Fitzwilliam still had a prominent bow of white and gold ribbon against her creamy shoulder.

I saw a groom, Joe, from the livery stables and rode over to ask him where Amos was. He grinned and nodded towards the stable block.

'Hiding hisself. Not easy when you're the height he is.'

'Hiding?'

I'd never seen Amos scared of man or beast. Before I could ask Joe to explain, he was swept aside by one of the knights.

'Miss Lane, I'm glad you're here. Why aren't you on the dais with the other beauties?'

It was Miles Brinkburn, his voice as cheerful and smile as wide as the first time I'd met him, a world away from the depressed man at the inquest. His head was bare, the rest of him encased in the hired armour from Pratt's.

'I'm looking for Amos Legge,' I said.

He disregarded it.

'Miss Fitzwilliam doesn't seem happy,' he said.

Indeed, the smile on Rosa's lovely face was growing strained. Another knight had just claimed a silk scarf from the lady next to her and the Marshal of the Lists was mounting his horse.

'Why not?'

'My brother's leaving it late to make his entrance. Squeezing the last drop of drama from it, I suppose.'

A harshness in his voice and a twist to his mouth showed that this was more than casual chat.

'Drama?'

'Riding up in Sir Gilbert's armour.'

'But I thought that was in Pratt's workshop,' I said.

'So it was, until yesterday afternoon. You mean you haven't heard?'

'I've been out of town.'

'I was supposed to be wearing it today. Pratt was making the alterations. All it needed was a few finishing touches.'

I noted that if Miles had felt any delicacy about wearing the armour after Handy's death, it had only lasted for a day or two.

'So what happened?'

'Day before yesterday, middle of the afternoon, some-body turns up at Pratt's and shows them a note saying he's authorised to collect the armour. Pratt himself is out of the shop, up here, and his damn-fool – excuse me – his assistant lets him cart it away, no questions asked. My dear brother, needless to say.'

'But I thought your brother was . . . away.'

I'd hesitated, about to say 'missing'. He noticed it.

'Gone away to sulk, you mean? I don't mean it was Stephen in person turning up with a wagon to collect it. It must have been somebody acting on his authority.'

'So your brother still hasn't been seen?'

'As I said, just waiting to make the great entrance in the ancestral armour. Only, if he doesn't look out, it will be too late.'

A trumpet sounded. The other knights began to form into a line, facing the ladies on the dais.

'Almost too late for me too,' Miles said.

His tone changed to antique formality. He bowed to me from the saddle.

'My lady, will you rescue me from shame and favour me with your token?'

His eyes were on the ribbon belt at my waist.

'Indeed I will not. I need that belt,' I said.

He laughed, gave me another bow and cantered away to join the rest of the knights. From their gestures, he was being mocked for not having a lady's token, as he'd predicted.

There was still no sign of Stephen. Rosa Fitzwilliam was staring fixedly ahead. You could see the tension in her neck, from not letting herself turn and look towards the road.

The trumpet sounded again. The marshal rode to the centre of the list, facing the ladies' dais, and opened his mouth to speak some no doubt sonorous and suitably

196

medieval words. Instead came a shout of 'Hold on a moment' and general laughter. Miles cantered up beside the marshal, pulling his horse up so sharply that it stood on its hind legs, and half fell, half threw himself to the ground, managing to land on one knee.

'My lady, will you rescue me from shame and favour me . . .'

This time he was speaking to Rosa Fitzwilliam. Her mouth fell open in surprise, though even that didn't spoil her beauty. At last she turned towards the entrance. Still no sign of her fiancé. Her white gloved hand went to the ribbon on her shoulder and hesitated there. For a moment her face took on an expression as stern as an emperor's statue. Then she untied the bow and held it out to him. Her arm started trembling. She had to fight to steady it and to fix a gracious smile on her face.

Her decision took Miles by surprise, everybody could see that. What had started as an act of bravado had become more serious altogether. The laughing and chattering had stopped and everybody was staring at them. For long moments he stayed on one knee. When he did stand up it was the abrupt and ungraceful movement of a clockwork toy. He took a step towards her, staring from the ribbon to her face and back again. He darted forward, took the ribbon and stepped back, the way a nervous colt might snatch a piece of carrot from the palm of a hand, still looking at her. Then he raised the ribbon to his lips and kissed it, not in a brief and formal way as the other knights had done, but fervently, keeping it at his lips for a long time. There were no 'aaahs' or applause this time. In total silence he mounted his horse and rode back to the other knights. Rosa Fitzwilliam had already returned to her seat. Although the ladies on either side of her had not visibly moved their chairs, it seemed that there was a larger space round her than before. The marshal, visibly annoyed, began his speech.

'My ladies, my lords, good gentlefolk . . .'

Beside me, Joe whispered, 'If the brother rides in now, that's gone and torn it.'

I thought it had gone and torn it in any case. If the Brinkburns had been a normal family, what Miles had done might be been seen as a simple courtesy. The elder brother is unavoidably delayed and, rather than leave his lady without her knight, the younger brother temporarily fills his place. But they weren't a normal family, and what had just happened didn't look temporary. It had the feel of a small social earthquake that had rearranged familiar scenery so that it would never be the same again. Miles's action had looked impulsive, and probably was. (On the other hand, perhaps that request to me had been a rehearsal.) Rosa Fitzwilliam was a different matter. The moment to make her decision had arrived sooner and more publicly than she'd expected, but it must have been in her mind for some time. However annoyed she'd been by Stephen's absence, what she'd done didn't look like impulsiveness. Having concluded, or been persuaded, that Miles was the more likely heir, she had publicly acknowledged him as her knight. That was the way it had looked to the crowd and how it would look to Stephen.

I didn't blame Rosa Fitzwilliam. Renowned beauty, in a man or a woman, is a gift like a fine singing voice or skill on the violin. It comes close to being public property, and makes its own rules that it would take an unusually strong nature to disobey. A fine singer would rather perform on the stage at Covent Garden than in a smoky room at a tavern. A great beauty marries the heir to a title, not a scandalously disinherited bastard son.

As far as I was concerned, one of the interesting points about her decision was that the pro-Miles party must have gained ground in the few days that I'd been away from London. Were there rumours spreading that I didn't know about? I watched the first pair of knights ride against each other, each managing to strike his opponent's shield and stay in the saddle, then turned Rancie towards the stable block, wondering why Amos was hiding. On my way I passed a girl of around sixteen, fashionably dressed in pink silk and ivory lace, pretty enough but with a disappointed twist to her mouth. She had a prominent knot of pink ribbons on her shoulder and stood leaning on her parasol, looking wistfully towards the stables. When I wished her good afternoon, I got nothing but a resentful look. I rode on into the yard. A few horses looked out from their boxes, but with everyone watching the jousting it seemed deserted of people.

As I sat looking round, a low whistle sounded from a box in the corner.

'Amos?'

I rode across and looked over the half-door. Sure enough, he was there in the shadows, sitting on a heap of straw. I slid down from the saddle.

'What in the world are you doing in there?' I said.

He put a finger to his lips.

'Is she still out there?'

'Who?'

'The pink one.'

'Yes.'

He groaned. I asked him what was the matter.

'She's took it into her head that I'm going to be her champion. I've tried to tell her it won't do, but she's as stubborn as a mule in a clover patch.'

I burst out laughing. Amos was accustomed by now to attentions from fashionable ladies, but they weren't usually as young and blatant as this.

'How did you meet her?'

'I've been teaching her brother. I've sent word to him to come and take her away, only he's waiting his turn to joust, so I've gone to ground here.'

'Don't worry, I'm here to chaperone you now. Will you help me put Rancie away, then we can talk?'

We found an empty box for her, slackened the girth and ran up the stirrup. Amos was still wary and suggested the fodder room as a place for our conference. He threw a horse rug over a pile of hay for me to sit on, and perched on the edge of a feed bin.

'What's this about Stephen being missing?' I said.

'The day you went down to the country, he was supposed to meet me at the stables about those horses he wanted to buy, but he didn't turn up. I didn't think anything to it at first, but the next day somebody comes to the guvnor and wants to know if we've seen anything of him.'

'Somebody from the family?'

'No. Clerk type of a man, the guvnor said.'

From Lomax, I thought.

'And Stephen hasn't been seen since the day Handy's body was found?'

'That's right, eight days ago. He's not been here to practise and he hasn't been near the stable that keeps his horses, apart from the one time that nobody saw him.'

'But if nobody saw him, how do they know?'

'I'm coming to that. Handy's body was found on the Tuesday, look. On the Wednesday morning, Mr Brinkburn's groom comes in as usual and finds his best horse gone and its tack too. Nobody but him and Mr Brinkburn had the key to the tack room, so he decides he must have come in, saddled and bridled his own horse, and ridden off somewhere.'

'You've spoken to the groom?'

It hardly needed Amos's nod to confirm it. He always spoke to the groom in the case.

'And if Stephen was there before the groom, he must have taken the horse very early,' I said.

'First light.'

Distant cheers came from the direction of the lists. I told Amos what had happened between Miles Brinkburn and Rosa Fitzwilliam. He whistled.

'Miles was expecting his brother to come riding up at the last minute in the ancestral armour to claim the favour from Rosa,' I said. 'He'd convinced himself that's why Stephen had the armour collected from Pratt's.'

'I know, he's been telling me all about it. I said I'd see what I could find out for him.' He gave me a side-long look. 'I knew you'd be wanting to know.'

I could see the signs. Amos had a story to tell. I settled myself more comfortably on the rug, resolving to try not to interrupt.

'There's a friend of mine runs Bond Street,' Amos said.

'What!'

Resolution broken at once. I was becoming used to Amos's network of contacts in circles high and low, but luxury shopping was hardly part of his world.

'I don't mean the shops and so on.' He waved them away, like swatting at a fly. 'I mean the horses and carriages. Place like Bond Street, hundreds of carriages and thousands of horses up and down all day, some-body's got to keep them sorted or it would be like a flock of geese with a fox loose, look. So my friend fixes who holds the horses and what they charge for it, and how long a carriage can stay in one place without having to pay more, and so on. And then the shops pay him if they want a place kept clear in front of them so that the carriages can draw up easy.'

'Is all this official?'

''Course not. That's why it works as well as it does.'

'It sounds highly profitable. Do the police know about it?'

'Yes, only they pretend not to as long as it all runs to order, which it does. Any road, my friend has to know what's coming and going. If you get somebody offering to hold horses he doesn't know about, or carriages not accounted for, it all breaks down.'

'And your friend saw the carriage collecting the Brinkburn armour from Pratt's?'

'That's what I'm telling you. It was the day before yesterday, Monday, about four in the afternoon. Not the busiest for traffic because most of the gentry had gone to get their tea, but enough about still. Anyway, he notices this horse and cart going up the street because he hasn't seen it before, and it's so out of the ordinary he'd have remembered. It was a piebald cob, Gypsy-like, feather-footed, well enough turned out in its way, pulling a closed cart shaped like a coffin.'

I started to say something then bit my lip.

'There was one man driving it, and another one sitting on top of the cart,' Amos went on. 'They drew up outside Pratt's and both men went inside. One of my friend's boys comes running up to hold the horse. Minute or two later, both men come out with a crate, open the cart and put it in, then go back for another two. The man driving gives the boy his tuppence, turns the cart round as neat as you like, and they go back towards Piccadilly. My friend asks the boy where they'd come from. The boy didn't have time to ask, but he noticed two things. The man who'd been riding on the cart had a left arm that hung funny, so he could only do the lifting with his right arm. And the cob had a brand on its hindquarters. Like a butterfly, the boy said. Neither my friend nor me had seen one like that, so we did a bit of asking around. I reckon I've come up with the answer.'

'Which is?'

He gave me one of his wait-and-see looks.

'Do you fancy going to the circus?'

I knew his ways well enough to understand I'd get no more answers until he was ready. Playing him at his own game, I said yes, thank you, I should be delighted to come to the circus, and he said he'd call for me at Abel Yard at five, going to the early performance on account of him having to be up early in the morning.

We left the stable yard together, Amos leading Rancie and both of us keeping an eye out for the pink girl. She seemed to have given up her vigil, but Amos was still wary and wouldn't part from me until we were safely back among the spectators. The jousting was still going on. The knights who'd already run their courses had taken off their helmets and were red-faced and sweating from the heat. Under their canopy, Rosa and the other ladies still looked as serene as swans. We found Joe, who held Rancie's bridle while Amos helped me mount. Both of them had to stay until the end of the proceedings, because there were horses to be taken back to the stables. I assured them that I'd be perfectly safe on my own and rode out of the gateway, back towards town.

As I came near the north side of Regent's Park, I saw a policeman walking in front of me. He was a tall man, striding along at a good pace, in the usual uniform of tall hat and tail-coat, the tails of the coat weighed down by the bulge of a truncheon and the smaller bulge of handcuffs. I had some instinct about him and was tempted to keep behind, but the tedium of checking Rancie's long easy stride would be too much for me. Besides, I had nothing on my conscience. Why should I be nervous of encountering a policeman, even an intelligent one? I rode level with him.

'Good afternoon, Miss Lane,' he said, raising his hat.

'Good afternoon, Constable Bevan. Have you been out to see the jousting too?'

'I have. Most instructive.'

I guessed from his tone that he'd witnessed the Miles and Rosa incident. He kept pace with us, walking close to Rancie's near shoulder.

'Were you there on duty?' I said.

'No, simply out of interest. I'm on night duty this week.'

'Yet you're in uniform.'

'Regulations. A police officer must always be in uniform.'

'You weren't, in Buckinghamshire.'

205

'That was in the country. It doesn't count. It's some-what ridiculous, isn't it?'

'What?'

'We must wear a uniform signifying police and yet no regulation says the other side must wear uniforms saying *Wrongdoer*. It puts the side of law and order at a disadvantage, wouldn't you say?'

'So you'd have the wrongdoers in uniform too, or the police in plain clothes?'

'I think the latter would be more practical, don't you? Some of us, at least. It will come, I'm sure.'

'If I may say so, you strike me as a very unusual policeman,' I said.

He laughed.

'I don't intend to be patrolling the streets of London by night all the rest of my life, if that's what you mean. Still, night duty has its interest.'

Something about the way he said it made me wary.

'Oh?'

'I've been talking to a colleague who was on patrol in Bond Street on the night of the Monday before last. That's the night before Mr Brinkburn made that regrettable discovery at Pratt's, if you remember.'

I said nothing.

'It was around two o'clock in the morning,' he went on. 'Our duties include keeping an eye on the doorways and windows of premises, in case anybody is attempting to break in. My colleague disturbed somebody at the side door of Pratt's.'

206

'Trying to break in?'

'Certainly loitering in a suspicious manner. My colleague shone his lamp on him and he ran off to a gig parked round the corner and drove away at speed. On close inspection, it turned out that he had been trying to force the lock.'

'I'm sure Bond Street attracts a lot of thieves,' I said.

'At a shop dealing in armour? And a thief in a gig? I asked my colleague to describe the man. He only had a fleeting view, of course, but his account was interesting. He said the person was a young gentleman with very dark hair.'

He emphasised the word 'gentleman'. We walked on a few strides.

'I saw the younger Mr Brinkburn at the inquest,' Constable Bevan said. 'He has dark hair. I gather that his brother's is lighter.'

'Half the men in London have dark hair,' I said.

Constable Bevan nodded, as if he'd expected my reaction.

'Quite so. We mustn't jump to conclusions, must we? Shall you be going back to Buckinghamshire, Miss Lane?'

'That's my business, Constable Bevan.'

I let my heel press lightly against Rancie's flank and she moved instantly into her faster walking pace, leaving him behind in a few strides. He had been intolerably familiar, but what annoyed me more was his obvious belief that I was close to Miles Brinkburn.

*     *     *

207

When I got home, there was another annoyance of the same kind, in the form of a note from Celia, with two rectangles of deckle-edged pasteboard enclosed in it. The date was that day's.

*Dearest Elizabeth,*
*Are you back in town yet? I've had no answer*
*to the note I sent you in the country, so*
*perhaps it missed you. I'm still confined to my*
*sofa and am almost dying of boredom. Philip*
*and I were invited to the Fair Ladies ball at*
*Lady D's this evening, but that tyrant of a*
*doctor won't hear of my going even if I*
*promise faithfully not to dance, and of course*
*dear Philip won't go without me, even though I*
*told him he should and at least bring me back*
*a few crumbs of gossip. So I am enclosing our*
*tickets in case you can make use of them. I*
*know one is not supposed to pass them on, but*
*everybody does and there'll be such a scrimmage*
*there that nobody will ever notice. If you do*
*make use of them, you are to visit me*
*tomorrow without fail and bring me not just*
*crumbs but whole slices of gossip, especially*
*about you know who and you know who else,*
*who have definitely been invited. Please do not*
*fail your affectionate friend,*
    *Celia*

I was about to throw the tickets away then, on second thoughts, tucked them into my reticule. If Celia had seen that, she'd have drawn quite the wrong conclusion.

# CHAPTER TWELVE

Amos drove into the yard at five minutes to five in a black-lacquered phaeton with cream leather upholstery and primrose yellow wheel spokes, drawn by a strawberry roan cob. He wore his brown top hat with a silver cockade, and his neckcloth and the rosebud in his buttonhole were yellow to match the wheel spokes. He swung himself down to hand me to my seat.

'I'm not sure I can live up to all this splendour,' I said.

He grinned, spun the phaeton in a circle as tight as a good skater's on ice and off we went by Mount Street and Park Lane, along Piccadilly at a spanking trot and down Haymarket. For all my worries, I couldn't help feeling in holiday mood as we bowled along overtaking less nimble vehicles. London on a fine June evening makes you feel more alive than any other city in the

210

world and I've always loved the circus from the time my brother Tom and I were taken there as children. At the far end of Whitehall, I stopped myself from looking to the right at the sad wreckage the fire had made of the lovely old palace of Westminster, like a rotten tooth in a beloved face. We trotted on across Westminster Bridge, with the river glinting in the sun beneath us. I hadn't needed to ask Amos where we were heading. What other circus would it be than Astley's Royal Amphitheatre?

Once we were over the river, Amos turned into the yard of an inn, had a word with the ostler, and left the cob and phaeton in his care. We strolled together to Astley's and Amos insisted on paying for seats in one of the boxes in the middle of the house. Astley's prides itself on being a theatre and circus combined, so first we had to sit through a comedy about two young lovers and a wicked guardian who wanted to marry the girl to a rich old man instead. I found it tedious, but Amos laughed. At last the lovers were united, the scenery cleared away and the area became a circus ring, with a troop of horse acrobats whooping on, dressed as Red Indians, riding bareback with long feather head-dresses streaming out behind them. Their tricks were amazing: hanging down at full gallop to pick up flags from the sawdust with their teeth, ankles locked round their horses' necks, leaping on and off each other's mounts and forming a pyramid of ten riders on the backs of two cantering horses. Three of the horses were piebalds and Amos craned forward for a closer look at them, then shook his head.

The Indians were followed by a comic routine between a clown and the riding master who was dressed like a cavalryman in white breeches and frogged jacket, then a girl acrobat in ballerina costume, pirouetting and somersaulting on the broad back of a dapple grey. After her, more clowns, a whole troop of them this time. They chased round the ring, assaulting each other with cardboard truncheons, strings of sausages, buckets of water.

One of the clowns fell over backwards, pretending to be knocked unconscious. To laughs and cheers from the audience, a doctor's cart came galloping to his rescue.

'There we are.'

Amos gave a sigh of satisfaction. The cart was rectangular and might at a pinch be described as coffin-shaped, drawn by a piebald cob. The doctor, in black top hat and white make-up, opened the lid and produced a giant syringe and a gallon-sized bottle of red medicine. He managed the routine neatly, although his left arm hung useless at his side. The victim was revived and, after more comic business, the doctor's cart galloped out. As it passed beneath us, the angle of the gaslight showed a butterfly-shaped brand on a dark patch of the horse's hindquarters. We stayed for the rest of the performance because it would have been impossible to get out from where we were sitting without creating a disturbance and, as Amos said, the doctor wouldn't be going anywhere. After the finale, as soon as the audience began to move, Amos cleared a path through them and I followed him into the street.

'There'll be a back way in,' Amos said.

There was, surrounded by street urchins trying to get a look at the horses and riders. We walked past them to a yard at the rear of the arena, full of horses and performers. The rectangular cart was standing by the wall with the piebald, unharnessed, eating from a bucket beside it. The man who'd played the doctor was watching it, still in his chalky make-up and smoking a clay pipe.

Amos walked up to him.

'Didn't I see you in Bond Street, day before yesterday?'

The man jumped and dropped his pipe, but caught it deftly on its way to the ground.

'What's it to you?'

'Just interested,' Amos said. 'Nice horse you've got.'

The man glanced from Amos to me and back again, wondering what to make of us. I decided to leave the questioning to Amos.

'There's plenty of people don't care for coloured horses,' Amos said. 'I reckon most of them have got more sense than the rest.'

'Horse sense,' the man said, grinning uneasily at his own joke. 'And most horses have got more sense than most humans.'

Amos laughed, took a pigskin tobacco pouch from his pocket, opened it and held it out to the man.

'Like a fill-up?'

'Don't mind if I do.'

They filled up their pipes, lit them and puffed away for a while without saying anything. The man was visibly relaxing. After a few minutes, Amos introduced himself and gathered in return that the man's name was Stanley Best.

'I know the gentleman who owns the armour,' Amos said.

'Armour?'

'That was what was in the crates you and your friend collected. Didn't you know that?'

Stanley shrugged.

'Didn't know and didn't care.'

'Did you have to take it far?' Amos said.

'Belle Sauvage, Ludgate Hill, to await collection.'

I remembered that the Belle Sauvage was another of the big coaching inns.

'Who was it addressed to?' Amos said.

'Who wants to know? We wasn't stealing it. My friend had a note, giving us the authority.'

'Who from?'

'You're asking a lot of questions. What's it got to do with you?'

Amos plunged his hand into a pocket and brought it out holding a handful of coins. Stan's eyes went to them.

'You get gentlemen playing jokes on other gentlemen,' Amos said. 'Maybe your gentleman's playing games with mine.'

'Maybe.'

Amos spun a sovereign into the air. Stan's good hand came up and caught it, quick as a swallow taking a gnat.

'Wasn't addressed to anybody,' Stan said. 'We just had to leave it there, that's all.'

Amos nodded, as if he'd guessed that.

'Your friend who drove you to Bond Street, is he in the circus too?'

'One of the Red Indians. I was too, till I got ridden over and this happened.'

He flapped his useless left arm like a penguin's wing. Amos spun another sovereign and Stan plucked it from the air, deftly as the first.

'Play this game all night, if you like.'

'Who was the gentleman told you to collect the armour?' Amos said.

'We never met him. It was a fellow acting for him.'

'What happened?'

Stan waited for another sovereign but Amos's hand went back into his pocket.

'There's a place we drink at,' Stan said at last. 'You get all sorts there. One night, there was this fellow in there we hadn't seen before, putting it around he'd pay good money for somebody who'd do little jobs for him, no questions asked.'

'Against the law little jobs?'

'That's what everybody thought. They were all stringing him on, laughing at him behind their hands. So my friend and I let him buy us a beer or two and we ask him what he wants. We were having him on.

215

If it had been against the law, we didn't want nothing to do with it.'

'Stands to reason,' Amos said, straight-faced.

'Only it turns out it wasn't. This fellow works for a gentleman who wants to play a joke on another gentleman, like you said. All we have to do is run errands now and then, and not ask questions. He says do we have access to a horse and cart, and we say yes.'

'You didn't mention it was a circus horse and a clown's cart?'

'Why should we? He didn't ask. So we say, all right, and he goes away and says he'll let his gentleman know and we'll be hearing from him. For a long time, there's nothing and we forget about it. Then last Saturday there's a note waiting for us at the public house, saying we're to collect the crates on Monday and take them to the Belle Sauvage, like I said. We're to give the note to the man at the shop, to let him know it's above board.'

'Who signed the note?'

'Couldn't make it out. Began with D or might have been B.'

'Was there money with it?'

'A few quid.'

'How many quid?'

'Five times more than I've had from you.'

'Ten pounds, for a little job like that?'

Stan looked defensive.

'The fellow said there was money in it if we did what we were told.'

Amos glanced at me. There was no doubt in my mind that the fellow in the public house had been acting on behalf of one of the Brinkburn brothers. The question was which. I tried a question of my own.

'And the man never said anything about who his employer was?'

Stan hesitated, less at ease with me than with Amos. 'No.'

'You said it was a long time from when he approached you to when the message came about collecting the crates. How long?'

Stan wrinkled his forehead and seemed to be counting up in his mind.

'A good three weeks, I'd say. Back at the start of the month or even late May.'

'Can you describe him? Was he tall?'

He looked at Amos. Another sovereign flipped through the air into his hand.

'No, short as what I am.'

Below average height, then.

'How old?'

'Not young. Thirty or a bit more.'

'What did he look like.'

'Nothing remarkable.'

'You must remember something. What colour was his hair?'

He thought about it.

'He didn't have much of it. I remember noticing that when he pushed his cap back. He was bald up to the top of his head and he had this funny mark where the hair would have been.'

'What?'

I must have yelped it out because he looked startled.

'Funny mark?' I said. 'What sort of funny mark? Was it the colour of a liver chestnut horse?'

'Pretty much.'

'And this shape?'

I picked up his whip from where it was leaning against the wall and used the end of it to draw a rough outline of the map of Ireland in the dust.

'That's the one. You know him then?'

I nodded, mind whirling. It must have been Handy who recruited them, but the note on Saturday couldn't have come through Handy, who'd been dead six days by then.

'And you never saw this man again, after the first time in the public house?'

'No, ma'am.'

I looked at Amos. We'd got as much from the man as we were likely to get, for the while at least, and I wanted time to think. We thanked Stan, who looked wistful at the thought of no more sovereigns, and walked back towards the yard where we'd left the phaeton.

'That man he saw,' I said, 'he was the dead man in the crate. Handy.'

'Certain of it?'

'Certain. How many men have birthmarks that shape?'

'What was his game, then?'

'I'm nearly sure he was working for either Stephen or Miles. It makes sense, when you think about it. There he is, their father's old servant with a not very good reputation, kicking his heels and wondering what to do with himself. When this question over the inheritance started, it must have occurred to one of them that it would be useful to have a spy in their mother's house.'

'He wouldn't need two men and a cart for that,' Amos said.

'No, but suppose it didn't stop at just spying? We know Miles played at least one nasty trick on Stephen that day at the Eyre Arms.'

'If the man Stan's got it right, it was a while before that when Handy went looking for helpers.'

'That would fit. Either of them might have been thinking up ways to annoy or humiliate his brother from weeks back.'

'So why does Handy make himself as conspicuous as a rook in a dovecot, going to people from the circus?'

It was a fair point, and I'd been doing some thinking about it while we'd been walking.

'Because I don't think Handy was as clever or worldly wise as he thought he was,' I said. 'He might have boasted to whichever brother was employing him that he had useful friends in low places. But after all, he's spent most of his life abroad. Who would he know in London? So when Stephen or Miles took him at his word, he had to do the best he could. He probably decided that people who worked round circuses were not always models of respectability . . .'

'He just might have been right there,' Amos said.

'. . . and didn't realise he'd gone and recruited a clown.'

'So which of 'em was he working for then: Miles or Stephen?'

'Stephen, I'd say. Miles was angry that the armour had been carted away.'

'Or pretended to be.'

I looked at Amos.

'You really think Miles is that clever?'

'I reckon there's more under that one's hat than he lets on.'

We were going up Haymarket on our way home when another thought came to me. I had to shout it to Amos above trotting hooves and jingling harness, but with no danger of anybody outside our phaeton hearing because of the noise of the traffic.

'Suppose it wasn't one or the other. From what I've heard of Simon Handy, he was quite capable of double-crossing them and working for both.'

'Wondered when you'd get there,' Amos said, looking straight ahead.

'If he was, and if one of them found out, that might have been why he was killed.'

'If it was Miles, he'd have been a cool customer, standing there while that crate was opened, knowing what they'd find inside.'

'He seemed genuinely shaken. And Stephen's the one who hasn't been seen since Handy's body was found,' I said.

'Reckon he killed him and done a bunk somewhere abroad, then?'

'It's possible, isn't it? After all, by disappearing like this, he's left the field open to Miles in every sense. There must be some serious reason for that.'

When we got back to Abel Yard, I insisted on refunding to Amos the three sovereigns he'd given Stan.

'No necessity for that,' he said.

'Don't worry. It's a lawyer's money, not mine.'

He nodded and pocketed the coins.

'Not many folks get money out of lawyers. Shall I be seeing you tomorrow then?'

'Not tomorrow. I think I must go back to Buckinghamshire. I'll be in touch.'

I didn't want to leave Tabby to her own devices in the country for too long.

'Staying in the same place as before?'

'Same place. And thank you, Amos.'

I watched him drive out of the yard and went upstairs. Mrs Martley was posting snippets from magazines into her Queen Victoria album at the kitchen table. We chatted for a while about nothing in particular, then I went up to my room, opened the window and looked out over the rooftops towards the trees in the park. Somebody was growing sweet peas on a nearby balcony, in pots squeezed behind wrought-iron railings two storeys

221

above the street. The smell of them filled the air. A woman's laughter rose from the pavement, along with the music of a waltz, from one of the big houses fronting on to the park. I felt my feet twitching. I had no business to want to waltz but, for a moment, I envied dancers with nothing more serious to worry about than whether their shoes would last the night. That reminded me that I still had Celia's ridiculous invitation cards in my reticule. I'd had no real intention of using them. I hadn't been invited, had no partner to go with and was not in a position to honour Celia's condition that I must carry whole slices of gossip to her.

I re-read her note: *you know who and you know who else, who have definitely been invited.* One of the *you knows* must be Miles. Was the other one meant to be his brother or Rosa Fitzwilliam? I needed to talk to Miles. In spite of their long day, my feet needed to waltz. Quite wrong, of course, to let my frivolous feet have any influence on the matter, but after all it was a June night in Mayfair.

The invitation card said *costume medieval.* There was nothing of that description in the wooden chest where I keep my best clothes, but it did contain my favourite blue-green silk dress, the shade of the sea on a fine day, with long white lawn sleeves, gathered in a series of puffs all the way down the arm and trimmed with ribbons to match the rest of the dress. It was an extravagance, compounded by matching silk slippers with bows. I swept my hair up high at the back and pinned it in place with a dragonfly made of amethysts and emerald-coloured enamel, a present from a satisfied client. Mrs Martley blinked as I rushed past.

'Going out again at this hour?'

'Yes. Don't wait up.'

I slowed to an easy walk once I was outside, careful where I placed my silk slippers. It was past ten o'clock, but still almost full light. The house where the ball was taking place was only a short walk away, quite possibly the one from which I'd heard the music. I was gambling that by this time of night arrangements for greeting guests would be less formal than at the start of proceedings. If there was a footman in the hall, announcing people as they arrived, a single woman with a second-hand invitation card would not be welcome. The gamble succeeded. The double doors were wide open to Park Lane, light and music pouring out. The road was half-blocked by a confusion of carriages: some people leaving already, others just arriving. Ladies and gentlemen in evening costume congregated on the steps, chatting to friends or cooling their faces in the fresh air from the park.

I went up the steps into a wide hallway lit by hundreds of candles and draped with bright new heraldic banners. A footman moved towards me but made no attempt to bar my way and instead offered a glass of champagne from a tray. I accepted it and followed the sound of music through two more sets of double doors to the

223

ballroom. A polite form of country dance was in progress, three lines of people the length of the room, bowing, bobbing and twirling. The ladies were showing inventive variations on the medieval theme, from muslins and conical hats with scarves that floated out as they danced, to stiff brocades, jewelled stomachers and embroideries that would have weighed down a pack pony. The men had mostly opted for conventional black and white evening wear, except for the few who considered their legs were shapely enough to risk doublet and hose. Miles Brinkburn was one of that minority. I noticed him almost at once, dancing opposite one of the muslin girls, and had to admit that the costume suited him. I could see no sign of either Stephen or Rosa.

'Miss Lane, how delightful to see you.'

I turned to see one of my singing pupils and her husband. He was an amiable man who fancied himself as a poet, but was handicapped by an indecently large annual income. They'd just left the floor and she was leaning on his shoulder, looking puffed.

'Please do me a kindness and dance with Roderick,' she said to me. 'He positively loathes having to sit out, and I want a chance to talk to my friends.'

The band struck up a waltz. Roderick bowed, offered me his arm and we were at once in a rainbow whirlpool of silks and satins. Roderick danced well and steered us expertly round clumsier couples. I laughed, from the exhilaration of the speed and the music, and a glass of champagne drunk too fast on an empty stomach.

'I do believe we're going as fast as the *North Star*.'

He misunderstood me and quoted a line of his poetry about shooting stars. I don't think he'd heard of the locomotive. As we danced past the orchestra, I recognised the flautist as one of Daniel's friends and waved my fingers to him over Roderick's shoulder. He winked at me. We manoeuvred past Miles and his partner, a redhead in white satin.

'Just as well the brother isn't here tonight,' Roderick said cheerfully. 'We don't want blood on the dance floor.'

'What about Rosa Fitzwilliam?' I said.

There was no point in being discreet and avoiding the subject, since the whole town would be talking about it.

'Came with her aunt and left early. Didn't dance. My wife says she looked out of spirits.'

I wondered if she was regretting that impulsive gesture at the jousting. The waltz came to an end. Roderick escorted me to where his wife was chatting with a group of other ladies and suggested we might all go through to the dining room for a buffet supper. I said I'd stay in the ballroom for a while. I'd noticed Miles returning his partner to her group of friends or family. He was now lingering on his own at the edge of the dance floor, looking thoughtful.

There were two questions above all that I wanted to ask him: Was Simon Handy working for you? Were you the dark-haired gentleman disturbed by a constable while trying to break into Pratt's? I decided to ask the second question first. The fact that I had information from the police might scare him into some unguarded reaction. I began walking over to him, but I'd only taken a few steps when two gentlemen appeared in the ballroom. They'd come from outside. The elder of them, an upright gentleman with steel-grey hair, was still holding his top hat and walking cane. The younger man beside him, with dark flowing ringlets and a gold brocade waistcoat, might have fitted in more appropriately with the other guests, except there was a purposeful air about the pair of them that made it clear they hadn't come to dance. The elder man was Oliver Lomax. The even greater surprise that stopped me in my tracks was the identity of the younger one – Benjamin Disraeli. Our eyes met. He said something to Lomax and started walking towards me. Other eyes had turned his way as well. He always had that effect on people. Various men and women greeted him and several obviously wanted him to stop and talk. He smiled and nodded, but kept walking towards me.

'Good evening, Miss Lane. What a coincidence to find you here.'

Nothing in the words would cause surprise to anyone overhearing, and it looked as if a few bystanders were trying. But a glint in his dark eyes signalled conspiracy, inviting me to admit the intimacy of a shared secret. Those eyes weren't missing anything about my appearance, from silk slippers to swirled-up hair.

'You're looking very well, if I may say so,' he said.

I guessed he was wondering if I'd arrived with a male escort or female chaperone, and possibly how I came to be on such a distinguished guest list. He could never quite place me in the scheme of things and that piqued him.

'A useful coincidence,' I said. 'I want to speak to Mr Lomax. I think he's avoiding me. Could you persuade him to come over, do you think?'

He placed a hand gently on my sleeve and guided me towards a great vase of lilies on a pedestal, away from the throng of dancers.

'What do you want to know from him?'

His voice was more serious now.

'I want to ask what he knows or suspects about the murder of Lord Brinkburn's valet. He made it very clear that I wasn't supposed to meddle with that, but it's no use. I'm sure it's linked with the other question.'

'And have you made any progress with the other question?'

'Yes. I've spent some time with Lady Brinkburn. I don't understand what she's doing, but she's not mad. Did you know Mr Lomax was trying to put blinkers on me?'

'I assure you, Miss Lane, no man in his senses could mistake you for a cart horse.'

'It's no joke. When you recommended me, did you tell him that I could be relied on to find or fabricate the evidence he wanted to keep everything tidy? Was I being paid to make sure the House of Peers could go on dozing comfortably, with no vulgar scandals?'

He raised his eyebrows, refusing to be annoyed.

'No. I recommended you as a person remarkably skilled at discovering awkward truths.'

'Then hiding them?'

He looked me in the eyes for a moment before answering. We both knew that our association had started with something that must stay hidden.

'I told him you could be discreet, when necessary.'

'There's a long distance between that and lying to order, and I want to tell him so. So will you please ask him to come and speak to me.'

Another waltz was in progress, the floor full of whirling couples. Oliver Lomax was working his way round the fringes with some difficulty, barged into by dancers, blocked by groups of people laughing over their champagne. He seemed to be trying to get to where Miles Brinkburn was standing, still on his own. Disraeli's eyes followed mine.

'I'm afraid Lomax is rather preoccupied.'

His voice was grave.

'Why? What's happening to Miles?'

My mind went to the intelligent policeman and the probability that Miles knew something about Handy's death. Was the family lawyer coming to warn him of imminent arrest?

'Lomax has some sad news to deliver,' Disraeli said. 'He asked me to come here with him because I know our hostess. A ballroom is not the ideal place for passing on such news, but we can hardly have a son dancing the night away when his father's dead.'

'Dead?'

'Yes, at the asylum this afternoon. The message was brought to Lomax's chambers this evening.'

We watched as Lomax skirted a chattering group and came alongside Miles, who didn't seem to have noticed him till that moment and looked surprised. Lomax said something and put a hand on Miles's shoulder. The young man's face turned pale and he hung his head. After a few more words they began walking towards the door together. People were looking at them now, aware of something wrong.

'What about Stephen?' I said. 'Does he know?'

'We can't find him. Lomax is hoping Miles might have some idea where he's gone.'

'Unlikely.'

The death of the of old lord had raised the stakes. Now Stephen was the new Lord Brinkburn. Anything the younger brother might do to overturn that would have to be done decisively, with even more eyes on him than in this crowded place.

'I'll go back to Buckinghamshire first thing tomorrow,' I said.

Disraeli looked surprised.

'I thought you wanted to speak to Lomax.'

'I do. But whatever the answer is, it's there, not here.'

Somehow, in a way I still couldn't fathom, the answer lay in a twenty-three-year-old journal in a green-shaded library. I didn't tell Disraeli about that. There was too much to explain. Miles and Lomax had vanished through the doorway into the hall.

'I must go,' Disraeli said. 'Lomax came in my carriage.'

'Is somebody telling Lady Brinkburn?'

'Lomax thinks that should be Stephen's duty, if they can find him. If not, Lomax or Miles will have to tell her. You'll excuse me, Miss Lane. Let me know what's happening. And good luck.'

He gave a quick bow, as if we'd just finished the waltz together, and walked away through the now subdued dancers. I supposed my friends were expecting me in the supper room, but I'd lost my appetite. After waiting ten minutes or so for Disraeli to get clear away, I walked out of the ballroom and past the heraldic banners into a summer night still humming with music from half a dozen wide-open doorways.

Early the following morning the *North Star* from Paddington whirled me back to the bank of the Thames.

# CHAPTER THIRTEEN

By mid morning I was walking from the Dumb Bell to the village, planning to collect Tabby from Mrs Todd's. I walked fast, still gripped by the urgency of the night before. Very soon the news of Lord Brinkburn's death would be brought to his widow, if it hadn't arrived already. Lady Brinkburn could hardly be expected to grieve deeply, but the decencies would have to be observed and it might be more difficult to find out what I needed from a household in mourning.

I found Mrs Todd in her garden, picking gooseberries. When I asked after Tabby she sniffed and told me she was at Violet's.

'She's been round there most of the time you were away. With respect, you should watch out or Violet will be getting her into bad ways.'

I didn't tell her that Tabby was in bad ways already.

When I got there, Tabby was with Violet in the weed patch in front of her cottage, the baby kicking and gurgling on a blanket in the sun.

'Violet's been showing me a lot of things that belonged to Mr Handy,' Tabby said, without greeting or preamble.

'What sort of things?'

'Writing and stuff.'

'Would you show me?' I said to Violet.

She gathered up the baby and we all went inside, to a fug of boiled cabbage smell and the ever-circling flies. While Tabby tucked the baby in its crib, Violet opened a door in the cupboard part of the dresser and brought out a bundle loosely wrapped in clean sacking. I hoped for letters, even another journal, but when she put it on the table and undid the sacking, it turned out to be an assemblage of oddments: pieces torn from newspapers, prints, a few loose leaves of paper with handwriting on them. Violet and Tabby watched hungrily as I turned them over.

'What do they say?' Violet asked.

Like Tabby, she'd never been taught to read. If she'd hoped for any messages of tenderness from Handy, she'd have been as disappointed as I was. There were receipts from stagecoach companies in Italy, France and England for places booked, cheap prints of views in various Italian cities, paragraphs from English-language newspapers in foreign towns listing eminent arrivals of the week, with Lord Brinkburn's name underlined in black ink, a programme for a performance of *Don*

*Giovanni* in Venice given five years before, receipted food and drink bills from various hostelries – all the detritus of a travelling life. Four pages on better quality paper, its deckled edges slick and grey from much fingering, turned out to be prints of erotic drawings, showing women in a Turkish bathhouse. Those, at any rate, Violet could understand, though she didn't seem embarrassed by them.

'His lordship liked pictures,' she said.

'When did Handy leave all these things with you?'

'He had some every time he came back. He said he wanted to remember things.'

There were only half a dozen notes consisting of two or three sentences at most, all in the same black handwriting, the words sprawling across the page. They were the kind of notes a man might give his servant to deliver, fixing appointments or offering conventional thanks for hospitality. Presumably the people who received them had scanned them and given them back to Handy. One, dated three years before, read: *Sir, The bearer of this, one Handy, is a thorough rogue but may be trusted for our present purposes.* It seemed sad that this motley collection was all Handy had to show for a lifetime of travelling and service.

I was bundling them up so that Violet could put them away when a smaller piece of paper slithered out from between two of the erotic drawings. Both the thick, greyish paper and the drawing on it set this scrap apart from the rest. This was a sketch, in charcoal, of a boy perhaps twelve years old, with a round face and untidy dark hair. The artist had caught a malicious look in his eyes and a twist of his mouth that seemed at odds with the round face and childish posture, hunched on a rock with his knees drawn up. A few pine trees were sketched in behind him. If you looked closely at the boy's hairline, there was a patch that might have been the edge of a birthmark or, equally probably, a smudge of charcoal.

'Is this Handy?' I said to Violet.

'Yes. Somebody drew him when he was a boy.'

'Who?'

'Don't know. He never said.'

But I knew the moment I saw it. The observant, nervy quality of the sketch was so like Lady Brinkburn's work in her honeymoon journal that it might have come from its pages. Only the texture of the paper was different. It looked as if it had been torn from one of the small pads that artists carry with them to jot down impressions. Lady Brinkburn had drawn Handy as a boy and must have liked him enough to give him the picture – unless he'd stolen it, of course. So when and why had she come to hate him?

I asked Violet if I might borrow the drawing. She was reluctant at first, but relented after I promised to take good care of it. Finally Tabby and I said goodbye to her and set off for the village shop to place an order for some provisions.

'I want you to go to the hall for me,' I said to Tabby. 'The steward there is Mr Whiteley. Go to the back door, say Miss Lane presents her compliments to Mr Whiteley and would be grateful for a word with him tomorrow about the cottage. Have you got that?'

She repeated it, word perfect.

'Then you wait there until somebody brings you out his reply,' I said.

'Wouldn't it be easier if I just found him and asked him?'

'Yes, it would be easier, but it's not how things are done.'

From her expression, she accepted it, but grudgingly.

'Were Violet's old things any use then?' she said.

'Possibly. You did well to find out about them, at any rate.'

She grinned.

'I've found out something else as well.'

'From Violet?'

'Nah, from Polly. It's about her ladyship.'

'Have you found out about her old maid Suzy?'

'Oh, she died years ago. Something else.'

I opened my mouth to ask what, then remembered that we were standing in the middle of the village street with probably half a dozen people watching from gardens and porches.

'Good, you can tell me when you get back from the hall.'

I watched her walking briskly along the road under the hot sun, then turned back to the woodland path and made my way to the cottage. Everything seemed as we'd left it, with no trace of intruders. After the hurry of travelling and London it was blissful to be back with the sound and smell of the river. I sat watching the swans, planning the conversation I'd have with Mr Whiteley. It would have nothing to do with the cottage and, if my suspicions were right, he wouldn't expect it to be.

Tabby was back sooner than expected, while I was still sitting on the river bank, dabbling my toes in the water. She came bouncing through the hollyhocks, humming with news, like a honeybee coming back to the hive loaded and dusted with pollen.

'Did Mr Whiteley send a message?' I said.

She nodded, and delivered it in a mock-pompous voice.

'Mr Whiteley sends his compliments to Miss Lane and will do himself the honour of calling on her at ten o'clock tomorrow morning.'

So the steward preferred to have his conversation with me at the cottage rather than the hall where we might be overheard. That was no surprise.

'Were they busy at the hall?' I said, wondering if a messenger from London had arrived.

'Not particularly, no. I heard one of the maids saying they must draw the curtains because his lordship was dead, but they didn't seem that bothered. Oh, and there's another message for you.'

She felt in her pocket and produced a folded square of paper, good quality and delicately scented. It was addressed to me in Lady Brinkburn's hand, but with less than her usual neatness. The writing inside looked equally hasty.

> Miss Lane,
> Would you do me the kindness of coming to tea tomorrow? I shall send for you. Please don't bother to reply.
> Sophia Brinkburn

'Did Mr Whiteley give you this?' I said.

'Nah, a lady. I think it might have been her ladyship. She came running across the grass to give it me.'

That sounded wildly unlikely.

'What did she look like?'

'She was wearing a green dress with white lace. She was quite old, more than forty probably, and her hair had a bit of grey in it, but more brown. She spoke in a deep sort of voice, like this.'

The last two words were a passable imitation of Lady Brinkburn's soft and low voice and the description fitted. From the description of her dress, she'd been in no hurry to change into widow's weeds.

'And she came running across the lawn to you?'

'Well, more walking fast, I suppose. But she was hurrying and panting.'

'Did she say anything to you?'

'She asked was I your maid.'

'How would she know that?'

'They kept me waiting at the back door long enough for the whole house to know it. I thought they might give me a cup of tea at least, but no. Any rate, I said yes, I was your maid. And she said would I give you this note and be sure I put it in your hands and nobody else's.'

The urgency, and the abrupt tone of the note, suggested more than a wish to take tea with me.

With the air of a job well done, Tabby sat down beside me on the bank, peeled off her stockings and dabbled her toes beside mine.

'So, do you want to know what Polly told me about her ladyship?'

'Yes. But how does Mrs Todd come to know anything about her?'

'She helps with the cleaning up at the hall when they're short-handed. She was there the autumn before last, when the lordship and the ladyship had this quarrel. Everybody heard it, Polly said. They couldn't help hearing it, even if they didn't want to, though I don't think they tried very hard not to.'

'This was when Lord Brinkburn came on his usual visit, I suppose.'

'S'pose so. Polly says her ladyship doesn't like him being there and shuts herself in her room.'

That fitted with what I knew, so was at least some support for whatever story Tabby had heard.

'Anyway, one night his lordship got roaring drunk,' Tabby went on. 'Polly says he always drank a lot, but usually he could take it like a gentleman; only that night he had toothache and he drank a lot of brandy for the pain, so what with the brandy and the toothache he was rampaging up and down the corridors, roaring like a bull.'

'Did Polly see this for herself?'

'Yes. She'd been told to stay over in the servants' attic that night, because of being needed to help with breakfast in the morning. She said she was terrified, most of them were. Anyway, after this has been going on for a while, he takes it into his head that he wants to see his wife.'

'Poor woman.' I imagined her shut in her room, hearing the roaring and stamping going on. 'Were either of the sons at home?'

'No. Polly said some of the men servants were trying to calm him down, only it made him worse. One of them tried to stop him going up the stairs to her room and he punched him in the face. Then he started rattling the door handle and shouting at her to come out. When she wouldn't, he told one of the servants to get an axe and break the door down.'

Tabby looked at me, biting her lower lip, face full of excitement. You could see how much she and Mrs Todd had enjoyed the story. Something in her expression said that the best part was still to come.

'So did anyone go for the axe?' I said.

239

'Didn't have time. While they were all standing there, the door to her ladyship's room opened and out came a man.'

'Good heavens!'

'He gave his lordship a piece of his mind, Polly said, for all the world as if he owned the house. Asked him what he was doing, kicking up such a row. His lordship didn't say anything, but his face turned the colour of beetroot. Then he went down a step, drew his arm right back and hit the other man in the chops so hard he fell back and banged his head on her ladyship's door.'

'Was he knocked out?'

'No. Polly said he should have been, after a hit like that, but he stood up, blood all over his face, and hit his lordship back even harder. His lordship wasn't expecting it, so he fell all the way downstairs. This other man followed him, stood over him and threatened he'd tell everybody.'

'Tell them what?'

'Polly says she can remember it word for word. Everybody else had gone quiet, see, after all the noise and shouting. They couldn't believe what was happening.'

'So what did this other man say?'

'"If you dare do anything like this again, I'll make sure all the world knows."'

'Knows about the way he treated his wife, did he mean?'

'I suppose so.'

But I knew that as a threat it did not make sense. There were other husbands, high and low, who treated their wives worse and still held up their heads in the world. Given that Lady Brinkburn was harbouring a man in her room, if the story were true, plenty of people would have said that Lord Brinkburn was within his rights, and the law courts would agree with them. If the story were true. In spite of the circumstantial detail, I found it hard to imagine quiet, fastidious Lady Brinkburn doing any such thing.

'So what did Lord Brinkburn do then?'

'He called the other man a filthy adulterous f . . .'

'Fornicator, I dare say.'

'. . . then he walked off into another room and slammed the door. Early next morning, he had his carriage called before it got light and went off.'

'Just like that, without saying or doing anything else?'

'That's what Polly said.'

That didn't make sense either. The mildest husband in the world would hardly take himself off from his own house, leaving an adulterer in possession of the field, and nothing I'd heard suggested Lord Brinkburn was pacific in temperament. I began to doubt Mrs Todd's story more and more.

'What about the other man?'

'Oh, he stayed.'

'Went back into Lady Brinkburn's room?'

'Yes, only Polly says he didn't stay long and he didn't spend the night there. Not that time, anyway.'

'So she saw him in the house at other times?'

'Oh yes. He's there all the time. He lives there.'

'What! Who is he?'

She shrugged. 'His name's Carmichael. Polly says he looks after Lady Brinkburn's books.'

# CHAPTER FOURTEEN

Mr Whiteley arrived promptly at ten o'clock next morning. He came on foot through the woods, a powdering of dust on the toes of his highly polished shoes, a briar rose leaf sticking to the shoulder of his black jacket. His complexion was greyish, like a man who had been ill or worried for some time. I'd sent Tabby to the village with a message to Mrs Todd saying she needn't come to clean that morning. At some time, I'd need to speak to Mrs Todd about the story of Lady Brinkburn and her librarian, but it would have to wait. I invited Mr Whiteley into the main room of the cottage and asked him to sit down, indicating the most comfortable chair. He chose one of the less comfortable ones and sat, knees together, elbows at his sides and gloved hands on his thighs, as if trying not to take up too much room.

'We've received some sad news, Miss Lane. Lord Brinkburn is dead.'

I offered formal commiserations, not mentioning that I'd known some time before the news had reached him.

'I understand that there is some problem with the cottage,' he said

I'd taken the chair opposite him.

'There's no problem with the cottage. The problem is with the evidence you gave at Handy's inquest.'

He said nothing for a long time. His eyes were fixed on mine, but I'm not sure he was seeing me. There was a downward slant to his eyelids that gave him a look of weariness. Gradually, his whole body seemed to give in to that weariness, shoulders relaxing, hands falling to his sides. He gave a long sigh, like the breath going out of a dying animal.

'It wasn't your fault,' I said. 'Did Mr Lomax suggest it to you?'

He gave the faintest of nods.

'You couldn't have seen Simon Handy outside the old dairy just after eight o'clock on Sunday evening,' I said. 'He was somewhere else entirely then, and I can prove it. And you didn't leave the old dairy unlocked with the crates of armour inside. You're careful with keys, and the padlock on that door had been freshly oiled to make sure it worked. Why did Mr Lomax persuade you to tell lies at the inquest? '

'Who are you? Why are you asking me questions?'

244

There was no anger in his voice, just wistfulness, as if hoping it would all go away.

'I'm working for Mr Lomax too,' I said, telling myself that it was true, more or less. 'He thinks I might be able to help the family. Goodness knows, it needs help, but I can't do it if people are lying to me.'

'I've never told a lie in my life before,' he said. 'Not since I was a boy, at any rate, and then I was no good at it and got a whipping.'

His formal voice was slipping, a countryman's accent coming through.

'You've improved then,' I said. 'The coroner didn't doubt you, but of course he had no reason to. You were the loyal family steward, doing his best in a bad business.'

'I am loyal,' he said. 'That's what I am – loyal.'

'I don't doubt it, but if you . . .'

But he was determined to make me understand. He leaned forward in his chair and went on talking in a quiet but intense voice.

'When Lord Brinkburn made me his steward, I thought it was the proudest day of my life. That was thirty years ago, before he married. My father had been one of the tenant farmers on the estate, and Lord Brinkburn bought the hall to have a place nearer London.

'It wasn't easy, even back then, but I kept things together through the bad times, and he appreciated that, I'm sure he did, even if he never said so.'

I thought back to what Disraeli had told me about the family finances.

'Were the bad times because Lord Brinkburn was short of money?'

He nodded.

'There were debts. Some people reckoned he'd over-reached himself, buying the estate. But then he made a good marriage, so we thought we were all nicely settled.'

He said *good marriage* entirely without irony, though he must have known better than most people how it had turned out, and went on like a man pleading his own defence.

'I've been a good steward all these years. There isn't a penny piece in the rents or a teaspoon in the kitchen or a bushel of corn in the barn I couldn't account for. But how's a man supposed to be loyal when he doesn't know who he's supposed to be loyal to? Can you tell me that?'

'The business of Stephen and Miles, you mean?'

'I've got used to Master Stephen, with his lordship being abroad so much. How could I look ahead, not knowing whether it's going to be Master Stephen or Master Miles?'

'But it must be Stephen now, mustn't it?' I said. 'He became Lord Brinkburn the moment his father died. Will that mean things are easier for the staff?'

He took a long time to decide whether to reply.

'It might, if we knew it was going to stay that way. I've nothing against either of them. It's setting one of them against the other that's doing the damage.'

'Lady Brinkburn, you mean?'

'I'm not saying a word against her ladyship.'

But the way he dropped his eyes said it for him.

'Did one of the sons come down to break the news to Lady Brinkburn?' I said.

'No. Mr Lomax sent his head clerk down.'

Which told me two things: Stephen was still elusive, and serious events were keeping the family lawyer in London.

'It must be difficult for a household when the husband and wife are at odds,' I said.

'It's never been the other way, with them. When they were off on honeymoon, all the staff were looking forward to the happy couple coming back. When we got word they were on their way down from the north we had the arch and the "Welcome Home" banner all ready to go up over the drive, the gardeners had the greenhouses so full of flowers and fruit they were bursting with them, the maids and kitchen staff all had new dresses, nearly mad with curiosity to see what the new mistress was like. We might as well not have bothered.'

'They didn't come?'

'Oh, they came all right. Only his lordship sent word on ahead that there was to be no arch, no banner, nobody but me out on the steps to welcome them. It was raining when they got here, and nearly dark. He didn't even get out of the coach. I had to go and hand her ladyship down myself, with nobody to introduce us. As soon as she and her maid and the luggage were out, the coach was off again.'

I imagined a young woman in the damp dusk, outside a house she'd never seen before, a staff of strangers who'd probably been watching from the windows as her husband deposited her there with less ceremony than he'd leave a dog.

'And it's been like that all along,' Mr Whiteley said. 'He didn't even come home when Mr Stephen was born. Now and again he'd visit us, but never for more than a week or ten days at most.'

I thought that on at least one of those occasions, he must have visited his wife's bed or there'd have been no Miles.

'Were they reconciled at all?'

'Not that we saw. After the first few times, she'd shut herself up in her rooms.'

'And the last time?'

'I suppose somebody's been talking.'

'You could hardly expect otherwise,' I said.

Perhaps I should have asked him outright: *Do you believe Lady Brinkburn is committing adultery with her librarian?* I think I held back partly from respect for him and his perplexed loyalty, but more because he was not the proper person to ask. Only two people would know for certain, and if I needed an answer it should come from one of them.

'How did Handy's body get into the crate?' I said.

Relief flickered in his eyes at the question I hadn't asked.

'I don't know, and that's the honest truth.'

'You told the inquest you weren't there on the Monday morning when the carter came to take the crates away. Was that true?'

'Yes.'

'So you wouldn't have noticed then that there was an extra crate. You said you glanced through the window at them on Sunday night, after you'd sent Handy packing. But Handy wasn't there. Are you still claiming you looked through the window at the crates?'

'I did, yes, just to check.'

'And the door was padlocked?'

'Yes.'

'You said everything seemed to be in order. Was that true?'

'It was only a quick glance.'

He'd said that he was no good at lies. It was true. I could tell he was keeping something back.

'So were there the right number of crates then – no extra one?'

He hesitated.

'I'm not sure. I told you, I only glanced.'

'So you can't be sure?'

'No.'

'Could anybody have put an extra crate in there without your knowing about it? You're a careful steward. You keep an eye on things.'

He said nothing.

'And what about the padlock on the door?' I said. 'Who keeps the key to it?'

'The keys to the outhouses hang on a hook just inside the scullery door.'

No hesitation this time. He was glad to have a question he could answer easily.

'So anybody in the household could have known about the key and used it?'

'Anybody, yes.'

'But it would have made a noise, wouldn't it? The door opening, a crate being carried in. Wouldn't somebody have heard?'

'We all go to bed quite early. Her ladyship doesn't keep us up.'

'So you're saying it would've had to be brought in after most people were in bed?'

'I'm not saying anything. I don't know.'

There was stubbornness as well as distress in his voice. I got up and opened the window on the garden. A bumblebee blundered in. Mr Whiteley's eyes followed it.

'I suppose Simon Handy knew in advance that the armour was going up to London,' I said.

'Yes, I doubt he cared about it, though. It all had to be carried down and cleaned and dusted, but he didn't do a hand's turn to help. He never did. Thought it was beneath him, I expect.'

Now he thought we'd moved away from a dangerous area, Mr Whiteley was more willing to talk.

'So he was idle?' I said.

'Bone idle. I never saw him put his hand to anything useful all the weeks he was here. He told me he was a valet. I said there was no gentleman in residence to valet for, so he'd better make himself useful in other ways. He never did.'

'And yet he was complaining of being given too much work to do,' I said.

'What!'

Mr Whiteley's mouth fell open. I quoted Violet's words without letting him know they came from her.

'He said he was being asked to do too much and it wasn't fair on a man.'

'That's nonsense. I've never known a man do less.'

His indignation was genuine, his cheeks flushed.

'So what do you think he meant?' I said.

'Goodness knows.'

'Could he have been working for somebody else?'

'I doubt it. It's true he'd be away for days on end, but I can't see that one doing honest work anywhere. Besides, there's not much call for valets round here.'

'It occurred to me that somebody might be paying him to report on what was happening at the hall,' I said.

I watched as he turned it over in his mind. He didn't hurry to deny it.

'Why do you think that?' he said at last.

'Something I found out in London.'

I decided not to give him the details of the man from Astley's.

'What have we come to?' he said sadly, addressing the bumblebee on the window pane rather than me. And again, with a sigh: 'What have we all come to?'

251

It was interesting that he hadn't asked me whom Handy might be spying for. I was about to ask him if he could hazard a guess, but at that moment the door opened and Tabby came shambling in like a disorderly dog.

'Polly says to send her respects and –'

'Tabby, visitors.'

But Mr Whiteley was already on his feet and reaching for his hat.

'Thank you, Miss Lane. I shall do my best to deal with the problems you mention.'

His performance of normality was entirely unconvincing and Tabby gave him a puzzled look.

'What did he want?' she said, as his stiff back and black hat vanished into the woods.

'Never you mind. What was the message from Mrs Todd?'

'Did you want her to come in tomorrow? She says she'll come unless you tell her not to.'

'That could have waited.'

I was annoyed with her. If she hadn't frightened him off, I might have got him to tell me more.

'Polly says he's a dry old stick, but fair minded.'

I set her to collecting salad leaves from the garden for our lunch and went down to stroll by the river, marvelling at where loyalty had led this dry old stick. Keeping faith with a family that seemed to have done little to deserve it, he'd lied on oath and hindered the investigation of a murder. He'd admitted that Oliver

Lomax had coached him to tell lies at the inquest. The risk that the lawyer had run was breathtaking. He'd committed a sin that would ruin him professionally if it became known. Surely the only thing that would persuade him to do that was an even greater risk to a member of his friend's family. Even then, it was hard to account for a loyalty even more extreme than the steward's.

In the afternoon, I changed into my blue cotton print, fit for another social call. For once, I didn't have to wear sensible shoes for walking because Lady Brinkburn was sending for me. I sat on the bench outside the door, enjoying the scent of the roses and waiting for the rumble of a gig or carriage wheels on the rutted drive through the woods. At half past three I began to think that she'd forgotten me and I'd have to walk after all. I was on the point of going upstairs to change out of my blue kid shoes when a rhythmic splashing came from the river, then the sound of oars clunking into rowlocks. So she'd sent a man with the rowing boat instead. What a good and sensible idea, much more pleasant to glide on the river rather than rattle along the dusty road. Footsteps swished through the long grass up the garden. I stood up, smoothing my dress, then must have gaped open-mouthed at the figure walking along the path. Robert Carmichael.

'Good afternoon, Miss Lane. I hope you have no objection to travelling by water.'

I managed to stop gaping and to wish him good afternoon, but my voice seemed to be coming from a long way off. In my mind, the picture of him standing over a bleeding Lord Brinkburn at the foot of the staircase was much more vivid than the smiling man standing there among the flowers. I'd known I'd have to meet him again, but had wanted time to be prepared for it, not allowing myself to be taken by surprise like this.

I followed him down the path to the river bank, saying nothing. The rowing boat was tied to the root of an alder tree. He pulled it parallel to the bank and offered a hand to help me in. I ignored it and settled myself on the seat in the middle of the boat. He took off his hat and jacket, folded them neatly in the prow, then cast off, stepping in lightly and settling himself on the rowing bench. A few strong strokes with the oars brought us through the water lilies at the edge to the middle of the current, facing upriver towards the hall. He rowed with a steady rhythm, still smiling as if this were the most delightful of pleasure trips. With his back to the direction of travel, he was facing me so that his face dipped towards mine with each stroke, then away again. In spite of the ease of his rowing, there was a sheen of sweat on his forehead, but then it was a hot day with no breeze, not even here on the river. I tried to keep my face impassive and look over his shoulder at the scenery, but was aware all the time of the bend and stretch of his arms in their fine white linen, the pale nape of his neck when he leaned forward. A mad impulse came to

me to ask him there and then, *Are you and she lovers?*
I fought it down. It had to be asked at some time, either
of him or her, but not now. The rhythm faltered.

'Look, a kingfisher.'

He was looking towards a willow, oars lifted from
the water.

'I missed it,' I said.

The look he gave me suggested he was aware that
something was wrong. He bent his head and resumed
rowing.

# CHAPTER FIFTEEN

As soon as we entered the house, Robert Carmichael handed me over to Lady Brinkburn's maid, Betty, and disappeared. Betty led me along the corridor and up the private flight of stairs by the library door. Lady Brinkburn was waiting in the doorway of her suite at the top. She wore a blue silk wrap and was barefoot, her hair loosely tied with a white ribbon. Her face was pale and papery in texture, with violet semi-circles under her eyes. The eyes themselves seemed remote and other-worldly, the pupils no more than pin-pricks.

'Miss Lane, I hope you will excuse my receiving you so informally. I'm so plagued by this heat I can scarcely think or stand.'

'You're not well,' I said. 'I'll go away.'

I was alarmed by the look of her, and even more by the nervous energy that seemed to charge the air round her.

When she put a hand on my arm I felt its heat even through my dress sleeve.

'Don't go. Please don't go.'

She kept her hand on my arm, her eyes on my face.

'Then I'll stay, if you want me to.'

She sighed with relief and drew me into the room.

'May I call you by your first name? I'm Sophia.'

'My name's Liberty.'

'Such a splendid name.' Then to Betty, 'It's all right. We have everything we need here.'

She closed the door on the girl's concerned face. All the windows of her sitting room were open, their white muslin curtains motionless in the heavy air, framing views of the lawn and river. She could, if she'd wanted, have watched Robert Carmichael and me walking up the grass. There were tea things set out on a table, a silver kettle on a small spirit burner. Waves of heat shimmered from it.

'We'll have tea here, just the two of us.'

She concentrated hard on making the tea, as if it were some dangerous scientific experiment. There were lines of pain on her forehead.

'You have a headache?' I said.

'Yes. I always do when the atmosphere is oppressive. Don't you find it so?'

'You should be lying down,' I said.

An inner door to her bedroom was half open, showing a broad white bed under a muslin canopy, the quilt as smooth and plump as a snow drift. A dark glass bottle and medicine glass stood on the table beside it.

'I'm tired of lying down. I've hardly slept for two nights.'

'I heard about your husband,' I said.

I could hardly fail to refer to his death, but formal commiserations did not seem in order, especially in the face of her obvious refusal to wear mourning.

'Do you think I should be in black for him?' she said, looking me in the face as if she really wanted an answer.

'No.'

She ran a hand down her blue silk.

'Betty put out my black bombazine, poor girl. I told her to take it away and burn it.'

She poured tea and handed me my cup. 'I hope you didn't object to arriving by boat. We thought it would be cooler on such a day.'

It might have been a brave attempt at social chat, only there was a shade of emphasis on the 'we' that invited me to notice it, and her eyes were fixed on mine.

'That was thoughtful of you.'

'Robert rows well, doesn't he?'

No doubt about it this time. She wanted me to notice the use of his Christian name.

'Yes, very well.'

'Robert is very dear to me. I don't know how I should manage without him.'

Her eyes were tired and full of pain, but there was challenge in them too.

'I think Mr Carmichael is very anxious to protect you,' I said.

'You've heard the story, of course?'

'Your husband threatening to break down the door with an axe?'

'Yes. This very door and that very staircase. It happened.'

There was a terrible openness about her face and her eyes, as if she were willing herself to be transparent. I said nothing.

'Miss Lane, if I were to tell you that Robert and I are not lovers, would you believe me?'

I thought about it, and all the time her eyes were on my face. In the end, I said, 'Yes.'

She nodded, as if that settled the point, but I noticed she didn't make the statement.

'Did what happened on your husband's last visit make you decide to tell people about Stephen and Miles?' I said.

'No. I kept silent about that dreadful business as about so many other things, only of course you can't stop the servants from talking. He went away again, as he always did, and left me in my tower by the river.'

It wasn't a tower, of course, but I guessed she was thinking of *The Lady of Shalott* again. In this mood, there did seem something fey about her, like a woman shut away from the world by a spell.

'So why did you decide to talk about it?'

She wanted to confide in me, or in somebody at any rate, but couldn't quite bring herself to make the irrevocable leap. All I could do was ask the questions that had been in my mind and see what happened. If she was angry with me and told me to go, then that was her decision.

'Because I knew my husband was dying and his mind was quite gone. I never expected that to happen. He was still a vigorous man when I last saw him. I was quite sure that I'd die first, then things would have to go however they went and it wouldn't be any fault of mine. Once I knew he was incapable of acting, the injustice would be my fault and I had to speak out.'

'But now he's dead, the title and the estate go to Stephen,' I said.

'If he's not his father's legitimate son, they'd have to alter it, wouldn't they?' she said. 'These things have to be done properly or the whole system of inheritance would fall down.'

Personally, I thought that would be no bad thing, only it wasn't the time to say so.

'Do you dislike Stephen?'

The pause before she answered lasted a long time. At last she said, 'No,' but uncertainly. Then, after a shorter pause, 'When he was a baby, I could scarcely bear to touch him. But I got past that. I told myself none of it was his fault. He was a little boy, like any other boy, laughing, bringing things for me to see, playing with his animals. How could I dislike that, whatever the circumstances? But then . . .'

She looked at me, biting her lip.

'Something changed?'

'Yes. He went away to school, of course. I suppose that makes all boys different, but it was more than that in Stephen's case. The year he was fourteen, he came home for the summer holidays. I can still remember it so clearly, it won't go out of my mind. I'd arranged a little tea party for the two of them as a welcome home, in the summer house. Stephen came striding in and glared at me, then before he even took off his hat he said to me in a terrible, cold, grown-up sort of voice: "Why did you drive my father away?"'

The pain in her eyes and voice was beyond help, but I tried.

'Boys can be cruel,' I said. 'They talk to impress each other at school, thinking they're adults. They don't realise . . .'

'He realised,' she said. 'It was his father coming out in him. Stephen is his father's son.'

I stared at her, trying to make sense of it.

'But . . . but the point of all this, surely, is that Stephen is not Lord Brinkburn's son . . . that is, unless I've totally misunderstood . . .'

'No, you don't understand, do you? A person can be his father's son in one sense and not in another.'

She spoke softly and sadly, but I felt that we'd just left firm ground and stepped on the quivering surface of unreason. Sensing my confusion, she touched my arm as if she were trying to comfort me.

'Don't look so sad. I still had Miles, after all. My little knight. He was only twelve years old at the time, but he stood up for me and tried to hit his brother. I had to stop him or Stephen might have hurt him.'

'But Miles is his father's son, after all,' I said.

'Yes, he is his father's legal son, but I don't believe he has a particle of his father's nature in him. Miles has all my qualities and probably all my faults as well. I willed that. Don't you think women can will qualities into their children?'

'I don't know. The fact of his birth – does it mean you and your husband were reconciled for a while?'

She laughed.

'We were never reconciled. You'll have heard Lord Brinkburn came here now and then to inspect his property. The property included me: a husband's rights, you understand. After those first few times, I locked myself away. He never tried to break the door down, until that last visit.'

'So Miles was the result of . . .?'

'One of those first property inspections, yes. I lay there in the dark, thinking that if there was a child it would be mine and only mine. I tried not even to think of his father all the time I was carrying him.'

'And the man who came to the tower, did you think of him?'

She shook her head and, for the first time in the conversation, dropped her eyes.

She offered more tea. I accepted.

262

'I read your journal,' I said.

'All of it?'

'Every word, and I enjoyed the pictures too. You have a great talent for sketching.'

She thought I was guiding us back to the shallow waters of social chat. There was both relief and disappointment in her eyes. I put down my cup and picked up my reticule.

'I came across another example of your work the other day.'

I unrolled the sketch of the boy Handy and put it down among the tea things, weighting it with the sugar tongs. She leaned forward to look at it, simply curious at first, then with an intake of breath and a flinch as if I'd hit her.

'Where did you get this?'

After the first shock, she was angry with me.

'Handy was friendly with a woman named Violet in the village,' I said. 'He'd given her some papers to keep for him. This was among them.'

She picked it up with the sugar tongs and held it in the flame of the spirit lamp. The thick paper was reluctant to burn at first and writhed and twisted, but she held it steady until it fell to the table in curled leaves of ash.

'You didn't always hate him,' I said. 'There was kindness for him in that sketch. And when he was wet and cold at Antwerp you had him wrapped in a blanket and made tea for him.'

When I'd first seen the sketch in Violet's bundle, it had reminded me of something. Hours later my mind had made the connection with the boy in the journal, 'wet as a herring'.

'I didn't know him properly then,' she said. 'I didn't know until later.'

'He was with you on the honeymoon tour, the boy riding on the back of the coach. I suppose he'd have been no more than twelve or thirteen then.'

'Yes, clinging on the back of the coach like a demon in a nightmare. All the way to Italy and back.'

'How could a boy that young be a demon?'

'It was born into him, I think. My husband saw that in him. That's why he chose him.'

The fierce energy was draining out of her, as if burning the picture had taken it away. She lay back on the couch, eyes half closed. I offered again to call Betty, but she shook her head.

'I want to tell you, I think. You've guessed so much already. Only, give me a moment.'

A sudden breeze came through the open windows from the river, whipping the light curtains into the room, then died away as rapidly as it had come, leaving the air feeling even more heavy. Still with eyes half closed, she started speaking.

'He was a birthday present to my husband. When he left school, his father told him he could have his own servant. His father thought he'd choose somebody from their estate in Northumberland. Instead, he picked out this ragged boy pulling a truck in a coal mine they visited.'

'A generous impulse,' I said.

'There wasn't any generosity about it. He saw Handy playing some mean practical joke on one of the other boys. Cornelius's sense of humour was always childish. It appealed to him and he took the boy on a whim. When he got his own carriage, he called Handy his tiger, dressed him in a suit of livery and had him riding on the back. Naturally, he came with us on our tour. Cornelius would no more have left him behind than one of the wheels. But Cornelius wasn't always kind to him. Some days he'd cuff him for no particular reason, other days he'd be feeding him cakes and letting him drink wine as if he were some kind of pet. I was sorry for him at first, as you saw.'

'What made you change?'

'It came gradually. I noticed him looking at me side-long, and grinning as if he knew something I didn't. Then Suzy came to me one day and said he'd tried to put a hand up her skirt – a boy of that age. I spoke to Cornelius about it and he only laughed and said that's what you'd expect a boy to do and Suzy was making a silly fuss about it. It was almost as if he was pleased to hear about it. After that, I tried to keep a distance between Handy and myself, but I couldn't help noticing things.

'What sort of things?'

'If we stayed in a place for more than a day or two, Cornelius would always go out in the evenings. He seemed to find acquaintances everywhere, though he wouldn't always introduce them to me. Handy would invariably go with him.'

'That was natural enough, I suppose. He'd need a boy to carry a torch and so on.'

'It was more than that. Sometimes they'd come back very late. I'd hear them laughing and singing, as if they were equals rather than master and boy. Then, next day, they'd be catching each other's eye and grinning as if there were some secret between them.'

'Did you say anything to your husband?'

'I tried not to think about it and to focus all my mind on the places we were travelling through. Even then, I had a presentiment I was seeing them for the first and last time.'

For a woman in her early twenties, that seemed intolerably sad. Perhaps even then she had a tendency to melancholy.

So you didn't ask questions?'

'Not until some time after we'd arrived by Lake Como. There was one occasion when they weren't back till dawn. Cornelius didn't get up till the afternoon. I told him that he was corrupting the boy and he'd have it on his conscience. I'll always remember what he said: "The boy was born corrupt, that's why I like him." I told him it was indecent to make a joke of something so serious, but I believe now he was telling the truth. Handy was born corrupt, and so was my husband.'

She lay back on the chaise longue, eyes closed. Telling all this seemed to have exhausted her, but I knew it was only half the story. Bad though it was, it couldn't explain the intense hatred she'd felt for Handy.

'You must have been furious when he arrived with that note from your husband saying he must be employed here,' I said.

'I believe it was Cornelius's final piece of malice against me. His mind was going, but he used this last spark of rationality to humiliate me after his death. Whiteley was trembling when he told me about it. I said he must send Handy away, pay him off, do anything. But Whiteley's a fool in some ways. His master's orders must be obeyed, even if the master's malicious and mad.'

'So you were relieved when you knew Handy was dead?' I said.

Her eyes stayed closed.

'I thanked God for it, and I bless the hand of whoever killed him.'

'Do you know who killed him?'

'I don't, but if I did, no power on earth could make me tell anybody. It was an act of justice. It took more than twenty years, but it came in the end. I'm glad I lived to see it.'

'Justice for what?'

'For something he and Cornelius did.'

'What?'

'I'm not going to talk about it. There's no need now. The devil has driven Cornelius off where he belongs,

267

with Handy clinging to the back of the coach as he used to do.'

The curtains billowed again in an isolated gust of breeze, like a breath from some sleeping monster. The heavy feathers of ash shifted on the tablecloth.

'There'll be a thunderstorm tonight,' she said. 'I used to love thunderstorms when I was a girl.'

Until one particular thunderstorm by the shore of Lake Como. I waited, but she said nothing. I thought she'd fallen asleep and was about to get up and go, alerting Betty on the way out, when she spoke again.

'I haven't told you why I wanted to see you, have I? I want you to do me a favour.'

'If I can, yes.'

'Will you come and stay with me, here at the house?'

Her eyes were open now. She swung her bare feet to the floor and made an effort to go into hostess mode.

'Just for a day or two. It would be so much more comfortable for you than the cottage and we could talk about pictures and flowers and so forth.' She stretched out a hand to me. It was trembling just perceptibly, betraying her attempt to speak lightly. 'Please, do say you will.'

'What are you scared of?' I said.

Tears came into her eyes. She looked away.

'Somebody came into my bedroom the night before last.'

I stared at her, puzzled.

'Betty, perhaps?'

'No. I asked her this morning. But I knew it wasn't her. It would have felt different.'

'Felt? Did whoever it was touch you?'

'No. A feeling in the air, I mean. I woke up suddenly. It was dark, but I knew at once there was somebody in the room with me. I said, "Who's there?" It didn't answer, just went out of the room quite quietly.'

'Didn't you see it go?'

'No. I'd drawn the curtains most of the way round the bed.'

'A man's footsteps or a woman's?'

'A man's.'

'Could it have been Mr Carmichael, looking in to see if you were all right?'

I was trespassing there. It would have been very peculiar behaviour in a librarian, but she'd as good as admitted he was more than that.

'No. I had the strongest feeling that . . .' she hesitated, '. . . that whoever it was didn't wish me well. And then the message came from London that Cornelius was dead.'

After the hesitation, the last words came out in a rush.

'You thought there was some connection?' I said.

'I think it was Cornelius's spirit, making a last check on his property on his way to hell.'

Anger and misery came together in her voice.

'Have you said anything about this to anybody else?'

'I told Robert. I'm not sure he believes me. He's been telling me I'm taking too strong a sleeping draught, you see. But even with the sleeping draught, I still wasn't sleeping. I'll go mad if I can't sleep.'

I thought of the bottle and medicine glass beside her bed. Laudanum, for a certainty. Liquid opium. Plenty of people took it to help them sleep or to calm the pain of toothache or indigestion. But taken habitually and in large quantities, it brought strange dreams. I remembered one man had been haunted by visions of monstrous crocodiles. It might explain both Sophia's nervous state today and the visitor of the night before. I wondered if she'd taken laudanum that night by Lake Como.

'If you really want me to stay with you, I will,' I said.

I was certain that there'd been no intruder, but my agreement didn't stem entirely from kindness. I was sorry for her, but I sensed that she still hadn't told me the entire truth. She was on the edge of confiding something, but still couldn't bring herself to take the risk.

'Thank you. Thank you so very much.'

'But I'll have to bring my maid. I can't leave her in the cottage on her own.'

'Of course. There's a spare bed in the maids' room. I'll have the gig sent round at once. You can go and fetch her and your luggage.'

She jumped up and ran to the bell-pull by the fireplace, decisive again now she'd got what she wanted. When Betty appeared she gave clear orders for bringing the gig to the front door and having a bed made up in the room where we were sitting. If the maid was surprised at this arrangement when there must surely be a spare bedroom in the house, she gave no sign of it.

Within ten minutes I was bowling up the drive and an hour later coming back down it, with Tabby by my side and my hastily packed trunk on the back. Tabby had been unimpressed by our entry into society.

'We'd just got comfortable here.'

'You'll be comfortable at the hall as well. Just watch what the other maids do, don't talk too much, and don't ask questions.'

I couldn't keep her with me all the time, so would have to trust her to the mercies of the servants' hall. The look she gave me when we parted in the hall and she was led away by Betty was as resentful as an abandoned terrier's. Lady Brinkburn came to meet me and take me upstairs. A bed was already made up for me in the corner of the sitting room and a table for two set up by the window, laid with a damask cloth, silver and glassware. I imagined the concealed resentment of the servants at having to take such extra trouble.

'I've ordered supper to be sent up here,' she said. 'It's cooler than downstairs.'

I doubted that, but was relieved at not having to meet Robert Carmichael again that day. Now that Lady Brinkburn herself had confirmed the story about him and her husband, I'd have some trouble looking him in the eye.

'I've told Robert you're staying with me,' she said, as if guessing my thoughts. 'He's very grateful to you.'

271

'He has no need.'

A man brought up my small trunk and, on Lady Brinkburn's orders, deposited it in her bedroom. She asked if I'd like my maid called to help me unpack. When I said I'd manage by myself, thank you, she seemed relieved.

'So pleasant, just the two of us.'

From her voice, we might have been two schoolgirls on an escapade, but the strained look was on her face all the time. I asked if her head was still aching.

'Yes. It won't be better until the storm's broken. It's building up, look.'

I followed her to the open window. A cloud bank the colour and shape of a bunch of black grapes had appeared in the west, its edges outlined in gold by the horizontal sun. Thunder sounded, so far in the distance that it was felt as a vibration in the body rather than heard. She shivered.

'Once it gets in the river valley it rolls on and on for hours.'

Like a storm in the mountains. I guessed she was thinking about a late summer night by Lake Como. We stayed silently by the window until there was a knock on the door and Betty wheeled in the supper trolley and laid out dishes and a wine cooler on the table.

'That will be all, thank you,' Lady Brinkburn said. 'Leave the trolley. You can clear away in the morning.'

I caught a surprised, even concerned, look from Betty.

More disruption to the routine. We sat at the table and Lady Brinkburn helped me to trout in aspic with cucumber, asparagus, chilled Muscadet. I was hungry and ate with a good appetite, but she only picked at her food. Her spaniel, Lovelace, sat under the table with imploring eyes and got more of the trout than she did. The storm was coming closer, the rumbles of thunder louder and more frequent. She winced at every one of them but kept up a determined and entirely conventional conversation, mostly about travel, encouraging me to talk about the places I'd visited.

'Oh, you are so fortunate to have seen the Bay of Naples,' she said. 'I should have loved to visit the south.'

She put it in the past tense, as if she were an old woman already.

'There's time, isn't there? You could travel where you liked.'

She would presumably have some allowance from the estate and could, if she wished, marry her young librarian and fly south with him as freely as a swallow. The tutting of English society would mean nothing to them in Naples or Athens. But her husband's death, which should give her a widow's freedom, had brought the question of succession to a head. It could tie her down with legal proceedings for years and put her name in the mouths of gossips round every tea table and parish pump in England. She'd dug a deep ditch between herself and any chance of happiness. Perhaps I could help her step across it.

'It must have occurred to you to leave things as they are,' I said.

She frowned, as if she didn't understand. I pressed on.

'Surely Miles is well enough provided for, and he's a young man who will make his own way in the world. Is it so important to you that he should have the title?'

'It's not a question of what's important for me. It's a matter of justice and honour.'

'Your own honour or the world's idea of honour?'

'You're clever, aren't you?' she said, and it didn't sound much like a compliment. 'I suppose you've been talking to Robert.'

I was about to deny it, until I remembered that I had talked to him about her, or rather he'd talked to me. I could hardly tell her that he'd appealed to me to make the world believe she was mad, for her own protection.

'I'm not speaking for him, I'm speaking for myself,' I said.

'But you have talked about me, haven't you? What did he tell you?'

'Very little, except he was concerned for you.'

The hostility that had flared up in her seemed to be draining away. She looked relieved.

'He worries about me too much.'

We finished the bottle of Muscadet. Although she'd barely eaten, she'd matched me glass for glass. She stood up, gathered our used plates and glasses, and stacked them on the trolley. I helped her push it out to the landing. The room was quite dark by now because of the clouds blotting out the evening sun, but she made no move to light lamps or candles. After a while she went through to her bedroom and came back with a dark green bottle and a small glass.

'I shan't sleep without it.'

She poured carefully until the glass was half full, squinted at it, then poured again until it was three-quarters full and tossed it back defiantly. She put glass and bottle on a table then lay back on the chaise longue. Her eyes closed, but her body still quivered at every rumble of thunder and when the first lightning forked across the sky her eyes jerked open with a scared and lost look, as if she didn't know where she was. She made a small sound, like a newborn puppy. I went over to her.

'It's all right,' I said. 'You should be in bed.'

I got her to stand up and walked her through to the bedroom. Her nightdress was laid out ready on the white coverlet.

'Don't leave me.'

So I stood looking out of her window while she got ready for bed. As I was standing there, another flash of lightning seemed to rip the clouds apart and the rain started with the suddenness of slops being flung out of a bucket. It settled to a downpour, hissing down on the lawn and the gravel drive, and the smell of damp warm grass filled the room. The sash window had been open top and bottom and the rain was coming in. I pulled it down so that only a foot or so at the top was open and started drawing the curtains.

'No, leave them open.'

She was in her nightdress with her hair down, her voice slurred.

'But the lightning . . .' I said.

'Things can come in behind the curtains.'

The laudanum was obviously taking effect, but there was no arguing with her. I left the curtains as they were, held back the coverlet while she got into bed and smoothed it round her. Lovelace curled up at the foot of the bed. Her hand came out from under the covers and took tight hold of mine. I kneeled on the rug beside her and stayed until her breathing became slow and regular and the grip on my hand slackened, then carefully drew it away. I stood up and tiptoed out, leaving the door half open so that I'd hear if she called out.

Although dark, it still wasn't late. I could hear life going on in the rest of the house, footsteps and muffled voices. The footsteps sounded louder when somebody came into the library downstairs. Robert Carmichael, probably wondering what was going on above his head. I didn't blame him for anything, or not really. Certainly I didn't blame her. She'd been horribly badly treated by her husband and had a right to take her happiness where she could. As for him – perhaps he really did love her. A man might love a woman fifteen or so years older than he was. He'd defended her and was concerned about her. So, the nagging disappointment in my mind was unfair to him and quite unreasonable.

I stood at the window and concentrated on the storm. Six seconds between the lightning and the thunder, so the heart of it was six miles away. Five seconds, coming closer. I liked storms. She'd liked storms too, until a certain night in her Italian tower. I thought of the journal. *Now and then, distant lightning illuminates the undersides of the clouds on the far side of the lake with a sullen kind of glow.* Then, in the morning, *Lord Brinkburn has told me something terrible, terrible.* A sudden use of her husband's formal title. All I knew now to add to that was that somehow the boy Handy had been involved. Also, his master's opinion of him: *That boy was born corrupt, that's why I like him.* Between one flash of lightning and the next, an idea came into my mind. If I could have woken her up then and asked her, I'd have done it, but I couldn't expect sense from her laudanum-numbed brain.

The storm came to its climax with a burst of thunder that seemed to rock the chimney pots. I was sure it would wake Sophia, but in the quiet that followed it there was no sound from next door. The lightning was no more than an occasional throb on the horizon, the thunder a low rumble. I changed into my nightdress and climbed into bed. The scent and coolness of starched linen sheets were so soothing that my mind stopped racing and I let myself drift into a half sleep, gentle as the rocking of a boat on the water. The image of Robert Carmichael's extended arms and bent neck tried to intrude into my boat, but I blocked it out. The half sleep became a full sleep, until it was shattered by a scream from the next room.

# CHAPTER SIXTEEN

I jumped up and ran through to the bedroom. Sophia was standing at the window in her nightdress. The flat light between darkness and day and the rigidity of her body made her look like a stiff, archaic statue. There'd been only that one scream. Now she was staring silently at the lawn between the house and the river. I stood beside her, following the direction of her eyes. There was nothing there, not so much as a rabbit.

'He's gone,' she said. 'He disappeared into the bushes when he knew I'd seen him. I think he's been there, watching my window, all the time I was asleep.'

'How do you know?'

'I could feel it. I had a dream of things crawling over my skin. I was so scared in my dream that I made myself wake up, and I looked out and there he was, standing on the lawn.'

Laudanum talking, beyond a doubt. I thought it best to try and calm her.

'The light's odd at this time of the morning.'

'I'm not seeing things. He was there.'

'Then it might have been anybody – a gardener, up early,' I said.

I glanced at the gilt travelling clock beside her bed. Twenty past four; too early even for the most conscientious gardener. 'Or a poacher, perhaps.'

But would any poacher have crossed the lawn so openly?

'It wasn't either of those. He was wearing a long black coat and a low-crowned hat.'

'Did you see his face?'

'It was too far away, and I didn't want to see his face.'

She shivered. I put a hand on her shoulder.

'Go back to bed.'

I decided not to mention Robert Carmichael. If there really had been a person there, wasn't he the most likely one, keeping watch on her window from a distance? But then, wouldn't a woman have recognised the man she loved, even at a distance in dim light?

She stood for a while as if she hadn't heard me, then sighed, walked across the room and sat on the edge of her bed. The sheets and coverlet were twisted like washing from a mangle. I settled on the bedside rug, looking up at her.

'At least the storm's gone away.' I said.

'It's worse when the storm's gone.'

Her voice was remote, as if coming from the back of a cave. I guessed she was remembering that other morning after a storm, more than twenty years before, and sensed that she wanted to tell me, or at least was near the brink of a decision.

'What happened, that night by Lake Como?' I said.

'I slept,' she said, still sounding surprised about it after all this time. 'I didn't expect to, with the headache and the storm, but I slept.'

'In your tower by the lake?'

'Yes, in my tower.'

She suddenly swung her legs on to the bed, pulled the coverlet over herself from waist down.

'And then something woke you?' I said.

We were at the heart of her story now, whether it was true or false. The next event must be the entry of the lover who was not her husband.

'No. Nobody woke me. I slept till Suzy came in and drew back the curtains in the morning. There was mist all over the lake, right up to the windows. It was like being on the inside of an enormous pearl, one of those misshapen ones. Baroque, is that what they call them?'

She stared at me from those eyes that were nearly all iris, as if she were still looking out at a mist. I answered her as gently as possible.

'So nobody came? You slept all night.'

'Yes. I woke up knowing something dreadful was going to happen. I don't know how I knew.'

281

'And nobody had come to you in the night?'

'Nobody.'

I settled back on my heels, wondering if she knew the significance of what she was saying. There'd been no daemon lover. My work was done. The story that had made her sons each other's enemies and been the talk of society for weeks was no more than an opium fantasy. I could take the *North Star* back to London in the morning and report to Mr Lomax that I'd heard her deny it. But I knew one thing would stop me: *This morning Lord Brinkburn has told me something terrible, terrible.* Terrible enough to destroy the rest of her life.

'That morning, your husband came to you and told you something,' I said. 'You wrote that much in your journal. What was it?'

She curled up and turned away from me, scrunching her head deep into the pillow as if in pain. I put a hand on the coverlet over her shoulder, trying to comfort her, but it was like touching stone.

'I'm sorry,' I said. 'It's all right. You don't have to tell me.'

I was angry with myself, both for hurting her so much and taking a hasty step and making her draw back at the last minute. For what seemed like a long time I knelt there, murmuring pointless things that were meant to be comforting. At last her shoulder softened, she gave a shuddering sigh and fell into a deep sleep. By then the sky outside was blue, the birds shouting their morning chorus. I drew the curtains across to keep out the light and sat in a chair by the window in case she should wake again and be scared. Two hours or so later, when there was a knock on the outside door, she still hadn't moved. I went across the sitting room to answer the knock, pulling the bedroom door closed behind me. Betty was waiting on the landing with a tray of coffee things.

'Is Lady Brinkburn still asleep, ma'am?'

'Yes. What time is it?'

'Half past seven, ma'am.'

She came into the room and put the tray down on a table.

'When her ladyship wakes up, would you ring and I'll bring her fresh.'

I said certainly I would. She hesitated.

'If you please, ma'am, Mrs Bream would be grateful for a word with you when convenient.'

'Mrs Bream?'

'The housekeeper, ma'am.'

'Please tell her I'll be downstairs as soon as I've had a cup of coffee.'

It was good coffee and I drank two cups at leisure, assuming the housekeeper would have some small domestic business on her mind and, quite possibly, a grudge against me for the inconvenience of making up an extra bed. Before I went downstairs I looked in on Sophia, but she still hadn't moved. I had no worries about leaving her, now that the household was up and about. When I asked for Mrs Bream I was directed to the linen room, where she was talking to one of the maids. As soon as she saw me, she sent the girl outside.

'You wanted to speak to me?' I said.

Mrs Bream was a comfortable pudding of a woman, with frizzy grey hair under her white cap. She looked as if she'd normally have been a cheerful body, but this morning she was worried.

'It's about your maid, ma'am.'

'Oh dear, has Tabby done something wrong?'

My conscience was pricked because I hadn't given her a thought all night. Goodness knows what sins against domestic order she'd committed. 'I'm sure she didn't mean any harm. She's inexperienced but good-hearted.'

Mrs Bream wiped her hands down her apron.

'The fact is, ma'am, I'm afraid she's run away.'

She looked at me from moist round eyes. My first reaction was to comfort her because she could hardly know about Tabby's wandering background.

'Don't worry, I dare say she woke up early and has gone out for a walk without telling anybody,' I said. 'Quite wrong of her, of course, and I shall speak to her about it when she comes back. Was that all?'

But she was looking even more miserable.

'I'm sorry to tell you, ma'am, things were said last night that probably shouldn't have been said, and I think she might have taken them more seriously than was meant.'

'What things?'

This was more worrying, and I suppose I must have spoken sharply because she was near tears.

'I said they shouldn't pick on her, but you know what girls are like these days, and how were they to know she'd take it like she did?'

I tried to make myself sound calmer than I felt.

'Mrs Bream, would you please try to tell me exactly what happened.'

She took a deep breath.

'It was at servants' supper. We all sit down when we've cleared the dinner things and have a bite or two of what's left over before the kitchen staff do the washing up. Nothing we're not allowed to. Lady Brinkburn knows about it.'

'I'm sure she does. But Tabby . . .'

'I told her to sit down with the others. The housemaids were all right to her at first. They don't often get people coming down from London, so they were asking her all about the fashions and so on, but she didn't seem to know as much as they thought she should. Then they started teasing her about the way she spoke and calling her a cockney, and one of them took exception to her table manners because she helped herself to a slice of ham without being asked. It was mostly fat and they'd turned their noses up at it anyway, but when she just grabbed for it . . .'

'Oh dear.'

Her table manners needed work, I knew that. I should never have exposed her to the snobberies of a servants' hall.

'And I know it wasn't right of our girl to make grunting noises at her, like a pig. But, with respect, it wasn't right of your girl. either, to do what she did.'

'Which was?'

'Rubbed the slice of ham in her face.'

'What happened then?'

'Your girl ran out and slammed the door. I told our girls they shouldn't have behaved like they did, and that was that. I thought she'd go up to bed when she got over her temper and I'd speak to you in the morning. Only this morning, she wasn't here.'

'Had she slept in her bed?'

'No. We'd given her a bed of her own, in the room with Ruth and Dora. They say she didn't come to bed all night.'

'Who was the one who made grunting sounds at her?'

'Dora.'

'Well, it wasn't surprising she didn't want to sleep in the same room as her, was it?'

I was trying hard not to take out my anger on the housekeeper. It wasn't her fault. If anybody's, it was mine for not thinking harder before transplanting Tabby from her home ground. In her place, I doubted if I'd have behaved any better.

'Mrs Bream, I'm very sorry if she upset your girls. The important thing now is to find her. What time was she last seen?'

'It was after eight o'clock when we sat down to our supper, and I'd say half an hour more before she ran out.'

'Into the thunderstorm?'

'Yes.'

'And nobody saw her after that?'

'No.'

'What time are the doors locked?'

'I lock the kitchen door from the inside before I go up to bed, when cook's finished. Cook was putting the oatmeal in to soak for the morning, and she and I were talking, so I couldn't rightly say.'

'Whenabouts?'

'Half past ten, perhaps a bit later.'

'And the front door?'

'I saw Mr Whiteley locking that as I was going upstairs.'

'And nobody checked whether Tabby had come back?'

'No, ma'am. We thought she'd have come back in and gone straight up to bed.'

'And Ruth and Dora didn't say she was missing until morning?'

'No, ma'am.'

I thought the two of them had probably lain awake giggling for a while, thinking of the cockney girl getting scared and wet outside. I'd have liked to bang their heads together. If it hadn't been for the storm, I shouldn't have been so worried. Tabby had probably slept rough for most of her life and was quite capable of surviving a short summer night in an outhouse. But she wasn't used to the country and might never have experienced thunder and lightning in the open. She could have flown into panic, run anywhere, with the river only a few hundred yards away.

'I'm going out to look for her,' I said. 'Would you please find Mr Whiteley and ask him if any of the gardeners have seen her. You might search the rooms in the house, in case she's come back in and is hiding.'

She nodded but looked uncertain. I had no right to give orders in somebody else's house, but it was not the time to be concerned with etiquette.

I went straight out to the back of the house and stood by the kitchen door, trying to put myself into Tabby's mind. She might instinctively make for somewhere that looked like her familiar shed in Abel Yard. The old dairy was still firmly padlocked, with nothing visible through the window but a scatter of wood-shavings. The two doors next to it weren't locked and opened on to a wood shed and a coal store. Either could have given her a night's shelter, but if she had been there, she'd left no sign. As I was closing the coal shed, a maid in black and white opened the kitchen door then ducked quickly back inside when she saw me. Dora, I supposed. I'd have liked to tell her what I thought of her, but it would have been a waste of time.

I stood with my back to the house, wondering what might have caught Tabby's eye by lightning flashes. The obvious possibility was a tall lean-to greenhouse alongside the wall of the kitchen garden. When I pushed the door open I found myself in heat that was already almost tropical at this early hour of the morning, breathing the yeasty smell of warm earth rising like a gas from freshly watered earth. Dark green melon vines rampaged up strings and hung down in swags, with dozens of ripening melons, each supported by its own miniature string hammock. Further on, velvety red-and-gold peaches gleamed between orderly rows of leaves, so perfectly ripe that even in my worry I found my mouth watering. I might have risked offending by picking one if I hadn't glimpsed through the leaves an elderly gardener, peering closely at a nectarine tree with a brass spraying machine in his hand. He pressed the spray button and a nicotine-smelling mist set me coughing.

'Dratted greenfly,' he muttered.

'Have you seen a girl?'

'Made out I didn't do them proper. I told him, if you can find a greenfly after I've been through them with the spray, I'll eat it, I will. He wasn't having it though.'

'A young girl, quite small.'

He shook his head and went on muttering. I left him to his work and walked out to look at a group of brick lean-to sheds, surrounded by orderly stacks of flower pots, nets and boxes. A glance through the window of the first one showed lines of wooden shelves for storing fruit and vegetables, mostly empty now, big metal bins, hessian sacks of root vegetables, stacks of baskets, but no sign of Tabby.

'What are you looking for, miss?'

The voice was angry. A dignified man in suit and waistcoat with gold watch chain, obviously the head gardener, arrived at a fast walk. I introduced myself and explained I was looking for my maid.

'Well, you won't find her in there.'

I insisted on going in to look under sacks, but he was right. When he saw I was genuinely worried he helped me search the other sheds, but was certain that no girl, however small, could have spent a night in his domain without his knowing about it. He'd been out inspecting the garden at first light, in case the storm had damaged anything, and found not a stick out of place. I thanked him and went back to the house, sure now that Tabby hadn't spent the night in any of the obvious places. Mr Whiteley was in the hall, talking to the housekeeper. I interrupted them.

'Have you found her?'

He looked apprehensive at seeing me.

'No, Miss Lane. Your maid isn't anywhere in the house. Might she have returned to your cottage?'

It was quite a sensible suggestion. Tabby might have sheltered somewhere from the storm, then, rather than go back to the house where she'd been mocked, found her way home as soon as it was light.

'I'll go and see,' I said. 'Please give my apologies to Lady Brinkburn and say I'll be back later.'

I decided to go to the cottage along the river bank. It was the shortest way, even though it would be muddy after the rain, but that wasn't the main reason. The picture I couldn't get out of my head was of Tabby running out of the house, so humiliated and angry that she didn't care where she was going, rushing through the storm to the river bank, catching her foot and falling. Her life on the London streets couldn't possibly have taught her to swim. I walked across the lawn at the front of the house, turning back once to look up at Sophia's window. Her curtains were still closed, as I'd left them. The path led me down to the landing stage, where the rowing boat that had brought me there was tied. I walked to the end of the jetty. Only a pair of swans on the water, nothing else. They were paddling hard to stay in place against a current that was running fast after the storm. There was about a foot of rainwater in the bottom of the boat.

'It will need baling out before it goes anywhere.'

I jumped round. Robert Carmichael was standing at the landward end of the jetty. He was wearing light indoor clothes, with no hat or overcoat, hair disordered and shoes clotted with mud. I was sure he hadn't followed me across the lawn, so must have been walking on the river bank.

'Have you seen my maid?' I said.

He shook his head and came along the jetty towards me. He looked tired, deep lines across his forehead and circles round his eyes as if he hadn't slept.

'Were you looking up at Lady Brinkburn's room early this morning?' I said.

The question came out before I had time to think about it. He stopped, looking startled.

'Looking up from where?'

291

'From the lawn. She says she saw somebody. She thinks it was the same person who came into her room the night before.'

He sighed.

'She's terribly scared, isn't she?' I said.

He nodded, looking at the swans. They'd given up their attempt to fight the current and were letting themselves be carried downriver, very stately, as if that's what they had intended all along. He was standing close to me, his sleeve almost touching mine.

'It was good of you to stay with her, Miss Lane.'

'I want to help her, if I can. She was asleep when I left. She says you're concerned that she's taking too much laudanum.'

I said it experimentally, wondering if he'd feel it as an intrusion. He looked away from the swans and up at me.

'I am worried, yes. I suppose she took her usual draught last night?'

'About three-quarters of a glass. She said she wouldn't sleep without it. The storm had brought back memories.'

Something in his eyes changed. He was alarmed now, as well as concerned.

'Did she talk about them?'

'Yes.'

He held my look, knowing I was waiting for him to ask. He was the one at risk of intruding now. It took him a long time to make the decision.

'Miss Lane, I hope this doesn't sound as if I'm expecting you to break a confidence. Believe me, I have a good reason for asking. Did she talk about . . .' A long hesitation. 'Did she talk about an event on her honeymoon tour?'

His hesitation had given me time to make my decision. Above all, I believed he loved Sophia and wanted to protect her. Soon, all of society would know that she'd changed her story. He had a right to know first, and in any case she hadn't sworn me to secrecy.

'You know about that night by Lake Como, the other storm?' I said.

He nodded and looked away.

'She told me last night that nobody came to her. She slept, she woke up, that was all.'

'Ah.'

One of the deepest sighs of relief I'd ever heard. His whole body seemed to relax completely. For a moment his hand rested heavily on my shoulder as if to prevent him from falling. Then he gathered himself together and took a step back, apologising.

'Forgive me. Did she say anything else about that night?'

'No. I was clumsy. I asked her a question that must have hurt her very much.'

'What?'

'I asked her what that entry in her journal next morning meant,' I said. 'The one about her husband telling her something terrible.'

293

I couldn't read the expression on his face. His eyes were like black stones.

'And did she answer you?'

'No, she was too upset. I shouldn't have asked it.'

A long pause, then he said: 'No, you shouldn't.'

His voice was cold, almost brutal. I felt as if I'd been invited in somewhere then had the door shut in my face.

'I must go and find Tabby,' I said.

I walked along the jetty, back to the grass, and turned along the river-bank path towards the cottage. I supposed he was still there on the landing stage, but I didn't look back.

# CHAPTER SEVENTEEN

When I got to the cottage, Mrs Todd had just arrived
to do her morning's cleaning. Any hope that Tabby might
have found refuge with her vanished in our first few
words. When I asked if she might be with Violet, Mrs
Todd sniffed and said she had no idea. I practically ran
to the village and, from Violet's bleary-eyed look, must
have roused her from her bed. She came to the door
with her bodice unbuttoned and the baby on her hip.

'I couldn't sleep for the storm. I can't abide lightning.'

She hadn't seen Tabby since the day before yesterday
and had no idea where she might be. I said if Tabby did
turn up, she should tell her to go to the cottage and
wait for me, but had no great hopes of it. I was beginning to think that Tabby might be trying to get back to
London. Its back streets and yards were the nearest thing
she had to a home, and the speed of our coach journey

295

had probably given her no idea of how far away it was, twenty-five miles or so. I imagined her small, resolute figure trudging the dusty road.

I walked up to the coach station at the Bear but nobody had seen a girl of her description. She certainly hadn't tried to board any of the London-bound coaches, but then she had no money. I tipped the head ostler and asked him to tell all the drivers to look out for her and, if they found her, bring her back. From his attitude, he thought it was an ordinary case of an absconding maid and I didn't waste time trying to persuade him otherwise.

On the way back, I stood for some time on the old bridge, looking down at the fast-flowing river. A dark bundle turning in the current set my heart thumping, but when it came nearer it turned out to be a mass of twigs and reeds. After that, I wasted an hour or two making inquiries around the village and outlying cottages. All I achieved were various promises to watch out for her and a false hope about a girl stranger seen on a footpath, who turned out to be a child visiting an aunt and nothing like Tabby.

A visit to the cottage produced nothing but well-tidied emptiness. If Tabby had come back, she'd have left some trace. The next hope was to go back to the hall, in case anybody had news of her now. I felt tired and weighed down with worry. The freshness of the air after the storm had been burned away as the sun rose higher, and everything felt hot and sticky again. But that was only part of the reason for my reluctance to go back to the hall. I didn't want to return because Robert Carmichael was there. His last words to me had been a reproach, and an undeserved one. Come just so far but no further, had been the message. He must have known that Lady Brinkburn was coming close to confiding in me and would surely have had enough influence with her to stop her if he'd really wanted. But then, she was stubborn in her way and had shown me the journal, even though he disapproved. He'd been unmistakeably relieved when I told him that she'd denied the story of the daemon lover. Then just one more question, and a perfectly justified one in the circumstances, had changed his attitude entirely. I'd been invited to share at least some of the family secrets, then  treated like a trespasser.

Still, no help for it. My responsibility to Tabby would have to come before the Brinkburns' problems. I drank some water, nibbled at a slice of yesterday's bread, then threw the rest for the ducks and went back through the woods to the road.

I'd chosen that way in preference to the river bank because there were two cottages on the way I hadn't covered in my search, but they were as useless as the rest and I began to regret my choice. The road was rutted and dusty, the sun beating down so that my head felt hot even under the straw bonnet. The only people I saw were four farm workers, taking a break from their work in the shade under the hedge, their scythes propped up beside them. Then, perhaps half a mile from the hall, the sound of galloping hooves came from along the road in front of me, and a horse and rider appeared.

It was too hot for galloping and the road was too hard, but that didn't seem to matter to this man. At first he and his horse were no more than shapes in a dust cloud. As he came nearer I could see that he was dressed like a gentleman in a black jacket and top hat, but he was riding like a jockey, swinging his whip hand to urge the horse on, though not actually hitting it. If he saw me, it didn't make any difference to his speed or direction, and I had to jump aside on to the grass verge as he went past. I recognised the horse as a blue roan I'd seen in the livery stables at the Bear, useful-looking but not accustomed to this pace and labouring hard. Then, in the one glance I had at his face, I recognised the rider, too. It was Stephen Brinkburn and he looked furious.

I waited for the dust to settle, then walked on slowly. Nobody had seen Stephen for ten days. He hadn't been at the hall the night before, so must have arrived while I was looking for Tabby. Lady Brinkburn had not said anything about expecting him. In normal circumstances, there'd have been nothing out of the way in the elder son rushing to comfort his bereaved mother, but normal circumstances didn't apply here. Besides, his visit must have been indecently short.

Whether or not he'd arrived in a bad temper, he was certainly leaving in one. That was the biggest puzzle of all. If he'd spoken to his mother, he must have received good news. She was no longer claiming that his conception was the result of a visit by somebody other than his father. Therefore he was what he'd always believed himself to be – legitimate successor to a title and a fortune. There'd be no embarrassing revelations in the House of Lords, society gossips would lose a good story and the fair Rosa would transfer her wavering affections back to her true knight. Even allowing for the death of a father who had not played a large part in his upbringing, Stephen Brinkburn should have been beaming like a man who'd just had all his birthdays come at once, not beating the dust out of the road as if he hated the world. That is, unless his mother had decided to change her story again. The possibility of that was at least a diversion from worrying about Tabby. Had Sophia understood the significance of what she was saying to me? I'd believed she had at the time, but a laudanum-hazed brain is a strange thing.

I'd thought yesterday that my work for the Brinkburn family had finished, but now it might be all to do again.

The maid who opened the front door to me looked hangdog, like a girl who'd had a scolding.

'Are you Dora?' I said.

'Yes, ma'am.'

It was a mutter with her eyes on the floor.

'It was unkind to tease poor Tabby,' I said. 'Still, I'm sorry about the ham. Has she come back?'

'No, ma'am.'

I was about to ask if Lady Brinkburn was receiving

visitors when Mr Whiteley came down the stairs, nearly tripping over in his hurry.

'Has your maid reappeared, Miss Lane?'

'No.'

'We've looked everywhere for her. I'm quite certain she's not on the estate.'

He looked scared of me, as if I'd hold him personally to blame. I asked him if he'd kindly send up to Lady Brinkburn and let her know I was back. He looked even more unhappy.

'Her ladyship is resting. Mr Carmichael said I was to ask you if you'd be kind enough to call back tomorrow, if convenient.'

It was another slam of the door, just in case I hadn't been deterred by the first one. The day before, Sophia had implored me to stay and protect her from whatever phantoms were haunting her dreams. Now she was treating me like an annoying and distant acquaintance. Dora was still standing by the front door, ready to open it again. I was practically being thrown off the premises. I stood my ground and looked Mr Whiteley in the eye.

'Mr Brinkburn has just passed me on the road,' I said, forgetting to give Stephen his new title. 'He seemed in a hurry.'

He gulped. Always, in his dealings with me, he must have it in mind that I knew he'd committed perjury. In my anger, I was prepared to use that shamelessly.

'Yes, I believe he was.'

'Was his mother expecting a visit? She said nothing about it to me.'

'I understand Mr Stephen's visit was unexpected.'

'And they quarrelled?' I said.

He couldn't bring himself to say so in words, only dropped his eyes and nodded. That confirmed what I'd expected from that glance at Stephen's face. I thought he'd wanted something from his mother and hadn't got it. In spite of what she'd said to me, she'd refused to confirm the legitimacy of his claim.

'Please give Lady Brinkburn my compliments and let her know that I shall come back tomorrow,' I said.

Then I released him from his misery by turning on my heel and walking out of the door. Anger took me halfway up the drive at a pace too fast for a hot day. I stopped to adjust my bonnet and, against my better judgement, looked back at the house, wondering if anybody was watching me from a window. If so, there was no sign of it. The serene red-brick façade framed by its close-cut lawn gave no hint of the suspicion and unhappiness inside. I looked at the place on the lawn where Sophia's eyes had been fixed the night before and an odd idea came to me. Suppose it had been a real man and not a laudanum vision after all. Could it be that Stephen had arrived before daylight and gone walking round the grounds of his old home, preparing for a crucial interview with his mother? I imagined him, staring up at her window in the half light, knowing that his whole future might depend on what she told him in

301

the morning. Then, in the morning, they'd quarrelled and nobody was going to tell me more than that.

For the rest of the afternoon I dragged myself round on my fruitless search for Tabby. I was becoming convinced that she was on her way back to London. First thing tomorrow I'd send a message to Abel Yard and ask Mrs Martley if she'd reappeared there. For now, I didn't even have the energy to lift a pen. I'd had precious little sleep the night before and had walked so many miles in the day that the seam of one shoe was bursting. I made some soup, dragged myself upstairs, undressed and went to bed.

From anxiety over Tabby and anger with Lady Brinkburn, I'd expected a restless night, but must have slept for eight hours or more, because when I woke up it was broad daylight and the birds were shouting their morning challenges to each other. I looked at my watch and found it was half past five, plenty of time to write my note and take it to the Bear to go by an early London stage. But it was stuffy in the cottage and the morning outside looked so clear and beautiful that I decided to give myself a few minutes by the river first. I changed from my nightgown into a chemise and petticoat and walked barefoot down the garden path to the bank. The cool river smell was all over the garden, early bees buzzing in the marigolds. The water was cold to my toes so I drew my feet up and sat on the bank, watching willow leaves eddying in the current. A kingfisher darted out of an alder tree, swift and bright as a rapier. My eyes followed its flight upstream. There was a rowing boat coming down.

My first thought was that it might be Robert Carmichael, coming to explain or apologise, and I prepared myself to be angry with him. But he was skilful with boats and would never have allowed one to proceed in such a disorderly way. It was drifting in the current like the willow leaves, sometimes coming straight on, at other times turning almost sideways. Nobody was rowing it. I thought it must have come unmoored from somewhere further upstream and stood up, looking for a pole or tree branch in case there was a chance of pulling it into the bank. There was nothing suitable to hand, so I ran back to the porch where I'd noticed an old clothes prop leaning. By the time I got back with it, the boat was almost level with the garden, but on the far side of the river. It headed for the opposite bank, then was caught by a counter-current that twitched it back midstream and carried it on with more speed than before. In that moment, I saw that it wasn't empty. Somebody was lying in it, white face upturned, body swathed in some dark fabric.

I only had one glance before the river carried it on, but was certain that the face was female. The first fear about Tabby and the river came rushing back. Instantly, I was sure she was the figure in the boat, unconscious or dead.

I slid down the bank into the river, taking the clothes

prop with me, and waded out waist-deep, petticoats floating out round me, toes sinking into the mud. I flailed after the boat for a few yards, but it was useless. There was no hope of catching it. Mud rose to my knees, flinging me forward into the water, head and shoulders under. I managed to keep hold of the clothes post and lever myself upright, then leaned on it to thrash my way back to the bank. Once clear of the water I lay on the grass, gasping and sobbing, until it occurred to me that the figure in the boat might have been only unconscious, not dead. I didn't truly believe that, but while even a slim hope remained I had to get help for her. I ran inside, crammed my wet feet into shoes, grabbed a cloak from the back of the door to cover myself then ran towards the road, hoping against hope to meet somebody with a horse or cart.

The path through the woods felt endless, with brambles like snares that seemed to have grown overnight. When I got to the road, there wasn't a person or a cart in sight. I remembered then that it was Sunday, with no farm workers out early. It was no use wasting time asking for help around the cottages. My only hope was that the boat might come to a stop at one of the piers of the new railway bridge, or at least that there'd be somebody there with a boat. I hitched up my cloak and ran, welcoming the stitch in my side as a distraction from the pain of my conscience. If I hadn't interfered, trying to save Tabby from her precarious style of life, she'd have still been sleeping, happy and louse-ridden, under a pile of old sacks in Abel Yard.

When at last I came to the bridge there were workmen with a pony cart and handcart, on some railway task so vital that it had brought them in on a Sunday. But they weren't working now. Some of them were on a substantial wooden jetty stretching a long way into the river, others clustered at the landward end. They were all looking in the same direction. I ran up to them and asked what was happening.

'Woman drowned,' one of them said.

I ran on to the jetty. The men there had their backs to me so I couldn't see what they were looking at. I touched the shoulder of the one nearest and he turned.

'Who's drowned?'

'She's not drowned,' he said. But my surge of relief didn't last for more than a heartbeat, because he went on: 'She's in a boat, stone dry. But she's dead.'

'I think I know who she is. May I see her?'

The men made way for me. They'd moored the rowing boat to one of the posts on the jetty. Both the post and the rope, designed for barges carrying bricks, were too large for such a small vessel. A long boat-hook swathed in waterweed was spreading a damp stain over the dry planks. They must have used it to catch the boat as it went past. For a moment I couldn't look past that stain, knowing what I'd see when I did.

I made myself look at the boat. Dark fabric, entirely

dry as the man had said. It seemed to be a cloak wrapped round her. They'd drawn it up over her face.

'Please let me see her face,' I said.

One of the men kneeled down on the jetty and moved it gently aside. The pale face was as tranquil as a wax mask, framed in thick swathes of hair that were only a little disordered. Hair that had been well tended for a lifetime, lightly streaked with grey.

'You all right, miss?'

'Your mother, is she?'

Rough murmurs of male sympathy round me, a hand on my shoulder.

'No, she's not my mother. It's not who I thought. She . . .' I hesitated, still not quite believing it. 'She's Lady Brinkburn.'

# CHAPTER EIGHTEEN

The first relief that I hadn't, after all, brought Tabby to her death gave way to shock and incomprehension. Lady Brinkburn's eyes were closed. She might have been asleep in her white bed where I'd last seen her. There were no obvious signs of violence. I found I was trembling and let the workmen guide me to a pile of timber and sit me down. They were kindly men, but brought in by the railway company and not local, so when I asked if somebody could take a message to Brinkburn Hall, I had to explain where it was. One of the younger ones volunteered to run there. I'd have preferred to break the news myself, but had no strength left and was realizing what a sight I must look, feet stockingless inside my shoes, hair wet and muddy, nothing but underwear beneath the cloak. I told the young workman to ask for Mr Carmichael.

'Tell him that there's been a serious accident and ask him to come to the railway bridge at once. Say the message is from Miss Lane.'

He ran off. One of the men who seemed to be their foreman folded the cloak back over Lady Brinkburn's face.

'Should we take her out of the boat, miss?'

I said I thought we should leave her as she was until somebody came. Two of the workmen stayed by the boat, while the rest of us walked slowly back to the bank. I asked the foreman the time and found it was still only seven in the morning. Back at the hall, they might not even know that Lady Brinkburn was missing. Her absence wouldn't be discovered until Betty brought in her coffee, or even later than that if the maid decided not to disturb her.

It seemed a long time before anyone came. The workmen drew apart and formed little groups, first talking in hushed voices and then more normally, lighting pipes. One of them laughed at something and was shushed by the others. I sensed they'd had enough of this drama and wanted to get back to their work.

At last a horse and rider appeared, in a cloud of dust. They reined up sharply and Robert Carmichael practically threw himself out of the saddle.

'Sophia's missing,' he said to me.

I looked towards the boat. He must have seen from my face, because he didn't say anything else, only strode along the landing stage to the rowing boat. The foreman and I followed. He kneeled down, drew back the cloak and took a long look. Then he covered her again and sat back on his heels, hands to his face, drawing long breaths. When he looked up at us at last, his expression was quite blank.

'We could have her taken to the main road at the old bridge, sir,' the foreman suggested.

Robert Carmichael stood up, visibly taking on responsibility.

'If you would, yes. Who found her?'

'Two of my men were out on the jetty and saw the boat. They managed to hook it in. They thought she was just asleep at first.'

Robert looked at me. I explained about seeing the boat going past on the current and trying to catch up with it. I said nothing about thinking it was Tabby. He listened to me, but only nodded.

Robert and the foreman lifted her out of the boat, on to a wide plank that some of the other men had brought. Her body wasn't quite bone dry, as the workman had said. When they lifted her, heavy drops of water fell on to the landing stage from her cloak. There were a few inches of water in the bottom of the boat. I remembered looking down at it moored to the landing stage at the hall, and Robert saying it would need baling out. The water must have soaked into her cloak while she was lying there. Almost against my will, my mind started moving again. *They thought she was asleep at first,* the foreman had said. A deep laudanum sleep.

Might she have taken an overdose, wandered down to her boat in the night or early morning and fallen into that last sleep, so deeply that she didn't notice the water seeping into her clothes? Had the boat somehow become unmoored by accident? Two days after I first met her, when we were on no more than conventionally polite terms, she'd talked about her boat. *I sometimes lie on cushions in my little boat moored to the landing stage, look up at the sky and imagine I'm floating along like the Lady of Shalott.* There was another possibility. If, in her fear and confusion, she'd decided to end her own life, it would have been typical of the romantic and dramatic streak in her nature to do it that way. I checked that nobody was looking at me, then felt under the seat and in the prow of the boat, anywhere that a bottle might have rolled. Nothing.

Back on land, they'd loaded her into the pony cart. One of the men drove, with the foreman, Robert Carmichael and myself forming a makeshift cortège on foot behind. Robert led his horse and said nothing to either of us. A workman must have gone on to the inn by the old bridge to warn them, because as soon as we got there the innkeeper came out and directed his ostlers to carry her into an outbuilding on the far side of the yard. I think from its long chimney and the lingering smell of malt that it might have been their brewhouse, but I'm sure they intended no disrespect. The innkeeper was kind, too, and offered me the use of one of his private parlours, '... if you'd like somewhere quiet to wait, miss?' I accepted gratefully because my legs were still shaking but thought: 'Wait for what?' They all assumed, from my shock at the sight of her body, that I was something to do with the family. Robert Carmichael disappeared into another room. I knew there would be a host of formalities. The coroner would have to be informed and there'd be formal identification and the opening of an inquest before her body could be carried home.

The parlour where I sat had a window giving on to the stable yard. The curtains were drawn across and I was too dispirited to open them, but the sound of hooves and wheels gave me an idea of what was happening. A rider went out of the yard at a canter, with shouted instruction from the innkeeper to ask for a constable. Then a stagecoach ground in over the cobbles, and driver and ostlers talked about it while they were changing the horses. I caught a word or two over the sounds of stamping hooves and jingling harness.

'. . . no blood, no nothing, just as if she'd gone to sleep . . .'

'Perhaps her heart gave out.'

'In a boat on her own, a lady like her?'

'No telling what they'll do.'

The coach rolled on its way towards London. By lunchtime, Lady Brinkburn's death would be the talk of the capital. Amos Legge would probably be one of the first to hear about it. I wished he were here.

\* \* \*

311

Later there was a knock at the door and Robert Carmichael walked in. He'd made an attempt to brush the dust of riding from his clothes and tidy his hair, and seemed reasonably self-possessed at first glance, but taut as a piano wire. There was no point in conventional sympathy. I put to him something that had occurred to me while I was waiting.

'Did you find her dead and put her in the boat?' I said.

'Why should I do that?'

There was no surprise or anger in his voice, only a faint puzzlement.

'As a last romantic gesture, perhaps. That's how she saw herself all her life, isn't it? The victim in her tower, the lady under a curse. Perhaps you thought a last journey down the river in her boat was a fitting end to the story.'

A flash of anger in his eyes.

'A fitting end – is that what you think it is? Lying there in a brewhouse, waiting for a cart to take her to the public mortuary and a jury of tradesmen and shop-keepers to view her body. Is that what anybody who loved her would have wanted?'

His voice dropped so low on the last sentence that I had to strain to hear it. The shock and grief seemed genuine, and yet I suspected he'd been trying to shape my view of events ever since he'd listened to my conversation with Lady Brinkburn from the top of the steps in the library. A man who knows secrets is powerful. Did he enjoy that power, and could his protectiveness

312

of Sophia hide something darker? I still didn't know the identity of the man who'd rowed to our cottage by night, with a message calculated to scare her, had I chosen to deliver it. He wouldn't be the first man who'd tried to keep a woman afraid so that he could act as her protector.

'So was it laudanum?' I said.

'It makes no sense. There wasn't enough to kill her. I swear to you, yesterday afternoon there was no more than a quarter of a glassful in the bottle. I know because I made her show me.'

Made her? What gave him that right? I was going to say that a quarter of a glassful sounded a large dose, until I remembered that I'd seen her drink three times that amount and still not sleep through the night.

'Could she have got more from elsewhere?'

'It's delivered from the chemist shop in town. Another delivery was due tomorrow. She was worried about running out. I'm convinced that was all she had.'

'Might she have sent Betty to town for some?'

'Betty wouldn't have done it without telling me.'

'Did she have to ask your permission to do errands for her mistress?'

'It wasn't a normal state of affairs. Betty was as worried as I was.'

'When did you know Sophia was missing?'

'When Betty took her coffee up this morning. Lovelace was there on his own, whining for his mistress.'

'When did you last see her?'

'I told you, yesterday afternoon.'

He hadn't told me, but I let that pass.

'How was she then?'

'Distraught. Keyed-up.'

'Was that because of the argument with Stephen?'

He said sharply, 'How did you know about that? She couldn't have told you.'

'No, because you kept me from seeing her yesterday. Why was that?'

'It was her idea.'

'I don't believe you.'

We stared at each other.

'Miss Lane, what have I done to make you so angry with me?' he said.

His voice was quiet and puzzled, as if he really couldn't see.

'Don't people usually become angry when they're lied to? You've been concealing things all along, and you're still doing it now.'

'Do you think I enjoy that? If they were only my secrets, all the world could have them and welcome. But they're not.'

I was tempted to admit the truth, that I was as angry with myself as with him. Together, we'd failed to protect her. But that would come too close to giving sympathy, or even asking for it.

'I suppose there will have to be some story for the inquest,' I said, deliberately harsh. 'Have you sent a message to Mr Lomax yet? He'll have to coach Mr Whiteley in his part like last time. Or will you be taking on the role?'

He made a surprised movement, then looked away.

'So you did know about that,' I said.

He didn't reply, just stood there looking down at the floor. When he spoke again, it was with a question of his own.

'Even if you don't trust me, would you do something for me, if I asked you?'

'What?'

It was an ungracious response, but I thought he was trying to lead me into another swamp of secrecy.

'Would you go to the hall and tell Whiteley what's happened?'

He must have seen the surprise on my face, for he explained:

'I have to stay here. I want to have her brought home, if they'll let me. And I must send messages to Stephen and Miles the fastest way I can find. I don't want them to hear this from anybody else.'

I didn't tell him that it was probably too late for that anyway. It struck me that he was talking more like a senior member of the family than their librarian, and I wondered how Miles and Stephen would react to that.

'All the staff knew when I left was that there'd been an accident. I promised poor Whiteley I'd send news to him as soon as I found out what had happened,' he said. 'He'll have to break the news to the others. Please ask him to tell Betty alone, before the rest. She was devoted to Sophia. Then I'd be grateful if you'd look through Sophia's rooms and see if she left a note of any kind.

315

The coroner is sure to want to know that, don't you think?'

The more he talked, the more surprised I felt. I'd accused him outright of trying to conceal things, but here he was giving me free range of the house and its staff before he had the opportunity to talk to any of them. Was he trying to prove to me that he had nothing to hide? If so, he was playing a dangerous game.

'If you really want me to, yes, I'll do it,' I said.

'Thank you.'

But his face was grim.

'What makes you think she may have left a note?' I said.

'I don't think she left a note, but if you look for it, nobody can say I found one and destroyed it, can they?'

He looked at me as if waiting for an answer. I didn't give him one.

Another knock on the door, then the innkeeper's voice.

'Mr Carmichael – the constable's here, sir.'

'I'll get the landlord to arrange a gig to take you to the hall,' Carmichael said to me as he went out. 'Thank you, Miss Lane.'

I'd have preferred to walk, but not in my dishevelled state, so I accepted the offer of the gig and got the driver to call at the cottage, where I changed my clothes and tidied myself. When we arrived at the hall drive, Mr Whiteley was waiting by the gate. He looked surprised and apprehensive as I got down. I told him that Mr Carmichael had sent me, and delivered the news in the most humane way I could manage. Big, slow tears ran down his face. He let them fall unashamedly, like a weary child.

'So it's come to that,' he kept saying. 'It's come to that.'

I didn't ask him what he meant, thinking it would be inhumane to question him so soon after the news. I told the gig to drive away so that we could walk together, allowing him a chance to recover himself before facing the rest of the staff. To my surprise, he wanted to talk.

'Him dead and now her dead. You spend all your life trying to hold things together, then it all comes apart in a few days.'

I thought the Brinkburn family had been coming apart for much longer than a few days, but only said that three deaths in such a short time were hard for any household to take. He stared at me through his tears.

'Three?'

'There was Simon Handy too.'

'Him!' His tone swept Handy aside. 'He never belonged here. You'd think it was him coming brought all the bad luck.'

We walked in silence for a while. He took out a big handkerchief and mopped his face dry.

'Was it her heart gave out?'

I'd told him only that Lady Brinkburn had been found dead in her boat near the railway bridge.

'I don't know. Did she suffer from heart trouble?'

317

'Not that I knew of, but what else would it be? If she wanted the boat out, she could have told me and I'd have got one of the boys to row her as usual, no matter how early in the morning it was. She had no call to do it herself.'

Again, the grief and puzzlement seemed genuine, and yet I'd heard the man lie. Not very skilfully, it was true, but I knew he could do well enough when coached. But then, who would have had the opportunity to coach him this time?

Since he wanted to talk, as many people do in shock, I asked when he'd last seen Lady Brinkburn.

'I saw her walking on the lawn yesterday evening with her little dog, like she usually did.'

'Not after that?'

'No.'

'Did you hear anything out of the way last night or in the early hours of the morning?'

A grim set came to his mouth and he looked sideways at me.

'No. I locked up last night like I usually do, and after that I didn't see or hear anything out of the way. Don't look at me like that. I'm not lying, not now. I've done with all that, and I don't care what anybody says. I don't care about my position either, now she's gone. I'll see things as right as I can for her sake, then I'll give notice and go to my pigs.'

'Pigs?'

'I own a cottage and three acres from money I've put by over the years. Nothing grand, nothing I didn't work

318

for and earn above-board. I like pigs. They don't ask anything from you beyond what's reasonable.'

We were nearly at the front door. I could see faces peering out from the window curtains, then drawing back. Staff discipline was already breaking down. He was on the defensive now, so there was nothing to lose.

'Just one thing,' I said. 'Who besides you has keys to the outside doors?'

He sighed. 'Mrs Bream has a key to the kitchen door, in case the scullery maid needs to take rubbish out early. That's all.'

'None of the family?'

'Certainly, the family has keys. Her ladyship has one . . . had one . . . in case she takes a fancy to go out early.'

'And Mr Stephen and Mr Miles?'

'Of course. If they happened to come down from London late one night, they'd want to get in without waking everybody up.'

'Did that happen often?'

'Not lately, no.'

We went up the steps. He paused with his hand on the door, as if reluctant to go inside.

'Mr Carmichael said to ask you to break the news to Betty first,' I said.

Another sigh from him. I guessed he was fearful of women's tears.

'Would you like me to do that?'

'If you would, miss. It might come better from a lady.'

'Perhaps you'd ask her to come out here,' I said, pointing to a garden bench in the shade at the side of the house. 'I can tell her while you're talking to the others inside.'

'Very well, miss.'

He squared his shoulders, pushed the door open and walked in. I waited on the bench, looking across the lawn to the line of yellow irises fringing the river.

After a minute or two, Betty came along the gravel path. She was pale and already crying. I patted the bench. She hesitated and sat down on the edge of it, as if she had no right to be there.

'I'm afraid it's true,' I said. 'Lady Brinkburn is dead.'

She put her hands over her eyes and started rocking to and fro on the edge of the seat. When I moved closer and slid my arm round her shoulder, she leaned against me and sobbed without reserve. We stayed like that for some time before she pushed herself upright.

'I'm sorry, ma'am.'

'I'm the one who's sorry, to have to tell you. Do you want me to call Mrs Bream?'

I thought the housekeeper might be better at comforting her than a near-stranger like me, but she shook her head.

'Her ladyship liked you.'

I was surprised.

'She said so?'

'After that first time when you came to tea. She said you were the sort of woman she could trust.'

It hit me hard. At that meeting, Lady Brinkburn couldn't have trusted me in the least. I was a hired investigator, sent to discredit her.

'Did she drown, ma'am?'

Betty asked the question in a small voice, looking down at the gravel. I could have turned the question back on her as I'd done with Whiteley, but decided against it.

'No. It isn't certain yet, but it looks as if she'd drunk too much laudanum.'

'Oh.'

She sounded sad, but not surprised.

'You knew she was in the habit of taking laudanum?'

'To help her sleep, yes.'

'You were concerned she was taking too much?'

'Yes, we were, ma'am.'

'We?'

'Mr Carmichael and me.'

She seemed open and trusting. The garden and house were silent, as if the shock had stunned them. Distant Sunday bells sounded from across the river. I thought about it for a while, then decided to repay trust for trust, hoping I wasn't making a mistake.

'Did Mr Whiteley tell you anything about where we found Lady Brinkburn?'

'No. Only that there'd been an accident and she was dead.'

'She was in her boat, on her own. It had drifted down the river. Nobody seems to know how it happened. Do you mind if I ask you some questions?'

Her mouth had dropped open in surprise. She closed it, then nodded permission. I knew I was taking advantage, but the questions would have to come at some time.

'Did she say anything to you about intending to go out in the boat?'

'No.'

'What time did you last see her?'

'Half past seven yesterday evening, or thereabouts, when I went up to collect her supper things. She said she wouldn't be needing me after that.'

'Was that unusual?'

'No, ma'am. Quite often, when she didn't need me in the evenings, she'd let me know so I didn't have to listen for the bell all the time. She was always kind about things like that. Always so kind.'

The tears started again. I put my hand over hers and waited until she was calmer.

'Were you there when she drank her laudanum last night?'

'No. She usually took it just as she was getting into bed.'

'When you saw her yesterday evening, did there seem anything at all unusual about her manner?'

She thought about it.

'She was sad. Sadder than usual, and mortally tired.'

'Did she seem nervous or frightened?'

'Her poor nerves were bad. She was always jumping at loud noises, if a door slammed or anything. I always tried to move quietly round her, not drop things.'

'Worse than usual yesterday evening?'

'I think so, yes. And the storm had upset her nerves.'

'Did she say anything about her son's visit?'

'No, ma'am.'

I didn't think Betty was concealing anything. If Lady Brinkburn had quarrelled with her son, it would hardly be something she'd discuss with her maid.

'Did she say anything about what she intended to do with the rest of the evening after you left her?' I said.

'No. I supposed it would be as usual.'

'What was usual?'

'About eight o'clock or half past, while the servants were having their supper, she'd take Lovelace out for a walk out on the lawn before they settled for the night.'

'Did she do that last night?'

'Yes, ma'am. I didn't see her, but Ruth had to go outside for something, and she did.'

'Was Lady Brinkburn alone?'

'Yes.'

'Did she always walk the dog on her own in the evening?'

'No. Sometimes Mr Carmichael was with her.'

She blushed but looked me in the eye, as if challenging me to say something. I guessed that she'd had to defend her mistress against gossip among the other servants. It would be cruel to embarrass her any more on that score.

'Did you notice her writing anything yesterday?'

'I didn't see her writing, but she had been.'

'How do you know that?'

'She had ink on the inside of her finger, where you get it when you hold a pen.' She held up her fingers to demonstrate. 'I noticed because sometimes when she gets ink on her fingers she asks me to bring a bowl of warm water and a pumice stone to get it off. She didn't last night.'

'Did she give you a letter to post or deliver to anyone?'

'No, ma'am.'

I still didn't believe I'd find a suicide note, but this was a trail that had to be followed.

'Betty, Mr Carmichael has asked me to go through Lady Brinkburn's rooms and see if she left a note. If you can bear it, I'd be very grateful if you'd come with me.'

She bit her lip and nodded. We went together into the hall. The maid Dora was polishing the stair rail. Her eyes were pink and the edge of her white apron crumpled as if she'd been using it to mop up her tears, but the stare she gave us was greedy for more news. We went past her and up the stairs by the library. Sunlight was streaming through the windows of Sophia's sitting room, on to a pot of auriculas on a table. Instinctively, Betty ran to the curtains to shut out the light.

'Leave them for a while,' I said. 'Is there anything here that looks different from when you saw it yesterday evening?'

She looked round and shook her head. To me, it was almost exactly as it had been when I'd had supper with Sophia. Even a novel on the window seat was splayed open, cover uppermost, just as I remembered.

I picked it up, just in case there should be a note underneath it. Nothing. She'd been in the middle of a chapter.

Betty and I made a fairly systematic search, though I could see her heart wasn't in it. I opened the drawers of the writing desk and found nothing but blank paper, wafers for sealing letters, a half-used stick of wax. After a while we went through to her bedroom. A green afternoon dress with ribbon trim was flung over the back of a chair. Automatically, Betty gathered it up and shook out the creases in the skirt.

'Is that what she was wearing when you last saw her?'

'Yes.'

The coverlet on the bed was smooth and unrumpled.

'Would anybody have come in to make the bed this morning?' I said.

'No, I always made her bed myself. I knew just how she liked it.'

So the bed hadn't been slept in.

'Where did she keep her nightdress?'

'In here.'

She opened the top drawer in a chest of drawers, on to lavender-scented emptiness.

'It's gone.'

I thought I'd caught a glimpse of white lace under the cloak when they'd moved Sophia out of the boat. So she'd taken off her dress, changed into her night-dress and drunk her dose of laudanum. At least that much made sense. The empty bottle was there on a

325

cabinet by her bed, the glass beside it. Why, having drunk it, didn't she get into bed? I turned back the coverlet and felt under the pillows, the bolster and the sides of the mattress for a note. Nothing, of course.

Betty was crying again, still holding the green dress in her arms. Before we left, she insisted on hanging it up in the wardrobe.

We were walking out of the bedroom into the sitting room when a thought came to me. I turned back into the bedroom.

'Betty, would you come here and look at the bottle, please.'

She came, looking puzzled. An ordinary empty dark green glass bottle of the kind you find by the dozen in any chemist's shop. I'd seen it in Sophia's hand the night before last. Only I hadn't.

'Does anything strike you about the shape of it?' I said.

She peered at it, then made a shape with her hands. 'It's got . . .'

The shape she was making was of a bottle with shoulders.

'And what was it usually like?'

'Straight down, like this.'

This time the shape was of a smoothly tapering bottle.

'What were they usually like, her bottles?'

'The smooth ones.'

'Not like this one, then?'

'No, ma'am.'

'Can you recall ever seeing her take laudanum from a bottle this shape?'

'No, ma'am.'

'Have you any idea at all where this bottle might have come from?'

'No.'

She looked both puzzled and scared. I told her to leave the bottle and glass as they were, and asked whether she could lock the bedroom. She nodded, went back to the sitting room and took the key from the drawer of a table. Once the door was locked, she insisted on drawing the heavy curtains of the sitting room to shut out the sunlight before we left. We went back down the stairs that led to the library door.

'What shall I do now?' Betty said.

I felt like telling her I had no idea. I supposed there were a dozen places I should be looking, hundreds of questions I should be asking, but my mind was a blank.

'I think you'd better ask Mrs Bream,' I said. 'I'll wait in the library for a while.'

Wait for Robert Carmichael to come back. I knew that most of those questions should concern him.

It was a relief to walk into the high, sunlit library, not so full of her intimate presence as the rooms upstairs. For a while, I simply walked from bay to bay, among the ranks of tooled leather spines and gold lettering, books nobody had read for generations, old sermons, county records, European genealogies with quaint crests. My wanderings took me towards the table where I'd read her journal, thinking of the secret that she'd come close to telling me and now never would. Sunlight was coming through the window under the half drawn-down blind, just as it had been on the morning when I'd last sat there. A leather-bound volume was lying closed on the reading desk. At first I thought I was imagining it because I'd been thinking about her journal. But it was the journal itself. I was sure Robert Carmichael had put it back on the shelf after I'd read it. Who had taken it out again?

I sat down at the desk, opened the journal at random and found myself looking at the Antwerp entry with its picture of the boy wrapped in a blanket, holding the cup of tea she'd brewed for him. The young Handy. Now that I knew his name and her opinion of him, it seemed that there was something shrewd and knowing about the eyes, too old for his round boyish face. I read on, hoping to find something I'd missed on first reading that might give a clue to the story she'd almost told me. There was nothing new, except my sense of loss for the observant and talented young woman she'd once been and how all that had ended.

Her account of the storm by Lake Como was almost unbearable now, reminding me of the night I'd spent with her. I turned the page, steeling myself for that diagonal scrawl across the two pages: *This morning Lord Brinkburn has told me something terrible, terrible.* It was still there, but it wasn't alone any more. Both pages, above it and below it, were filled by neat and level lines of writing, in what was unmistakeably her hand. At first I wondered if I'd made some ridiculous mistake and the writing had been there all the time. Then, at the start of the line in the top left-hand corner I saw yesterday's date. I read on.

*I'm going to write it now at last. I feel time is running out. The storm last night was a sign, I think, like the first one. I am not sure who will read this, or whether anybody will read it, but I'll write it and fate will have to decide. I'm too tired to decide things myself any more. I've had to make too many decisions that nobody should be asked to make. Here's what happened. My husband really was away that night. There was nothing new in that. Time and time again on our tour, he'd spent nights away from me. At first he'd make excuses about meeting old friends and suchlike and I'd believe them, or at least try to believe them. He always took the boy Handy with him. After a while, I'd catch the boy looking at me sidelong and grinning, as if he knew something I didn't. Then my husband would make sudden changes of plan – staying in some place days longer than expected or hurrying us on to the next.*

*I tried to enjoy the travelling and my sketching and not think about him. I succeeded for much of the time, but it was almost as if it* made him angry to see me in anything like contentment. He took to dressing very carefully and ostentatiously before these nights away, as if to make clear that whatever was happening elsewhere was more important than his life with me. I began to ask questions. He never answered them. Once, when I became angry and demanded an answer, he slapped my face and said it was no business of mine. I thought it might be better when we got to Lake Como and established ourselves in the villa, but it was worse. He was away several nights a week and often did not come back till the afternoon.

That morning after the storm, I was determined to have it out with him. Perhaps the electricity had stirred up my brain. I woke up early in the morning, just as it was getting light. It seemed as if the storm had drained all the beauty out of things. The lake was a dull pewter colour, the pine trees without the sun on them were greenish-brown, the colour of moss in winter. It came to me suddenly that, if I didn't challenge him, my whole life would be like that, without warmth or colour. That gave me a kind of desperate courage. He came back earlier than he usually did after those nights away, about ten o'clock in the morning. I heard the wheels of his coach on the cobbles. Then his voice yelling for the groom to come and take the horses.

*He sounded to be in a bad temper. Somehow,*
*that made it easier to keep to my resolution. I*
*didn't care if he hit me again. Even pain would*
*be better than nothingness.*

That brought us to the bottom of the double page. I looked at the neat lines of writing, with the entry from twenty-three years ago slashing across the paper like a brand on an animal's smooth hide. I turned the page, holding my breath in case there was no more, but the neat writing went on down the page that had been blank when I last read the journal.

*I knew he'd come to me straight away in my*
*tower. Although he left me alone so often and*
*paid me little attention when we were together,*
*he'd always come to see me when he returned,*
*much in the way a man might check that his*
*horse or hound hadn't run away. I waited for*
*him in my sitting room, in a chair by the*
*window. As soon as he came through the door I*
*said to him, quite coolly, I believe: 'I wonder*
*why you took the trouble to marry me, since*
*you seem to prefer anybody's company to mine.'*
*He closed the door and stood there looking at*
*me for a long time, with a strange smile on his*
*face. I think even at that hour in the morning he*
*had taken drink, and when he spoke at last, his*
*voice was slurred. Clear enough though for me*

to hear what he said, although at first I simply couldn't understand it. 'Oh, but I haven't married you, my dear,' he said. I think I accused him of being drunk, upbraided him for saying such a wicked and monstrous thing, even in jest. He went on smiling. 'I assure you, I'm not jesting,' he said. He went to the door, opened it and yelled for Handy. The wretched boy was never far away from him and appeared in seconds. C told him to go to his dressing room and bring his black leather portfolio.

While he was away I sat frozen, unable to move so much as a finger. C straddled the arm of a sofa and lit a cigarillo. Handy brought back the portfolio. C untied it, sorted through it and gave Handy a piece of paper to bring across the room to me. It was a record from a church in. Northumberland of C's marriage to one Natalie Stevens, dated nine years before. I write down this fact calmly now. Even after this gap of time I cannot begin to describe the sensations of anger, bewilderment, incredulity that made me more like a mad thing than a rational being. Two things, though, I must bring myself to write down. The creature I had thought of as my husband informed me that he had a son by this woman, then eight years old. Also, in reply I suppose to some sobbed-out question from me as to how he could do this thing, he said: 'She is a

*very beautiful woman, much more so than you*
*are, my dear.' The Handy creature had been in*
*the room all the time this was going on.*
*Cornelius asked him, asked a malevolent child:*
*'Is not your other mistress much more beautiful?'*
*And Handy looked into my face, laughed, and*
*said, 'Yes.'*

There the writing ended, halfway down the page. It
had been a warm day when I came into the library, but
I was shivering as if it had become midwinter. Like
Sophia, I couldn't take in what I was being told.

'Is she telling the truth now?'

I must have said it aloud because a voice from behind
me said, 'The truth about what?'

Just as when I first read the journal, Robert Carmichael
had come quietly into the library while I was too
absorbed to notice and was standing a few steps behind
my chair.

# CHAPTER NINETEEN

After that first glance behind me, I didn't look at him. When I turned back the page to show him the start of what she'd written, I had to force my hand to stop trembling. He must have read quickly, because within seconds his arm came over my shoulder and turned the page onwards. The sleeve of his jacket brushed my cheek. I gave him enough time to read to the end.

'Did you know she'd written this?' I said.

I still didn't turn and look at him, not trusting my face to hide the horror I felt.

'No.'

'Had she talked about it to you?'

'Yes.'

'So is it true?'

'Yes, it's true.'

The reply came without hesitation, his voice heavy.

'Why didn't she denounce him? He'd committed bigamy. She could have had him sent to prison.'

I thought he wasn't going to answer, but he was moving round the desk to face me.

'Is that what you'd have done, Miss Lane?'

'Yes. Isn't it what any woman would have done?'

He shook his head.

'Imagine her circumstances. She'd been living with him since the wedding as his wife, with all that implies. Yes, if she could have proved the earlier marriage, he'd have spent a long time in prison, but would that have helped her?'

'She'd have had her freedom.'

'*Freedom*. It's a grand word, isn't it, Miss Lane? A dog dying in the gutter has all the freedom in the world to get up and walk away, if only he could.'

'She was an intelligent woman. Surely she had friends and family?'

'Her father was dead and she'd never been close to her mother. Besides, what could they have done? She was neither wife nor maid, and nothing could change that.'

I met his look, willing myself not to blush.

'Are you telling me her reputation was gone, through no fault of her own?'

'As the world sees it, yes.'

'Then the world's a donkey. Surely, when the truth was known, anybody whose opinion mattered would pity her.'

'Pity, yes. If you'll permit me, you are probably about the same age now as Sophia was then. Would you want to spend the rest of your life being pitied?'

His way of bringing the conversation back to me was disconcerting. I didn't want to put myself in her place, but there was an intensity about his voice and his look that was forcing me to do it.

'There's something else,' he said. 'Forgive me if I'm being indelicate, but for her sake you should know it. By the morning he told her about the marriage, Sophia had good reason to know that she was in a certain condition.'

'She was expecting his baby?'

'Yes.'

'Stephen?'

'Yes.'

I dropped my eyes again, not so much from delicacy as from pain for her.

'You see, when he put his terms to her, she really had no alternative,' he said.

'Terms?'

'The terms on which she lived for the rest of her life. She should have this house, a comfortable income, freedom to travel if she wanted. He and she would remain married in the eyes of the world but live separate lives.'

'As long as she didn't denounce him as a bigamist?'

'Yes.'

'So she accepted?'

'As I explained, she really had no choice,' he said.

I wanted to scream out that, yes, of course she had a choice – child or no child; that she'd have been better begging for their bread, singing in the street for their supper, than living with the bargain she'd made. If he was waiting for me to agree with him, he'd be waiting a long time. Perhaps he realised that.

'In a sense, she won in the end,' he said.

'In what sense? Living with her books and her auriculas?'

I felt like adding . . . *and with you*, but stopped myself in time.

'She married him after all,' he said. 'A year later, Natalie Stevens died. She and Lord Brinkburn had been living in Rome. He came back here and showed Sophia the death certificate. It said she'd died of a fever. Then he took Sophia off to Germany and married her. It was a perfectly legal marriage this time. Unlike his elder brother, Miles is his father's legitimate son.'

'He was protecting himself when he married Sophia,' I said. 'Once he'd made her his legal wife, she couldn't be asked to give evidence against him in court, so he was safe from a bigamy charge.'

'Yes, and of course he had her money. That was probably what weighed most with him. I think that occurred to Sophia later. At the time, she even hoped he'd had a change of heart and regretted what he'd done to her.'

'Why did Lord Brinkburn take such a risk in the first place? He must have known he was risking prison. Or was the man always mad?'

337

'No, not as the world sees it. But almost insanely arrogant. Believe me, I've thought about the man's character a lot. I wanted to understand how he could cause such harm. I decided that he believed anything he wanted must happen, more or less as a natural law. He wanted Natalie Stevens, so he married her. He might even have acknowledged the marriage sooner or later. I'm sure society would have said he'd married beneath him, but he never cared much for public opinion. That changed when he learned of his father's debts. The almost worthless state of the inheritance must have come as a shock to him. A reasonable man might have sold off the estate and lived economically with the woman he'd married. But that wasn't in Brinkburn's nature. He hadn't told his friends about the marriage, so when they pointed him in the direction of a rich bride to solve his problems, he seized on that, as he'd always seized on anything else he wanted. Perhaps that long honeymoon tour gave him an opportunity to see what a tangle he'd made for himself.'

He spoke without a pause, not looking at me for understanding or approval, as if Lord Brinkburn's character had been a life study with him.

'Did you discuss this with Sophia?'

'Yes.'

His reply was simple and dignified. Perhaps I was being unfair to him, almost blaming him for the wrong another man had done. And yet there'd been too many evasions for me to trust him.

'So is that where this wretched business started?' I said. 'She knows Miles is legitimate, as the world sees it, but Stephen isn't. So she thought Miles should inherit, but couldn't bear to tell the real story.'

'Yes.'

'In any case, according to her account, neither of them's the heir. If his son by the other woman has survived, then he must inherit. Didn't she see that?'

'Condemn her for not thinking clearly, if you must. God knows, I tried to talk her out of doing anything about it.'

'You thought she should keep quiet and let Stephen inherit,' I said.

'Yes.'

'Of course she loves Miles but doesn't love Stephen.'

'She told you that?'

He seemed surprised.

'Yes. She said he'd accused her of driving his father away. It seems hard that she should go on blaming him for something he said when he was not much more than a child.'

'It was. Believe me, I tried to tell her so. But you've seen how stubborn she could be when she thought she was in the right.

'She thinks Stephen takes after his father.'

'No more so than Miles does. Believe me, I know the pair of them very well. But there was no convincing her.'

'Because of what he said when he was fourteen?'

'There was something else. She didn't tell you that

Stephen went to visit his father in Italy during his first long vacation from university?'

'No.'

'It was natural enough. He was a young man with money and freedom to travel for the first time. He hadn't seen much of his father through his childhood, and I believe Brinkburn had thrown out some casual invitation. But, as Sophia saw it, he was enlisting on his father's side, and that was that. Ironic, in its way.'

'Why?'

'From hints thrown out by Stephen, I gathered that the visit had not gone as well as he'd hoped. He seemed depressed in spirits when he returned. I think he'd seen the sort of life his father led in Italy and didn't like it. Sophia didn't see that. She chose to think Brinkburn had let Stephen in on some terrible secret.'

'The first marriage? Did he?'

'No, I'm quite certain of that.'

'Something else?'

He said nothing for a while, as if making up his mind. Then he put his hand on the back of the chair at the other side of the desk, glanced at me to ask permission and sat down.

'I'm going to tell you this because there is no point in not telling it now, and it may explain something to you. Sophia believed there was something worse. As you know, she was a highly imaginative woman, and she had been thinking about all this for more than twenty years.

340

She'd convinced herself that Natalie Stevens did not die of natural causes.'

'What!'

'She thought that once he found his first wife inconvenient, he poisoned her, with Handy as his accomplice, and bribed a doctor to write the death certificate he showed Sophia.'

I stared at him.

'That last day I was with her, she said Handy's death was justice being done,' I said. 'Was that what she meant?'

'Almost certainly.'

'Is there any proof?'

'None at all.'

'Do you believe it?'

'No. But it fitted with Sophia's mood in the last few days. She told me she thought things were coming full circle. She believed she was going to die soon.'

'Was she ill?'

'No, apart from the reliance on laudanum. It started when she knew her husband was near death. She got it lodged in her mind that, because he was so possessive, he'd somehow take her with him when he went. When Handy arrived here out of the blue, that was the last straw. I remember what she said to me: *He's sent his homunculus to claim me, like a daemon come from hell. Handy helped him kill one wife, now he's come for the other.* There was no reasoning with her.'

I looked up at him.

'So did she kill Handy?' I said.

He looked at me.

'I don't know.'

His voice was so quiet that the words seemed no more than a rearrangement of the air around us.

'It wasn't Mr Lomax who coached poor Whiteley to lie at the inquest,' I said. 'It was you, wasn't it?'

He nodded.

'That was a bad thing to do to an honest man,' I said.

'Do you think I didn't know that? I wanted to give the evidence myself, but Lomax said it would come better from the steward. If my first plan had succeeded, we wouldn't have needed Whiteley.'

'What was the first plan?'

He hesitated.

'If she did kill Handy, would you blame her – knowing what you know now?' he said.

I knew I wouldn't get a response to my question until I answered his. I thought about it.

'I don't think I should blame her, or not much. Not enough to see her hanged for him.'

'Yes, it was my idea. Lomax knew about it, but it was my idea.'

'So what was this plan?' I said. 'And how did Handy die?'

I expected him to demand some promise of secrecy, but he settled himself on a chair and told me.

'There's a fruit store by the garden wall. It's not much used at this time of year.'

It was one of the places I'd searched for Tabby. I remembered empty shelves and a lingering smell of apples.

'The head gardener does his rounds every night,' he said. 'He noticed that the door had been left ajar and went to close it. That's when he found Handy's body on the floor, with his head battered in. There was a coal hammer beside him, with blood and hair on it. The hammer had been left there from the time they'd been repairing a shelf back in the autumn. The head gardener went and told Whiteley, and Whiteley told me. As luck would have it, that was the same evening they were packing up the armour to go to London.'

'And it was your idea to pack up Handy's body with it?' I said.

He looked me in the eye.

'My idea entirely. Whiteley helped. I think the poor man was in a state of shock. Our coachman came round in the morning, as arranged. I watched him and one of the gardener's boys loading the crates, hoping against hope nobody would smell or see anything unusual. They didn't.'

'Then you went up to London to consult with Lomax,' I said. 'By the locomotive, I suppose?'

'How did you guess? Yes. It had already struck me that, with the advent of the *North Star*, a man could virtually be in two places at once: I could see the crates off, in apparent innocence, then reach London while he was still on the road.'

'You were planning to intercept him before he got to Pratt's, say there'd been some mistake and reclaim the crate with Handy in it, somewhere near London and well away from the hall?'

'Yes.'

'So what went wrong?'

'Even the *North Star*, it seems, is not entirely reliable. Between here and London it did whatever the locomotive equivalent is of a horse casting a shoe. We were delayed for three hours at Slough. By the time I reached London, the load was delivered and Pratt's closed for the night.'

'So you tried to break in,' I said.

Up to then, he'd been telling the story calmly. Now his eyes widened and his body tensed.

'Were you watching me?'

'Of course not. At that time, I didn't even know you existed. But a policeman scared you away. He happened to talk to the officer who gave evidence at the inquest, Constable Bevan. Bevan's been down here, asking questions.'

He sunk his head into his hands.

'Does he know who I am?'

'I don't think so. All he has is a description of a dark-haired gentleman. But he's a clever man, and I think he'll be back.'

He raised his head to look me in the eye and gave a nod, accepting what I'd said.

'Tell me, what would you have done with Handy's

body if you'd managed to get it from the coachman or away from Pratt's?' I said.

'Thrown it in the Thames at night. Bodies of unknown people are being taken out of the Thames every morning, you only have to look in the newspapers. So the assumption would have been that he died in London.'

'And might never have been identified or associated with the Brinkburns?'

'If the fates had been kind, no.'

'But they weren't. I suppose once you'd been almost caught by the police, you had to give up the idea. He had to be left for Miles to discover next day.'

'I never intended to involve poor Miles. I thought he'd simply be found by one of Pratt's workmen when they unpacked the armour.'

'So when did you know about Miles finding the body?'

'As soon as it happened. I was watching.'

'What?'

'There's a jeweller's across the road from Pratt's. I was in there, pretending to take an interest in bracelets. I saw Miles go in, but was too late to stop him. Soon afterwards, a young woman in a blue dress came tripping down Bond Street without a care in the world and went inside. I wished I could protect her from what was going to happen.'

'Me?'

'You. I still wish it.'

'Too late now.'

'It's all too late.'

He closed his eyes and leaned back, looking nearly dead from tiredness.

'How much did Lomax know about this?' I said.

'Once the body was discovered, I had to tell him. He was angry, but we were too deeply in by then.'

'Protecting Sophia?'

He nodded.

'So what happened?' I said. 'Did Sophia somehow decoy Handy to the fruit store, jump out from the shadows and batter him to death with a hammer, then go quietly back to her room?'

'I've told you, I don't know.'

His eyes stayed closed.

'Then, some time later, she's overcome with remorse and commits suicide. With a dose of laudanum that you yourself said wasn't enough to kill her.'

'What else am I to think? Until I saw that entry in her journal, I doubted it. Why did she write that after all this time?'

'I think she came very close to telling me the story on the night of the storm,' I said. 'Perhaps, if she hadn't been killed, she'd have given me this to read.'

His eyes snapped open.

'Killed? You're saying she didn't kill herself?'

'I am, for two reasons. There's an empty bottle that probably contained laudanum by her bed. But it's not the one I saw, or that Betty ever saw. It's a different shape.'

I sketched with my hand in the air the shape of the bottle with shoulders. His eyes followed my hand.

'Do you know anything about that bottle?' I said.

He shook his head.

'And you still think she couldn't have arranged an extra supply without your knowing about it?'

'I'm sure of it,' he said.

'Suppose it contained a stronger solution of laudanum than she usually took? Enough to kill her.'

'But the boat – who put her in the boat?' he said.

'I don't know.'

He said nothing for a while, then: 'You said there were two things.'

'The man on the lawn. Very early that morning I was with her, she screamed out because she'd seen a man standing on the lawn, looking up at her window. I thought at the time it was a figment of her imagination. I'm wondering about that now. If somebody wanted to change that laudanum bottle, he'd have been spying on her, looking for his opportunity.'

'You thought it might be me.'

'Yes, but you wouldn't have needed to spy on her. You knew her routines better than anybody.'

'So I'd have been ideally placed to substitute the bottle,' he said. 'I suppose that has occurred to you too?'

'Why would you do that, when you'd gone to so much trouble to protect her?'

'Perhaps because I thought I couldn't protect her any more and wanted to spare her suffering.'

'Is that the case?'

He looked at me.

'No.'

'If there was a man spying on her, he was either an outsider or a person who doesn't come here very frequently,' I said.

I didn't need to mention names. He knew that neither Miles nor Stephen had been frequent visitors to their mother's house.

'We still don't know a man was really there,' he said.

'No, but there's something that makes me almost sure of it. My maid Tabby hasn't been seen since that night. I'm becoming very much afraid that she saw something she wasn't meant to and has . . .' I hesitated, not wanting to say the worst, '. . . has come to some harm.'

We said nothing for what seemed like a long time. Then he reached across and closed Sophia's journal.

'What are you going to do with that?' I said.

'Burn it.'

'No.'

My cry of protest was instinctive, not because of anything that might happen now, but for the final destruction of what she might have been.

'It could do harm,' he said.

'Not to her, not any more. Is it Stephen you're thinking of? You're still worrying about a smooth succession and no scandal. You loved her and somebody's killed her. Doesn't that matter more?'

He was angry now.

'I don't think you're the best judge of what matters.'

'No, I don't suppose I am. But I know this matters.'

I tied the tapes of the journal, stood up and tucked it under my arm. For a moment I thought he was going to wrench it away from me.

'Where are you taking it?'

'Somewhere safe. Don't worry, I don't intend to show it to policemen or lawyers. If that changes, I'll give you warning.'

He could have got it from me quite easily if he'd really wanted. In spite of his protest, I sensed a relief in him that it was being taken out of his hands. He stood back and let me walk out of the library and out of the house without saying anything. The journal sat on my lap on the railway journey back to London.

# CHAPTER TWENTY

Abel Yard was in its summer evening state of drowsiness, hens scratching in the dust, Mr Colley's bone-idle son-in-law straddling an old chair in front of the carpenter's shed where he pretended to work. The chair only had three legs, so at least he had to exert himself to the extent of keeping it balanced. I asked him if he'd seen anything of Tabby.

'Neither hide nor hair of her.'

Not taking his word for it, I looked in her outhouse. The sacks were just as I'd last seen them, so she hadn't slept there. I took my bag and the journal upstairs and found a note from Mrs Martley on the table: *If you get back, I'm sleeping over at Mr Suter's just in case.* There was the heel of a loaf in the bread crock and the remains of a ham in the meat safe, so it was just as well I was too tired to be hungry. I brewed tea and drank a couple of cups, then went upstairs. It had been a long day. I took off my dress and corsets and lay down on the bed, dozing in the golden evening light that filled my room.

I was almost asleep when a sharp knock sounded on the door downstairs. I thought it might be Mrs Martley, back for some reason and having forgotten her key, so I opened the window giving on to the yard and shouted down, 'Is that you?' No answer. I couldn't see whoever it was standing at the door because of the angle of the roof. Then a man's voice:

'Miss Lane?'

Surprise jolted me back from the window. It was either Stephen or Miles Brinkburn. Their voices were alike, but goodness only knew why either should come and seek me out, on a Sunday evening in a place like Abel Yard.

'Wait there,' I called down.

I took my time putting my clothes back on, trying to give myself a chance to think. I was so mazed with drowsiness and the events of the day that it was hard to get my thoughts in order. Finally I went downstairs and opened the door on Stephen Brinkburn. He was a tall streak of black: black gloves, black cravat, black top hat.

'I'm Stephen Brinkburn,' he said. 'I need to talk to you.'

At least he didn't say Lord Brinkburn, though I supposed he would be entitled to, but there was arrogance in the way he spoke, as if I had no choice in the matter.

'What about?'

He's surely have been told by now about his mother's death. Though he'd lost both parents within five days, still I didn't feel it was my place to offer condolences. We hadn't even been introduced, though he'd been in my thoughts most of the time.

'May we go inside?' he said.

He was possibly aware of Colley's son-in-law gawping at him open-mouthed from the end of the yard.

'Very well.'

I led the way upstairs, relieved to note that he left the bottom door open and unlatched behind him. It wasn't so much the propriety of being alone in the house with him that bothered me as the fact that he was a man of uncertain temper who looked strained to breaking point.

When I invited him to sit down he took off his hat and plumped himself in Mrs Martley's chair at the kitchen table, apparently unconscious of his surroundings. I took a chair opposite.

'I thought you might still be down at the hall,' he said.

It sounded like a declaration of hostilities, letting me know that he had been following my movements. I supposed Lomax must have told him. Well, two could play at that game.

'We just missed each other,' I said. 'I saw you galloping along the road from the hall yesterday morning.'

He frowned. I looked back at him with a tilt of the head, inviting him to state his business.

'It seems that you managed to gain my mother's confidence very quickly.'

'Did she tell you that?'

No answer. I had the impression that he'd decided in advance what he was going to say and wanted no diversions.

'I understand you take money for your services, Miss Lane.'

Either he intended an insult, or didn't care one way or another.

'I'm an investigator. I charge a fee as a doctor or lawyer does.'

'I want you to work for me.'

'I'm choosy about my clients.'

He blinked, at least recognising an insult when it came in his direction, but kept doggedly to his purpose.

'I want you to give me a statement in writing, that I can show to a lawyer, about how my brother managed to exert unfair influence on my mother.'

I stared at him.

'How could I, even if I wanted to? I only met Lady Brinkburn for the first time two weeks ago. If there was influence, it must have been going on well before that.'

'I'm talking about three days ago, very early on Thursday morning.'

My first thought was the figure on the lawn, but that had been early on Saturday morning. On the Thursday morning, I'd been on my way back from London.

'I wasn't there,' I said.

353

'Did my mother talk about it to you? Did she tell you he'd got her to sign a paper?'

'No. She said nothing about him.'

He looked disbelieving.

'As soon as he knew our father was dead, he went hurrying down to the hall and made her sign. He must have bullied or threatened her in some way, and I'm determined to prove it.'

'Was that what you and your mother quarrelled about on the day before she died?' I said.

He looked furious. I calculated my chances of getting out of the room and downstairs if he turned violent. Then his attention was taken by something on the table.

'What's that doing here?'

The journal. I'd put it straight down on the kitchen table when I came in, too tired to find a better place for it. There was no doubt from his expression that he'd recognised it.

'Did you take it or did she give it to you?' he said.

I didn't answer.

'It's family property,' he said. 'My property.'

Since that was undeniable, I expected him to pick it up. He just sat there staring down at it, thinking hard. When he spoke at last, his voice was surprisingly calm.

'It's no use as evidence, you know, neither one way nor the other.'

I realised then that he knew nothing about the new entry his mother had made just before she died. That was evidence, and very damaging to his case. He was right that the old entry helped neither brother, supporting the fact that something had happened on the night in question but not mentioning an unknown lover.

'You've read it then?' I said.

'Of course I've read it. I suppose Miles has too.'

I held my breath, waiting for him to open it and see the new entry. He shrugged.

'I suppose Miles paid you to steal it. I might have known he'd get here first. Well, much good may it do him.' He stood and picked up his hat from the table.

'I'll wish you good evening then, Miss Lane. I'm dis-appointed in you. I'd been told you were a woman of some intelligence, but you're missing something as clear as noonday. You'll find out soon enough, and so will everybody else.'

Then he marched away downstairs, heavy-footed as if he were still wearing armour, leaving his mother's journal unopened on the table. I took it upstairs with me and kept it within touching distance through the night, on a chair by my bed.

In the morning, I decided to call on Celia. I owed her a visit, but that wasn't the reason. I wanted to know about the paper that Miles Brinkburn had allegedly forced his mother to sign, and Celia was the perfect source of society gossip – even better than Amos when it came balls and salons. I dressed carefully, waited until the socially acceptable hour of eleven o'clock, then walked the short distance to Grosvenor Square

355

where Celia and Philip had their town house. As I arrived at the front door, two beautifully dressed young women were getting into their carriage, giggling and chattering. Celia's harvesting of the latest news obviously began at the crack of dawn by Mayfair standards. I gave my name to the footman and was shown upstairs almost at once. Celia was reclining on an Egyptian-style couch, in a light and airy sitting room decorated in dusky pink and ivory. She wore a housecoat of pink and silver brocade and matching slippers with turned-up toes, her hair tied with a pink ribbon, and was clearly in blooming health. She sat up to throw her arms round me.

'Elizabeth, darling!' (One of these days I'd manage to implant my real name in her butterfly mind, but it wasn't going to be today.) 'You've positively saved my life. I am literally dying of boredom and as solitary as what-was-her-name after whoever it was abandoned her on Naxos or somewhere.'

It was hardly kind to the girls who'd just left, but perhaps five minutes' solitude was a long time by her standards.

'Now, sit down here beside me and tell me everything you've been doing. I've heard you were the belle of the fair ladies' ball, or would have been if you hadn't got there so terribly late. What were you doing? Emilia says that dragonfly of yours is the most delicious thing she's seen all season and she wants to know where you got it, or is that a secret? Be an angel and ring that bell for me, would you? The doctor says I positively must not bend or stretch and I'm fainting for a cup of chocolate.'

Chocolate was duly ordered and arrived in a silver pot with two cups of delicate porcelain, large as soup bowls. While this was going on, Celia kept up a scatter-fire of questions.

'Is your aunt better? Did you see old Lady D at the ball with her protégé? That's what she calls him, at any rate. A quarter of her age, and her grandson was his fag at Eton. Have you ever known anything so entirely shameless? Tell me about the costumes. Is it true that the Laverick girl came covered head to foot in real roses then had to exit *en courant* when the petals started falling? Probably too good to be true, these things usually are, don't you think?'

Once we'd finished the chocolate and the maid had taken the cups, she got down to serious business.

'My dear, you've heard the latest about Miles?'

Her voice was low, her look commiserating.

'I thought you might be able to tell me,' I said.

'Then you haven't heard? I'm afraid things are serious between him and La Rosa. You know the father's dead?'

'Yes.'

'Well, it turns out Lady Brinkburn's just died too. Some people are saying she killed herself out of grief when she heard her husband had died, only that doesn't seem very likely since they'd been living apart for ages, but then women do sometimes do strange things at her age, don't they? Anyway, the point is that just before she died she signed this paper saying Miles is her only legitimate son. And you know what that means.'

She paused for breath. So that was the paper Stephen Brinkburn had been talking about. No wonder he was so angry. He'd have been even angrier if he'd known that the claim was supported by what his mother had written in the journal.

Celia must have mistaken my look for disappointment.

'So of course, that changes everything, my dear. Miles came rushing back to town and showed the paper to Rosa. She'd already compromised herself by that business at the jousting – you surely must have heard about that – and it turns out that she'd preferred Miles all along, only her aunt persuaded her she shouldn't take the younger son when she could have the one that mattered. So the engagement with Stephen is off and it's only a matter of time before she and Miles let it be known that theirs is on instead, though I suppose they may wait until all the business of the title goes through the law courts and Philip says that may take years, which would be hard on her since complexions don't last forever, but there it is.'

Her hand came out and rested lightly on my wrist.

'I'm sorry, my dear. If things had gone the other way, he really would have done very well for you, and I know he was interested. Still, other fish . . . I shall plan a campaign for you. It will be something to pass the time in my dreary cell while I'm held prisoner like this.'

She leaned back against her silk cushions, almost consoled for my imagined loss. I knew it was useless to try to protest and that she was already riffling through *Debrett's* in her mind for possible younger sons. I thanked her, kissed her on the cheek and left, promising to come back as soon as I could.

On the walk home, I thought over what Celia had told me and ran through a timetable of events in my head. Late on Wednesday night Miles learned that his father was dead. Early next morning, by Stephen's account, he'd rushed down to the estate and got his mother to sign the statement. I assumed, as seemed likely, that it was this knowledge that had put Stephen into such a fury when I saw him galloping away from the hall on Saturday morning. The news would have spread round London in a short time. Stephen was in danger of losing title, fortune and fiancée. It would hardly have been surprising if he'd been the figure on the lawn at first light on Saturday, staring up at his mother's window and wondering how to persuade her to change her mind. But she hadn't changed her mind, and by first light on Sunday morning she was dead.

Considered that way, Stephen had a strong motive for killing his mother. But there was another way of looking at it. Which brother had most to gain? Not Stephen. With his mother dead, there could be no change of mind.

That statement Miles had secured was her last word on the subject. Had that occurred to Miles? His mother was impulsive and stories could be changed back again. He had an equally strong motive to make sure that it really was her last word. Was that what Stephen had meant when he taunted me with missing something as clear as noonday?

As I walked along Adam's Mews I met various vagabond boys, known to me by sight, who hung around the stables and picked up the occasional coin by running errands and holding horses. Tabby would have been a familiar figure to them, but when I asked if they'd seen her recently, the usual answer was 'not for a long time'. That probably meant not since she'd gone away with me, ten days ago. I promised all of them a reward if they could bring me information that helped me find her, and watched their eyes light up, but couldn't feel hopeful. If Tabby had been alive and well, she'd have found her own way home by now.

Mr Grindley the coach repairer was outside his workshop smoking a pipe as I passed by, and he greeted me with a smile.

'What you been up to, Miss Lane?'

'Up to?'

'Policeman been round inquiring for you.'

'Policeman?' My heart somersaulted. 'How long ago?'

'Not half an hour since. Said he'd be back.' He gestured with his pipe. 'Here he comes now.'

And strolling through the gates to the yard, top hat and brass buttons gleaming, came Constable Bevan, with a smile on his face like a man who expected people to be pleased to see him. I wasn't.

# CHAPTER TWENTY-ONE

'Good morning, Miss Lane. I gather you've lost your maid,' said Bevan, raising his hat to me.

No point in gratifying his vanity by asking him how he knew. He must have seen me talking to one of the street boys and got the information from him. It was hardly a secret, after all.

'Are you going to help me find her?' I said.

He shook his head. I noticed that there was a smear of soot down one side of his nose. He seemed unaware of it.

'Absconding servants aren't a police matter. Unless they've taken some of their employer's property with them, that is.'

'She hasn't.'

He nodded, still smiling, as if that confirmed something he'd already discovered.

'Well, I'm sorry she's not come back,' he said. 'There are a couple of things I'd have liked to ask her.'

'To ask Tabby? What?'

I couldn't keep the surprise out of my voice. He glanced at Mr Grindley, standing within earshot, and looked pointedly down the yard. Unwillingly, I walked a yard or two and he followed.

'Anything you wanted to ask Tabby, you'd better ask me,' I said. 'Or if you know anything, please tell me.'

He looked down at the hen coop beside us as if thinking of sitting on it, then remembered his manners.

'So you'll answer for her, will you?'

'If I can, yes. But what is this about?'

He squinted down his nose.

'Have I got soot on my face?'

'Yes, you have.'

I felt meanly pleased to have a chance to unsettle him, even in this small way. He took a handkerchief from the pocket of his uniform tailcoat and dabbed at the smear, not seeming much concerned.

'Dirty place, Paddington.'

He looked at me over the handkerchief.

'Are you trying to tell me you've just come back from Maidenhead?' I said.

'Oh no. Can't go running around like that on the public's money. They don't even like paying us back for omnibus tickets.' He tucked the handkerchief away. 'Just as well some people are more public spirited.'

'Please tell me what all this has got to do with Tabby.'

He pretended to be surprised by the sharpness in my voice.

'I'm about to tell you. You remember we had the pleasure of meeting when I was on my little fishing trip?'

'When you wanted me to believe you weren't on duty. Yes.'

'Well, I wasn't on duty, in a manner of speaking. But a man naturally gravitates towards his own trade. A barber, for instance: put him down in a strange town and, a pound to a penny, before the hour's out, he'll be talking to another barber. You must have noticed it yourself, observant lady like you are.'

'So what you're telling me is that you just happened to get into conversation with a local policeman?'

'Coroner's officer, in this case. An older trade, as it happens, but much the same line of country when it comes to unexplained deaths, as in the case of the late Simon Handy.'

'And I suppose this coroner's officer, whom you just happened to meet, came rushing up to Paddington by railway train first thing this morning, for the pleasure of your conversation. Suppose you tell me what this has to do with me and my maid?'

He sighed, as if my impatience offended him.

'He's a conscientious man. Some people, a death on a Sunday morning, it would be a case of let it wait till Monday. Of course, he might have been taking into account that it was a member of the aristocracy.'

'Lady Brinkburn?'

'Lady Brinkburn. He went out to the hall, spoke to the servants – "Who'd been the last one to see her alive?" and so on. One of them he spoke to was her ladyship's maid. Clever girl, by his account. She pointed out that the lady's laudanum bottle wasn't her usual pattern. She even had it safely locked up there in the bedroom. He wondered who'd told her to do that. She remembered the name from when the lady had come visiting. Good description too.'

He paused and looked at me.

'Yes, I advised her to,' I said. 'It seemed a reasonable precaution. I knew somebody would have to make official inquiries.'

In fact, I hadn't been thinking so far ahead. It had been an instinctive reaction after the discovery about the bottle. He nodded.

'Very proper and public spirited. Bit of a coincidence though, wouldn't you say?'

'Coincidence?'

'Simon Handy's found dead in London. You're there. His late employer's found dead in Buckinghamshire. You're there again. Has it struck you that you might be a kind of natural magnet for coincidences?'

I'd been doing some quick thinking, not liking the way things were heading. On one hand, my client was entitled to confidentiality. On the other, I couldn't have envisaged these complications when I took on the case. I compromised.

'It's not coincidence. I've been involved in professional

inquiries concerning the family. That's all I'm prepared to tell you.'

'It's a serious offence to withhold information about crimes.'

He said it in a tone that made it sound like a casual observation, rather than the threat it was.

'If you think I'm withholding information, then say so outright.'

He nodded, as if accepting that was as far as he'd get, and glanced towards the gates. I thought I'd called his bluff and was relieved to have got off so easily.

'Well, I'll wish you good day then, Miss Lane.'

He half-raised his hat, turned away, then pivoted back.

'But I was forgetting where we started, wasn't I? Your maid.'

'If you've anything to tell me about Tabby, then say it.'

The look he gave me then was like the expression on an angler's face when he stares at the circles fish make on water, all the while weighing up where to cast his line.

'Another coincidence – the biggest of the lot, you might say. When and where did you last see this Tabby?'

My brain clammed up with fear, so I had to struggle to count back the days. I thought he was about to tell me she was dead.

'Friday evening, or afternoon, rather. Three days ago. There was a storm you see and . . .'

I managed to collect my wits enough to give him a

short account of Tabby arguing with the maids and rushing out.

'Did you ever send her to do shopping for you?' he said.

'What's that got to do with it? Yes, she ran the occasional errand for me here in London. When we were at the cottage, she bought food at the village shop.'

'Food. You didn't by any chance ask her to buy laudanum?'

I stared, wondering if I'd heard aright.

'Of course not. I don't use laudanum.'

'Then how do you account for the fact that on Saturday afternoon a young woman who sounds very like your Tabby walked into a chemist's shop in Maidenhead and bought a bottle of laudanum? An unusually strong solution of laudanum, as it happens.'

'There must be some mistake.'

The words sounded lame even in my own ears. The sceptical look on Constable Bevan's face showed what he thought of them.

'Another coincidence, then. Short, skinny girl of fifteen or so, dark hair, good teeth, a bit of an impudent look about the eyes. Sounds very much like the young woman I spoke to down at your cottage by the river.'

'That description could fit a lot of girls.'

'True enough. Still, there was one thing the chemist noticed in particular. Her voice. Broad cockney, he said. Proper broad cockney. Doesn't that sound like your girl?'

I looked down in the dust where the hens were pecking.

Somewhere among them was the one she'd tied up, just to get my attention. I didn't try to answer him because there was nothing I could say.

'If you decide there's anything you want to tell me, my beat's the south side of this end of Oxford Street,' he said.

He tipped his hat again and this time really did start walking away. I called after him.

'The girl – what happened to her?'

He turned.

'She bought the laudanum, left the shop, that was that. As far as my friend could make out, nobody's seen her since.'

Then he walked on and out of the gates, leaving me looking down at the chickens.

I spent a bad hour up in my room, trying to make sense of what he'd told me. The girl in the chemist's had been Tabby. Either that, or Constable Bevan was playing some complicated game for his own purposes, but I couldn't see why. Looked at one way, there was a horrible logic to it. Tabby quarrels with the maids, walks out, and next morning is seen in the nearest town buying a bottle of laudanum. Was it with some idea of poisoning Dora and Ruth in revenge, or killing herself, in despair at being made a mockery? An outsider would say that either was possible, but – when the shock began to wear off – I couldn't believe either. Tabby had taken her revenge in a direct and characteristic way, rubbing ham in her tormentor's face. If she'd decided that wasn't enough, she was far more likely to have stormed back and knocked both girls down than used some sophisticated method like poisoning. As for self-destruction, it was beyond belief that a girl tough enough to survive homeless on the streets of London would be driven to end her life by two silly housemaids. Besides, what would she know about laudanum? It was an indulgence above her class. In her world, if people wanted to drink themselves into temporary insensibility, it was gin not laudanum in the glass. And where would she get the money for laudanum? I'd never given her more than a copper or two at a time. When she went shopping, she was scrupulous about bringing back my change. If Tabby had bought laudanum, somebody else had given her the money for it.

That raised quite a different possibility that turned the whole case on its head. Lady Brinkburn was increasingly dependent on laudanum. Both Robert Carmichael and her maid were worried about that and trying to limit the amount she took. Suppose Lady Brinkburn had encountered Tabby wandering in the grounds. She'd already used her to run one errand, in delivering a note to me. Why not borrow her for her own purposes? So Tabby had bought the laudanum for her and delivered it, probably at some secluded place chosen by Lady Brinkburn so that nobody else would ever know. Then later Lady Brinkburn drank the full bottle, lay down in her boat and died, without anybody else being involved, and my suspicions of Stephen and Miles were moonshine. That seemed to me much more likely than any other possibility, but it left one great question unanswered. After she'd run her errand, what had happened to Tabby?

I puzzled at it until my head was spinning so much that only a walk across the park would clear it. It was high time I called on Amos Legge. His practicality and commonsense were an antidote to too much theorising, and there was always a chance that he'd know what to do next.

It was mid-afternoon by this time, the drives so packed with fashionable carriages that a nimble urchin could swing from one to the other the length of the park without setting foot on the ground. I saw several who seemed to be trying it, until footmen noticed and dislodged them. The urchins simply rolled themselves into balls, stood up and shook off the worst of the dust, then dived for the back of the next carriage. The stables where Amos worked seemed quiet in comparison. The door of Rancie's box was open, a boy forking fresh straw inside, so she must be out in the park, earning her oats with some suitably gentle-handed lady rider. I was sorry to have missed Rancie, because she always managed to calm me when I needed it, and that day I needed it very much. Rancie's black cat, Lucy, came up to me and rubbed against my skirt. I bent to stroke her and noticed that there was some new smell around the yard, making her twitch her sensitive whiskers. The smell had nothing to do with horses. In fact it reminded me, against my will, of what Constable Bevan had been saying about barbers.

The door of the office next to the tack room opened and Amos Legge walked out, holding a small bottle. He was dressed with less than his usual elegance, in breeches and shirtsleeves, with a leather farrier's apron over them. He seemed pleased to see me, but had a slightly guilty look and put the hand with the bottle behind his back. Then he looked at my face and his smile faded.

'You were there when they found the lady, then?'

'Yes.'

'I'm sorry for that.'

I wanted to tell him about Tabby, but somebody shouted to him from inside the office, telling him to hurry up. He gave me an apologetic look.

'We've got to get it done so it dries in time, but the way the lad's fuddling about, the funeral will be over before we get there.'

'Funeral?'

But he was striding away towards a loosebox. I followed. I supposed a horse had some small injury, and it was always useful to learn from Amos's expertise.

The occupants of the box were a stable lad, looking nervous, and a very large black gelding, not in the best of tempers. I'd seen the lad before, but not the horse. Amos opened the half door and went in, making reassuring sounds at the horse. It rolled its eyes and flared its nostrils at him.

'He won't let me put the twitch on him,' the lad said.

'We don't need no twitch for this. It's not as if we're hurting him. It's only the smell of it bothers him.' He gave the bottle to the boy. 'You be careful you don't spill it. The guvnor says it costs more than French brandy. I'll see he stays quiet.'

He put his hand on the horse's neck and murmured a string of words to it in his deep Herefordshire voice. There was no particular sense to them, but even to my ears they were as soothing as the cooing of doves. Soon the big horse had dropped his head and was standing quietly. He was a fine beast, sixteen hands high or more, and pure black apart from one white sock on the near hind and a small white blaze.

At a nod from Amos, the lad squatted down by the horse's near hind, poured liquid from the bottle on to a cloth and dabbed it on to the horse's white sock. The smell I'd noticed outside filled the box and the horse shifted a little, but stayed calm enough under Amos's hand for the white to be turned black. Then Amos took the bottle and cloth from the lad and quickly did the same to the small white blaze on the animal's forehead, before it had a chance to realise what was happening.

'Thar lad, good lad.'

He produced a carrot from his pocket, snapped it into pieces and fed it to the horse, murmuring quietly to it all the time. When he was sure it was completely calm, he opened the box door and the three of us filed out. I waited till the lad had gone about his business.

'Are you turning horse thief then?' I said to Amos.

He laughed.

'Undertaker, more like. You've surely seen that trick done before.'

'Yes, but isn't it usually with boot polish?'

I knew that some people were very fussy about having the horses that drew their carriages matched to perfection. A groom could do a lot with black boot polish to even up markings on legs and foreheads. Amos shook his head.

'Quality job, this one. A very particular customer.'

'He can't be so very particular if he's dead, can he?'

'Left instructions in his will: six coal-black geldings to draw the hearse, four coal-black mares for the mourning coach, all geldings to be matched at sixteen hands or above, all mares at fifteen two. Now how many pure coal-black horses have you seen in your life?'

'Not many.'

'And then not as many as you think. Even the ones that look black usually have a touch of white on them somewhere. So any stables with a horse for hire that's big enough and can be made to look black enough is in a good market. It's not just the one stage, either. The hearse and mourning coach have got to go all the way from Kingston to Portsmouth, and that's three changes, even going slow like they will be.'

Until then, I'd been laughing at the absurd vanity of it, but the name Kingston rang a hollow bell with me.

'Do I know this late gentleman?' I said.

'You know his sons, any road.'

'Lord Brinkburn?'

'That's the one.'

'He was in a private asylum near Kingston upon Thames. Why are they taking his body from there to Portsmouth?'

'As far as I gather, he's said in his will he's to be buried in Rome, so they've got to put him on a ship. They'll have had him embalmed, I reckon, this weather.'

'He thought he was the Emperor Hadrian,' I said. 'I suppose that's why he wanted to be buried in Rome.'

Then I thought that a madman's will would have no legal force, so Lord Brinkburn must have laid down all these arrangements while he still passed for sane. Had he chosen his final resting place because his first wife had died there? If so, it was the first and last sign of softness I'd heard of in the monstrous man. I supposed there'd be no such pomp for Lady Brinkburn. As soon as the coroner allowed, she'd probably be buried in the village churchyard as quietly as she'd lived, with the hated Handy just the other side of the wall. It was odd that three of the people who'd set out from Newcastle on that not exactly honeymoon tour twenty-three years ago had died within two weeks of each other.

'When's this cortège setting out?' I said.

'Midday tomorrow. Soon as he dries off, I'm taking this one and the mare over to Kingston, to be ready.'

'I suppose the Brinkburn sons will have to be there tomorrow?'

'Bound to be.'

Amos strolled up a few doors to another loosebox. A broad black face looked over the door and accepted a piece of carrot from him.

'Quiet as a cushion, this one,' he said. 'Didn't give us no trouble. Useful mare, schooled to side saddle as well as driving.'

He looked at me.

'Nice ride to Kingston, across Richmond Park. I was going to ride the other one and lead the mare, but I could just as easy have a saddle put on her.'

I was about to say I couldn't go jaunting out to the country. I'd lost Tabby, my case had collapsed round me so I could expect no fee, and I had no idea what to do next. Then I thought, *Why not?*

'So I'd better go home and change into my riding costume,' I said.

He grinned.

'I'll have her ready by the time you get back.'

As I walked to Abel Yard, I realised that the attraction of a long ride in the country was not the only reason for my decision. The absurd funeral cortège was the nearest I'd ever get to the man who'd been the cause of so much trouble. I wanted to see him on the road behind his six black horses, with his sons paying their last respects to a man who'd done nothing to deserve respect. Since I'd followed him, through the journal, on one decisive journey of his life, it was fitting in its way that I'd see him set out on his last one.

# CHAPTER TWENTY-TWO

A man was waiting outside my locked door at Abel Yard. He had the look of a superior domestic servant who'd been unfairly put upon, standing with bent head and drooping shoulders as a protest about being kept waiting. He'd have been more comfortable sitting on the mounting block in the shade, but that would have deprived him of his sense of grievance.

'Miss Lane? I was instructed to deliver this directly into your hands.'

He handed me a folded and sealed paper, with an air that said he wasn't accustomed to being used as a messenger boy, and left without asking whether there was a reply. I recognised the handwriting as Disraeli's. The message was short.

*Dear Miss Lane,*
*There has been an unexpected development in*
*the case which concerns us. If a certain report*
*which has come to me is true, matters are not*
*as we have been led to believe. I should be*
*grateful for a chance to discuss the situation*
*with you. I am escorting Mary Anne to a recital*
*this evening. I enclose a ticket in the hope that*
*we may meet there.*

I unlocked the door and went upstairs, not knowing
whether to be annoyed or amused. It was typical of my
association with Disraeli that he should have suggested
a public place for our meeting, including, in this case,
his bride-to-be as chaperone. I could never decide
whether this was from concern for my reputation or his
own. From experience, he would contrive a few minutes
for us to be alone among the fashionable crowd and
have our conference. It was typical, too, that he should
assume I had nothing better to do with my time and
not tell his servant to wait for a reply. He'd count on
my curiosity, if not my obedience, to ensure that I did
as he wanted. Well, this time he was wrong. I was
looking forward too much to my long ride with Amos
and my curiosity wasn't in the least piqued because I
was sure I already knew what Disraeli wanted to tell
me. He prided himself on knowing what was happening
everywhere and would have heard by now that Lady
Brinkburn had signed a paper naming her younger son

as legal heir. Old news, as far as I was concerned. I looked forward to telling him so when we met, but that could wait now until after the funeral.

By evening, Amos and I were cantering together across Richmond Park, with the sun going down behind the old oak trees and red deer running beside us. Amos had to hold the big gelding back so that my mare could keep up, and I missed Rancie's speed and lightness of foot. Still, she was a kindly animal and obviously enjoyed a day out of her usual routine. When we slowed to a walk on the Kingston side of the park, I told Amos all I'd discovered about the Brinkburns. He'd been considerate as ever on the journey, not pressing me, but I wanted his opinion because he sometimes seized on things I'd missed. He listened and shook his head.

'So the lady killed herself, after all?'

'What else can I think? It was Tabby buying the laudanum, I'm afraid there's no doubt of that. I'm convinced she wasn't buying it for herself, so who else would have asked her to do it but Lady Brinkburn?'

'Meaning to kill herself with it?'

'That's what I can't decide. She might just have been desperate for sleep and taken too much. But there's the question of the boat. I doubt if it would have come untied accidentally. If she'd decided to die, it would be just like her to untie it, lie down and float away.'

He turned his big gelding out of the park gates, on to the road.

'And you reckon she might have done away with herself because she killed Handy and regretted it?' he said.

'I don't think she did regret it, if she did it. As far as she was concerned, it was retribution on Handy for helping Brinkburn kill his first wife.'

'Do you reckon the first wife was killed, then?'

'I don't know, but she'd convinced herself they'd killed her, and that's what matters.'

'So if she did it and wasn't ashamed of it, why kill herself?'

'I doubt if she was being so rational. The problem for her was that it all seemed to be part of a pattern: Handy suddenly appearing again, this notion of hers that her husband intended to take her with him when he died. Or perhaps she was just tired of it all.'

'You said she had a stubborn streak. Would she have killed herself, leaving things as they are between the sons? Wouldn't she want to see it settled before she went?'

'So perhaps it was accidental,' I said.

He whistled a few bars of 'Over the Hills and Far Away'.

'You don't think so, then?'

'I'm not saying anything.'

'You have a way of not saying anything. Out with it.'

'You said yourself, either brother had a reason. I've gotten to know the pair of them quite well over the jousting, and as far as I can tell they're both calves from the same barn.'

380

'Meaning?'

'According to you, their mother was stubborn and their father was crazy. Breeding's the same with people as with animals – what goes in comes out.'

'But their father wasn't always mad.'

I said no more. Amos would have heard, as I had, that it was syphilis that had eaten away the old lord's brain, but even in our free and easy conversation there were things not to be discussed.

'Two wives at a time doesn't sound too sensible to me,' he said.

'In any case,' I said, 'there's one big objection to either Stephen or Miles killing their mother. Tabby bought the laudanum. It's far more likely that she'd do that for Lady Brinkburn than for either Stephen or Miles. She knew who Lady Brinkburn was. If Lady Brinkburn had met her wandering round the estate it would have seemed quite natural to Tabby to be asked to run an errand for her.'

'Where's she gone, then? That was Saturday, this is Monday. A girl like that would have got herself back to London in that time.'

'But suppose she heard somehow that Lady Brinkburn had died? She might make the connection with the laudanum and think she'd be blamed.'

That ended the conversation for a while, because we were coming near Kingston and the road was busy. I noticed several more large horses whose total blackness looked suspicious, though we didn't get near enough to smell them until we turned into the yard of the coaching inn at Kingston, when distinct whiffs of barber's shop and bootroom scented the air.

A harassed-looking ostler with a list and a measuring stick pounced on us as soon as we rode through the gateway.

'Geldings to the left, mares to the right.'

Amos told him he should take it easy because it was a funeral and not starter's orders for the Derby. He made a point of helping me down from the mare and treating me like a fine lady, which was his habit when in company, no matter how companionably we'd ridden. Within minutes I was being escorted inside the inn by a lad who carried my saddle bags. I'd supposed that rooms might be hard to come by because Lord Brinkburn's friends and associates would have come down from London to see off the cortège, but the landlord seemed glad of my custom. He had a list on his desk of rooms occupied and it looked no more than half full. One name, though, leaped out at me even though I was reading upside down: O. Lomax Esq. So at least Lord Brinkburn's old family friend and lawyer was among those present. Come to think of it, he was probably Lord Brinkburn's executor, thus responsible for overseeing all the pomp and complexity of the funeral cortège. Neither Stephen nor Miles was on the list, so they must be staying overnight elsewhere.

I took possession of my room, washed hands and face in water from the pitcher and replaced my top hat with a bonnet that had suffered from being cramped into a saddle bag. Supper of cutlets and a glass of claret was served to me in a private parlour, alongside a mother and daughter who were on a coach journey from Godalming to London. They said little and ate quickly. I'd have much preferred to share my meal with Amos, but when he was about his professional business there was no chance of that. After I'd eaten, I looked out to the yard and saw him chatting happily with a group of grooms and ostlers in the evening sunshine, beer mugs in their hands, surrounded by rows of black equine faces looking out over loosebox doors.

It was still too early to retire for the night, so I decided to stroll. On a whim, I asked the landlord for directions to the private asylum where Lord Brinkburn had died. He looked surprised but gave me clear directions – down the main road southward for half a mile, then first right. The place was called Newlands, and it was set back from the road. A walk of less than half an hour brought me to the top of its drive. From appearance, it might have been any country house, admittedly rather a gloomy one, in red brick, standing in lawns and shrubberies that produced dark green leaves rather than flowers, even in late June. But the gates that closed off the drive were perfectly ordinary gates, with no chain or padlock, and as far as I could see there were no bars at any of the windows. Obviously losing one's reason, like so many other things in life, was much more discreetly managed with plenty of money.

As I stood looking down the drive, a man came hurrying up it. I stepped back against the hedge, not wanting to be noticed. He was a working man, a gardener possibly, with powerful broad shoulders and a discontented expression. He opened both gates wide, and waited. Hooves and wheels sounded on the road, from the direction I'd come, and a dark carriage drawn by two heavy horses came swaying into sight. I stayed where I was, thinking that this was how things were done. Lord Brinkburn's place was being filled immediately by another paying guest, similarly afflicted. To avoid embarrassment or unpleasantness to his relations, he was being brought at the end of the day, to be stowed out of sight. It was not something I wanted to see and I regretted the curiosity that had brought me there, until I realised it wasn't a carriage for the living. It was the hearse. It rolled along slowly and heavily and turned in at the gates. Tomorrow it would be driven by a coachman all in black, with a black scarf round his hat and a black ribbon on his driving whip. Tonight it was in the hands of a delivery driver in plain brown jacket and gaiters. A straight-sided mourning coach, as black as the hearse, followed at the same slow pace behind two mismatched brown cobs. As they went down the drive, the broad-shouldered man closed the gates behind them and followed. Hearse and mourning coach drew up one behind the other at the front of the house and the drivers jumped down.

By now, the light was starting to go. I stepped out

from the hedge to walk back to town, then caught my breath and prepared to run. A man was standing a few yards away. He must have come along the road from the other direction while I was watching the hearse. For a moment, surprise at finding him there kept me from recognising him, though I sensed at once that his presence wasn't friendly.

'You again,' he said.

Stephen Brinkburn. I said nothing, partly because my heart was beating so hard. I was embarrassed too at being found there, with no proper reason.

'What are you doing here? Or can I guess?'

His first question was reasonable at any rate. He'd last seen me in London and couldn't have known about my impulsive decision to ride out on the black mare. I couldn't even turn his question back on him, since it was only to be expected that a son should take an interest in his father's funeral arrangements, though it was odd he'd chosen to do it from the road rather than up at the house.

'I suppose my brother sent you,' he said.

To that at least I had a response.

'I'm not working for your brother.'

'I don't believe you.'

Although he made no move towards me, his hostility filled the air round us.

'If you don't believe me when I tell the truth, there's no point in talking, is there?' I said.

I turned and walked slowly in the direction of the

main road, expecting with every step that he'd come after me. Instead he called out.

'You can give Miles a message from me.'

I walked on. He shouted again.

'Tell him he can ride the black horse tomorrow, and I wish him joy of it.'

I stopped and turned then, caught by the oddity of the message. Stephen was still standing there by the gates of the asylum, a tall black figure against the pale road. I decided not to ask him what he meant by it and walked on quickly, relieved when I came to the main road with people and horses going up and down.

My heart was still thumping hard, so I made myself walk slowly back to the inn. Instead of going in by the main door, I went through the arch into the yard. As I'd hoped, there was the glow of a pipe in the twilight and the unmistakeably tall silhouette of Amos by the back door.

'Where've you been then?' he said to me, without even turning to look.

'Walking.'

I was still too disturbed by the meeting to want to tell anybody, even Amos. Instead I asked him how the horses were settling.

'Well enough. They're most of them used to being in different quarters. Our two ate up their feed like good 'uns.'

It was soothing, being among the horses. We strolled together from box to box, watching one nuzzling its hay manger, one asleep with legs folded in neatly like a cat, one swaying gently on its feet. As we went, I counted them. Four black mares for the mourning coach, then the row of taller geldings to pull the hearse, . . . four, five, six, seven.

'There's too many,' I said to Amos, pausing by the last box. 'Or are they keeping one spare?'

'No, that's the saddle horse. Mr Lomax was down after dinner to see it's all being done right, and he told us. One seventeen-hand gelding to be ridden on the first stage in front of the hearse, making seven altogether.'

'So who's riding him?'

Amos gave his pipe a long pull to keep it glowing and looked at me.

'His heir. That's what Mr Lomax said. His son and heir.'

So that was what Stephen meant. By letting Miles ride the black horse at the head of the funeral procession tomorrow, he'd be publicly acknowledging his brother's right to title, fortune and bride. After all this, total surrender.

Only the way Stephen had said it hadn't sounded like surrender in the least.

# CHAPTER TWENTY-THREE

I told Amos about meeting Stephen and we discussed it until the last of the light went and bats were flying across the stable yard. The essential decency of Amos made him believe there were limits to what a man would do.

'I could understand Mr Stephen wanting to knock Mr Miles down,' he said. 'He's done that once already. But they're brothers. I don't reckon he'd do worse than that.'

'You said yourself it's all in the breeding. And you didn't see Stephen tonight.'

'Did he threaten anything?'

'Not as such, no. But . . .' It was hard to put into words the impression he'd made on me. 'It was as if he'd decided something and there was no going back.'

'I don't see there's much he can do,' Amos said.

'There'll be enough people watching. Not unless he rides up to the procession tomorrow and challenges Mr Miles to fight him.'

'Oh gods, Amos. You don't think he'd do that?'

The idea hadn't occurred to me, but once spoken it seemed all too likely. It was what they'd been practising for weeks, after all. It even came as something of a relief after what I'd been imagining.

'And there's the business of the armour,' I said. 'We still don't know what's become of it. Suppose Stephen's planning to arrive on a pure white charger in the ancestral armour.'

'Worth seeing,' Amos said.

I was tempted to agree with him. Also, it would puff this absurdity of a funeral procession into the laughing stock that Lord Brinkburn's life deserved.

'It's still dangerous,' I said. 'Miles won't be wearing armour. If Stephen has got his hands on a lance with a point to it, he could run him through.'

Amos still wasn't convinced.

'Only if Mr Miles is daft enough to sit there and let him do it. What are you thinking of doing, then? Telling Mr Lomax to watch out tomorrow?'

'I don't trust Lomax. Besides, he's a lawyer and he'd want evidence. All I have is a feeling.'

Amos tapped out his pipe.

'Tell you what I'll do, if it'll make you sleep better. I'll borrow a horse tomorrow and make sure I'm not far away from Mr Miles.'

I said, meaning it, that yes it would make me sleep better. With Amos on the alert, Miles should be as well protected as if he had a squadron of the Household Cavalry round him. I only hoped he deserved it.

Next morning, I was down at the stable yard before six o'clock. The cavalcade wasn't due to set out from the asylum until eleven, but the grooms had been up and active from first light, putting a final polish on to the horses' already gleaming coats with linen cloths, oiling hooves to jet blackness. Amos was in the gelding's box, plaiting his mane. He told me nothing had been seen yet of Miles or Mr Lomax. He'd heard that Miles was staying with a friend in another part of the town. I went inside for breakfast. By the time I came out, the first two pairs of horses were on their way to Newlands. Amos went out next with our two, riding the gelding bareback and leading the mare. He winked at me as he went and promised to be back in plenty of time to pick up another horse so that he could keep an eye on our man. Soon after the last of the ten black carriage horses had left the yard, a groom came from wherever Miles was staying to collect the big saddle horse.

The yard seemed empty with them all gone, but then people started arriving with bags and baskets because the London to Chichester stage was due. It arrived in the usual hurry, with a confusion of passengers and luggage descending and alighting and grooms pushing people aside to change the horses. It left full up inside, with three riding on top. As it was grinding out of the yard through the archway, a man came running up. Behind the coachman's back, he jumped on the passenger step then bounded up, grabbed the rail round the top of the coach and swung himself on to an outside seat. It was done as deftly as a circus trick. He sat down with the other outside passengers, coolly raising his hat to acknowledge the laughter and ironic cheers of people watching.

'There's a fellow doesn't believe in paying fares,' someone said.

The man's athleticism was all the more surprising because, from the glance I'd had of him, he wasn't young and had the use of only one arm. The left one had flapped limply at his side as he jumped. I might have thought more about it at the time, but one of the passengers from London who had got out of the coach was standing and staring at me.

'Miss Lane.'

Robert Carmichael seemed as surprised to see me as I was to see him. He was dressed in black and looked near exhaustion, face pale and eyes feverish.

'What are you doing here?' I said.

Not a polite question, but I couldn't help it. Of all people, he seemed one of the least likely to want to honour the late Lord Brinkburn.

'I suppose I owe it to him,' he said.

In a conventional situation, it would have been perfectly reasonable for the tutor of the late lord's sons to take a modest place in his cortège. Did Carmichael really expect me to believe that was the case here? Then I remembered that he didn't know I knew that he'd knocked his late lordship downstairs.

'Is Lomax here?' he said.

'Yes, but I haven't seen him. He may have gone straight to Newlands.'

'Newlands?'

'The asylum.'

He looked ready to drop from weariness.

'It's not far,' I said. 'If you like, I'll walk with you and show you. You'd just have time for a coffee first, if you wanted.'

I wasn't simply being charitable. Whatever his reason for being there, he might have some influence on his former pupils, though I doubted if it would be enough to prevent whatever Stephen intended. He nodded, thanked me and disappeared inside.

I found Amos in the tack room and told him about the man jumping on the stagecoach.

'He looked very much like the clown from Astley's,' I said. 'If he's here, he's working for one of them, probably Stephen.'

Amos agreed. By daylight, he seemed disposed to take my suspicions more seriously.

'Still, why was he getting out before anything starts?' he said.

'Perhaps he's done whatever Stephen wanted him to do.'

'In that case, why isn't he just taking himself back to

Astley's? He's going in the wrong direction. Unless he's planning to meet us next stop.'

'Next stop?'

'Esher's next stop for the stagecoach. Next stop for the coffin too, but with the speed that'll be going, it'll be evening before it gets there.'

'At that rate, it will take them a week to get to Portsmouth.'

He grinned.

'Today's the slow day. After that, the mourning coach and the first lot of horses go back and they pick up a bit of speed, by hearse standards any road. Mr Lomax is staying with them all the way to the boat to see things are done properly, but the rest of them go home tonight.'

'So will today be the only day Miles is riding with them?'

'That's right. If Mr Stephen is planning anything, it's got to be here or at Esher, or somewhere in between.'

He quickly tacked up the cob he'd arranged to borrow and set out again for Newlands.

Soon after that, Robert Carmichael emerged from the inn, looking refreshed by the coffee. It was twenty to eleven, so we set out briskly along the road. As we walked, I told him my theory about Stephen. He shook his head.

'No, I don't believe that of him. If it were the other way round, I might. There's a wild streak in Miles, but apart from anything else, Stephen wouldn't make himself look ridiculous.'

'I think he's beyond worrying about that. He's on the point of losing everything. Did you know Sophia had signed that paper for Miles?'

'Not until it was too late, no.'

'And that Miles has taken Stephen's fiancée?' I said.

'Nothing has been announced officially.'

'But all of London is talking about it. You must know Stephen better than most people. Have you any idea what he'll do?'

He shook his head. I was letting myself grow angry, oppressed with the idea that something was going to happen and we could do nothing about it.

'What in the world was he doing last night, on his own by the gates to the asylum?' I said. 'Where was he all the time he was missing from London?'

'I can't answer that. All I can say is if you expect me to believe Stephen is going to try to kill his brother, I simply don't.'

'Somebody killed Simon Handy,' I said.

We walked in silence for a while. Then he said quietly: 'We buried Sophia yesterday.'

'Have they held the inquest on her?'

'Yesterday morning. The verdict was accidental death. They decided she drank too much laudanum, meaning only to sleep, and was sufficiently confused to get into the boat, as she sometimes did.'

With a country jury, sparing the feelings of a prominent family, the verdict hardly came as a surprise.

'I suppose you gave evidence,' I said.

'Yes, I did.'

It was a simple statement. There wasn't a trace of combativeness or evasion in him. He was too tired for that, as if he'd been living on his nerves for a long time. As before, I was caught between feeling liking and pity for him, but still nagged by a sense of something hidden.

I asked him if anything had been said at the inquest about the extra bottle of laudanum.

'It was mentioned that there was an empty bottle her maid couldn't account for. Nothing more.'

'The police think they know where it came from,' I said. 'Perhaps it wasn't mentioned at the inquest because they couldn't prove it.'

I told him about Tabby, and my theory that Lady Brinkburn had met her and asked her to buy the laudanum. He shook his head.

'Sophia had more pride than that. She'd rather have gone without than got some girl she hardly knew to run errands behind Betty's back and mine. She was a deeply honourable woman.'

Perhaps he caught some doubt on my face.

'Miss Lane, some time ago I asked if you'd believe me when I told you that Lady Brinkburn and I were not lovers. You were kind enough to say that you would.'

'Yes.'

'I didn't say it then. There were reasons. But it's only just to her memory to say so now. Sophia was more kind and generous to me than any man had a right to expect, but we were never lovers. She lived and died an entirely faithful wife to a husband who treated her shamefully.'

We turned into the side road.

'So, do you believe me?' he said.

'Yes.'

'Thank you for that.'

We said nothing more until we came within sight of the asylum. Its gates stood open to the road.

'Even if you don't believe me about Stephen and Miles, please do what you can,' I said. 'Keep as close to Miles as possible.'

Most of my trust was in Amos, but it was just possible that Robert Carmichael might have some effect. When we came to the top of the drive, I told him he should walk on ahead.

'You're here by right,' I said. 'I'm not.'

But I was still puzzled about his presence there. He nodded, and to my surprise, reached out and touched my hand.

'Thank you for being concerned, for Sophia and for them too. I hope to see you when it's over.'

I watched him walk down the drive. A group of people and three vehicles stood in front of the house. The hearse and mourning carriage now had their teams of horses attached to them and were a fine sight in their way, like some great monument in ebony and silver. The hearse had broad glass panels at the back and sides to give a clear view of the coffin, which was draped in black velvet with gold braid edging. A knight's helmet, brightly burnished and looking remarkably like the ancestral one that had belonged to Sir Gilbert, stood on top of the coffin. There was even a small page, or 'tiger' standing on the step at the back of the hearse, dressed in black velvet breeches and tunic and a black tricorne hat. Lord Brinkburn had contrived a grand spectacle for himself, perhaps in the knowledge that nobody cared enough to do it for him.

Apart from the two principle vehicles there was only one other carriage, an old-fashioned travelling chariot. Since a society funeral usually included a train of at least a dozen carriages bearing friends and relations, and even empty carriages sent to represent their owners, this was a sign of how few friends Lord Brinkburn had left in his native land. One of them, Oliver Lomax, was standing by the travelling chariot, looking at his pocket watch. Even from this distance he looked less upright and confident than when I'd last seen him. Perhaps he was genuinely mourning the death of his old friend. Miles was beside him, holding his tall black horse by the bridle. There was no sign of Stephen.

Miles glanced at Lomax and, at a nod from him, mounted the black horse and rode to take up position in front of the hearse. Under his black top hat with its crepe streamers, his face was pale and expressionless. The driver of the hearse, red-faced and sweating in his heavy funeral cape, flicked the reins and the six black geldings came to attention. Lomax opened the door of the travelling chariot and seemed to be inviting

Carmichael to get in with him, but Carmichael glanced towards Miles and stayed on foot. I looked round for Amos but couldn't see him. My guess was that he'd be waiting on his horse by one of the shrubberies, ready to join the procession once it moved off. Miles pressed his heels into his horse's side and set off at a slow walk. The hearse driver let him get three lengths ahead then set his team in motion, in a slow grinding of wheels on gravel, creaking of leather and jingle of harness chains, the page clinging to a strap on the back. After another three lengths' gap, the mourning coach followed. By then, I was close enough to glance inside and wasn't surprised to see it was empty. All part of the show. Robert Carmichael paced beside it, his eyes on Miles. The travelling chariot followed, with Lomax as its only passenger. I fell in behind it. If we went on as slowly as this, it would be easy to keep up on foot.

Halfway up the drive, a tall shadow of man and horse fell across me and there was Amos.

'Best if I ride on ahead of them, see if there's anyone up to anything,' he said.

Before he'd finished speaking, he was cantering along the grass beside the drive, passing the hearse. Carmichael gave him a startled look and moved up closer to Miles, then visibly relaxed as Amos rode on and out of the gates. Inside his carriage, Lomax would probably be annoyed at this informality, but there was nothing he could do about it.

As we'd guessed, turning six horses and a hearse

through the gateway proved a difficult business and the whole procession slowed to a halt. On foot, I was able to squeeze past to the road. Amos, as the unofficial outrider, was well in front, going at a walk now and turning his head from side to side to see over the hedges. He looked back at me and gave a thumbs-up sign. All clear so far. I stood back as Miles rode out of the gateway, with Carmichael on foot by his side. They were deep in conversation, with Miles leaning down from the saddle. Behind them the hearse manoeuvred itself through the gates, followed by the two carriages, and they rolled slowly behind Miles and his horse towards the main road. From the point of view of anybody intending an attack, that was a good opportunity missed.

I walked behind Oliver Lomax's carriage, thinking about what Carmichael had said. If he'd spoken the truth in saying that he and Sophia weren't lovers, what explained this devotion to the family? Then both my thoughts and my feet were brought to a sharp halt because the carriage had stopped so suddenly I'd almost walked into the back of it. Lomax's head came out of the window, shouting to his driver on the box to ask what was happening. I pushed my way past, walking on the bank close to the hedge through swathes of buttercups and red campion. The whole procession had also come to a stop. The small page on the back of the hearse was swinging out on the hand-strap, trying to see round. I pushed past the mourning carriage and hearse to where Miles, still on horseback, and Robert Carmichael on foot were standing in the middle of the narrow road. In front of them, blocking the way, was a tree trunk that certainly had not been there when we'd walked along the same road about a quarter of an hour before. It wasn't a particularly substantial tree trunk, but since six horses and a hearse could hardly be expected to jump, it blocked the way as effectively as a larger barrier. There was no possibility that it could have fallen accidentally on a calm day, with not enough breeze to stir a grass blade.

Amos had dismounted from his cob and was standing in front of the fallen tree.

'Get back,' he shouted at Miles and Carmichael. 'Get back behind the hearse there.'

Carmichael took the point at once and grabbed the bridle of the black horse, trying to drag it round, but Miles hauled on the rein, resisting him and demanding to know what was happening. The hearse driver echoed the demand more plaintively, and the alarmed voice of Oliver Lomax sounded from two coaches back. Nervous horses started whinnying and fidgeting, jammed in the narrow road and sensing the unease of the humans round them. Amos bent his legs, hooked his arms under the tree trunk and began to raise it. Two men might have found it a heavy burden, and at first it looked as if even Amos's strength couldn't shift it alone. The hearse driver clambered down from his box with the intention of helping, but before he got there Amos straightened his legs and stood upright. For a moment he stood with the tree balanced across his forearms, then pivoted and tossed it alongside the hedge, leaving the road clear.

Even as the grass was still quivering from the impact of it, and before the hearse driver could clamber back on his box, a man appeared from a gateway just beyond where the tree had been. He was hatless, hair plastered to his forehead with sweat, leaves and earth clinging to his black jacket. He was carrying a large woodman's axe. Miles was looking in his direction and saw him first.

'Stephen, what are you doing here?'

Stephen made no reply. He walked out into the centre of the road, stopping in front of the hearse.

'Better let me take care of the axe, sir,' Amos said peaceably.

Stephen ignored him. I could see Amos debating with himself whether to take it off Stephen by force. When Stephen grounded the axe, its head down, but kept his hand round the shaft, Amos glanced at me and moved close to him.

'Not yet,' I mouthed.

Stephen was facing the funeral cavalcade like a man about to make a speech. I for one wanted to hear what he had to say. Oliver Lomax had left his carriage and pushed his way through to stand alongside Miles and Carmichael.

'There's no necessity for this,' Lomax called to Stephen.

'There is every necessity.' Stephen's voice was loud,

but sounded calm. 'You wouldn't listen to me any other way. This whole funeral is a fraud and a farce. You are burying a man who's not dead.'

'Get out of the way,' Miles shouted at Stephen. He kicked his horse into a trot and came riding at Stephen, barging Carmichael aside. Stephen shifted his weight and began to raise the axe. Amos grabbed for Stephen's arm a moment too late. His momentum took Amos swinging past Stephen so that he was standing between the two brothers, off-balance. The axe rose. Amos let himself fall back against the black gelding's chest. Whether he was most concerned to save the horse or Miles there was no telling. But either they'd never been the targets or Stephen had misjudged his blow. The axe swung and struck, not at Miles but at the glass side panel of the hearse.

Even the glass seemed frozen by the suddenness of it. For one heartbeat, the cracked pane hung in its place, defying the laws of gravity. Then it split apart and slithered down to the packed earth of the road, hissing and tinkling. Stephen dropped the axe and took his stand by the shattered panel.

'Just come here and look, if you don't believe me.'

He yelled it to everybody. Carmichael was the first to move. He put his hand on Stephen's arm.

'What is it you want us to see?'

His calm and the quietness of his voice came like cool water in a fever. Stephen looked to be on the point of clambering into the hearse but he stopped and turned to his old tutor, trying to match his reasoned tone.

'What Lomax won't admit is that we've all been led by the nose . . .'

Miles threw himself down from the horse at and came towards them.

'Don't try and reason with him, Carmichael. He's taken leave of his senses.'

Any hope of calm flew away. Stephen seared a look of hatred at his brother, pushed Carmichael aside and started running. Before any of us could see what was coming, he'd vaulted on to the driver's box of the hearse and grabbed the reins. The startled horses flung their heads up and down like black sea waves. I had just a second before the wheels started turning to make my decision, so I suppose it should be called more of an impulse. I ducked my head down, wrapped my hands in my skirts to protect them from the glass, and dived inside the hearse. As it lurched forwards I heard shouts from outside, Amos's deep tones loudest among them, but Stephen had put the scared horses straight into a canter, so there was nothing anyone could do about it.

There'd been no time to explain, and precious little that would have sounded reasonable even if I'd tried. Simply, I was taking a gamble: a gamble that – in spite of what his brother had said – Stephen had not after all taken leave of his senses, and based on his behaviour of the last few minutes, I'd have had to admit that the odds did not look promising.

# CHAPTER TWENTY-FOUR

I crouched on the floor, everything rattling and bouncing round me like an ironmonger's shop in an earthquake. Clouds of brown dust from the road whirled in through the shattered side, setting me coughing and stinging my eyes. I doubt if a hearse had ever moved so fast. A mere coffin was no burden at all for six excited horses, and Stephen was driving like a man trying to win a bet. Through the small window at the front of the hearse, I could see his back as he sat on the driver's box. He didn't turn and had no reason to suppose I was on board. Looking through the back window, I glimpsed a shape in the dust clouds that looked like the mourning carriage coming after us, with a figure large enough to be Amos on the driver's box. It was travelling fast but not gaining on us, having four horses instead of six. As well as the dust, my view of it was restricted by what seemed to be two black columns on the outside of the window. It took me some time to realise that they were the legs of the unfortunate page, forgotten by everybody and clinging to the back of the hearse for dear life.

Through it all, something was clanging like a funeral bell gone mad. The knight's helmet had fallen off the coffin in the first few strides and was now rolling round the floor, striking against the corners of the vehicle and the coffin sides. On one of its revolutions, I caught it and looked at it. I couldn't be certain that it was the one I'd seen in Pratt's workshop in Bond Street, but it certainly looked like it. My theory, still forming among the whirling dust clouds, depended on the idea that it was one and the same. The clowns from Astley's – acting on somebody's behalf – had taken the armour from Pratt's to an unknown destination. One of the clowns had been at Kingston that very morning and might well have been sent on to meet the hearse at its first stop at Esher. These two facts, combined with Stephen's claim that we were burying a man who wasn't dead, had formed the wild idea that sent me diving into the hearse. I wished Miles hadn't interrupted Stephen, or that there were some way of talking to him. *You're missing something clear as noonday.* I thought I knew what he meant now. I'd no idea where he was heading, but he'd surely have to stop at some time. He could hardly drive a hearse and six horses for long on the public roads at this speed. Soon we'd have to turn out of the side road and on to the main highway with heavy traffic. Did he have a plan at all?

The helmet was in my hands, but there was still a metallic clashing noise somewhere. It took me a while to realise that it was coming from inside the coffin. So the rest of the armour was in there. It made sense of a kind, the way that some madness makes sense if you follow the thread patiently enough. A change in our speed sent the velvet pall slipping from the coffin top, hanging askew with the gold braid grazing the floor. We'd slowed from a canter to a trot and the shape behind us was gaining. It was indeed the mourning carriage with Amos on the box, getting all the speed possible out of his four mares. The black legs of the page were still there on the other side of the window. Then as I watched the legs canted over to one side because we were turning left, still at a trot and dangerously sharply. I thought the poor lad must fall and be badly hurt, and then that the hearse itself would topple over and all of us, people and horses, be killed. A vehicle less broadly based would have gone for a certainty, but somehow we were past the turn, out on the high road and cantering again, and the legs of the page had returned to upright. Amos and his team managed the turn better and gained some ground. I guessed that his plan was to overtake us and force the hearse to stop, but there was still a lot of ground to make up.

The pall was crumpled on the floor now, the gleaming coffin top bare. It had shifted. The sharp turn had dislodged it so that it was at an angle to the coffin itself, a triangle of blackness gaping at the corner. Surely coffin lids were screwed down? This one wasn't. There were holes all round the lid, expensively brass lined, but no screws in them. That made sense too. It gave me just enough confidence to do the thing that would prove my theory right or wrong. I moved from a crouch to a kneeling position, accustomed enough now to the motion to risk a move, and put the helmet on the floor. Still on my knees, I shuffled towards the end of the coffin and gave the lid a push to open it a few inches wider, heart hammering in case I was wrong. My reward was a gleam of burnished metal – a pair of greaves, lying neatly side by side.

'Leg armour, but no legs.'

I said it aloud, wild with relief. Stephen was right. All this funeral pomp for a suit of empty armour. The person who thought he had a right to wear it wasn't dead at all, but alive and enjoying his bitter joke. Anger as well as relief made me shove the whole coffin lid aside. The thump it made as it fell off jarred through my body. I looked from the greaves, up to the swell of the corselet, and a scream jagged through my head, through the interior of the hearse, so that the whole world was ringing with it.

I screwed up my eyes and put my hands over my ears, but it was no use because it was my own scream. A hand had risen slowly from the coffin. It was a bony, liver-spotted hand, appropriate to a corpse. My first horrified thought was that my theory was wrong after all. There really was a body in the coffin under the armour. The jolting of the journey, and my own desecration, had provoked it into this last parody of life. But as the scream died away I managed to grab another scrap of thought: *corpses do not hold pistols.*

When I opened my eyes, sure enough, the hand was holding a pistol. At first sight, it had been holding it awkwardly, as if grabbed in a hurry. Now the pistol was level and there was a face behind it – an elderly face surrounded by sparse white hair, with eyes that were all pupil from the darkness inside the coffin so that they looked hard as obsidian.

'Lord Brinkburn,' I said. 'You killed your wife.'

Not a wise thing to say, if there'd been any hope of pacifying him, but the look on that face was beyond reach of argument and I knew he intended to kill me or anyone else who was in his way. I tried to get off my knees, with a faint hope of throwing myself out of the hearse. The eyes and the pistol followed me, the bony hand tightening on the butt. Then the air broke into a spray of diamonds and something hard and black hammered into my chest, hurling me backwards into darkness. As I went, I was aware of somebody saying something. Even in the circumstances, it struck me as odd that the Angel Gabriel should speak with a cockney accent. It took several repetitions for me to grasp that what the voice was saying was *Enerund*s?

I opened my eyes. Still darkness. There was something over my eyes. I pulled it away and found it was the page's tricorne hat. The first thing I saw was Tabby's face inches away from mine, mouth open in a gape that was either horror or laughter. She was lying on her stomach on top of me. The broken glass all round us on the hearse floor and air coming from a different quarter showed that she'd come diving in through the back window.

'Out,' I gasped.

Lord Brinkburn and his pistol must still be there in the coffin, though I couldn't see him and there on the floor together we were an easy target. I grabbed Tabby by her page's coat and rolled us over towards the shattered side panel, just aware that the hearse was now going slowly and jerkily. Stephen's voice was shouting from the box. Glass jabbed at me through my clothes as we rolled over the broken rim of the panel and thumped down on the road, Tabby uppermost. The back wheel of the hearse ground slowly past us, then the vehicle juddered to a halt, just beyond where we were lying. Tabby rolled away from me and helped me up.

'He said it was a joke. He said it was only to have a laugh on all of them.'

She spoke pleadingly, as if expecting rebuke from me. Trickles of blood ran down her forehead and cheek.

Stephen had jumped off the driver's box and come running towards us, but before he got to us the mourning coach arrived at a canter. Amos pulled the mares back on their haunches, knotted the reins round the rail at the front of the box, then made an almighty vault to land on his feet beside Tabby and me.

'What's happening, girl?'

'Lord Brinkburn, in the coffin. He's got a pistol.'

I gasped the words out as he was helping both of us to our feet. Even Amos's quick mind couldn't have understood what was happening, but on the word 'pistol' he started walking towards the hearse.

'Stop,' I said. 'He's dangerous.'

The door of the mourning coach opened. Robert Carmichael and Miles bundled out, falling over each other, and came running up to us.

'Lord Brinkburn isn't dead,' I said. 'He's in the coffin, but he's alive. He's got a pistol. Make Amos stop before he shoots him.'

They stood stock still.

'Your father's still alive,' I shouted. 'But for heaven's sake . . .'

The look of stupefaction on both their faces showed that they hadn't known. I rushed after Amos and grabbed the back of his coat, just out of pistol range of the hearse.

'No need to rush in and tackle him,' I pleaded. 'He can't get away.'

'He will, if somebody doesn't get hold of those horses,' Amos said.

The six black geldings were a churning, whinnying mass. In stopping the vehicle so suddenly, Stephen had slewed it sideways. The front pair were in a ditch at the side of the road, though still on their feet, a shaft splintered, traces twisted like seaweed.

'You keep back,' Amos told me.

He ran to the horses, drawing the knife he always kept in a sheath at his waist, and slashed through the front traces, freeing the pair in the ditch. They clambered out and bolted away down the road. Amos managed to grab what was left of the traces and pulled the others round before they could follow. This slewed the hearse so that the open side was towards us. The coffin was still there, with no sign of anybody inside it.

'He can't have got away,' I said. 'We'd have seen him.'

Stephen faced Carmichael and Miles.

'Perhaps you'll believe me now. Go and look. That coffin's empty,' he said.

'It's not empty,' I yelled. 'He's in it. Don't go in there.'

I was desperate, wondering what I could say or do to make them understand the danger. Then the problem solved itself. The face with the obsidian eyes reared itself up over the edge of the coffin and the hand pointed the pistol at the group of us.

Somebody screamed. Not I this time; it was Miles. After that, silence. Stephen took a step towards the hearse. The pistol moved so that it was pointing at him. He stopped.

'He's done you no harm.'

That was Robert Carmichael's voice, remarkably steady, speaking to the man in the coffin. He walked forward, past Stephen. The pistol aim shifted to him. Stephen, voice hoarse, told Carmichael to stop, but he went on walking towards the hearse.

411

'It will only make things worse,' Carmichael said, as if reasoning with a difficult child. 'Give it to me.'

And he added two syllables that none of us had expected to hear. Beside me, Miles gasped and Stephen jerked his head round and stared at Carmichael. Carmichael took another step forward. The pistol cracked. He fell to one knee and the hearse lurched forward. I ran to Carmichael. His head was down, fists clenched against his chest with blood seeping between them.

Amos came running up too, shouting to somebody I couldn't see to keep hold of the horses. Carmichael raised his head and looked at me.

'Not dead.'

He sounded surprised. Gently, Amos took Carmichael's hands and moved them away from his chest, then drew the jacket aside. Carmichael winced.

'Yes, you'll live,' Amos told him, as casually as if they were discussing a hurt hound. 'Glanced off the collar bone. We'll get you lying down in the coach there.'

He helped Carmichael to his feet.

'The pistol,' Carmichael said. 'Get it before he reloads.'

Amos nodded.

'You all right with him?' he asked, transferring Robert's weight to me.

Like a man on a routine errand he strolled across and into the hearse. Lord Brinkburn hadn't moved since firing the shot.

'I'll take that, sir,' Amos said, quite politely, and removed the pistol from his unresisting hand.

Stephen walked over and helped me support Robert. 'Did he say . . .?'

'Later,' I said. 'Get him to the coach before he loses any more blood.'

Between us, we walked Carmichael towards the mourning coach. Lomax had just climbed out of it, looking as if the events of the morning had aged him ten years. He glanced from the disabled hearse to Robert and back again, opening his mouth to ask what was happening. Lord Brinkburn chose that moment to crawl out of the coffin, stiffly as a clockwork toy, face expressionless.

'Cornelius,' Lomax said.

The horror on his face and in his voice left no doubt that he hadn't been included in the plot. Lord Brinkburn glanced once in his direction, then concentrated on manoeuvring himself out of the hearse, shuffling over the floor on his buttocks, setting his feet unsteadily on the ground. He was wearing a shirt and old-fashioned black breeches, dragging the velvet pall cloth after him. Stephen looked at me over Carmichael's head and made a move as if he wanted to go to his father.

'Cornelius?'

Lomax's voice quavered, begging for reassurance. Lord Brinkburn glanced at his old college friend as if he didn't recognise him, then straightened himself up as best he could, leaning on the side of the hearse, and tried to drape the pall round himself like a toga.

'*Hadrianus imperator sum.*'

'No more of that,' Stephen said sharply. 'You're not the emperor Hadrian. You were never mad, not in that way. You deceived everybody, except the keeper of the asylum. I suppose you made it worth his while.'

'Why?' Miles said plaintively. 'What was he doing?'

For probably the first time since childhood he was appealing to Stephen like a perplexed younger brother. Stephen didn't answer. Lord Brinkburn said nothing, hunched under the pall more like a soft-shelled turtle than an emperor.

'He killed your mother,' I said to Miles. 'I think he probably killed Simon Handy too.'

After what had happened, there was no gentle way of saying it. Besides, the urgent thing now was to get Robert to medical help. Amos had seen that. He'd managed to find a couple of bystanders to hold the hearse team and was already on the box of the mourning coach, turning it round towards the town. He shouted to Miles and Stephen to look after the other horses then brought the coach to a halt and signed to me to bring Robert on board. Tabby helped.

'Am I coming with you?' she said, sounding remarkably unconcerned.

She'd even managed to retrieve her tricorne hat and jam it on her head at an inappropriately jaunty angle.

'Yes, you are,' I said. 'You have some explaining to do.'

414

I made Robert lie back on the seat and wouldn't let him talk on the short and fast journey back to Kingston. As soon as we came to a halt in the yard of the inn, Amos jumped off the box and told one of the stable lads to run for a doctor. The yard was crowded as usual. Various curious people came to gawp as Amos helped Robert inside. Intent on the two of them, I took no notice until a familiar voice sounded behind me.

'Good morning, Miss Lane. In the middle of the excitement as usual, I see.'

I spun round, and there was Mr Disraeli, elegant as ever, with the faintly amused air he cultivated. But there was just a shade more anxiety in his expression than was appropriate for a cynical man of the world. I tried to match his calm.

'Have you come down for Lord Brinkburn's funeral? If so, you've wasted your journey. It's been cancelled.'

'For lack of a body, I presume.'

I stared at him.

'How in the world did you know that?'

'I didn't know. There were rumours. Didn't you receive the note I sent you?'

'I thought . . .'

I started to explain and gave up.

'I believe we need to talk,' he said.

We walked side by side towards the door of the inn.

'Am I still coming with you?' said a cockney voice from behind us.

Disraeli looked over his shoulder. When he saw the

funeral page, with blood-streaked face and hair coming down under the piratical hat, his jaw dropped. I'd never seen that happen before and didn't expect to again.

'Is that yours?' he said.

I nodded. Tabby followed us in.

# CHAPTER TWENTY-FIVE

'So how did you know?' I said to Disraeli.

He and I were sitting on either side of an empty fireplace in the inn's back parlour. I'd told him what had happened as briefly as I could, trying not to shudder when it came to the hand rising out of the coffin. Tabby stood by the door, dabbing at her face with a damp cloth, which was all she'd accept in the way of medical attention. Luckily, the scratches weren't deep. Disraeli answered my question in a low voice, obviously uneasy about her presence, but I wasn't letting Tabby out of my sight.

'I didn't know anything for certain, but there were rumours around legal circles,' he said. 'There'd been an argument between Stephen and Oliver Lomax, and one of the clerks must have been listening. Stephen was claiming that the madness was a pose and his father

417

wasn't really dead. Lomax thought Stephen was talking nonsense, trying to muddy the waters about this inheritance business. I thought you should know what was being said, but it seems you were ahead of me.'

I didn't disillusion him, having my professional pride.

'I think all the time Stephen was away from London, he was keeping watch on that so-called asylum,' I said. 'He had a much clearer idea of what his father was capable of than any of us realised.'

'Brinkburn must have been planning it for a long time,' Disraeli said.

'Yes. Probably ever since Robert Carmichael knocked him downstairs.'

Disraeli's eyebrows rose.

'The tutor?'

'Yes. Brinkburn thought he and Lady Brinkburn were lovers.'

'Were they?'

'No.'

He gave me a look as if asking how I could be so sure.

'So Brinkburn had decided to kill his wife?' he said.

'Yes, but he had no intention of hanging for it. He pretended he was mad to have a chance to do his plotting without interference and set up an alibi, then announced his own death and confirmed it in people's minds with this very elaborate funeral. If there were any doubts cast on it or questions asked later about how Lady Brinkburn died, he'd have been safely out of the way in Italy. I dare say he'd conveyed a fair amount of the family money over there to live comfortably for the rest of his life.'

'And the title?'

'In his own eyes, he'd still be Lord Brinkburn. It might even have amused him to think of Stephen and Miles fighting over a title that belonged to neither of them, just as it amused him to take the family armour with him.'

'A strange sense of humour.'

'Very strange. But then, not many men witness their own funeral procession. That would have appealed to him. His original idea might have been to travel quietly to Italy and have the armour sent out in the coffin, but he couldn't resist an extra touch of drama by being there in person.'

'So you say he'd decided to kill his wife,' Disraeli said. 'Did he actually do it?'

'Yes.'

For the second time that day, I saw Disraeli taken aback. That firm 'yes' hadn't come from me. It came from Tabby, in her corner. Disraeli might have been trying to speak quietly, but his discretion was no protection from ears made sharp by street life.

'You'd better come here and tell us,' I said.

She came and stood beside me, giving Disraeli stare for stare.

'Starting with the night you walked out,' I said.

Tabby glared at me.

'It wasn't my fault. They were making fun of me.'

'Never mind that now. Tell us what happened after you left the house.'

She took a deep breath.

'It was raining. I didn't know where I was. They'd got me so angry, I just walked round for a bit, thinking what I wanted to do to them. It started thundering and lightning, so I thought I'd find somewhere to curl up till it was over. I was walking along by a wall near some bushes, then this man spoke to me.'

'What did he say?'

'He asked what I was doing there. I didn't know nobody was there until he spoke, and he had a dark coat and a hat on, so I didn't see him against the bushes. But I recognised the voice.'

'Recognised it from where?' I said.

'That first night, at the little house by the river, when I thought it was a ghost and he said something about somebody coming back to haunt somebody. It was the same voice.'

Disraeli was leaning forward, listening intently but leaving the questioning to me. I told Tabby to go on.

'Anyway, when I didn't answer all at once he said did I work for Lady Brinkburn. So I told him I hated all of them in that house and I wouldn't work there even if they paid me a pound a week.'

She paused for another deep breath.

'What did he say to that?'

'He laughed and said he supposed I'd just been

dismissed for insolence. So I said he supposed about right. I didn't think you'd want anything more to do with me, see, because you'd expected me to behave proper with the rest of them, and I hadn't. So he said would I like to work for him.'

'Just like that, only a moment after he met you?'

She shrugged.

'Why not? So anyway, I said yes, and he put his hand on my shoulder and said that from now on I was his handy girl and not to forget it.'

'*Handy* girl, those very words?'

'That's what he said. I didn't think nothing to it at the time. It was only later I remembered that Violet's man, the one that died, was named Handy, and I only remembered that after him and me had the falling out over the bottle, so . . .'

'Don't get ahead of yourself. You've just agreed to work for him. Did he tell you who he was?'

'He said his name was Lord Brinkburn and he owned the ground we were standing on and the house and everything, though it didn't suit him to live there at present. So I asked him where we were going and he said I was to wait where I was because he had things he wanted to see to, then he'd come back for me.'

'He didn't say what things?'

'Nah. Anyway, I waited in the bushes there for a long time. It was getting light when he came back. He said I was to follow him and we went all the way along the river bank, past where our little house was, to a place where he had his carriage waiting, parked out of the way under some trees. He said he was going to sleep inside for a bit and I was to sleep underneath it, so I did. Then later he woke me up and told me to harness the horse because we had some shopping to do. I didn't know how to harness the horse, so he cuffed me round the head and said I wasn't very handy after all and did it himself.'

Tabby said it in a matter-of-fact way, as if cuffs round the head were only to be expected. I tried not to let my anger show.

'And what was this "shopping"?'

'He drove us up near a chemist shop, gave me some money and said I was to go inside and ask for a bottle of laudanum, the strongest solution they had. He made me say it over and over until I got it right. So I went in and got it and gave it to him, and we went back to where the carriage was parked and waited there all day, until evening. Then we walked back to the hall. He gave me the bottle and said I was to take it in at a side door he'd show me and put it by Lady Brinkburn's bed. I said I didn't know where her bedroom was and I wasn't setting foot in that house again, no matter what he did. I wasn't going to have them laughing at me again.'

Even now, with Tabby standing beside me, my heart lurched at the danger she'd been in.

'He must have been very angry with you.'

'He was, first go off. He got hold of my ear and

twisted it till I thought it would come away from me head. And that was when he said about Handy.'

'What exactly?'

'"I had another servant called Handy. He got above himself and wanted a lot of money before he'd do as I told him, so I took a hammer and cracked his head open like cracking a boiled egg."'

She even managed an approximation of that elderly, arrogant voice.

'So what did you do?'

'I told him if he tried that with me, I'd take the hammer to him first.'

Again, the voice was matter-of-fact. She wasn't boasting. In her world, that was how things were done.

'Weren't you afraid he'd kill you there and then?'

She shrugged again.

'He didn't in any event. He just started laughing.'

'Laughing!'

'Yeah. He was still holding on to me ear, so he was jerking it up and down from laughing. Then he said I had the cheek of the devil, so perhaps I was Handy re-in-something or other.'

'Reincarnated?'

'Something like that. So then he let go of me ear and took the bottle back and said he supposed he'd have to do it himself and to wait there. Then he came back and we went and found his carriage again, and he drove us all day, to the big house.'

'What big house?'

'The place where we started from this morning.'

'The asylum?'

'I didn't see any mad people there, it was only us and some people who looked after the place. Unless he was mad.'

'Do you think he was?'

She considered.

'Dunno. We talked about it one day, when he'd come back from somewhere and was in a good mood. He gave me a glass of wine and said he supposed I thought he was mad. So I said I thought he was no madder than a lot of other people, and he laughed and said I was right and he just liked to live the way he wanted to, and that other people were always out to stop people like him living the way they wanted to. But they were ordinary people, so didn't matter, and him and me weren't ordinary.'

I wished, for several reasons, that I could have heard that dialogue between the lord and the gutter urchin.

'Was that when he told you about the plans for his own funeral?'

'Yes. He said there were a lot of people wanted to see him dead, so he was going to give them what they wanted, only he didn't plan to die just yet. So we'd have this big funeral, and he'd travel in the coffin for the first stage to make sure things were being done the way he said, then someone would come and help me let him out and the coffin would go on a boat with nothing in it but a suit of old armour. By then, we'd be on the other side of the water, laughing at them.'

'So you were you supposed to go away with him?'

'He said I could go with him to Italy. Is that a long way?'

'Yes.'

'He said it was always warm and sunny there and a man could do what he wanted.'

How long would it have stayed warm and sunny for Tabby if his plans had succeeded and she had gone with him? Weeks or possibly months before she'd done something to annoy him again, and that time he would have killed her instead of laughing, just as he'd killed Handy when he'd baulked at helping his employer commit murder. But in spite of everything, there'd been a touch of regret for a lost adventure when she'd talked about going to Italy.

'I got the surprise of my life when I saw you in there with the coffin,' she said. 'Until you screamed, I thought you was all part of the plan.'

'You saved my life, diving through that window,' I said. 'You took a risk. He could have killed you instead.'

She shrugged.

'I didn't think about it. I just went.'

Disraeli caught my eye. His look said, *Can we believe her?* I nodded and stood up.

'You sit down and wait here, Tabby. I'll be back in a moment.'

Disraeli and I walked into the corridor.

'She'd be a good witness,' I said.

He made a face.

425

'I hope to God it won't come to that.'

'Why? For the good name of the aristocracy?'

'It's not as simple as that.'

'It seems to me quite simple. He's killed two people at least. If he were some poor tradesman, they'd hang him without thinking twice.'

'Lord or tradesman, the man's insane. We don't hang madmen.'

'So what will happen? Will he be allowed to go off to Italy, or be shut in some other so-called asylum with freedom to come and go?'

'We'd have to make sure that didn't happen again.'

'We?'

'I'll have to speak to his sons, of course.'

As before in our acquaintance, it struck me how much Disraeli needed to be at the hub of things. Favours to friends, or even friends of friends, who might be useful in his political career were only part of it. He wanted to know how society works, the way a clock-maker wants to know about cogs, springs and ratchets. That knowledge was power to him, though what he hoped to do with the power wasn't clear to me.

'I shall speak to Lomax when he's recovered,' he said. 'You've earned your fee and it should be paid.'

'I'm sure he won't see it that way. I was supposed to help settle the question of succession smoothly and quietly. It's still not settled.'

'Ah yes, the succession. I have an idea that the old man won't outlive the humiliation for long. Of course the eldest son will have management of the estates as soon as Brinkburn's declared officially insane.'

His tone was musing, almost absent minded. My question had been a test to see how much he knew.

We came into the stable yard. It was full of grooms and lads dealing with a mass of over-excited black horses. Amos stood head and shoulders above the rest. He gave the halter ropes he was holding to a couple of lads and came over to us, raising his cap to Disraeli. Disraeli, who knew Amos's worth, returned the compliment with a tip of his silk top hat. I asked Amos if any of the horses had been hurt.

'Nothing worse than a strain and scratch or two. They'll be all right when we get them settled.'

'Is the hearse here?' Disraeli asked him.

'Couple of draught horses are bringing it in now. I sent the carriage back for the gentlemen.'

Disraeli said he would wait inside, and please to tell him when the gentlemen arrived. I had a word with Amos, then went to reclaim Tabby. She jumped up when I came in.

'Are we going back to London now?'

'Not quite yet. I'm going to ask them to send you in something to eat and drink, but I want you to do an errand for me first. Would you please find the landlord and ask how the gentleman is who was brought in wounded.'

She grinned and went. I settled into a chair, thinking that even Disraeli didn't know anything. With his appetite for secrets, he'd have relished those two syllables I'd heard from Robert Carmichael. But I'd no intention of telling him. Not yet, at any rate, and perhaps never.

Tabby was back within minutes, grin even wider.

'He wants to see you.'

'Who? The landlord?'

'Nah, the gentlemen who got shot. I couldn't find the landlord, so I asked somebody where the gentleman's room was and went in. He says . . .' She screwed her face up, trying to remember accurately. 'He says, "My compliments to Miss Lane, and if she can spare a few minutes I'd be very grateful for a talk with her." Second room on the left, it is, top of the big staircase.'

No point in lecturing her about keeping to instructions, so instead I took mine from her and went.

# CHAPTER TWENTY-SIX

I knocked on the door. It was opened by a man carrying a doctor's bag. He was on the point of leaving.

'He'll do very well,' he said to me. 'Nothing but gruel and toast for the next twenty-four hours and total rest. I've left him a sleeping draught. Make sure that he takes it. I shall return tomorrow to change the dressings.'

He obviously took me for a relative. I didn't disillusion him. The room was dim, curtains drawn. A maid stood at the washstand, piling bloodstained cloths into a bowl. Robert was in a bed by the wall, propped up on pillows.

'Miss Lane, thank you for coming.'

His voice was strong but his face was as pale as the borrowed nightshirt he was wearing. He glanced at the maid then looked a question at me. I asked her if she would be so kind as to tell the kitchens to make gruel. She left, taking the bowl of cloths with her.

'Thank you. Are they back yet?'

'On their way.'

'Would you come over here – I'm sorry I can't get up.'

I sat on a chair by the bed.

'Are you hurt at all, Miss Lane?'

'No.'

'I want you to do me a favour.'

'What?'

'Forget what you heard me say to him.'

'You called Lord Brinkburn father.'

He tried to smile.

'A man may say anything when somebody's pointing a pistol at him.'

'It's true though, isn't it?' I said.

He didn't answer. I shifted the chair round so that I was looking him in the face.

'If I'm supposed to keep your family secrets, you'd better tell me why. You're his son by the first wife, Natalie Stevens, aren't you?'

'Yes.'

'Did Stephen and Miles know?'

'No.'

'And she?'

'Sophia knew from the day I walked out of the blue and into her life. It's unbelievable, that woman's generosity. That's why I'm asking you to do this, in her memory. It's all a wreck and a horror, but we must save something for her sake. You liked her, didn't you?'

'Yes. So did you just come to her and tell her who you were?'

'I didn't intend it to be as brutal as that, but heaven help me, it must have seemed that way to her. I grew up knowing Brinkburn was my father, I even have a few faint early memories of him. I was too young to know or care about legitimate or illegitimate. Then my mother died. Brinkburn paid for my education, public school, Cambridge, but always through lawyers and on condition that I used another name, not his. I chose my mother's father's name, Carmichael. I never saw Lord Brinkburn in all that time. As I grew older, I was curious enough to make a few inquiries about him. I found out that he was married with sons and assumed that I was a by-blow, perhaps one of many.'

'Weren't you unhappy about that?'

'Boys are tough creatures. I thought he was behaving quite generously in the circumstances. I assumed that, when I'd finished my education, he'd send word of what I was supposed to do. I had some idea of going into the army, but I'd need his approval and a little of his money if I wanted a commission. So I hiked blithely from Cambridge to Buckinghamshire to see him, not knowing he was living in Italy. I'd no intention of embarrassing him, of course. My idea was to deliver a note asking for the favour of a meeting. I was walking up the drive with it, and met Sophia.'

'And told her, just like that?'

He moved awkwardly and winced.

'Almost. You saw how quick she was to form impressions. She guessed there was something. And she made it clear from the start that there was no affection left between her and Lord Brinkburn, if there ever had been any. I told her he'd paid for my education. When she suddenly asked me if I were his son, I saw no reason to lie to her. I said yes.'

'What did she do?'

'She asked me to stay. She said she needed a tutor for her sons.'

'Your half brothers. Wasn't that awkward?'

'They didn't know, of course. Oddly, it wasn't awkward. I liked her and I liked them. And I suppose I was young, not knowing much of the world. It seemed a reasonable arrangement to me. I'd tutor them, put by a little money, then off to the army. Only, when I'd been with them a few weeks, Sophia said she couldn't in honour keep quiet about it any more. She told me the story you've read in her journal. She said my mother had been legally married, I was my father's legitimate heir and she knew enough about that first marriage to help me prove it to the world.'

'What did you do?'

'Told her she must do no such thing.'

'Didn't you believe her?'

'Yes.'

'Didn't you want a title and a fortune?'

'No.'

He said it with a force that set him coughing. I poured

water. He drank it and leaned back on the pillows, and talked without taking his eyes off my face, as if he needed very much to convince me.

'After what she'd told me, I didn't want my father's name, whether it had a title in front of it or not. As for a fortune – I'd always expected to earn my living. I shouldn't know what to do with a fortune, particularly one I'd taken from a boy who'd done me no harm.'

'Why did she tell you, do you think?'

'That quixotic sense of justice of hers. And another thing . . .' He hesitated.

'Yes?'

'She was already beginning to convince herself that Lord Brinkburn had poisoned my mother when it suited his purposes to have her out of the way so that he could marry Sophia legally. She thought she owed me a debt.'

'Do you think she was right, that he did poison your mother?'

'I don't suppose I'll ever know for sure. I doubted it until today. Now I think he was quite capable of it.'

'Was Sophia surprised that you wouldn't claim what was yours?'

'I think she was already beginning to know me by then. I said if she tried to do anything about it, I'd go abroad and never come back. She had to accept that. I thought nobody would ever know but the two of us; Stephen would succeed to the title and that would be that. Then she developed this prejudice against Stephen and . . . well, you know the rest.'

I couldn't help glancing at the small bottle on his bedside table that held the doctor's sleeping draught. His eyes followed mine.

'Yes, that affected her judgement too. Would you please put that wretched bottle somewhere I can't see it. I'd rather lie awake for the rest of my life than touch laudanum.'

I took it away and put it in a cupboard. His eyes followed me there and back.

'So, will you do as I ask and forget what I called him?' he said.

'Stephen and Miles heard.'

'I shall deal with them. Stephen will succeed, Miles will be properly provided for, and that will be an end of it.'

It was their tutor's voice speaking as well as their elder brother's. I believed him.

'I can't forget,' I said, 'but I won't tell.'

Particularly not Disraeli.

Amos, Tabby and I stayed at the inn overnight. Late in the evening a message was brought up to say a gentleman wanted to see me downstairs. Stephen was waiting in the private parlour. I'd never warm to the man, but came near to pitying him. His face was haggard, with a nervous twitch to the mouth.

'I apologise to you, Miss Lane. I should never have implied that you were in my brother's pay.'

I nodded acceptance of the apology. I wanted him

to go. He stayed, shifting his weight from one foot to another.

'I'd been driven half mad. I'd watched my father. I knew something was happening, but nobody would listen to me.'

'What's going to happen to your father?' I said.

It seemed to me I had a right to know. His reply was reluctant.

'Lomax says no legal offence has been committed, although the funeral was a joke in very bad taste. It has been agreed that my father's mental condition makes it necessary that he should be kept in a secure establishment for the rest of his life. That is being attended to.'

In his words I heard the soft thuds of the upper classes closing doors against unpleasantness. I wanted to scream that two people had died. No use. Stephen added, in a voice so low I could hardly hear it: 'And Robert says we are to thank you.'

Before we left next morning, I went to inquire after Robert's health. He heard my voice at the door and called to me to come in. The doctor stayed tactfully in a corner packing up his bag. Robert looked better and claimed to have slept well.

He smiled and put out his hand to me.

'Stephen spoke to you?'

'Yes. I guessed you'd sent him.'

'I had a talk with both of them yesterday evening. They've seen sense, I'm glad to say.'

If the doctor had been listening, nothing in Robert's manner or voice would have told him his patient had just talked his way out of fortune and title. Trying to keep my own voice as light, I asked what he intended to do now, as if we were simply discussing plans for the next few days. His reply showed he knew I meant more than that.

'In all honesty, I don't know. Nearly all my adult life has been looking after Sophia. I feel as if I'm coming out of a chrysalis and I don't know yet what kind of creature I am.'

'I think a good one,' I said.

He glanced to make sure that the doctor's attention was on his bag, then raised my hand to his lips and kissed it, not in the exaggerated chivalrous way as Miles might have done, but quite simply.

'I shall travel, I think, when I'm well,' he said. 'I'd appreciate it very much if you'd allow me to write to you.'

'Yes. Yes, please.'

He was still holding my hand. A knock sounded on the door.

'Her journal,' I said. 'I still have it.'

The door opened to let in a maid with a steaming bowl of gruel. He let go of my hand slowly.

'Keep it. I think it's safer with you than anybody. To our next meeting.'

'To our next meeting.'

\*     \*     \*

Tabby and I saw off Amos, riding the gelding and leading the mare, and later took our seats inside the coach back to London. I'd negotiated to buy garments from one of the maids at the inn, so that Tabby could be decently dressed. She'd been ungratefully reluctant to exchange her page's costume for skirts and a mob cap, but was more cheerful by the time we arrived back in the city.

'So what's happening next?' she asked, as we turned into Abel Yard.

'I hope nothing for a week or two,' I said.

She looked quite disappointed. Again, that dreadful feeling of responsibility struck me. As far as I'd had any plan for her, it was to give her a more orderly life. I'd done quite the reverse. All I'd achieved was to feed her voracious appetite for drama. When I watched her putting down our bags and looking round the untidy yard with the air of somebody coming home, I knew Tabby had added herself to my list of unsolved problems.

# CHAPTER TWENTY-SEVEN

A few days later I paid another social call on Celia.

'My dear, where have you been? Surely not another aunt? Country relatives are all very well, but one shouldn't take them too seriously. Now, I want to know everything you've been doing.'

So for the next twenty minutes or so I savoured the taste of chocolate and the scent of roses without saying a word, while she prattled on happily about people I didn't know. Then:

'. . . and you must have heard the latest on the Brinkburns, even down in the country. It turns out that the old man wasn't dead after all! I can't think how that rumour started, but perhaps it was a mix-up at the asylum. And all that business about the mother was a mistake as well. It seems that she was writing a novel, poor woman, and there was this young bride in it who

438

was on her own in a tower by a lake in a storm and well . . . you know. She talked to her friends about this novel and I suppose they were only half listening, as people do, and they got the idea into their heads that she was talking about herself, which I suppose should be a lesson to all of us. Anyway . . .'

She paused for breath and took a sip of chocolate.

'. . . Stephen will inherit when the old man really does die at last, as everybody thought he would, and he and Miles have made up their quarrel. They were actually seen at a private dinner party together last night, though of course they can't go to balls and things because of being in mourning for their mother. I must say, Stephen is being very gallant and forgiving about the whole thing, which is . . .'

I managed to break into the flow, though I had to raise my voice to do it.

'What do you mean, Stephen's being forgiving? Stephen's the one who's won, isn't he? It should be Miles being forgiving.'

'Oh, my dear, you have been out of things, haven't you?' She looked at me pityingly. 'I thought everybody knew. In spite of Stephen being the heir, Rosa Fitzwilliam has decided to stay with Miles. Of course, Stephen is broken hearted, though now everybody knows the inheritance business is settled, I'm sure there'll be plenty of girls just queuing up for a chance to console him. Of course, everybody's saying Rosa could have done better, but she does love Miles, so I suppose it's all very right and romantic.'

I sat there marvelling at how easily the social order seemed to repair its wounds, and wishing it were the same for people. Celia must have mistaken my expression for shame at being so far behind-hand with the news that mattered.

'My dear, it really does puzzle me how you manage to know so little about what's really happening in the world.'

'I suppose I have a kind of talent for it,' I said.

A+

AUTHOR
INSIGHTS,
EXTRAS &
MORE...

FROM

**CARO
PEACOCK**

AND

**AVON A**

# Knights in a Time Warp

Suits of armour are part of the furniture of my working life. Where some people might come in to the office of a morning and stroll past computers, water coolers, filing cabinets, and hardly notice them, I do much the same with a line of figures covered from their toes to the crests of their heads in shining steel. Some have elbow and knee plates so ornate that they look like fins on the kind of fish you see on *National Geographic* programs. One wears a natty little gold crown on top of his helmet. Other helmets stick out at the front like crows' beaks, as if the person inside intended to peck his opponent to death if all else failed. They are, in a sense, my bread and butter because, when not writing books, I work as a guide in stately English homes. My present place of work is Hampton Court. No, not that Johnny-come-lately of a place on the Thames just outside London, lived in by Henry VIII. Our Hampton Court is a hundred years older than that one, and around a hundred sixty miles west, near the city of Hereford. Its foundation stone was laid by Henry IV, and it goes back six hundred years.

Visitors tend to gasp at this lineup of armour in our cloister corridor, and I guess they're imagining the clang, crash, and bloodshed of battles five hundred years ago. They often gasp again when I explain that the suits of armour in this part of the house were made only about a hundred and seventy years ago in the nineteenth century, when steamships were crossing the Atlantic, railways extending all over Britain, workers mass-producing things in factories, and an ingenious chap named Babbage was inventing the forerunner of the computer. Also, the only clanging, clashing, and bloodshed most of these suits are likely to have experienced is when sweating workmen carried them into the newly built castles of men who'd made their money in trade and wanted some instant ancestors. Far from being disappointed by this, many visitors are intrigued. What's going on here? When, in *Henry V*, Shakespeare wrote, "Now thrive the armourers," he's alluding to the coming Battle of Agincourt in 1415. To find armourers still thriving more than four hundred years later takes some explaining.

The root of it is the Victorian passion for things medieval. Probably it was a reaction against what many Victorians saw as the increasing pace and pressure of modern life and the loss of the old world virtues of loyalty, honour, and chivalry. Of course, from Homer onward, every age has assumed that its ancestors were braver, better, more honourable than their successors. The breathtaking thing about the Victorians is how far they were prepared to go to try to recreate the architecture and customs of that lost world. The unmissable example is the British Houses of Parliament. In 1834, the old buildings burned down. MPs and peers set up a committee to decide in what style they should be rebuilt. They chose the Gothic style, with the result that the Houses of Parliament, inside and out, have many of the architectural features of a medieval cathedral. Many landowners up and down the country followed suit, competing with each other in cloisters, vaulted ceilings, arched doorways. And, of course, the suits of armour to match.

"So these were never actually worn in battle?" some of our visitors ask, a little regretfully. Now we come to the really odd part. It's possible that they might have been, or at any rate worn in a joust. Jousting in the nineteenth century? Yes, in the nineteenth century. A joust at Eglinton Castle in the Scottish lowlands and jousting in London too, very close to where Lord's Cricket Ground is today. In 1839, a group of young noblemen spent a year or so of their time and large sums of money in re-creating their idea of a medieval joust. That's the starting point for Liberty Lane's third adventure, *A Family Affair*. The shop run by Samuel Luke Pratt at 47 Bond Street that sold suits of armour really did exist. So did the London jousting ground in the garden of the Eyre Arms tavern and even the Railway Knight that ran on metal tracks. As an advanced young woman, Liberty regards all this with wry amusement. By background and inclination, she is not cut out for just watching and being beautiful and inspirational, which tended to be the role of the ladies in all this.

The moving spirit in the Eglinton Tournament was Lord Eglinton himself, a wealthy and fast-living young aristocrat who could trace his family history back nearly seven hundred years. His younger half brother, Charlie Lamb, was so fascinated by knighthood and heraldry that as a small boy he even designed coats of arms for his pet guinea pigs according to strict heraldic rules. The announcement that they intended to hold a tournament, with knights in armour riding at each other with lances, caught the public's imagination. Excitement spread well beyond aristocratic circles. Souvenir plates and milk jugs were produced with pictures of tournament scenes. Even tailors got in on the act. The Victoria and Albert Museum in London has a beautiful gentleman's waistcoat from the period with miniature knights on horseback galloping across it.

As for the event itself, people from all over the country begged for tickets—and even some from abroad, including two gentlemen from Baltimore. Special excursion steamboats and trains had to be laid on to take thousands of spectators to Eglinton Castle. The knights at the centre of it all, thirty-five wealthy young men, dressed their servants as medieval men-at-arms, invested as much as a working man might earn in a year on hiring accessories like knightly pavilions and camp beds, and spent days debating which aristocratic lady should be chosen as the tournament's Queen of Beauty. (The honour went to the lovely Lady Seymour. We can only imagine the backbiting that must have gone on from the other candidates.) Most of the young men had titles in their own right, but they adopted poetic noms de guerre: Knight of the Golden Lion, Knight of the Swan, Knight of the Burning Tower. On the morning of the tournament, the road to Eglinton Castle was blocked for miles back with carriages.

Then it started raining. This was Scotland, in August. It went on raining and raining. The banners and costumes were sodden, the ground under the chargers' hooves turned to thick mud. The roof of the grandstand where the Queen of Beauty and her ladies were sitting with the other celebrity spectators let in the rain, and everybody was soaked. The knights managed to ride a course or two, but by then conditions were so appalling that they mostly missed their opponents' shields altogether. The rain kept on, the tournament ground flooded, the wet and cold spectators spent most of the night trying to unstick their carriages from the mud or stagger back to their excursion trains. The knights admitted defeat by the weather and went back to being ordinary Victorian aristocrats. The story is told in a wonderfully entertaining book called *The Knight and the Umbrella* by Ian Anstruther. It was published in 1963, and secondhand copies can still be found on some online book sites. Many of the details of the tournament frenzy in *A Family Affair* come from that source.

Apart from the sheer absurdity of the enterprise—and the possibilities it offered for murder and mayhem—what fascinates me about the Eglinton Tournament is the way that every age has to form its own view of history. The past is so complex that no single historical view can comprehend all of it. So in viewing the past we have to pick and choose, and there are fashions in the way we view historical periods, just as there are fashions in music, clothing, entertainment. Lord Eglinton and his friends made up their idea of what the Middle Ages were like, often using genuine medieval sources but interpreting them in their own way. Similarly, we make up our idea of what people in the nineteenth century were like, following the sources as best we can but, necessarily, picking and choosing from an overwhelming amount of material to make a partial picture. We may be nearly right, or wrong, or even ridiculous, but the one sure thing is that we can never be entirely right about anything from the past. That's why, for all its ridiculous aspects, I can't help admiring the railway-age knights of the Eglinton Tournament for their head-on determination to bring alive their take on a lost age. In a way, I suppose we're all in the same business.

Karolina Webb

**CARO PEACOCK** acquired the reading habit from her childhood growing up in a farmhouse. Later she developed an interest in women in Victorian society and from this grew her character of Liberty Lane. She rides, climbs, and trampolines and also enjoys the study of wildflowers.

# BOOKS BY CARO PEACOCK

### A FOREIGN AFFAIR
**A Novel of Victorian England**
ISBN 978-0-06-144589-7 (paperback)

"A plucky protagonist who refuses to back
down as an increasingly murky plot surfaces..."
—London's *Sunday Observer*

### A DANGEROUS AFFAIR
**A Novel of Victorian England**
ISBN 978-0-06-144748-8 (paperback)

"Peacock skillfully interweaves figures of real
Victoria London, while avoiding the genre's
typical focus on aristocracy.... The mystery flows
smoothly, with well-placed red herrings, excellent
reveals and pleasing surprises."
—*Publishers Weekly*

### A FAMILY AFFAIR
**A Novel**
ISBN 978-0-06-144749-5 (paperback)

"Great period detail and heaps of energy...feisty."
—*Daily Mirror* (London)

"As satisfying as one could wish."
—*The Times* (London)